Season of the Cats

Pamela Sargent

WILDSIDE PRESS

In memory of the cats:

Molasses, Taffy, Bogie, Falstaff, Miller, Cadbury, Slater,
Greystoke, Maxwell, Hennessey, Nickers, Sox, He-Man, Muffin,
Cocoa, Munchkin, Kitmus, Macia, Spencer, and Ellie

Published by Wildside Press LLC.
www.wildsidepress.com

Season of the Cats

"Pamela Sargent's *Season of the Cats* opens the door on what seems a quiet domestic drama and then draws us in by giving an odd psychological turn to the surface ordinariness of her main characters, husband Don Martinson and wife Gena Lawlor—who, we learn, have more going on in their lives than their unique personal quirks, their unsatisfying day jobs, or their shared fondness for cats. Indeed, Sargent's novel qualifies as an eerie entry in the Alfred Hitchcock suspense sweepstakes. It stalks its readers from first page to last with a self-possessed feline single-mindedness that brooks no resistance and affords little respite. Even its satisfying resolution contains within it the admonitory possibility of further raised hackles and claws still ready to unsheathe. A deliciously unsettling performance."

—Michael Bishop, author of *Who Made Stevie Crye?*

"Pamela Sargent has given us a delectable confection, wrought from an irresistible recipe: a dash of Fritz Leiber, a touch of Neil Gaiman, a dollop of Roald Dahl—plus a full measure of her characteristic adroit plotting and compelling prose. At once whimsical and sardonic, *Season of the Cats* will enchant all fans of offbeat fantasy."

—James Morrow, author of *Galápagos Regained*

"Pamela Sargent's latest novel *Season of the Cats* might be called fantastic realism. With the lightest of touches, Sargent reveals what shivers and glitters just below what we think is familiar, ordinary, and comfortable. The author's trademark attention to detail and step-off-the-page characters are all here, as well as her deft plotting. Sargent is a major American author whose work slips in and out of genre…whose work transcends genre."

—Jack Dann, author of *The Man Who Melted*
and *The Memory Cathedral*

"A gifted social critic, Pamela Sargent draws the lives of a dysfunctional suburban couple as seen in a fresh, sometimes funny, often macabre light. Which is the bigger threat to the marriage, the evil spectre they call Household or the countless furry citizens of Catalonia, their imaginary Magic Kingdom who show up in real life? The race threatens to be a photo finish; finding out what happens, and how, is half the fun."

—Kit Reed, author of *The Story So Far* and *Enclave*

"This is a sneaky book. You think you're reading it; it's actually stalking you. This is a story that may seem familiar at first but that's only how it pulls you in. Trust me, you're about to be unsettled in ways you never imagined."

—Pat Cadigan, twice winner of
the Arthur C. Clarke Award

ALSO BY PAMELA SARGENT

Novels
Cloned Lives
The Sudden Star
The Golden Space
The Alien Upstairs
The Shore of Women
Alien Child
Ruler of the Sky: A Novel of Genghis Khan
Climb the Wind: A Novel of Another America

The Watchstar Trilogy:
Watchstar
Eye of the Comet
Homesmind

The Venus Trilogy:
Venus of Dreams
Venus of Shadows
Child of Venus

The Seed Trilogy:
Earthseed
Farseed
Seed Seeker

Short Fiction
Starshadows
The Best of Pamela Sargent
Behind the Eyes of Dreamers
The Mountain Cage and Other Stories
Eye of Flame and Other Fantasies
Thumbprints

Dream of Venus and Other Stories
Puss in D.C. and Other Stories

Nonfiction
Firebrands: The Heroines of Science Fiction and Fantasy (with Ron Miller)

Anthologies
Women of Wonder
Bio-Futures
More Women of Wonder
The New Women of Wonder
Afterlives (with Ian Watson)
Women of Wonder, The Classic Years
Women of Wonder, The Contemporary Years
Nebula Awards 29
Nebula Awards 30
Nebula Awards 31
Conqueror Fantastic

Star Trek Novels (with George Zebrowski)
A Fury Scorned (The Next Generation)
Heart of the Sun (The Original Series)
Across the Universe (The Original Series)
Garth of Izar (The Original Series)

One

Gena sensed it. Something had taken up residence in her home, invisible and malign.

She argued more often with Don over trivial matters. Sometimes it seemed as though she wasn't speaking to her husband at all, but to someone else entirely.

When they had first moved in together, Gena and Don vowed that they would avoid the disputes that broke up other couples. In particular, they solemnly swore, their finances would never become a bone of contention. A small part of Gena's money was hers to spend as she pleased, as was Don's. He would have his own checking account, as would she, but they would also maintain a joint household account for savings and shared expenses.

That seemed fair to Gena, even if it meant leaving Don largely in charge of their fiscal affairs. He knew more about such matters than she did, so it was better to let him make the big decisions, even if lately that meant overlooking the flashes of resentment that afflicted her whenever he grew too controlling.

Their household account was used to pay the rent, phone, and electric bills, and also covered the cost of groceries and other essentials. When Gena and Don decided to get married, which was after they had agreed that she would continue to use her own last name of Lawlor as long as she was "Mrs. Martinson" to Don's parents, the household account was also paying for any new furniture. After they moved from their apartment into one half of a rental in a two-family house, their meager savings were consigned to a household savings account. When they finally managed, with the help of a loan from her parents, to make the down payment on a small brick house that had felt like the perfect home for them the first time they had set foot inside it, "Household," as they now called their joint savings account, bought them a new lawnmower.

By then, Don and Gena had been married for over five years, and determining what was and what wasn't a household expense had become more complicated. If Gena rented an evening's entertainment, the cost came out of her own money; if she and Don were together and agreed on the choice of a movie, they split the cost. Gradually it dawned on her that since Don often worked late and she was usually the one to rent the DVDs on her way home, she was paying for most of the movies on top of coughing up half the monthly cable bill and half of whatever they spent with Netflix.

It wasn't fair. She was making a good deal less than Don to begin with, and the expense of the movies left even less for her to spend on herself. If both of them watched the movies, why wasn't their admittedly modest cost a household expense?

"I think," Gena said to Don one night, "that it's time Household took over paying for something I've been paying for." She said it playfully, in the same way Don spoke of the household account, almost as if it were a person sharing their home with them. They sat on the floor in front of the sofa, with a pizza they had both paid for sitting on top of their glass-topped coffee table. They had just finished watching "Die Hard with a Vengeance," one of Don's favorite movies, and it occurred to her that she was usually guided by his taste and not her own when selecting their entertainment.

Don said, "I was thinking the same thing. I mean, about Household covering an expense I've been handling."

"Oh?" The grim tone of his voice disturbed her. Their personification of Household had begun as a joke, but lately Don sounded more serious whenever he invoked the name of their joint account.

"You first," he said as he reached for another slice of pizza.

"It's about the movie rentals. I'm the one who always pays for them."

"Not always."

"Almost always. The last time you brought home a movie and paid for it was almost a month ago."

"Three weeks ago if you count from yesterday," Don said, with a certainty and exactitude that annoyed her. "Besides, it's easier for you to pick one up. You get off the bus at Chock Full o' DVDs on your way home."

That was true. Since moving to this house, she had found that it was easier to take the ten-minute bus ride to her job at the financial offices of St. Luke's Hospital; using her car meant either a major hassle finding a place to park in the nearby neighborhood or else paying for a space in the hospital's parking lot. The bus stopped at a strip mall two blocks away on the return trip, where the Chock Full O' DVDs store was located. She could walk home from there and feel virtuous about supporting a struggling local business.

"It's not picking them up that's the problem," Gena said, "it's paying for them. Seems to me that if we both watch them, it's a household expense."

"That's ridiculous."

"Household paid for the TV." She waved a hand in the direction of the flat screen on the wall.

"That's because it counts as furniture, and Household covers furniture. Movies—well, that's a recreational expense, like a concert or going out to dinner."

Gena frowned. Don shouldn't have mentioned that. Whenever they went out to dinner, they split the bill fifty-fifty, and that increasingly struck her as unfair. She almost always ordered one of the lighter entrées, or else an appetizer and the soup of the day, while Don loaded up on appetizers, steak or prime rib, and colossal salads, often followed by coffee and dessert that they could have fixed for themselves at home, where the expense would have been covered by Household. Even with reasonably priced ethnic food of all varieties at restaurants around town, Don managed to find the most costly items on the menu. Whenever he dined out, he ate as though he might never eat again, as though his plain and scanty childhood meals, prepared by a mother with only the most rudimentary cooking skills, still haunted him. His meals always cost more, and yet Gena was paying half the bill, which amounted to subsidizing his overindulgence.

"Maybe Household," she said, "should pay for dinners out, too. After all, it already pays for groceries. And if it paid for the TV, it ought to pay for what we see on it."

"Household didn't pay for the DVD player," Don said, "and that's what we use to watch the movies." He tilted his head. Don looked very appealing when he tilted his head, cute and blond and just adorable, as if he really were still a boy instead of rapidly closing in on thirty-five. "But you have a point. Let's leave Household out of it and split the cost of the movies from now on. Besides," he continued, "there's another expense I think Household should cover."

Gena lifted the top of the pizza box, but Don had already devoured the last slice. "What?"

"My car."

"Wait a minute." She drew up her legs and wrapped her arms around them. "Why your car? Why not both our cars?"

"Because you almost never use yours except on weekends. That makes it personal. Almost every time you drive, it's personal business."

"Not when I go to the supermarket."

"You do that once a week, and I pick up plenty of groceries myself. And when I drive, it's mostly to go to work or get stuff we need or pick you up after work when I can get out early enough. I mean, I could make a case that I almost never use my car for purely personal things."

"I don't drive to work," Gena said, "because it's easier to take the bus."

"Then how about this? Household covers my car and your bus fare."

"No."

"Why not?"

"Household doesn't cover transportation."

"It covers household expenses," Don said, his voice rising.

"A car isn't a household expense."

"It is if it's used for household business."

Gena leaned forward and rested her arms on her knees. "Give me a break, Don. You can call almost anything we do household business." Keep going down this road, she thought, and pretty soon they might as well have joint accounts for everything, which was what they had hoped to avoid. Joint accounts for personal expenses only meant more opportunities for arguments, and they were not going to contend with each other on the financial battlefield where so many other couples had fallen in combat. So they had hoped, but now Household was becoming an entity threatening to dominate them.

Household. Just hearing that word rattle around in her mind seemed ominous. For a moment, she again felt that something else was in the living room with them.

Don shouted, "All right, all right!" He picked up the remote and turned on the local news.

They were just in time to catch the end of the first story, which appeared to be about a murder. Some man had allegedly strangled his wife and been arrested while weeping hysterically over her dead body. There was a quick shot of a ranch house that looked vaguely familiar and then the face of a young blonde female reporter appeared.

The newscaster said, "Neighbors are shocked at the tragedy. There are reports that Harman was still screaming that someone else had committed the act even after he was restrained by the police. There'd been some trouble lately between him and his wife, and reports that police had been called to the house, but nothing to indicate the potential for such violence."

The face of an older woman filled the screen. She said, "They seemed like such a nice young couple. I remember when they moved in last year, why that Pete Harman came over to clear my driveway with his snowblower after that big storm and didn't even ask for anything in return. And then, well, after a while they started having more fights and I guess things just weren't going so well."

The blonde newscaster reappeared. "And now Peter Harman is in custody, his wife Brenda is dead, and their neighbors on Carlton Street are left wondering about two people they thought they knew. Kerry Saletan for WKTG News."

"Carlton Street," Gena said. That was just around the corner from where she and Don had been living before they bought their house. That fact was unsettling, as if such violence might erupt anywhere without warning.

They watched the rest of the news in silence, until WKTG's chief meteorologist Vince Fantuzzo promised them warmer and sunnier weather for tomorrow, and then Gena meowed softly.

"Meow," Don responded.

"Here, kitty, kitty."

Don crawled to her side and rubbed against her, raising his rump as though to flick an invisible tail. "Meow."

"You are just the cutest thing," Gena said as she scratched Don on the back of his neck. As he curled up at her side, she began to purr, or at least to offer the best imitation of a cat's purr that she could muster.

But later, before they went to bed, Gena spent a few moments studying the two china cats on top of her dresser. They were in their usual position, front paws and noses touching, so that they almost seemed to be kissing. Gena picked up one of the china cats, then set it down an inch away from its mate.

That was the first time she had ever separated them.

Two

On their first wedding anniversary, Gena and Don had adopted a cat from an animal shelter run by Operation Whiskers, a local organization of cat lovers. Gena had been a volunteer at the organization's shelter for several years, cleaning out cages, changing cat litter, feeding the cats, and soothing animals that seemed frightened or distressed. She was on the verge of adopting a pair of brother kittens when Don entered her life, and by the time she discovered his shared fondness for felines, the two kittens had found another home.

Almost a year after their wedding, a small long-haired male cat with black and white fur, a cute little face, slightly oversized paws, and beautiful green eyes arrived at the shelter.

The other cats were intimidated by him. With just a cold stare, he silenced even the most obstreperous of the kittens; the older cats shrank away or rested their heads submissively on their front paws whenever he glanced in their direction. When Gena held him, he gazed up at her face as if peering deeply into her soul. The cat had been at the shelter for only three days when Don dropped by, and the animal had immediately padded over to him and uttered a commanding meow. Impressed by the intelligence and self-possession of the furry little creature, he had insisted that they give him a permanent home, and she had quickly agreed.

Gena, who disapproved of cutesy names for pets, had given their cat the name of Vladimir. Gena's mother had a theory that people who gave their animal companions human names would be less inclined to treat them only as animated toys, and Gena had no reason to doubt that hypothesis. Her family's former cat, a much-loved and overindulged short-haired male with fur the hue of butterscotch, had been dubbed Cameron by her mother and was regarded as a member of the family for the fifteen years he had shared their home before kidney disease took his life.

Vladimir was given a diet of assorted dried and moist cat foods, served to him in his own ceramic and porcelain bowls, and his long fur was brushed and combed daily. His veterinarian, known around town as the Catwoman, was the appropriately named Dr. Caterina Lucci, who limited her practice to cats. Never would Gena and Don have dreamed of raising their voices around Vladimir. Gena would not even pick him up to pet him, but waited until Vladimir deigned to leap into her lap.

Vladimir was such an appealing little fellow that both Don and Gena were soon wondering aloud why people could not be as dignified, intelligent, and cute as cats. One thing led to another, and soon the two of them would be meowing at each other, crawling around the floor in imitation of Vladimir's movements, and curling up on the sofa—but only when they were alone; it wasn't the kind of thing to do when somebody might unexpectedly drop by, and they'd had to keep their voices down so that Mr. Bowes, their landlord on the other side of the two-family house, would not hear them. They had been relieved to move into their own house, where there were fewer impediments to their catlike conduct.

By then, they had developed a complex imaginary world populated entirely by cats, which Don, in a fit of inspiration triggered by a recent Discovery Channel program about Barcelona, had dubbed Catalonia.

In this feline utopia, small domestic cats of all kinds were the only inhabitants. Like the world dominated by human beings, Catalonia had cities and towns, resorts and restaurants, banks, businesses, and transportation systems; unlike the human world, Catalonia lacked injustice of any kind. This entire realm was ruled by an imaginary tomcat that had blond fur not unlike Don's hair in tone, and by a female cat with black fur, since Gena was a brunette. Don had hit upon Nicholas and Alexandra as appropriate names for these feline sovereigns. History was not his strong suit, so Gena refrained from reminding him that the historical figures of Nicholas and Alexandra had ruled Russia incompetently before being executed by Bolsheviks. No matter: their Catalonia had nothing to do with that region of Spain, either.

Vladimir had escaped the burden of a too-cute kitty name, but Catalonia was soon infected by cuteness. Within its environs, cats traveled to cities such as Mew York, Mew Orleans, Catlanta, and Los Angorales on the luxurious trains of CatTrak. They dined at a chain of restaurants called the Fish and Flagon that specialized in fresh seafood, took care of their financial affairs at Kittibank, and vacationed in Catcún or Kittybunkport. Catalonia, in all of its accumulated detail, rapidly became almost as real to Gena and Don as anything in the actual world around them.

Occasionally, objects in the real world seemed to be Catalonian manifestations, as if their imagined world were somehow leaking into the actual one. Gena definitely felt that way while in a stationery store buying a card for Don to mark their fourth anniversary. The card of course had a feline motif, and Gena was thrilled to discover two darling china cats among the store's collection of tchotchkes. Indeed, one of the cats had painted golden fur that looked just like the fur she envisioned for Nicholas, while the other was as black as Gena's feline alter ego Alexandra. Gena could not resist buying them and kept the pair on top of her bedroom dresser, where, every morning, she and Don could wake to the sight of the two china cats, the totemic representation of their marital bond.

The world of Catalonia would be theirs alone, never to be shared with anyone else. This was largely because anyone else getting wind of this invented cosmos of cats would assume that Don and Gena were not only besotted by cuteness, but deranged as well. But their private world was also a comfort to evoke after a bad day at work or during an episode of self-doubt. In the world of Catalonia, where cats were free to do as they liked, Don could forget that his main professional purpose in life was seeing that people collected as little as possible on any insurance policies they bought from his company. In Catalonia, Gena could envision herself as a fiercely independent feline in a position of authority instead of as a woman who still lived in a house only a twenty-minute drive from the home of her parents.

Catalonia bound them together. Gena often felt that she had fallen in love with Don because she had sensed his gentle and imaginative side at their first meeting. To break up with him would mean abandoning their beloved realm, which they had created together. Gena was convinced that any divorce would subject Catalonia to the devastation of quakes, storms, and environmental disasters, while Don viewed the inhabitants of their cat world as potential allies in a battle that he trusted would never come.

"If we ever broke up," he often told Gena, "I'd call you up and meow. I'd remind you that if we weren't together at Christmas, you'd miss decorating the tree at Rockefurry Center."

"And miss a visit from Santa Paws, too," Gena replied.

Catalonia became their consolation for Vladimir's treachery, when he escaped outside to wander the few blocks back to their old neighborhood not long after they had moved into their own home, abandoning them to take up residence with their former landlord Mr. Bowes, who had often fed Vladimir such forbidden foods as shrimp, albacore tuna in oil, and baked Virginia ham whenever Don and Gena were out. "A cat is a free being," Mr. Bowes had insisted when Gena went back to pick up some belongings she had stored temporarily in the two-family's basement. "You cannot hold a cat against his will, he is a free being," and Gena had reluctantly conceded the point. Vladimir, sitting in Mr. Bowes's bay window, had stared balefully through the glass at her as she left, perhaps comparing the healthy but more limited diet she and Don had offered him with the taste treats he consumed now.

If their actual cat had betrayed them, those in Catalonia would not. Those kitties were always there, ever prepared to welcome Gena and Don into their complex but kindly universe.

Even so, Gena missed Vladimir, especially when she was alone in a house that seemed colder and more oppressive in the cat's absence. Her home's good vibes, the warm and welcoming feeling she had experienced when the real estate agent first showed her the house, had departed with

Vladimir who, she now recalled, had taken up the habit of snarling at dark corners and howling in the night even after he had curled up between them on their bed. Perhaps another cat would restore the lost warmth; there were so many at the shelter that needed homes.

But Don seemed content with matters as they were, and adopting another cat would cost them. They and Household, since Vladimir had been treated as a household expense, already owed Caterina Lucci a fair amount of money they had not yet paid for Vladimir's medical care and repair of injuries he had sustained in battle with other cats; they didn't need to tap into the little they had been able to save to take on the expense of another cat.

Lately, the household accounts had taken over Don's conversation. She had thought he might ease up on that subject now that the last of his college loans was almost paid off; instead, he had grown even more obsessive.

"We have to think of the future," he would say. "Maybe it's time to cut back. I remember what it was like for my father, always having to worry and barely scraping by and not being able to get even a little ahead when Devlan and I were growing up. That sure as hell isn't for me." Occasionally she had the feeling that she was talking to some money-grubbing entity that had temporarily taken on Don's form, and imagined a figure much like the one depicted on Monopoly game boards but with a much meaner facial expression, a large fat man in top hat and morning coat with a walrus's fat mustache, looming behind Don and clutching a briefcase full of currency—Household, the device created to keep themselves from fighting over money, but now a creature who was too often Don's ally.

Three

A coworker of Don's had recommended that he start thinking about investments. Don made that announcement in what sounded to Gena like the voice of Household. Shouldn't they start to save more? Didn't they want to be able to provide for the children they might have someday? Didn't they want to get ahead and not have to live from paycheck to paycheck the way Don's father had for much of his life? Didn't they want to be prepared for harder times, given the ever shakier state of the economy? Didn't they want some financial security in their old age? Didn't Gena want to be able to consider a move later on to another part of the country, even if that might be a temporary drain on their finances?

That last argument had been the convincer. Maybe that was because Don had offered it right after Gena was off the phone with her mother, whose calls were always at least an hour long and often left her feeling totally bummed. If her mother just couldn't resist hinting that Gena had not quite measured up to her expectations, then living at some distance from her daughter might at least keep her from doing so three or four times a week.

Gena's resentment, simmering all day, finally boiled over during a trip to the mall with her best friend, Tracey Birnbaum. On a rack inside an emporium called The Clothes Horse hung a silk blouse in Gena's favorite shade of pale blue.

"Damn it all," she muttered as she tried on the garment in the fitting room, "this would go perfectly with my long navy blue skirt."

"Buy it, then," Tracey said. "It looks great on you."

"Can't afford it." But she could, if she borrowed from Household. If only she could figure out a way to make the silk blouse a household expense.

"Well," Tracey said, "are you going to get it?"

Gena took off the blouse and hung it up again. "Can't."

Tracey sighed. "Let's go get a soda. I'll buy." They left The Clothes Horse and headed toward the mall's Burger King. "My philosophy is that you buy what you want to buy, within reason of course, and worry about the bill later."

"Not Don's philosophy." Gena's voice trailed off. Tracey knew something about how she and Don handled their finances, although Gena had never gone into detail about how their joint account had morphed into an immaterial but increasingly dictatorial Household.

They picked up their diet sodas and sat down at a side table. Tracey looked a bit happier. That pleased Gena, whose main reason for going to the mall with Tracey was to cheer up her friend, who had admitted to being very depressed since the breakup of her marriage.

"I might as well tell you," Tracey said as she brushed back a lock of long brown hair. "It's definitely over between me and Johnny. We're going ahead with the divorce."

"I'm so sorry," Gena said, having long expected to hear that unsurprising news. Tracey, who occasionally had her own lapses into cuteness, used to refer to her soon-to-be-ex-husband as her "Poopsie Sweetums," even in public, before he had abruptly walked out on her, proclaiming that he needed his space. Her most frequently used term for him now was "that fucking bastard."

"The fucking bastard's already moved back to Chicago," Tracey continued. Her voice was hard, but her eyes glistened, as if she might suddenly burst into tears. "He doesn't have a job there, but he's moving anyway." She sipped her soda. "At least I won't have to go to that goddamn marriage counselor any more." Her voice shook, and Gena feared that Tracey's brittle exterior would crack. "I always had the feeling she was taking his side. And I'll be free of the son of a bitch forever in a year."

"Are you going to keep his name," Gena asked, "or go back to Tracey Sussman?"

"I don't know. Wish I could ditch Birnbaum, but that might not be such a good idea." Tracey was an artist and illustrator, a profession that still struck Gena as exciting and romantic even though Tracey rarely discussed anything that sounded even remotely artistic. She had done cover paintings for romance and mystery novels and illustrations for magazine stories, but most of her work was for children's books on such subjects as medieval clothing, the Plains Indians of the nineteenth century, famous racehorses of the twentieth century, elves, fairies, dragons, and flowers. Her conversations about her work consisted largely of complaints about contracts, fees, royalty payments, reproduction rights, copyright violations, online postings without permission, gallery owners who screwed artists on sales of paintings, and other financial and legal transactions, some even involving what sounded like blackmail and bribery.

"Trouble is that my audience," Tracey went on, "such as it is, knows me by that fucking bastard's last name now, so I may be stuck with being Birnbaum forever. You were smart to keep your own name. You won't have that problem if you and Don ever split."

Gena could not bear to contemplate such a possibility. To split up with Don—that was unthinkable, yet she was beginning to wonder if any of the couples they had come to know over the years would still be together ten years from now. Divorce might be like a contagious disease, easily spread to those who were exposed to it. She and Don were not immune.

But they couldn't break up. They loved each other too much. Besides, what would they do about Catalonia? Their shared world would be torn apart, its cities, towns, businesses, and contented, extremely cute cats banished to oblivion.

"Oh, my God," Gena murmured, feeling as though the black-furred Alexandra who was her Catalonian counterpart had suddenly been separated forever from her golden-furred mate Nicholas. Tears sprang to her eyes; she could almost hear Alexandra crying out to her with mournful meows of fear and despair.

"What's the matter?" Tracey asked.

"Nothing. Just a passing thought." Her marriage was now so bound up with a make-believe world that she was beginning to wonder what she cared about more, Don or their imaginary feline refuge.

Time, she told herself, for a reality check. Time to acknowledge that she still had a life apart from Catalonia and Don and Household.

"I've changed my mind," she said to Tracey. "I think I'll get that blouse after all."

* * * *

Don never asked Gena about her purchase, although he must have noticed the withdrawal from the household account. He never even seemed to see that she had bought a new blouse. Within a month, her guilt over buying the garment had vanished in the face of Don's far greater betrayal.

He had used some of Household's money to pay for a new Wii, even though they already had a PlayStation. Gena had discovered his treachery while perusing Household's records, something she had not done for a while. She was not one of those suspicious women who doubted her husband; couldn't she trust him implicitly? Apparently not, as the household accounts revealed, and he had admitted his deed as soon as she challenged him, without showing a trace of guilt.

"Okay, I bought a Wii," he told her.

"A Wii is not a household expense."

"Sure it is," Don replied. "Where are we going to use it? In the house. That's Household."

"It's not."

"Household paid for the TV, didn't it?"

"We decided a TV was furniture. A Wii isn't furniture, it's a—a—" Gena searched her mind for the proper terminology. "—an electronic gaming system," she concluded.

"So?"

Maybe, she thought, it wasn't worth arguing about. Judging by the relatively modest sum he had spent, he had gotten a very good deal on the Wii and its games and accessories. Still, it was the principle of the thing. Unfortunately, she was on morally shaky ground, given the devious way in which she had purchased her silk blouse.

The Wii, she realized then, was his revenge for her purchase. He had seen that she would be unable to object to his new toy.

"All right," she said, then batted her eyes. "This wouldn't happen in Catalonia. You'd never have such wonderful creatures as those cats arguing over a Wii."

"Of course you wouldn't," he said. "Their Wiis cost a fraction of what ours cost, plus they're made by Kitsubishi instead of Nintendo. They're so cheap that every cat and kitten can get as many as they like. You can't walk into a Catalonian home without finding a Wii, which makes it a household expense."

That wasn't fair. Gena was about to object, but an uncharacteristically icy look in Don's eyes made her hesitate. It was almost as if something else was suddenly sitting inside him, something cold and malign, looking out at her through his eyes.

The thought came to her, as it did more often lately, that she did not really know what her husband was like inside. Even here, inside their home, inside the house that had once seemed so welcoming, the man she loved often seemed alien, even threatening.

Household, she thought wildly. Household had enslaved Don—or perhaps her husband had bent Household to his will in preparation for taking over all of their financial affairs. Don, who had admitted early in their relationship that his parents had struggled financially, had always had a thing about money, but this recent obsession wasn't just about money but about control. If he completely controlled his life and their affairs, he could stave off the worst; that need to rule was what drove him at bottom. His father had ceded too much authority to others, Don had told her, which had only added to his troubles.

Household was now becoming the instrument of his dominion over her and everything else. Strangely enough, she found herself thinking that Don—if he were fifty pounds heavier and had white hair and a walrus's mustache—would look like Household.

"Meow," she said, testing him.

He tilted his head, then curled his fingers and swatted gently at her, as if his hands were paws, but she knew that he was not about to back down.

"Okay, Don," she continued. "You made your point."

He smiled, looking self-satisfied and not Catalonian at all.

Before bed, she picked up her black china cat and set it down several inches away from its mate.

Four

Yolanda Gutierrez said, "Yeah, he hung himself. Guard looked into the cell and there he was, hanging there with a noose made out of a T-shirt."

Gena sat at her work station, her St. Luke's ID badge hanging around her neck, entering data as she listened. Her coworker Yolanda was talking about Peter Harman, the man who had strangled his wife.

"Guess he really was sorry deep down," Jeannie Biggs added. "Saying it wasn't him but something else, and all of that stuff about something, like, taking him over, I guess he…" Jeannie fell silent, a sure sign that Barney Litzer, their supervisor, had stuck his head out of his office door and was staring down the aisle between the two rows of work stations.

Gena did not need to hear anything more about the unfortunate Harmans anyway, as she had seen most of the story on WKTG that morning. Peter Harman, in apparent grief and remorse, had managed to hang himself in his jail cell despite being on a suicide watch. The police and the district attorney could now admit that there was little doubt of Harman's guilt since there would be no trial. One lawyer had speculated that Harman might have offered an insanity defense, although such a strategy would have been unlikely to succeed. There had been no sign of any trouble between the Harmans until recently, when neighbors had occasionally overheard the couple arguing loudly; the police had been called to the house twice, with no charges filed. Family members and acquaintances were reeling in shock; finding out that a kindly, unassuming computer technician had strangled his equally nice and unassuming assistant librarian wife had stunned everyone who knew the Harmans. No one would have expected it, a self-proclaimed good friend of Brenda Harman's had asserted to the WKTG reporter, not even after Brenda had confided to her that she no longer felt safe in her home, that the atmosphere there had changed, that the house seemed creepier and that Pete had been acting strange lately.

"It happens sometimes," Margot Trammer muttered, and Gena knew that Barney was back inside his office and had closed the door. "People just go along about their business, and then suddenly something snaps." She slipped on her headset and adjusted her mouthpiece.

Gena turned back to her computer screen as the others donned their headsets. The murmuring of her colleagues as they made their first phone calls of the morning was a calming sound, as all of the women possessed pleasant, musical voices while Gary Liebow, their only male coworker, had a soothing baritone, and she had grown used to ignoring what the calls were actually about. She and the others worked in Billing and Accounts Receivable at St. Luke's Hospital, so Margot, Yolanda, Gary, and Jeannie spent much of their time dunning people who had failed to pay their often substantial bills. There was, Gena supposed, an irony in that the medical insurance St. Luke's offered its employees was almost as bad as having no insurance at all; one high-deductible trip to the emergency room and any one of them might have been on the receiving end of such a call. She could be grateful that Don's more generous benefits also covered her.

She had, over the past few years, also remained reasonably content with her job of reviewing forms, entering data, and proofreading long lists of accounts due, overdue, paid and unpaid, even though no promotion seemed in the offing any time soon. She felt a twinge, an inner wincing that afflicted her more often these days. Adapting to her routine work was probably yet another indication that she was as conventional, passive, and dull as she had always suspected, and insensitive, too, since she was able, most of the time, to ignore the true purpose of her work; extracting as much money as possible from people who, through no fault of their own, had suffered the bad luck of injuries or illnesses they could not afford.

Her employment was the sort of work Household might have picked out for her. That was a new thought, and not one to dwell on for too long; at least she had a job.

Gena forced her attention back to the screen and was soon lulled into a familiar and comforting semi-hypnosis by the green symbols scrolling up on the black screen.

* * * *

Alexandra was on the prowl, padding swiftly up one of the picturesque hills of San Furcisco, one of Catalonia's most beautiful cities. The overhead twittering of birds made her ears twitch and flatten against the sides of her head. To chase birds was a pleasure, but no inhabitant of Catalonia would ever dream of killing one; Catalonian cats had sublimated that instinct.

Yet there were times when ancient instincts awoke and the blood ran hot, when the desire to tear and rend and bite into flesh would overcome her. That thought so startled and disturbed Alexandra that she quickly suppressed it, even while knowing that she had often been in the grip of such urges, when the calm surface of her thoughts gave way to anger, rage, and the need to lash out at whatever…or whoever…happened to be nearby.

Sharpening her claws, she slipped toward a bush and concealed herself to wait until an unwary bird landed on the sidewalk in front of her—

"Whooo!" shouted a passenger from a speeding car. The hills of San Furcisco became again a tree-lined street of assorted Colonials, Victorians, split-levels, and two-family homes with postage-stamp-sized yards. Gena's small red brick house again stood on the corner of Ackley Avenue and Bancroft Street. Her mother's blue Volvo waited at the side of the house, just clearing the driveway, while her mother stood on the small front stoop, jabbing at the doorbell.

Gena backed quickly toward a tree, trying to conceal herself as her mother turned in her direction. "Eugenia!" she called out brightly, the only person who still called Gena by her full first name. "Yoo hoo!"

Her mother was a small, pretty, delicate-boned woman with curly black hair and large brown eyes; Gena, at barely five feet four inches tall and only a few pounds overweight, felt huge and awkward in comparison. Laurie Lawlor could be merciless in her judgments of those whose behavior and deportment did not measure up to her high standards, and she always seemed to know what Gena and Don might be up to even before Gena became aware of it. Living near her mother was a little like having Stalin nearby.

"Uh, hi, Mom." Gena shuffled out from behind the tree. Alexandra's feline pride had fled from her. "You should have told me you were coming."

"Well, I just happened to be in town."

That was always the excuse. If her mother was within a couple of miles of Gena's house, she had no compunction about coming over without warning, not even a quick call on her cell phone. Gena sighed as she climbed the steps to the front door, thinking of the last time. She and Don had been in the middle of passionate lovemaking, accompanied by meows, on the living room sofa, when Mrs. Lawlor had started banging on the back door, calling out, "Yoo hoo!" They had barely had time to pull on their clothes before she had shoved the door open—Gena cursed herself silently again for having not double-checked the troublesome lock—and waltzed into the house. It would never have occurred to Gena's mother that any normal couple might be having sex on a sofa in the middle of a Sunday afternoon.

"Anyway, hello, dear." Mrs. Lawlor lifted her head for a kiss. "I see you've been shopping." She gestured at the box under Gena's arm.

Gena handed her mother the box, then unlocked the door, trying to remember if she had put the coffee mugs and breakfast dishes in the dishwasher that morning. Probably not, and she hadn't cleaned out the coffeemaker after unplugging it, either. Maybe Don had cleaned it, as he often did. With any luck, maybe she could keep her mother out of the kitchen.

"And what did you get?" Mrs. Lawlor asked as she handed the box back, then shrugged out of her coat.

"Nothing much." Gena set the box down on the chair in the alcove, hung up their coats in the entryway closet, and propelled her mother into the living room. "Can I get you anything?"

"A glass of white wine would be nice." Mrs. Lawlor frowned. "No, better not—I still have to drive home. Better make it a diet ginger ale." She perched gracefully at one end of the sofa. "Can't stay long, though. Your father will be a bear without his supper."

"He'll survive, Mom." Eugene Lawlor, unlike his wife, was tall, big-boned, and built along the lines of a promising draft pick for the National Football League; he would not starve without his supper. Gena wandered toward the kitchen with a feeling of impending doom. Her mother was being awfully cheerful, what Mrs. Lawlor referred to as "feeling chipper," and that was usually a bad sign.

She poured them two diet ginger ales on ice and went back to the living room. "I have something to say that concerns you, dear," her mother said brightly, and Gena's heart sank. "You know that your father and I have been thinking about whether we should move somewhere else after he retires."

"Oh?" Gena handed her a glass, then sat down at the other end of the sofa. Laurie Lawlor had left her job at the local office of the state health department almost a year ago, and Mr. Lawlor had decided to spring for an early retirement package now that the engineering firm that employed him was downsizing, but Gena had not known that her parents were considering a move. "Florida?" she asked, afraid to hope. "Arizona?" That would certainly solve a lot of problems. No more surprise visits, for one thing.

"Well, we talked about that, dear, and the more we thought about it, the more we kept thinking that it didn't make sense to move so far away. I mean, most of our friends are still around here, and we have our golf and tennis club and all our other activities, and you and Donald, of course. And I wonder if even a lower cost of living would make up for the disruption and expense of moving and having to adjust to another place."

"You could always visit." Even an extended visit of two or three weeks' duration was a small price to pay for having the rest of the year free of maternal intrusions. "And your friends could visit you, too."

"And then it struck me," Mrs. Lawlor went on, as though she had not heard Gena at all. "I thought about some of the nice new developments we have in the area now, those pretty townhouses and convenient condos and such. So I've been looking at brochures, and making some calls, and—"

"What?" Gena said, feeling suddenly hollow.

"—so I went over to Rolling Hill Acres today, and I was really quite impressed. For what you get, the prices are extremely reasonable."

Gena gaped at her, unable to speak. Rolling Hill Acres, a development of condominiums and townhouses for older upper-income couples, was sited on land that more closely resembled gentle slopes than rolling hills, and the gentle slopes on which those townhouses and condominiums stood were only a few minutes' drive away.

"You have to admit," Mrs. Lawlor continued, "that living in the city instead of out in the suburbs has its advantages, especially in a nice secure place like Rolling Hill Acres, and we'd still be able to see our friends and do all the things we usually do."

"Oh, God," Gena murmured.

"You look a little peaked, dear. Are you sure you're feeling well? Could it be that—" Her mother leaned toward her. "It would be nice to live so close by to my first grandchild."

"I'm not sick. I'm not pregnant, either, so don't get your hopes up. I just had a long day at work." Gena heard Don's car in the driveway. Help, she wanted to cry out to him: Save me.

Don came inside through the back door with much stomping of feet and began whistling and banging around in the kitchen. He would have seen her mother's car, but he was definitely taking his time about coming in to greet her. How fortunate Don was. His parents lived far away in a small town east of Seattle, while his older brother Devlan resided in Key West, where he owned a bar and restaurant.

"Donald?" Mrs. Lawlor chirped. "Is that you?"

Don appeared at the entrance to the living room. He had shed his jacket, loosened his tie, and clutched a beer in one hand. "Uh, hi, Laurie." He stood there, apparently unwilling to advance any farther. "How's it going?"

"Well, it's going just fine, Donald."

"Great." He swallowed some beer from his bottle. "Hope you don't mind my excusing myself. There's a couple of phone calls I promised to make."

"Well, you just go right ahead and make them, dear." Mrs. Lawlor was still smiling and chirping, but there was steel in her eyes. "I was just leaving anyway." She got to her feet. "I hope you two can come out to the house soon for dinner. You haven't visited for quite a while."

"Been busy, but we'll try to make time." Don noisily gulped more beer on his way back to the kitchen. "And give my best to Eugene."

Gena walked her mother to the door. "You haven't actually gone ahead and decided to move to Rolling Hill Acres," she said.

"Well, your father will inspect the place, and obviously there are things to work out. But we're giving it serious thought. You know, Donald ought to go a little easier on the beer. He's getting just a bit paunchy around the waist." Gena's mother had been giving the same advice to her own oversized husband for years, with little effect. "Good-bye, Eugenia."

"Bye, Mom."

"And do try to visit for dinner sometime."

"We will."

Gena closed the door behind her mother and went back into the living room.

"Coast clear?" Don shouted from the kitchen.

"Yes. You know how she hates it when you swig beer straight from the bottle."

"If I annoy her enough, maybe she'll stop coming over here unannounced." He wandered in, slipped off his loafers, and propped his feet up on the coffee table.

Gena said, "Let's go away. Let's put the house on the market, sell everything, and move to San Furcisco—San Francisco."

Don squinted at her. "Yeah, right. Dump my job and move to one of the most expensive cities in the country. That's kind of unrealistic."

"Somewhere else, then. Anywhere that'll be ours."

"But we can't just pick up and move. We don't even know how long it'd take to unload this place, and God only knows what kind of job I could find somewhere else, if I could even find a job. I mean, just the move would really set us back. If we can only wait—"

"I can't wait. Mom's thinking of moving to Rolling Hill Acres when Dad retires." Gena buried her head in her hands. "I'll go out of my mind, I just know it."

"Jesus."

"Why did we have to live here?"

Don let out his breath. "Number one, because I have a pretty good job here. Number two, because this town is relatively cheap compared to some places. And number three, because you seemed happy with things the way they were."

"Well, I'm not," she said. "I just thought that eventually you'd think of moving somewhere else, or get transferred, and I could be patient. Maybe I should have been clearer."

But she knew why she hadn't been clearer, why she had not admitted her discontent with living here right from the start. Her usual submissiveness had kicked in, the chronic passivity that seemed to have condemned her to accepting what was handed to her in life without making any effort to change it. She had been living in the first place of her own, a tiny apartment in the back of a remodeled carriage house, for only a year and a half when she had met Don; it had been almost a relief to love him, to be able to surrender much of the management of her life to him.

"You always said you didn't exactly want to die in this town," she finished.

"I don't. And it wasn't much fun when we were still living together to have Laurie pestering us about when we were going to get married and old Eugene glaring at me as if I was some sort of rapist or pervert who stole his little girl." He was silent for a while. "Look, maybe your parents will decide against moving to Rolling Hill Acres, and they'd still have to sell their house first. There's nothing definite, right?"

Gena nodded.

"No point in getting stressed out about it now." He drew his feet from the table and sat up. "What's in the box?"

"Oh." She had nearly forgotten about that afternoon's purchase. She felt a momentary twinge of apprehension. "Remember those nested dolls we saw downtown at Dunhill and Stein last week? The ones I thought were so cute?"

"No."

"Of course you do. The kitty cats, the handcarved and handpainted ones with all those Russian imports. You told me later that they looked like they could have been made in Catalonia. Well, I bought them." She opened the box, pushed aside the tissue paper, and lifted the nested dolls from the box, opening each to remove the smaller dolls inside until seven painted wooden cats sat on the tabletop. "I just couldn't resist them. Now I just have to figure out where to put them. Actually, I saw a nice wood and glass cabinet at Dunhill and Stein that would be perfect for displaying them, and we could use it for other—"

"Those cats must have cost a pretty penny."

"They weren't cheap. They're handmade."

"You must have spent a good share of what you made this week."

Gena took a deep breath. "I went to the bank and got the money from Household."

"Household?" Don's mouth hung open. "Household?"

"They're decor for the house. That's as much a household expense as your Wii is."

"So that's what this is about. I'd really like to hear how you decided that getting expensive imported handmade Russian nested dolls was a household expense."

"I told you. They're decor for our home." Gena batted her eyes, trying to look as cute as possible. "Besides, they're so Catalonian. Why, they might have been carved for Nicholas and Alexandra."

"I don't give a damn!" he shouted, startling her.

Household had driven him to this, to attacking Catalonia. Gena stared at him, unable to speak. What had Household done to him? She could almost sense Household lurking nearby, waiting for any chance to strike at her through Don, even if that meant delivering a massive and possibly fatal blow to Catalonia and its inhabitants.

"You obviously have no real understanding of what Household's purpose is," he continued in a deeper voice and considerably more hostile tone. "You can't go around throwing money away and trying to justify it as a household expense. That goes against the whole reason for setting up our household account in the first place. I thought we could handle that account together, but—"

She felt the Catalonian Palace Guard taking up position behind her, all of its members clothed in boots, long jackets, and furry hats much like those worn in "The Wizard of Oz" by the Wicked Witch of the West's soldiers, ready to come to the defense of Alexandra and her feline court.

Gena said icily, "So Catalonia doesn't matter to you any more."

"This isn't about Catalonia," he replied, still speaking in that weird deep voice. "It's about Household."

There was no help for it; she fell back on her last line of defense and burst into tears.

"Oh, Jesus," Don muttered, sounding more like himself. "Come on, Gena, I didn't mean it about Catalonia. See?" He emitted a few heartfelt meows. "Groomies? Want some groomies?" He moved closer to her and began to comb her hair with his fingers.

She allowed herself a few purrs, but was not entirely mollified. Striking at Catalonia was a grievous offense. Without Catalonia, their marriage might have been in serious trouble by now, what with their recent disagreements over Household and her mother's threatened move to Rolling Hill Acres. Catalonia was probably one of the few things she and Don had in common.

Not quite. There was also Household.

The air around her abruptly went cold.

Household was near, determined to control them both forever.

But she pushed her fears away, curled up, and rested her head on Don's lap as he continued to stroke her hair.

Five

Don was losing himself. Once he had dreamed of travel, seeing more of the world, but he had to consider Gena now. The marriage he had sought, that had promised him stability, warmth, companionship, and love, had turned him into a fearful, timid man who settled for things instead of reaching out for them.

Of course he still loved Gena. He had been in love with her ever since he had first glimpsed her curled up in a chair at Barnes & Noble with a volume of fairy tales. She had lifted her head and gazed at him with her soft hazel eyes, and he had known that he was a goner, that his previous two long-term relationships had been no more than infatuations, that it would be only a matter of time before he and that small and slender stranger were together. Yet he would have been content simply to go on living with her for the foreseeable future if not for some of the advantages marriage conferred, such as medical insurance for both of them through his employer and, given their disparate incomes, a more favorable tax situation.

Marriage had also eased his strained relationship with Gena's parents, even though they had been extremely upset that Gena and he had decided to tie the knot at the county courthouse with only a couple of friends as witnesses, informing the Lawlors a week after the event had taken place. Don had explained that big formal weddings were costly and wasteful, that for his brother to fly up from Florida and his parents to travel almost three thousand miles across the country for a lavish wedding would have involved considerable inconvenience and expense.

Don's father had been so relieved at being able to avoid his son's wedding without having to feel guilty about it that he had sent an overly generous check as a wedding present. Devlan had called to extract a promise that Don and Gena would visit him as soon as his business picked up and he had time to show them around. Eugene Lawlor, even while regretting that he had not been able to give his little girl away at a fancy shindig, had been impressed by his son-in-law's practicality.

But it was also true that Don lived in dread of ever having his parents and Gena's within a hundred miles of one another, let alone in the same room, and had known that having them all in attendance at his wedding would have been courting disaster. Old Laurie would probably consider his parents' lifestyle, which included such pursuits as bowling, weekend breakfasts at the local fire station, and avid viewing of professional wrestling matches and NASCAR races, along with his mother's boning up on current events by means of the *Star* and the *National Enquirer*, and his father's membership in a lodge named after a herd animal, beneath contempt. He had felt that way himself once, embarrassed by his mother's credulity and his father's heartiness, qualities that had remained unchanged in them even after their improved finances might have allowed for a bit more refinement, before his mother-in-law's snootiness had given him a new appreciation of his family's unpretentious ways. Lately he found himself recalling the bedtime stories his mother had read to him in her gentle, halting voice during his childhood, and how often she had embarrassed him during his teens with her enthusiastic hugs. Guilt pricked him; he would visit his parents more often; he missed them terribly sometimes, even though he would never admit that to Gena and could barely admit it to himself.

Yes, there had been good solid reasons for getting married, but lately he was having second thoughts. Not about staying with Gena, of course—he loved her and would give up his life for her, not that such a choice was likely ever to present itself during his uneventful existence. He could also escape to Catalonia with her, where he could forget about the insurance business and the damned district supervisor who seemed intent on making life as unpleasant as possible for him and his coworkers.

Maybe Catalonia was much of what still bound him to Gena at this point. He had always had a disgustingly sentimental side that he had concealed from everyone—his macho father, his sturdy if suggestible mother, his friends. He had even hidden his mushier side from his older brother, although Devlan, who had remained in the closet until long after he had moved away from home, coming out only after establishing his business in Key West and a home with his partner Rob, might have been sympathetic. Gena was the only person who was aware of his softer side, who had immediately welcomed the chance to elaborate on Catalonia with him. She might have almost no practical sense, but at least she could share Catalonia with him.

So he had always assumed, anyway, before she had started messing around with those two china cats on their dresser. He had grown so used to seeing them in their customary position—front paws and noses touching—that he usually ignored them. Now they had become a barometer measuring his wife's emotional state, perhaps even the state of their marriage. After they had argued earlier that week, he woke up to see the cats glaring at each other across an expanse of several inches. If their argument was especially bitter, or involved disputes about Household, the cats were often placed with their backs to each other. That morning, he had risen to find the black china cat behind a barricade of perfume bottles and her yellow-furred mate taking shelter near a grove of earring trees. Evidently Gena was still pissed off about those nested Russian cats and his insistence that she either return them to the store or return the money she had spent on them to Household.

Lately, thoughts of Catalonia, instead of amusing and consoling him, evoked darker thoughts. He would envision Nicholas and Alexandra sneaking off to separate wings of their palace, each meeting with favored courtiers and plotting against the other. He would recall how viciously content their former cat Vladimir had looked after sating his blood lust with a bird or some other innocent little creature, and begin to think that dreaming up a peaceful world of cats was stretching the limits of sanity to absurdity, even for such an imaginary construct as Catalonia. The sight of the two china cats that morning had made him feel uneasy, even threatened by something unseen, something that was stalking him and waiting to pounce. Maybe his imagination was getting the better of him, but Gena had looked unusually hostile at breakfast, pouring his coffee and looking as though she could as easily have hurled the cup at him as set it down on the table. Her hazel eyes had seemed greener, too, and colder, with almost the same gleam he had often seen in Vladimir's eyes.

"Don?"

He looked up and into the beautiful blue eyes of Stella Przhewalski, the newly hired underwriter. "Here's that file you wanted," she went on.

"Thanks," Don replied.

As Stella left his cubicle, he noticed a couple of his fellow workers ogling her discreetly as she passed their open doorways. If he hadn't been married, if the company didn't have all its detailed directives about employee relations and sexual harassment, maybe—

Nicholas, his Catalonian counterpart, would certainly be attentive to any good-looking female cat who crossed his path. Gena had insisted that the inhabitants of Catalonia, unlike the felines of the human world, had to be monogamous. Maybe, but Don had his doubts about that.

He opened the file, trying to concentrate. Most of his days lately were spent looking through files and staring at his computer screen as he tried to figure out if certain claims should be paid in full, or even paid at all, and his attention often drifted.

Maybe those rumors he kept hearing about the company downsizing this office, or even closing it, were true. If so, he could hope that he might be transferred to another city, the only practical way to move somewhere else, and that might be the best thing for him and Gena. She was counting on him; she sure as hell wouldn't be able to make an escape from her home town turf on her own. Once her dependence on him had made him feel important and needed. Now it was becoming a burden that he longed to shed.

He thought enviously of Nicholas, free to roam around Catalonia all night with his friends, knowing that Alexandra wouldn't worry about him and could take care of herself. He imagined cats roaming Catalonian streets, their old instincts roused, longing for blood and for prey.

* * * *

Don drove home earlier than usual, feeling depressed. Lately, he was beginning to look forward to those beers before dinner a little too much. As he came down his street, he saw his mother-in-law's blue Volvo pulling away from his house. He shrank back against his seat as he put on the brakes, but apparently Laurie hadn't noticed him; otherwise, she would have screeched to a halt, rolled down her window, and been hollering "Yoo hoo!" at him by now.

He drove toward his driveway and pulled in behind Gena's car. One of these days, Household would have to provide them with a carport, since the house had no garage. Summer was less than three months away; he might find somebody willing to do the work for a reasonable price by then. He didn't like the thought of depleting the household funds for a carport, but if they moved, such an addition would make it easier to sell the house.

Who am I kidding, he thought. They wouldn't be moving for a while, and even if they did, it would probably just be to another house in this city or its suburbs. His father, an unskilled laborer all his life, considered a reasonably well-paid white-collar job like Don's one of the pinnacles of human achievement, and even Don had once considered himself lucky to have landed his position.

Now he was thinking of opportunities that might have been lost. In college, he had indulged himself with courses in math, physics and astronomy before buckling down to courses in business; after all, he hadn't won a full tuition scholarship to a respected university in the eastern United States just so that he could blow all that largess on entertaining himself intellectually. He had toyed with the idea of getting a graduate degree, additional training that might have qualified him to teach or do research and feel as though he was of some real use to others. But that would have meant taking out another student loan before paying off the old ones, and he and Gena could never have survived on the comparatively low pay such professions yielded, especially if she continued to drift through life with her modestly paid position and her habit of throwing money away every time a silk blouse or some hand-painted Russian cat dolls struck her fancy, like a bullet shot at a bell.

"No practical sense," a voice said inside him, "that's her problem, and it's going to get worse. Maybe you'd be better off without her. Maybe you'd be better off if she—"

Don shook himself. Self-pity and rage were a volatile combination, especially when combined with beer. He took a deep breath, opened the back door, and went into the kitchen, which seemed darker than usual. For a moment, he felt as though he was being watched, but managed to shrug off the feeling. He was at the refrigerator before he heard the faint sound of sobs.

He crept toward the dining room. A bottle of champagne sat in an ice bucket on the table, flanked by two unlit candles in silver holders sent by one of Gena's aunts as a wedding present. Gena was slouched over the table at the other end of the room, her shoulders shaking, her head buried in her arms, a wad of tissues in one outstretched hand.

"What's the matter?" Don asked.

"Oh, Don." Gena raised her head. Her face was streaked with tears.

"And what's with the champagne?"

"I was going to celebrate. Barney told us at work that those pay increases were going to come through for everybody next month after all, and he hinted that I might get a promotion, too."

"But that's great," he said, bewildered.

"Then Mom came by, and she told me Dad just loves Rolling Hill Acres. They went there last weekend to check everything out. Dad didn't say a word to her after that, Mom said, and then this morning he suddenly jumps out of bed and says, 'I like that place, I really like that place.' What are we going to do?"

Don could not speak.

"I'll go crazy, I just know I will. Why did I have to be an only child? It's bad enough now, but Mom'll be coming over all the time then."

Don kept his voice steady. "We'll just have to set some rules. We'll just have to be firm." He wished that he could sound more commanding and convincing.

"Rules?" Gena wailed. "What rules has she ever listened to? We said don't come over without calling first, don't drop by on weeknights unless it's really urgent, don't call us late at night or really early in the morning. When has she ever paid any attention?"

"She'll have to pay attention now," he said.

"We have to move. That's the only way out of this."

"Gena, you know we can't—"

"We have to move! I don't care where it is, just as long as we're at least a thousand miles away!"

"Excuse me?" Don, still in his coat, sat down across from her. "I've got to throw away my job, this house, and everything else because you can't figure out how to handle your own mother? Give me a break! Why don't you just tell her that you think moving to Rolling Hill Acres is a lousy idea?"

"I can't tell her that!" Gena cried.

"That's your problem! You can't tell her anything! Maybe if you could, you'd start growing up!"

Gena let out a shriek, and then they were off, fighting the most vicious battle they had ever had. Don could not stop himself from blurting out that

Gena's mother was a true dyed-in-the-wool bitch, which of course required that his wife defend her mother's honor. She accused him of marrying her under false pretenses, of leading her to believe that they would be living in her home town for only a short time when he had actually intended to stay here permanently. He pointed out that she, having always lived in the same area except while away at college, had no practical understanding of what any move across the country entailed.

From this relatively high ground, they quickly descended into more brutal commentary about personal mannerisms, bodily hygiene, slovenly housekeeping, choices of entertainment, and weight control issues. Don declared that Gena's habit of clicking her tongue against the roof of her mouth to express disapproval drove him nuts; she responded by telling him that he could use a stronger mouthwash and could drink less fattening beverages than beer. He was about to retort that she could use an aerobics or Pilates class herself when his gaze fell to the champagne.

The bottle was still in the bucket, unopened; the ice around it had melted. Don leaned toward the bottle. "Moët and Chandon?" he asked as he read the label. "Isn't that kind of steep?"

"I wanted to celebrate!" Gena shouted, and then: "Besides, Household bought it!"

"You tell me how the hell champagne's a household expense!"

"All right, I'll tell you! The only way I can stand being in this household is by getting drunk enough to put up with you!"

They hurled more abuse at each other, and then somewhere in the back of Don's mind, a small voice started whispering for a time out, to put a sock in it, to remind his now enraged and red-faced wife that her parents had not yet made a final decision about a change in their abode.

But this fight wasn't about Gena's mother. It was about her own insecurities and lack of spine. Having failed to stand up to her parents in the past, she now let them walk all over her. She could not handle her own life, and depended on him to do that for her.

"Stop," the small voice inside him was saying, a feline voice, almost Catalonian. "You mustn't do this, I can't allow it." Nicholas would not be snarling and hissing at his beloved Alexandra as if he were no better than a lowly alley cat. Catalonians were not only better behaved than the cats of this world, they were also far more rational than human beings. Surely he could follow their noble example.

"Expensive champagne," another deeper voice murmured, "as a household expense," and Don recognized it as that of Household, or how he had often imagined Household would sound. "Next thing you know, she'll be dipping into my funds for such necessities as caviar and single malt Scotch."

The voice was so real that he could feel Household leaning over his shoulder to murmur to him.

"I don't know how you could have married such a fool," the venomous voice added.

"I don't know how I ever married such an idiot!" Don shouted.

"I don't know why I married such a creep!" Gena screamed back.

The cats scurried for cover. He could not see them, but sensed them running to hide in the living room or fleeing upstairs. All of Catalonia was going to ground. Even the carved Russian cats standing in a row on the sideboard looked as though they were desperately trying to remain inconspicuous until the storm blew over.

"Stupid impractical woman," the voice of Household whispered, "always sticking her hands into my moneybags at the slightest excuse. Before you know it, there won't be any of me left."

"Bitch!" Don got up from the table. "I hope you choke on your goddamned champagne! I hope all of Catalonia chokes on it!"

And then he stomped toward the kitchen and let himself out the back door.

Six

on drove around for a while before realizing that he was hungry. Spotting the light of a sign with golden arches up ahead, he headed to the drive-through and ordered supper.

As he devoured his Quarter Pounder with cheese, his resentment grew. His argument with Gena had been pointless, but he was still furious with her. He was not about to forget this little set-to even if her parents changed their minds about Rolling Hill Acres and moved to Hawaii. Now, instead of enjoying a meal in his own home, he was forced to sit in this parking lot chowing down in his car, and would probably have indigestion later, all because of Gena. He sure as hell wasn't going to pay for his burger and fries out of his own funds; this meal would for damned sure come out of Household.

He realized then that he was only a few blocks from Jeff Nardi's apartment. Jeff, his closest friend, had trained him in at the insurance office before abruptly quitting his job to go into business for himself. Jeff was a likeable dude, but absentminded enough to have forgotten to show up when Don had invited him to his and Gena's wedding, arriving just as they were leaving the courthouse with Johnny and Tracey Birnbaum. He was also impractical. At least Don had always thought of Jeff as impractical, given that Jeff seemed happy to drift through life with no thought of settling down and no solid plans for the future.

Now, thinking of how quietly contented his friend always appeared to be, it seemed that Jeff might somehow possess the secrets of the universe. Don needed some of those

* * * *

Jeff Nardi lived a few blocks from downtown in a new complex of twenty apartment units that resembled a college dormitory. Most of the spaces in the parking lot were taken, but Don found a spot at the edge of the lot.

As he left his car, a howl pierced the silence. The howl was answered by another shriek, and soon cries that sounded like those of newborn babies demanding to be fed echoed through the night.

He hurried across the lot toward the building's lighted entrance, feeling uneasy in the darkness. A screech louder and more piercing than the rest made him pick up his pace. Only cats, he thought, and there were a lot of them around, judging by the sound, but he still felt apprehensive.

"Hrrow!" a creature of some sort shrieked very close to him. He looked around hastily, but saw only the metal carapaces of cars, SUVs, and mini-vans. Maybe the cats were hiding under the cars, waiting to make their move.

He felt as if he was being stalked, ridiculous as that was. The howls and cries were giving him the willies, as if a multitude of cats were speaking to him, castigating him for his cruel remarks to Gena and the abuse he had directed at their private world of Catalonia.

He came to the entrance, pressed the buzzer, opened the front door to let himself into the hallway, then hit the button below Jeff's mailbox. After a few moments, a door at the end of the hallway opened.

"Yo, Don," Jeff called out; he was dressed in a T-shirt and jeans. "Come on in." He motioned Don inside the apartment and slammed the door. "Haven't seen you in a while."

"How long?" Don asked.

"Not since February."

Don took off his trench coat, then sat down on the sofa in front of a coffee table piled high with magazines, newspapers, and books. A computer and work station sat in one corner, surrounded by cables; scores of CDs in jewel boxes and a few flash drives were scattered next to a laptop on the dining table near the kitchenette, along with a cell phone, a couple of coffee mugs, and a few empty take-out food containers and pizza boxes. The disorderliness of Jeff's apartment was oddly comforting.

"So what's the deal?" Jeff continued.

"Gena and I had a fight."

"Want a beer?"

"Nope."

"Some coffee?"

"No, thanks. Somebody near your building must be hosting a feral cat convention. I never heard so much meowing."

"Oh?" Jeff looked absently toward the glass doors that led outside to the building's patio. "Hadn't noticed. Maybe they're in heat or else the spring weather's getting to them. They couldn't be attracted by any cats here, because the manager doesn't allow pets." He sprawled in a chair, hooking his leg over one arm, then brushed strands of black hair from his forehead. "Did you have your fight before dinner or after?"

"Before, but I grabbed a bite on the way over." Don sighed. "Gena found out today that she's getting a raise and might be in line for a promotion. Then her mother apparently dropped by and said she and Gena's father might be moving to Rolling Hill Acres. And when I got home, we got into a big argument about how much money she took from the household fund for a set of Russian dolls and a bottle of champagne, so here I am."

"That's really enlightening," Jeff said.

"The money's what did it," Don said. "That's what we were really fighting about. Gena has no money sense at all. I don't know how she ever got a job at St. Luke's in Billing and Accounts Receivable—the whole damn hospital'll probably go broke one of these days."

"I thought you worked all that out," Jeff said. "You used to brag about it. Gena has her own account and cards, you have yours, and you put the rest of your money into a joint account."

"Household. That's what our joint account is called. Except now we keep getting into arguments over what is a household expense and what isn't. The whole point was to avoid that."

"You want some advice?" Jeff asked.

Don nodded.

"Close the joint account, take out all the money, and split it down the middle. Then do what you want with your share, or even leave it where it was under just your name. If Gena blows her share, that's her lookout. It's a waste of time to fight over that stuff. Life is too short."

Life is too short. That was Jeff's favorite saying. Life was too short to buy a house and tie himself down with a mortgage and property to maintain, to stay at a job he hated, to get married and, even if he avoided a statistically probable divorce, to bring up children who stood an excellent chance of growing up to be extremely uncongenial, incompatible, and ungrateful adults who would have all manner of global environmental problems to contend with and wouldn't thank him for bringing them into existence only so that they could use up even more of the planet's shrinking resources. Once Don had found this a cold and overly bleak philosophy, but now he could almost discern its virtues.

"Can't do it," he said sadly.

"It's your funeral."

They watched an NCAA playoff game for a while, but Don found himself unable to concentrate on the players' moves. Anyway, if he stayed away too long, Gena might get hysterical and call her parents. He didn't want to arrive back home to find Gena weeping on Laurie's shoulder and Eugene getting after him about treating his little girl so badly.

"I'd better go," Don said.

"You can stay here, dude."

"I know, but I should go home."

Jeff got up and walked him to the door. "Look, if you need to come over, just give me a call. I'm usually here at nights except when I'm over at Rose's."

"Didn't know you were still seeing her."

"May not be pretty soon," Jeff said. "Now she's telling me our relationship isn't going anywhere. Whenever it's just about perfect, they tell you it isn't going anywhere, and then the you-can't-commit stuff starts, and then you break up. At least that's my experience."

As Don left the building, he heard more meows. The chorus of cats invisible was soon at full throttle, shrieking and yowling. He looked up, almost expecting to see a full moon in spite of the darkness, but the sky was black, so overcast that he could not see any stars.

The apprehension he had felt earlier seized him again. For a moment, he heard a sound like that of someone breathing near him, and then a soft growl. He stood still, listening, but discerned only the sound of distant traffic.

He would go home and apologize to Gena. That wouldn't settle anything, but they would have a cease-fire until he figured out what to do.

* * * *

The house was dark when Don got home. Gena's car was still in the driveway, and there was no sign of his mother-in-law's Volvo or his father-in-law's Escalade. He slipped inside through the front door, hung up his coat, then took off his shoes to tiptoe up the stairs.

A step creaked; he heard a sound that might have been a sigh. The thought came to him, not for the first time, that things had started going wrong between him and Gena not long after they had moved here, as if the house itself were exerting a malign influence on them. He could imagine, especially now, in the dark, that his house was haunted by some unknown entity.

The bedroom was dimly lit by the glowing numerals of the digital clock on the night table. Gena was asleep, the bedcovers pulled up over her head. He glanced at the dresser. The china Alexandra cat was still behind her fortress of perfume bottles, while Nicholas had been banished to the corner where Gena kept her makeup—not a good sign.

He lingered in the bathroom, reluctant to emerge from that strangely comforting refuge of antiseptic odors and fluorescent lighting, but finally forced himself to go back into the bedroom. He was in his pajamas and creeping toward the bed when Gena suddenly cleared her throat; he jumped.

"Jesus Christ, Gena."

"You stayed out long enough," she mumbled.

"I'm sorry," he said, meaning it. "I shouldn't have yelled at you. I'm sorry I made that remark about Catalonia."

"Got it on sale, you know," she said. "The champagne. The liquor store was having a special. And I didn't even open it after you left. I put it in the refrigerator. We can have it some other time."

"I'll look forward to it. Now go back to sleep."

He got into bed, still thinking. Jeff's suggestion about how to handle their money actually wasn't that bad, with a few modifications. The first order of business might be to tell Gena that she could handle a new household checking account by herself, since he could still look over the statements from time to time to see how much was being spent and make sure that particular account held only what they would need. Once they got that squared away, he could take full control of the savings account. There was really no good reason to keep it in both of their names, and maybe Gena would be so overjoyed at having Household's checking account in her keeping that she would not notice that Don was controlling most of their money.

Only fair, he thought. Think of practicalities, of their future, of Household. Once this money business was settled, they would be free to devote their efforts to more worthy ends, such as researching good potential long-term investments and deflecting Gena's parents from their threatened move to Rolling Hill Acres.

"Watch her," an orotund voice whispered as Don closed his eyes. He sensed its power, and the wretchedness that would surely be his if he ignored it. "She's been reckless in the past, so take care. Your future is at stake. Don't let her get out of hand. Don't be a patsy. I'll be keeping an eye on you both."

Be careful, Don told himself, ready to sleep at last.

Seven

"Caterina Lucci the cat doctor calling," the answering machine said as Gena picked up the phone.

"Hello?" Gena said.

"Gena! Glad I caught you," Caterina Lucci continued.

"I had some personal time to use up, so I don't have to be in until this afternoon."

"Good. I need to talk to you. Vladimir's here, along with a Mr. Elden Bowes."

"Is he all right?" Gena asked. "Vladimir, I mean."

"He's just as furry and cute as ever, but he did have quite an adventure, according to Mr. Bowes. Apparently Vladimir was outside when Mr. Bowes saw him with another cat, a large and extremely aggressive gray cat. They started hissing and snarling, and then they went at each other, and about two seconds later, some other cats suddenly showed up and chased the gray cat away, so luckily Vladimir escaped with just a couple of scratches. All he needed was some first aid, but Mr. Bowes insisted on having everything else completely checked out, and a good thing, too, because I noticed on Vladimir's chart that he was almost due for his rabies shot, so I gave it to him, and then I noticed that he was just about due for a feline leukemia vaccination, so Mr. Bowes is bringing the little fella back for that in a couple of weeks."

"Well, it was nice of you to call and let me know," Gena said, wondering why Dorothy, the veterinarian's receptionist, hadn't made the call for her. Caterina was a good vet, and deeply devoted to her feline patients, but she was also disorganized and could run on at the mouth. Gena had been at her office more than once when Dorothy had been forced to interrupt one of Caterina's lengthy soliloquies about Vladimir's cuteness and intelligence to remind her of her next appointment.

"I called," the veterinarian went on, "because naturally when Mr. Bowes came in, I assumed you'd asked him to bring Vladimir in for you, but he said, no, that wasn't the case, a cat is a free being and Vladimir had been keeping company with him for the past few months."

"He used to be our landlord," Gena said.

"Yes, that's what he said, and also that Vladimir had chosen to return to his house and take up residence there some time after you moved to your house, so of course I wanted to verify that."

"It's true," Gena said. "Vladimir has no loyalty at all."

"Cats give their affections freely," Caterina said, "you can't demand them." It sounded like something Mr. Bowes would say. "But I do sympathize with you. Anyway, when I gave Mr. Bowes the bill, he told me to call you."

"Why?"

"He said you and Don would pay it, so of course I had to verify that."

"We'd pay it?" Gena croaked, thinking of all the money they already owed the vet for treating Vladimir's earlier battle injuries.

"Yes, and for the feline leukemia shot, too."

"Why us?" Gena asked. "Vladimir's living with him now."

"Yes, I know, but he said that you and Don were the people who brought Vladimir into his life and that he shouldn't be penalized financially for that and that it wasn't his fault that the little guy decided that he preferred living with him instead of you because a cat is a free being."

"A very expensive being," Gena muttered.

"And he *is* paying for Vladimir's food and general upkeep. He even asked me for some suggestions on his diet, since he has gained a bit of weight. Anyway, he's still here, so do I bill you or extort the money from him?"

Gena sighed. "Send the bill to us," she said, feeling defeated. Maybe when she told Don about this, he would get angry enough to go over to Mr. Bowes's house, confront him, and return either with Vladimir or with reimbursement of the bill. She knew that she was not up to confronting the old man herself.

"Tell you what," Caterina said. "I won't send the bill until after he gets the feline leukemia shot. You can wait and pay the whole amount after that." That was quite generous of Caterina, considering how far behind they were on the substantial sum they already owed her.

"Thanks." Gena paused. "Did Dorothy take the day off?"

"Dorothy's taking the rest of her life off. She called me up and told me with absolutely no warning that she was quitting as of today, because her dog can't stand to be around her when she gets home from work. So now, except for my two part-timers, I have to handle everything by myself, and frankly, business hasn't been all that great lately, even with Wednesday evening and Saturday morning hours. Maybe this town isn't big enough to support a vet who only handles cats."

"I'm sorry to hear that."

"I may have to consider taking on dogs, and much as I love them, too, I really think they should see their own vets." Caterina was silent for a moment. "Say, you wouldn't be interested in taking the job, would you?"

"What job?"

"Dorothy's job. My office manager. I know you can handle the computer and the billing, and the scheduling and phone calls and the rest of it isn't that hard. And you've got experience with cats from your work with Operation Whiskers. I'll pay you whatever you're getting now and throw in two weeks of vacation during the first year."

Gena's heart leaped. A job, and in an environment not unlike her beloved Catalonia. Still holding the phone to her ear, she paced the kitchen, wanting to accept. She could be around cats throughout the week instead of staring at a screen of numerals and columns of figures, sending out letters warning of dire consequences if overdue bills were not soon paid, trying to decipher the boilerplate of various medical insurance policies, and lulling herself into a stupor as she went about the kind of work that would not exist in any just society. She could be of some service to people, or at least to their animal companions. She would no longer have to feel sullied and soulless.

If she did go to work for Caterina, though, she would be giving up any chance for a permanent position with St. Luke's, a job with considerably more potential benefits and opportunities for advancement than Caterina could offer, assuming that the occasional whispers she had overheard about St. Luke's outsourcing some of the work in Billing and Accounts Receivable were false.

"I wish I could," Gena said, "but—"

"Think it over. I'd much rather give the job to somebody I know."

"Um," Gena said, so as not to commit herself.

"Just let me know fairly soon, like maybe in a week or so. By the way, can I ask you something about Mr. Bowes?"

"Sure."

"Is he reasonably sane? Or would you call him a couple of wrenches short of a tool box?"

"He's eccentric," Gena replied, "but I wouldn't call him nutty. When we were renting from him, he kept the place up and always handled any repairs right away, so you'd have to say he's reliable. He was actually a pretty good landlord, even if he didn't exactly discourage Vladimir from moving back in with him."

"I asked because he said that those cats—the ones that chased the gray cat away, the cat that got into the fight with Vladimir—were still sitting around his house when he left to bring Vladimir to my office, and that they followed him to his car and then sat there staring at him as he drove away. He insisted there was something really strange about them, something weird about the way they were sitting there and watching him and Vladimir. I told him cats can give some people the willies and he shouldn't worry about that, but he said, no, he'd never been fearful of cats, and they were certainly free to stare at him as much as they liked, but these particular cats gave him the distinct impression that they were keeping him and Vladimir under, well, some kind of surveillance."

"Since cats are free beings," Gena said, "there isn't a whole lot he can do about that."

"I suppose not. Better go. I'll give Vladimir a scratch behind the ears for you. 'Bye."

Gena crossed the kitchen, put the phone back in its cradle, then poured herself another cup of coffee. There would be no Billing and Accounts Receivable departments at Catalonian hospitals, she thought, because Catalonian cats had universal veterinary services that were free to all. Nor would any cats dream of calling up other cats to dun them for unpaid bills, but would call only to offer unexpected discounts and refunds. After all, if they hassled their fellow felines over anything like accounts that were in arrears, the aggrieved parties would probably show up at their offices pronto and go for their creditors' throats.

She shook herself, startled at how vivid that thought had been, how suddenly her own anger had welled up inside her. Such thoughts of violence should have no place in her Catalonian musings.

Household could cover Vladimir's new vet bill, but she wondered if Don would agree to that. She could cite precedent, but he could counter that Vladimir was no longer a member of their household. She could feel another argument coming on, one that would begin with their former cat and this unforeseen expense and then quickly degenerate into personal accusations. Don would be after her again about her spinelessness, about how she should have refused to agree to pay Caterina anything for Vladimir's treatment, and soon she would be yelling at him about how he should have gone over to Mr. Bowes's house a long time ago and demanded that he give their cat back to them immediately, whether Vladimir was a free being or not.

The kitchen seemed cold, colder than usual. Don was always harping on how they had to save on their heating bill, which of course was paid by Household. Maybe that was why Vladimir, who often sought out spots near heating vents to take his catnaps, had gone to live with Mr. Bowes, who had always kept his furnace going full blast, regardless of the cost.

Someone was standing behind her. She could feel herself being watched. Gena looked around quickly, but she was alone in the kitchen. The air around her still felt too cold.

She finished her coffee, surprised at how little it had warmed her, and was about to head upstairs to take a shower and get dressed when the telephone rang again.

"Hello, Eugenia," her mother's voice said on the machine, "this is your mother. Are you there? If you're there, pick up." Gena sighed; her mother could never do anything so simple as to leave a message. "Pick up, dear. It's about Rolling Hill Acres and our plans."

More bad news, she thought, and picked up the phone, steeling herself for the worst.

* * * *

Gena sang to herself in the shower and hummed as she got dressed. Maybe things were finally going her way after all. She had just finished putting on her mascara when an inspiration suddenly came to her.

Her problem with Household could be easily solved. She was amazed that she hadn't thought of the solution before. Since Household had become a source of conflict rather than being a means to avoid battles, it was time to get rid of Household altogether.

Caterina deserved to be paid. A quick calculation told her that Household's meager assets would be much diminished if she paid the vet what she was owed, but that was only fair, especially since Caterina thought enough of her in spite of that debt to offer her a job. Household would have to be liquidated. This was such a daring and startling notion that the bedroom lights seemed to flicker for a moment, while a looming shadow behind the night table took on the aspect of a bird of prey. She could almost imagine that Household was preparing to take on physical form to strike her down for her presumption.

Doubt bit her. Don might not be so amenable to dispensing with Household.

Her gaze fell to the two china cats on her dresser. The painted Alexandra was still glowering at the china Nicholas from behind her wall of perfume bottles, while Nicholas cowered behind a makeup case. Gena picked up both of the figurines and set them down next to each other, knowing that reconciliation was now possible.

Getting rid of Household would save Catalonia. She had to look at it that way. Don had said cruel and unkind things about their shared world, statements he could never have made without Household egging him on. Maybe that was why Vladimir had deserted Gena and Don for Mr. Bowes; maybe Household had driven him away.

Well, a new day was dawning, she thought as she hurried down the stairs and through the kitchen to the back door. The morning fog had lifted and the clouds were parting, promising a sunny afternoon. She closed the door, made sure it was locked, then turned to see four cats sitting in a row in the small back yard.

Two calicos, a yellow-furred cat and a small gray cat with white markings, stared at her. She glanced at them, expecting them to scurry away, but they continued to watch her as she walked toward the sidewalk. She looked back to see the gray-furred cat and one of the calicos trailing after her.

She stopped and faced the cats. They gazed at her with an unnerving stillness, then sat down and began to lick their paws.

She thought of all the times she and Don had talked about how wonderful it would be if Catalonian cats suddenly showed up on their doorstep, their imagined world made manifest. They would of course have to invite them inside, and listen to their tales of Catalonia as they served them shrimp and spring water.

The cats stopped licking their paws and stared at her again, and she had the distinct feeling that they might attack if she annoyed them enough.

But she had nothing to fear from them. She could imagine that the cats were there to support her in her efforts to rid herself of Household, urging her not to back down.

"You live there, don't you?" a voice said. She turned. A white-haired old man in a baggy tweed coat stood on the sidewalk.

"Um," she said, thinking that it was none of his business.

"You do," he muttered. "I know you do." She walked past the old man, ignoring him. He looked like he was hard up, with his frayed coat and muddy shoes, and she wondered what he was doing in this neighborhood. Maybe he was casing the houses, looking for an easy target.

She looked back. The old man was gone, and she could no longer see the cats, either, only a strange dark shadow looming over her house. She watched as the shadow slowly faded, banished by sunlight. She was spooking herself, she thought, worrying about some old guy who was probably harmless and a few cats that had happened to wander into her yard.

Gena continued toward the bus stop. Perhaps her mother's news, good tidings for once, had unlocked her mind to inspiration, thus showing her the way to free herself from Household's tyranny.

Mrs. Lawlor had begun by saying that a townhouse in Rolling Hill Acres no longer seemed so enticing. "Your father got up this morning," she continued, "and announced that he couldn't think of moving to a place where he wouldn't have room for his workshop." Mr. Lawlor's workshop was a room in the basement where he stored his largely unused tools. He only went there to read, watch TV, have a drink at the room's small bar, call up coworkers on business, or entertain his buddies when they came over to watch sports events with him, yet he refused to call the room a study, hideaway, rec room, den, man cave, fortress of solitude, or any other more appropriate term than "workshop."

"So that's that," Gena's mother concluded, "and there isn't much chance of talking him into a condo, either, since there would be even less space for his workshop there."

"Maybe that's for the best," Gena had murmured. "You've put a lot of work into your house, and it's not so big that you'd have trouble looking after it later on."

"True. It also didn't escape me that you weren't exactly overjoyed at the prospect of having us nearby at Rolling Hill Acres. Now don't object, dear," she went on, even though objecting to that assertion was the furthest thing from Gena's mind. "At any rate, the more I thought about it, the more it didn't make sense to leave this house and go to all that trouble just to move a short distance away. So what we're considering now is a place in Florida, just for the winter, and we're already making plans to go down there and look around sometime after Christmas."

Gena had struggled to control her ecstasy; a few months free of her mother's surveillance was a truly enticing prospect.

There was a spring in her step as she approached the bus stop on the corner of Ackley and Rycroft. What a wonderful day, she thought as she nodded at the other two women waiting under the shelter for the bus. Now all she had to do was settle the business of Household. That would take courage and fortitude, but with one victory of sorts under her belt, she could handle Household.

She imagined herself handing Don a beer when he came home, then telling him the news. "Mom and Dad decided against moving to Rolling Hill Acres. Why, they're even thinking of going to Florida for part of the year. Wasn't I silly for getting so worked up about having them move closer to us? And guess what? Household is no more."

Gena shifted her weight from one foot to the other. A clean strike—that was the way to handle Household. Wipe it out and give it no chance to regroup. Don's most frequent complaint about her lately was that she was too dependent and lacked spine and initiative—well, she would show him that she had plenty of initiative. Whatever quibbles he might have, he would probably be relieved that she had taken the matter of Household into her own hands and decided it once and for all.

Eight

Don gaped at Larry Philmus. Larry, the local office manager, gazed back at him across the desk. Larry looked just about as miserable as Don felt, which was probably why Al Farris, the goddamned district supervisor, had picked Larry to convey the bad news instead of doing so himself. Al would never settle for making only one guy miserable when he could torment two.

"Shit," Don muttered at last.

"Could be worse." Larry leaned back in his chair. "You've got your severance pay, and unemployment, and you're bound to find something sooner or later."

"Really? In this job market?"

"I'll give you a glowing recommendation."

He should have seen it coming. That was the worst of it, that he had refused to see that his own job was in jeopardy, that he had let himself get so out of touch with the office grapevine that he hadn't had a clue. He had known that the company might decide to scale down this office, and that a few people would be let go when they did, even that the local office might be closed down entirely. And then he had dismissed such troublesome thoughts.

"I know it's a pisser," Larry said. "I'm not thrilled about moving to Illinois, either. Now I have to go home and tell Joanie she's got to give up that exercise class she teaches at our church and tell my kids that they'll be going to a new school away from all their friends. That's assuming we can even sell our house any time soon."

"At least you have a job," Don said.

"I know. I keep telling myself that. I'm really sorry, Don."

Don got to his feet. "But I'll bet that son of a bitch Farris isn't sorry."

"His days might be numbered. With all the offices we're closing, they won't need that many district supervisors soon."

Don left Larry's office and wandered back to his cubicle. Instead of sitting down at his work station, he grabbed his coat and headed for the elevator. What was the point of sitting around here tying up loose ends, enduring the pity of colleagues, and commiserating with other victims of the purge?

The elevator was mercifully empty. Don rode it to the lobby, which was also empty; noon was still a half-hour away. He hurried outside and crossed

Court Street to the sidewalk that circled the park in front of the county court-house. The weather had brought a beautiful spring day; in less than a month, the park's tulips would be in bloom. He wondered what he would be doing by then.

Don sat down on a bench. An old man in a baggy tweed overcoat was shouting incoherently at the sky, then stopped and shuffled over to Don.

"Got a buck?" the old man asked in a calm deep voice unlike his ranting tone. He rubbed at his spiky white hair.

Normally Don would have ignored him, but now he reached for his wallet and handed the man two one-dollar bills.

"Here," he said. "I just lost my job," he added.

"Got fired?" the man asked.

"Laid off, let go, axed, downsized, shoved overboard, totally fucked over—whatever you want to call it."

The homeless man looked up. "The woonkels will do that to you!" he shrieked to the heavens. "By the way," he said quietly in his deeper voice, "thanks for the money. Thought you looked like kind of a Scrooge at first."

"Just don't buy any booze," Don said, but the other man was already wandering away. Whatever problems he had in his own life, he was a lot better off than that poor bastard, and maybe it was good to be reminded of that. He would refuse to let fear of long-term unemployment get to him; he had his severance pay, could squeeze out the payment for health insurance through COBRA for at least a few months, and Gena was set with her job for the foreseeable future. With that and unemployment, they could get by if they scaled back, and maybe he would find something sooner than expected, especially if he got aggressive about checking out possibilities in other parts of the country. Gena wouldn't mind that, given that she was always bugging him about moving away from here.

In the long run, things might actually improve for both of them. He had to look at it that way. Change, as he had read in an article somewhere recently, meant opportunity. And no matter what happened, he and Gena would still have Catalonia.

At that moment, he looked down to see a large long-haired cat with thick brown fur sitting on the grass near him.

He should never have made his intemperate remarks about their private world of cats, comments that he knew had wounded Gena deeply, and vowed that he would never do so again. Something had got into him; he had spewed his hateful comments even as part of him was struggling to keep silent. Catalonia was sacrosanct, a universe inhabited by a better breed than humankind, a world where cats could roam without hindrance and no one was ever laid off or downsized.

The brown-furred cat was still staring at him. "Here, kitty, kitty," Don said. The cat gave him a look of disdain, then slowly walked away, tail held high.

He took a deep breath of the clear spring air. Things could have been much worse; at least they hadn't given him an hour to clear out his desk under the watchful gaze of a security officer. He could not have endured that final humiliation, and allowing him to stay on until Friday had to mean that Al Farris trusted him enough to know that he would not go berserk and trash the office, or mess around with any important computer files. As big a prick as Farris was, maybe he'd feel enough pity and respect for Don to cough up a good recommendation. It was important to look on the bright side and keep up his spirits; prospective employers would sense any lack of confidence.

Don got up and walked toward the food vendor who had just finished setting up his parasoled cart on the corner. A chili dog with the works would hit the spot right about now, and then he would go back to the office and figure out exactly what to tell Gena. It would probably be best to put it in Catalonian terms, with a lot of meows.

* * * *

"Sorry I'm late," Gena said as she sat down across from Tracey Birnbaum, relieved to see that her friend seemed in good spirits. "My business at the bank took longer than I expected."

"Don't worry about it. I'm glad you called and asked me out to lunch." Tracey sipped from a glass of wine. "I'm in a good mood today, and believe it or not, it's all about kitty cats."

Gena started. She had been thinking of Catalonia, imagining herself padding along the streets of Mew York among hordes of feline city dwellers, on her way to a Fish and Flagon café, just before she had entered this restaurant, a newly opened eatery recommended by Tracey.

She steadied herself. "What about kitty cats?" she asked.

"First of all, what about you, kiddo? You look like the cat that just swallowed the canary."

"Actually, I've just settled a big problem," Gena replied.

Household would never again disturb her peace of mind. She had mailed a check to Caterina on her way here, and Don would get what little had been left in the household account in the form of a cashier's check to spend as he pleased. He would be proud of her. Household consigned to oblivion, his in-laws having second thoughts about Rolling Hill Acres—it would be a red-letter day for him as well.

"It's a good day for me, too," Tracey said. "Shauna Leopold wants me to illustrate her next three books."

"Shauna Leopold?" Gena asked.

"The children's books writer. I'm sure I mentioned her to you. She had a falling-out with the artist who's been working with her, and anyway her publisher thinks it may be time for a change, and she just loved the illustrations I did for *Manfred and Beelzebub*, especially the ones where Beelzebub the cat is playing with a Venetian blind cord."

"Beelzebub the cat?" Gena said.

"You remember, that kids' book I illustrated a year and a half ago, when I was coming over to your old place and using Vladimir as the model for Beelzebub. This is a big break for me. Shauna Leopold sells a lot of books, and now they're thinking of doing a Shauna Leopold calendar, and if they do, I'll be in line to do the paintings for that, too. All her books are about this world of cats where the fish leap out of rivers and turn into fillets, cats chase mice and birds just for fun, without ever really hurting them, and thick streams of milk flow through gardens of catnip—you get the picture."

"Really," Gena said.

"And those kitty cats might really pay off for me. I'm looking forward to this. Maybe I should go over to Caterina Lucci's and scope out some of the Catwoman's patients for inspiration."

"Sounds like a good idea," Gena said, not sure of that at all. Tracey had spooked her with her talk of Shauna Leopold and the writer's fictional feline world, and there was something a bit unnerving about Tracey's being so enthusiastic about painting cats, as she had usually kept her distance from Vladimir when visiting. It was almost as if Catalonia's ambience were leaking into her friend somehow, to make her so eager to tackle this new project.

Tracey finished her wine, then signaled to the waitress. Tracey was lucky, Gena thought; she could drink in the middle of the day and not have to worry about heading to the office afterwards. However much she might complain about the uncertainty of her work and her relative lack of security, she had a freedom Gena envied. Maybe one of her reasons for having Tracey as a close friend was that Tracey was everything Gena wasn't. Tracey had left her mother's home in Boston to go to college in California, had dropped out after a couple of years to attend art school in Philadelphia, had bummed around Europe for a few months visiting museums, and had then come back to New York City to launch her career. She hadn't been stuck for her whole life in one place, accepting whatever Fate deigned to send her way; the only reason she was living in this city at all was that Johnny, the fucking bastard, had found a job here right after their wedding, where she would be only a three-hour drive from Manhattan.

A waitress suddenly appeared at Gena's side. Tracey could even get a waitress to come to her table promptly, a skill that had always eluded Gena.

"What'll it be?" the waitress asked.

"It's on me," Gena said, "so order whatever you like."

"I'll have another glass of wine and the lobster salad," Tracey said, then grinned. "Good solid cat food."

Gena ordered the same, with a glass of iced tea, then noticed that the salt and pepper shakers on the table were small glass cats. She was beginning to feel as though she had drifted into a Catalonian outpost.

"Now tell me about your big problem and how you solved it," Tracey said.

"Oh." Gena stiffened in her chair. Maybe it wasn't fair to tell her friend about her decision before informing her own husband. "Tell you what—as soon as everything's settled with Don, you'll be the first to know."

"Ooooh. Sounds mysterious.

"Let me put it this way. We won't be arguing over that ridiculous household fund any more."

* * * *

As she opened the back door, Gena glimpsed a movement from the corner of her eye. When she turned around, she saw only an empty back yard of short green grass bordered by shrubs just beginning to sprout leaves. She was sure that she had just seen a small furry body scurry under one of the shrubs.

It was probably a neighbor's cat, or else one of the rabbits or raccoons that occasionally ventured down from the wooded hillsides that overlooked this end of the city. She could not see any small animals in the yard now, yet still felt as though something was watching her.

How strange, she thought as she closed the back door, that she should feel so apprehensive now. She had spent the whole afternoon delighted with herself for being so decisive, scrolling through the figures on her computer screen at her work station and entering data without a care in the world, and here she was feeling uneasy about what she had done. The house seemed much darker and more forbidding than usual, even with the overhead fluorescent kitchen lights on, and she was suddenly afflicted with dread. She could almost imagine that Household was still here, seriously weakened but still ready to do battle, a badly wounded warrior preparing to wreak his vengeance upon her.

She crept into the living room, glancing from side to side, expecting an ambush. A draft of cold air rushed past her face as she heard what sounded like a sigh. Instead of feeling freed from an unnecessary burden, she was beset with the amorphous apprehension that usually meant a violent thunderstorm was pending. She went to the living room window, wondering if the weather was changing, but the rosy evening sky was still clear.

She had hung up her coat and removed the envelope from her purse when she heard the back door slam. "Gena?"

Don was home early. "How's the queen of Catalonia?" he continued. "How's that wonderful, furry creature?"

"I've got some good news," she called out. Maybe it would be better to tell him about her parents first.

"Glad to hear it, Your Majesty," he shouted back. "Mine's not so good."

It sounded as though he'd had a really bad day at work. "Then I'll tell you my news first," she said.

"That might be a good idea."

She went into the living room and sat down on the sofa. Don entered the room with a bottle of beer in one hand and a large glass of wine in the other. He had a grim look on his face as he handed her the wine, and then he flopped down on the sofa and heaved a loud sigh.

The feeling of impending doom still hung over her. "Guess what?" she said, hoping to cheer him but hearing her voice quaver. "My parents decided not to move to Rolling Hill Acres after all, because Dad wouldn't have any space for his workshop there. They're even thinking of getting something in Florida for the winter."

"Great," he said, not sounding very enthusiastic. She had expected elation.

"Mom said—well, she admitted that maybe it wasn't such a good idea to live that close by. And they're already planning to go to Florida after New Year's to check out some places."

Don lifted his bottle and took a swig of beer. "I guess that's good news," he said in a flat voice, "but in a way, that doesn't matter now."

"Oh." Gena looked down at the envelope in her hands. At this point, she had planned to meow and curl up in his lap, but had lost her Catalonian spirit. "I've got something else to tell you. I did a lot of thinking after that awful fight we had the other night. It's stupid to fight so much about Household, especially when the whole point of having a household fund was to avoid those kinds of arguments."

Don lifted his head, looking slightly more cheerful. "I'm really glad to hear you say that. I've been thinking the same thing. In fact, I was going to talk to you about it before—"

"I did something about it, too," she said, feeling more confident. "You'll be proud of me, Don. I really took the bull by the horns." She handed him the envelope. "Darling Don" was printed in large letters on the front of the envelope, followed by italics spelling out "H.R.H. Nicholas I" and a rough sketch by Gena of what was intended to be a cat wearing a crown.

"What's this?"

"Open it."

Don tore open the envelope and took out the cashier's check, then peered at it. "What's this?" Gena was suddenly afraid to answer him. "Where did this come from?"

"Household."

"Household?" His mouth was hanging open; he looked completely bewildered.

"The only way to settle this," Gena said, feeling her determination return, "is to liquidate Household. So that's what I did. That's what was left after I paid off Caterina."

Don's mouth was still open. He hadn't said anything. She had expected at least a meow.

"I mean, we owed her a lot," she continued, "and I know she said we could pay her off a bit at a time, but her practice hasn't been doing so well lately and I figured she could use it. Anyone else would have been after us a long time ago." Don was silent. "And you can take what's left and do whatever you want with it." Gena batted her eyes. "I just wish that I could have deposited it all in Kittibank. They pay much higher interest than human banks."

Don held up the check and peered at it.

"Meow," Gena murmured. "Meeeaaaaoooow." She slid over next to him and clawed his arm gently with one hand.

He recoiled from her and leaped to his feet. "What an idiot!" he shouted. "I'm married to a total moron!"

"I was thinking of you!" she retorted. "I was thinking of us! I didn't want us fighting over money all the time!"

"Gena, I can't take this," he said more calmly. "I was laid off today."

"What?"

"Laid off. Canned. Fired. Had my ass tossed out of the company. They're closing the local office. By the end of this week, I won't have a job."

"You lost your job?" Gena asked.

"Hello! That's what I just finished saying! Let me explain something to you." He picked up his beer bottle and stomped to the other side of the room, then turned to face her. "I was counting on that money to help pay for our health insurance through COBRA until I find another job. We'll have to worry about every penny, maybe for a while, and you take what little we saved to pay a bill we didn't need to pay. I don't suppose you could stop payment on the check."

She pointed her chin at him. "I wouldn't do that to Caterina."

"Of course you wouldn't."

"I was only trying to help!" she cried.

And then they were off, dragging out long-buried disputes that seemed ready to be disinterred. She was an overly dependent and fearful young woman who couldn't take charge of her own life and only succeeded in creating disaster when she tried. He was an unambitious man who should have secured himself a better job in a nicer city long ago instead of settling for the position he had now lost. He worried too much about money; she didn't worry enough about it. She spent too much time hanging around with Tracey Birnbaum and too much money on useless items for their home; he went to seed every weekend staring at football, basketball, or baseball games for endless hours, or messing around with electronic games. He also had a way at the table of handling his fork as if it were a steam shovel, a mannerism that he had no doubt picked up from his uncouth parents.

"You leave my parents out of this," Don said. "You only visited them once."

"And what a joy that was." Those cruel words could not be coming from her, but she could not stop herself. She gulped down some of her wine. "Do they eat in front of the TV every night, or only when they have guests?"

"They've got enough sense to leave their children alone most of the time, which is more than I can say for your mother. I'll bet your main reason for volunteering at Operation Whiskers is to make sure you aren't home on the weekend if she decides to drop by."

Gena stood up, shaking so hard with rage that she was afraid she might commit an act of violence. She thought of Alexandra, fleeing from the Catalonian royal palace to escape her mate's wrath, of cats taking up defensive positions behind barricades in their capital city's streets. Household might be dead, but his malign influence remained; Catalonia was at war.

"And I hope they all die," a deep voice said, sounding completely unlike her husband, although it had to be Don who was speaking. "I hope all of those cats finally meet their well-deserved demise."

"This is the end," she announced, "I'm leaving," and thought she was hearing an echo of her statement. Then she realized that Don had just said exactly the same words.

"I've had it," Don went on.

"I was trying to help!"

"Makes me wonder what the hell you would do if you weren't trying to help. Why did I ever marry you? Temporary insanity—that's the only explanation I can think of!"

Gena went to the front alcove, opened the closet, took out her coat, and then grabbed her purse. It was time to fire some bigger verbal weapons, to lay waste to the battlefield. "Fuck you, Don."

"Well, fuck you, too. I've had it. I'm out of here."

"*I'm* out of here!" she screamed as she opened the front door and ran outside, almost tripping when she reached the bottom step. She had brushed against something with her foot; she looked down to see a large cat with thick orange fur glaring up at her.

"Mrrow," the cat said, baring its teeth.

Gena backed away, keeping a wary eye on the cat. Don came outside, closed the front door, and then started messing around with the lock. That was another thing she couldn't stand, the obsessive and compulsive way he had of going around checking every last little thing before they went any-where. He had always claimed that the intelligent cats of Catalonia would be just like that, paying attention to every detail, being as fussy as cats so often were. The son of a bitch couldn't even break up with her without checking the damned door to make sure it was locked before he left.

The cat hissed at her. Gena fled around the house and was halfway up the driveway before she saw that she could not back out until Don got his car out of her way. She yanked her keys from her purse, got into her car, started the ignition, then beeped her horn. In her rear view mirror, she saw Don hurry toward his car, the strange orange cat at his heels.

Gena honked again, then rolled down her window. "Get your goddamn car out of my way!" she shouted.

"I can't do it fast enough!" he yelled back as he pulled his car door open. The cat retreated and hunkered down on the sidewalk. Mrs. Seligman, their neighbor on the other side of their driveway, peered through her living room curtains at them, and a few children were gathering across the street to watch.

Don rolled out of the driveway in reverse. By the time Gena had backed into the street, he was barreling down Bancroft Street toward the strip mall.

She headed in the opposite direction, eyes stinging with tears as she thought of what lay ahead—more bitter arguments, divorce, the destruction of Catalonia—everything they had always sworn to avoid.

Nine

Gena was only five minutes away from her parents' home when she realized that Don would expect her to go there, to cry on her mother's shoulder and ask her father which lawyer friend of his she should call.

Catalonians would never hire divorce attorneys. Divorce was rare in Catalonia. Even when cat couples separated, their fellow felines soon effected a reconciliation. Catalonians mated for life.

She drove onto the exit ramp, turned right, and continued climbing an increasingly steeper hill until she reached a small open space near a guard rail and came to a stop at the scenic overlook called Sacchetti's Cliff, after a legendary high school student who had allegedly scaled the escarpment after consuming a large quantity of beer. Sacchetti had completed this feat over three decades before Gena had graduated from the same high school, but his name had stuck to the edifice, where she and Josh Fedder used to make out in his car during their senior year. Below the scarp, the once small town south of the city had metastasized into a suburb of enclosed malls, strip malls, tract houses amid winding roads, McMansions on green hillsides, and long dark ribbons of highways.

Gena had grown up in that expanding suburb, in her parents' house, the only home she had ever known, before going away to college. She had returned after graduation, thinking that she would be there for only a little while, but it had grown easier to stay at home, especially since many of her high school friends had all regressed together, allowing parents to provide them with shelter and sustenance and moral support while they drafted their résumés. She and Josh had started seeing each other again before he left to take a job in Arizona. Now, most of her friends had left the area, their e-mails and phone calls becoming ever more infrequent until she was hearing from them only during the Christmas season. Of her closest friends from high school, only Trudy Whitbeck still lived nearby, and Trudy didn't really count as being overly dependent and homebound because she had moved back from California after acquiring both an M.B.A. and a divorce and was almost never at home, as her position with a firm of business consultants required a lot of travel.

Gena had longed to get away, and had nearly decided to leave with Josh when he moved to Tucson, but something had held her back, some deep fear of the unfamiliar, even as she continued to yearn for something other than what she had always known. Even after she had moved into her own apartment, she had been content to remain in familiar territory. Meeting Don and falling in love with him had settled the matter for the foreseeable future.

Maybe her timidity and inability to part from the overly familiar accounted for how she had so readily taken to conjuring up Catalonia, an exotic place to which she could always escape. It seemed to her now that when she and Don had first invented their feline refuge, Catalonia had been a more adventurous setting where cats prowled and plotted and warred against their enemies. Alexandra, with the aid of Nicholas and his scientific advisors, had even accompanied her mate on a number of dangerous missions to the human world, in order to gather intelligence about possible enemies and to rescue cats in peril; she was, or had been, a cat ready for battle. So Don had claimed while narrating stories of the pair bravely traveling across the continua. But lately, Gena had been concentrating on Catalonia's gentler aspects, making it a safer and softer place in her mind, tamed by her fears.

She might lose Catalonia forever. Tears trickled down her face, mocking the promises she and Don had made to each other.

* * * *

Gena drove back to the city and through its streets, past houses and apartment buildings filled, she imagined, with people sitting down to dinner in homes that provided a respite from the hassles of the day, happy to be with those whom they loved. Once, she and Don had been people like that. She remembered how quickly they had decided to buy their house, how right the place had felt to them both, how certain they had been that their search was over.

"Good vibes," the realtor had told them while showing them the house. "That's what the Aiellos always said, that this home had good vibes, almost as if some kind of guardian angel was living in it and watching over them. They really hated to give it up when they had to move out of town." Gena had felt that way during her first weeks in her new home, safe and protected, sometimes imagining that a kindly spirit was sharing the house with her and Don. What had happened to that atmosphere of warmth and security?

How could she have said what she had to him tonight? Swearing at him was bad enough, but she most regretted the remarks she had made about his parents. That was a touchy subject with Don, as she had seen during their one visit to the couple. Hal and Verna Martinson lived in a house in a neighborhood of yards littered with broken children's toys and dwellings in need of paint jobs or new siding. Gena and Don had checked into a hotel, since Don was in Seattle on a business trip, so they had evaded a stay in the parental abode, but duty had required a couple of days with Verna and Hal and taking them out to dinner. Verna had reciprocated with a supper of franks, beans, and Sloppy Joes, washed down with beer and large bottles of soda, eaten in front of the TV so that Hal could watch a Seattle Seahawks game. There had been a few cracks from Hal about his "college boy" son, but most of his witticisms had been gentle, and Verna had enveloped Gena in a farewell hug far more affectionate than any her own mother had ever offered her. The visit had gone far better than Don had anticipated, and she had promised herself that no critical remarks about Don's family would ever cross her lips. After all, she had reminded herself, Eugene Lawlor had one grandfather who was a prizefighter in his youth before shipping out with the merchant marine and another who had been a longshoreman on the New Jersey docks.

She had broken her promise. Her vision blurred as she struggled not to cry again, pulled over to the curb to wipe her eyes, and sighed as she saw that she was parked in front of the Saint Thomas Aquinas Church. Don had supposed that most Catalonians were agnostics and skeptics, as he was, but she had insisted that they would also allow freedom of religion to all cats. She had imagined Alexandra slipping out of the palace on holidays and special occasions to worship with the feline congregation of Saint Kitmas, or perhaps practicing the more ancient rites of Bast, the cat-headed goddess of ancient Egypt.

Gena was about to start her car again when a small gray cat padded up the steps to the closed doors of the church, followed by a calico and a long-haired black cat that might have been Alexandra's twin. The three cats sat down in front of the entrance, tails twitching, as if waiting for someone to let them inside. Gena felt twinges of guilt, trying to remember the last time she had gone to Mass—years ago, just before she had gone away to college, when she had announced to her parents that organized religion seemed to lack the essence of true spirituality.

The faint sound of a meow came to her.

At that moment, the black cat turned its head and looked right at her. Gena gazed back; the cat continued to stare at her in a way that was unnerving. She could almost believe that the cat knew exactly how messed up and unhappy she was.

Ridiculous, she thought. She continued down the street, then made a right turn. Tracey lived on this narrow street of cottages and small apartment buildings, in one side of the modest two-family stucco house she and her soon-to-be ex-husband had bought a couple of years ago. Gena parked in front, noticing that the city's cats seemed to be out in force tonight. Three kittens scampered past her on the sidewalk, a white Angora lounged next to a garbage can, two fat tawny cats rested on the hood of a parked car, and she could hear the distant cries of tomcats in heat.

Don, she thought wistfully, wondering if her husband was thinking of her at all.

She rummaged in her purse, then in the glove compartment, wanting to give Tracey at least a bit of warning that she was outside, before realizing that she had left her cell phone at home. She slipped out of the car and locked the doors, then walked up to the front steps.

The lights on Tracey's side of the house were on, although her tenant, as usual, seemed to be out. The tenant, according to the label on his mailbox, was Roland Tewksbury, which made Gena imagine a fussy old man. She had never met him, even though he had been renting from Tracey for almost four months; apparently he traveled a lot on business. The ideal tenant, as far as Tracey was concerned, since he paid his rent promptly and was rarely around.

Gena rang Tracey's bell. "I didn't order any food," Tracey called out through the door, "and if you're looking to yak at me about your religion or sell me anything, get lost."

"Tracey? It's Gena."

The door suddenly swung open. "Well, come in," Tracey said.

"If you're in the middle of something—"

"I'm done with work for now." Tracey drew her inside, then closed the door. The living room coffee table was covered with sketches of cats; through the open door to Tracey's studio, Gena glimpsed an easel with a painting of a golden-haired cat that might have been modeled on Nicholas, sovereign of Catalonia. She swallowed hard.

"What's the matter, kiddo? You look kind of bummed."

Gena took a deep breath as she handed Tracey her coat. "Oh, Tracey, I don't know what to do. Don and I had the worst fight of our lives, and now it's all over between us. That's what he said, or maybe I did, I can't even remember now. I closed the household account, and he lost his job, and now—"

"Back up a minute. Who lost what?"

"Don and I had this ridiculous argument," Gena said. "Then he told me that he was let go from his job today. Things sort of escalated after that."

"Oh, God. You poor thing. He didn't get violent or anything, did he?"

"No, just pissed off. He yelled and cursed at me, but he didn't hit me. Don would never do anything like that."

"Look, if you want to stay here for a while—"

She would have to go back to the house for some clothes, underwear, and toilet articles if she stayed with Tracey. Suddenly the tasks of having to organize herself, move her belongings to new quarters, and then figure out how she and Don were going to divide everything up seemed insurmountable. Maybe it was only inertia, habit, and laziness that kept a lot of marriages going. People on television or in movies and books didn't seem to have such obstacles; they just said everything was over and got the hell out.

Maybe that was what she should do, just throw her stuff into her car and head off for parts unknown.

Gena heaved a sigh. She would probably get about as far as her parents' house.

"What am I going to do?" Gena said.

Tracey replied, "I could call my lawyer tomorrow and see if he'll take you on. He handled my case pretty well, all things considered."

Gena lowered her eyes, remembering the times she and Don had discussed how they would behave if they were ever to separate. Never would they dream of using lawyers as gladiators in a vicious battle to the death. No scorched-earth, take-no-prisoners approach for them, no wasted time and money on counseling, either; the trouble with both counselors and lawyers was that it was in their financial interests to have the gap between estranged spouses yawn as wide as possible for as long as possible. She and Don knew better; they wouldn't fall for that trap. They would have enough respect for each other and enough fond memories of their shared past to conduct themselves rationally, as Catalonians might.

But neither of them had really believed that they would ever part when they had made such pledges.

Tracey left the room and returned with a couple of chocolate bars. "Here," she said, handing one to Gena. "Some solace for you. Chocolate does the job for me when everything's fucked. By the way, which one of you did the actual walking out?"

Gena bit into her chocolate bar. "What do you mean?" she asked with her mouth full.

"Which one of you walked out? Which one abandoned the house? I assume you did, since you're here."

"We both did."

"You both did?"

"I told Don I was leaving, and he told me the same thing, and then we both got into our cars and drove away. I mean, I had to scream at him to move his damn car so I could back out of the driveway."

"You *both* left the house?" Tracey set her half-eaten bar down on the coffee table next to a drawing of a cat lapping at a puddle of water. "My God—I never heard of two people abandoning the domicile together. You'd better get back there before he does."

"Why?" Gena sniffed, then searched her bag for a tissue. "What difference does it make? I can't stand the thought of being in that house."

"Listen to me. Do you want to go back there and have Don refuse to let you in? Do you want him claiming that you walked out on him and talking about desertion? That could cause you a lot of grief later. You'd be at a disadvantage for sure." Tracey stood up and pulled her to her feet. "We'd better get you back home right now."

* * * *

All the spaces in the parking lot behind Jeff Nardi's building were taken. Don drove back out and parked along the curb a half-block away, then walked back. Up ahead, a brown and white cat was sharpening its claws against a tree. Another cat with pale yellowish fur padded over to the tree; the two cats turned to look in his direction.

The fierce look in their eyes brought him to a halt. Don backed up and watched as both cats pawed at the grass. For a moment, he expected them to leap at him, and then they ran off into the darkness.

Weird, Don thought, and longed for lost Catalonia already; he could admit that much to himself. He desperately wanted that imaginary kingdom of cats to be real, to be able to move through some sort of fracture in reality to find himself among those cats, his lost Alexandra restored to him, his breach with Gena healed.

He shook off that thought. His marriage to Gena would never have lasted; her latest folly with the household account demonstrated that. Anyone that impractical and impetuous would only have dragged them both into ruin. Their world lacked Catalonia's confused but stable mixed economy as Gena had envisioned it, in which all cats had a guaranteed annual income, medical care was free, businesses of all kinds flourished, everyone had a comfortable place to live and enough food to eat, and the entire government was funded by voluntary contributions instead of taxes.

He and Gena lived in a much harsher world, something she tended to forget.

Maybe he should be grateful to Household for exposing the shaky foundations of their marriage and for allowing some reality and plausibility to enter even their escapist imaginings. The fact was that, reluctant as he was to admit it to himself, his vision of Catalonia had been diverging from Gena's in a few ways. His cats were a bit bolder than the ones she spoke of, more willing to acknowledge their fierce feline instincts. The Nicholas he imagined, although egalitarian, was prepared to exercise his authority if Catalonia required it, even if that meant acting alone rather than in concert with his mate Alexandra.

Don lengthened his stride, almost feeling that he was on the prowl. Nicholas, sovereign of Catalonia, would not be moping around if he lost his mate. As dear as Alexandra was to him, he would, like most male cats, be out looking for some action. As he came to the entrance to Jeff's building, the yowl of a cat tore through the night.

He hurried inside, wondering what he would tell his friend. Jeff didn't have a whole lot of space in which to put him up, especially since Jeff worked at home. Maybe, Don thought, I should have stayed in the house. He would have to settle that with Gena. She could stay with her parents temporarily, even if that meant a longer commute to her job. That was the only practical solution; it was also eminently fair, given that Gena was largely responsible for their dispute.

He knocked on Jeff's door. He heard a click near the door's peephole, and then it opened. Rose Cutler stood in the entrance, her short blond hair looking even shaggier than usual. She wore jeans, a denim jacket, and a bright red T-shirt.

"Hi, Rose," Don muttered, disappointed that Jeff did not seem to be at home. "Mind if I come in?"

"Fine with me. Jeff isn't here, though. He's out discussing the fine art of politics with Clifford Beaufort."

Don stepped inside. "Clifford Beaufort?" All he knew about the man was that he was a minister who ran a halfway house in the run-down north end of the city for drunks, drug addicts, homeless people, and other unfortunates, and that his principled but brief forays into local politics had accomplished little.

Rose closed the door. "Beaufort announced that he's running for mayor," she said, "and he's just hired Jeff to be his campaign manager and run his Web site. Jeff's really stoked about taking it on."

Don vaguely recalled hearing about Beaufort's announcement a few days ago. "But Beaufort doesn't have a chance against Mayor Dorff."

"I know, and he sure as hell can't pay much of a salary, but Jeff's been thinking about his civic duty and responsibilities lately, apart from the fact that Stan Dorff is also a major horse's ass."

"You can say that again."

"Jeff's a horse's ass, too. He's just a different kind of horse's ass from Mayor Dorff."

"You're in a good mood," Don said as he sat down.

"I only came over to get the stuff I left here," Rose said, gesturing at the coffee table, which held a large open duffel bag filled with paperback books, a hair dryer, and various articles of clothing. "Jeff and I have finally come to a parting of the ways. If he doesn't come over to my place to pick up his crap in two days, I'm tossing it. You can tell him that for me."

"Sorry to hear it." He thought of his parents, who had been married for almost forty-five years. How had they ever managed it? Probably by never talking to each other about anything except bowling, football, basketball, NASCAR races, celebrities, and the TV shows they usually watched.

"Jeff just can't make a commitment." Rose folded a long flannel nightgown and thrust it into the duffel bag. "He can't even let a commitment be a theoretical possibility. He'd rather just have somebody around at his convenience."

That didn't sound like such a bad idea to Don. "What a coincidence," he said. "Looks like Gena and I are breaking up, too. That's why I came over here."

Rose's eyes widened. "Jeez. I'm sorry. Do you want to talk about it or anything?"

"Not really."

She closed the duffel and pulled the bag's strap over her shoulder. "You can tell Jeff I left my set of keys on the dresser in the bedroom." She was silent for a moment. "I'm really sorry."

"It happens."

He stared after Rose as she left the apartment. She was one of the few women he knew who looked good in jeans, even from the rear, and Rose looked as though she had been working out lately. She had to be almost forty, an age that once might have put him off, since women over a certain age were more likely to be wary and cynical, but her maturity now had its attractions. He wouldn't have to explain certain things to Rose. A woman with some experience of life would not be as ditzy as Gena.

Don felt a pang at the thought of his wife, then reached into his pocket and pulled out the envelope she had given to him earlier. "Darling Don," she had written on the envelope, followed by "H.R.H. Nicholas" and a badly drawn penciled sketch of a blob with whiskers that was obviously supposed to be a cat.

A lump rose in his throat. There hadn't been all that much in the household account, certainly not enough to make much difference in his situation now. But it was the principle of the thing. The worst of it was that Gena had not even bothered to consult him before withdrawing the funds and closing the account. This was no time to give in to sentimentality and to his longing for lost Catalonia.

He put the envelope back into his pocket. His settlement and severance should be enough to see him through his present difficulties, if it didn't take him too long to find something else, and maybe he could sell the house by the time he found another job. He would have to sit down and do some calculations, figure out the most practical way to proceed.

Being practical suddenly repelled him. He should just blow what he had on a trip to Australia or some other part of the world while he still had a chance to see it. If there were such a thing as a one-way ticket to Catalonia, he would have been the first person aboard the flight, provided of course that he could morph into feline form. He thought of furry flight attendants coming down the aisles with trays of shrimp cocktails and fine wines. Every passenger on CatAir, needless to say, would fly first class, and there wouldn't be any of those baggage searches and security measures, either.

He shook himself. That was one of the problems with Catalonia; dwelling on that fanciful place enticed him into fits of whimsy and impracticality;

flipping back and forth between fantasy and reality was madness. Household had been a counterbalance to such imaginings.

Outside the slightly open window behind the sofa, a chorus of cats cried out into the night, wailing as though a world was coming to an end.

* * * *

Tracey followed Gena home in her car and pulled up behind her in the driveway. Gena did not see Don's car, but that might not mean anything. He might have parked somewhere nearby and then sneaked back to the house, ready to surprise her, even though that would be atypical behavior on his part. He would be far more likely to have his car sitting in the driveway, to announce that he was again in possession of the house and that she would have to deal with him while they decided what furniture and other belongings she would be allowed to take away.

She and Tracey entered the house through the back door, glancing quickly from side to side. Gena still feared that Don might be lying in wait, sharpening his claws, ready to leap out from the darkness as soon as they were through the door. But the house was dark, and apparently empty; Don, as usual, had turned out all the lights before abandoning their home.

"Don?" Gena called out, just to be on the safe side. "Don?" She hit the switch near the door, and the overhead light came on. "Don?" She cast an apprehensive look in the direction of the doorway to the cellar, torn between wanting to castigate him harshly for his cruelty and preparing to forgive him if he had decided to return.

Tracey said, "His car wasn't outside."

"Maybe he'll come back later." Gena sat down at the kitchen table.

"Want me to stay?" Tracey asked.

"You don't have to—I'll be fine. If he were going to come back here tonight, he would have been here by now. Besides, I'll have to face him sooner or later. Right now, I'd better get some sleep, or I'll never make it to work tomorrow."

Tracey looked relieved. "Guess I'll go home and spend the rest of the night with the kitties. Ever since I started working up my sketches, there seem to be more cats hanging around my neighborhood, so I've had more models to work with. Maybe they're all hoping to be immortalized in the pages of the next Shauna Leopold opus."

"Thanks, Tracey."

"Look, maybe it'll all blow over. After all, your parents are still married, and Don's parents never got a divorce, either. That gives you a big familial advantage over me and almost everyone else I know."

Gena got up and went to the door with her, said good night, then locked up. Still in her coat, she lingered in the kitchen, unable to face the empty house alone.

She would be on her own for the first time in her life. She had finished her four-year degree in literature and history at a small liberal arts college only fifty miles away, and there she had lived in a dorm, which wasn't exactly being adventurous. Her first apartment had been her residence for not much more than a year when she had met Don at the Barnes & Noble; it had been a relief to move into his larger place.

Together for almost seven years, if she counted the time they had lived together before their marriage. Appalling when she considered it; she was all of thirty-one years old and in all that time she had never led anything resembling a truly independent life. Alexandra, she had always insisted, had led a free and self-reliant existence of travel and adventure before being crowned as queen and settling down with Nicholas in Catalonia's royal palace.

There had to be something of Alexandra in her. After all, wasn't Alexandra her alter ego? Maybe splitting up with Don was for the best. Having to look out for herself would be a learning experience.

Confidence flowed into her, then a sudden stab of terror. What if she couldn't take care of herself? What if St. Luke's did outsource her job? What if she lost everything and had to crawl back to her parents' house?

Gena went to the front alcove, hung up her coat, and then crept through the house, making sure that the doors and first-floor windows were locked. She decided to leave one lamp on in the living room, afraid to be alone in the dark and empty dwelling, then went upstairs. She would force herself to get used to the dark, now that she might have to handle the electric bills all by herself.

She hadn't killed off Household at all, she realized. She had only put herself in a position where Household could torment her even more.

She sensed a presence in the house. A draft of cold, dank air touched her face. Household was waiting in the shadows, looking for an opportunity to strike. The creature might have gone off to lick its wounds, but was still waiting to take revenge. Household was still with her, and Catalonia, which she had hoped to save, was in grave danger.

She flicked the light switch on the wall just inside the door as she entered the bedroom. On the dresser, her two china cats were next to each other, sitting where she had left them that morning. Seeing them together like that gave her hope. Reconciliation with Don was still possible. He cared as much about Catalonia as she did.

The wooden floor creaked and shook. The two china cats flew at her; Gena threw up her hands to deflect them and felt something sharp against her palms. Too startled to scream, she stumbled backwards and collapsed on the bed.

For a while, she was afraid to move. She was spooking herself, imagining things. At last she forced herself to sit up.

The china cats lay on the rug next to the bed, still intact. She picked them up, grateful that they hadn't struck the floor.

Household was fighting back. She opened the top drawer of the dresser and put the cats inside on top of the layers of folded nightclothes.

She undressed and got ready for bed, but was afraid to turn off the light on the bedside table. The king-sized bed seemed empty without Don; she tossed and turned, trying to sleep. Alexandra would be roaming the palace, searching for her lost Nicholas while the rest of Catalonia slept, still unaware of the threat to their two sovereigns and their entire way of life.

Gena pressed her face into the pillow and sobbed until she was exhausted and tearless, then hovered between wakefulness and sleep. Her half-conscious mind insisted that something was sitting on the bed near her feet, the way Vladimir used to do when he was still living in this house. She knew that if she opened her eyes, she would see only a cat there, a small creature that meant her no harm, but she could not look because the cat would come after her if she did. Maybe others of its kind were under the bed, just waiting until the cat on her bed gave them a signal. She heard them under the bed, the soft sound of breathing that might become purr or snarl. They were waiting for her, ready to leap out and dig their claws into her and scratch out her eyes if she did not remain perfectly still. She lay frightened and unable to move, aware of the small extra weight on the bed, and finally drifted into unconsciousness.

Ten

Strange, Don thought, that almost every cat in town seemed to have crawled out of the woodwork. They climbed up trees, rooted around in gardens, rested under shrubs, sheltered under a couple of "For Sale" signs posted along Ackley Avenue, and bounded across lawns.

Gena's car was in the driveway, which meant that she had not gone to her parents' home and, as usual, had taken the bus to work. Today was Thursday, so chances were that she wouldn't go running over to the Lawlor house until the weekend. He could move back in on Saturday, call her up while she was with her parents, and tell her that they had to face up to a few things.

A large gray cat loped out of the way as he pulled up in front of the house. Others were hanging around his house; in fact, it looked as though they were now leaving other people's lawns and porches to congregate on his property. He opened the car door carefully and got out as several scurried up to him and came to a halt.

A few eyed the back door, while others peered at him from under the shrubbery bordering the back yard. Don shivered; the way they were staring at him was eerie, as if they knew his innermost thoughts. Vladimir had sometimes looked at him in that way, as if Don did not fool him at all, as if Vladimir could as easily decide to scratch out his eyes as leap into his lap. Don took a few steps back and four cats followed him, as if bound by a common purpose; they retreated in unison as he moved toward them.

"Scat," he said. "Get lost, you guys." The cats stared at him. He told himself that they would wander off eventually, and if they didn't, he would call the city's animal control department.

Right now, he needed a shower, and then he would grab his laptop and pack whatever he might need for the next couple of days or so. He would be late to work, not that it mattered now, given that Friday would be his last day on the job. Jeff had been amazed at Don's run of bad luck, but maybe it was just as well to have everything hitting him at once. After he worked out a settlement with Gena, his life would essentially be his own again, and he wouldn't have to worry about her while he hunted for another job. Gena might think that this fight was all about money and Household, but he was now convinced those were only symptoms of a basic incompatibility. They would have broken up sooner or later; better to have it happen now, while they were both still young enough to start over.

He felt tough-minded and practical as he opened the back door and went inside. The hand-painted Russian cats, he noticed as he glanced into the dining room, still stood in a row on the sideboard. That was what had started all the trouble, arguing over how much she had spent on those damned hand-crafted cats.

Catalonia, he thought longingly. How could the imaginary world they had created together survive? They could not divide it up, leaving Mew York to Gena while he kept Mew Orleans and San Furcisco, or trying to decide whether Nicholas or Alexandra would remain in the palace. Perhaps both fe-line sovereigns would have to abdicate and leave the governing of Catalonia to some other cat.

His neck prickled. Shadows in the corners of the dining room darkened, as if reflecting his mood. He sighed as he started up the stairs to the bedroom. What a deluded sap he was, deep down. Gena had played on that sappiness, probably believing that getting her hooks into his soft side would keep them together. Well, maybe it was time to become as tough as he sometimes pretended to be, and forget about Catalonia and all its darling cute little kitties. Gena had done everything possible to smooth any rough edges from Cata-lonia, any hint of the troubles and travails of this world. Catalonians were always kind, socially responsible, sweet-tempered, and adorable; Alexandra was brave, independent, and decisive; and Nicholas was courageous and intelligent while remaining benevolent and gentle. Neither cat had to worry about finances because the ludicrous Catalonian economy designed by Gena provided them with everything they could possibly want. Well, she sure as hell didn't resemble Alexandra all that closely, and he wasn't that much like the Nicholas she had conjured up. Maybe trying to pretend that he was had only distracted him from more important practical concerns. Imagining a world as implausible and icky and cute as Catalonia had only made him weaker and more foolish.

"That's all I need," Don said to himself sarcastically, "to live like a cat and not think about the future at all. That'd really put me on the right track." Odd, he thought, that his voice sounded so much deeper and more resonant in the empty house, as if, in Gena's absence, it had taken on more strength and power, amplifying his anger. Not his voice at all.

A yowl sounded through the house. Don started, then heard a screech from the back yard. It sounded as though some of the cats he had seen out there were having a territorial dispute.

He pounded up the stairs, hurried into the small home office across from the bedroom where he kept his desktop computer, file cabinet, and treadmill, and peered out through the window at the patch of lawn below. A compact black and white long-haired cat with large paws was in the middle of the yard, fur up, back arched; the other cats backed away from the angry feline.

Vladimir, Don thought. That cat was a dead ringer for him. But this cat couldn't be the disloyal creature who had abandoned them for the blandishments of Mr. Bowes. There was no reason for Vladimir to make the trek back to this neighborhood when he could stay where he was and indulge himself with all the tuna and shrimp old man Bowes would be lavishing upon him.

Cats scurried across the lawn, fleeing from his property until the yard was empty. The cat that might have been Vladimir's twin looked up at the window where Don was standing, then bounded away.

* * * *

The spring weather was as warm and beautiful as it had been the day before, so Don decided to take a long lunch break in the park next to the county courthouse. Going to work had been a mistake. The six other people in the office who had been laid off either expected him to commiserate with them at great length or else were too deep in self-pity and depression to do anything but glower at anybody rash enough to approach their cubicles. The fortunate ones who still had their jobs, including Larry Philmus, insisted upon offering sympathy and condolences with a sincerity that did not entirely hide their relief at having been spared his fate.

The only exception to such behavior had been the bodacious Stella Przhewalski. "I'm really sorry you got the axe," she said as she stood in the entrance to his cubicle.

"Sorry you did, too," he had replied.

"Yeah, but I haven't been here that long, you know, so as soon as I started hearing the rumors, I knew my days were numbered, being the last hired and all."

"I'll get past it," Don said.

"Oh, I know you will, and any other company would be lucky to have you, too." As Stella gazed at him with her lovely blue eyes, a sudden impulse to have her on his desk came and went too quickly.

Maybe, Don thought, he should ditch work tomorrow. But he had used up all his sick leave and personal days in a savage bout with flu that past winter, and did not want to mess up any chance for a good recommendation. "Worked conscientiously right up through his last day." That ought to look good to any prospective employers in a recommendation. He would be a tough guy, too macho to let a little downsizing get to him. Besides, Larry had promised to take him out for drinks on Friday evening, hinting that Don and all of his unfortunate soon-to-be-unemployed colleagues would get a nice send-off.

As he walked through the park, Don recalled the day he had come here with Gena to get married, how beautiful she had looked in her off-white suit and carrying her small bouquet of white roses. He looked toward the county courthouse, where he would probably wind up ending the marriage that had begun there. Coming over here to eat lunch had been another mistake. At least not having to come in to work would make it easier to avoid the courthouse and the white-columned memories of his wedding day.

His marriage was over. The absence of the two china cats from the top of the bedroom dresser had only underlined that fact. He wondered if Gena had smashed them in a fit of fury or merely hidden them somewhere, not that it mattered. In either case, she had clearly meant it as a signal that there was no hope left for them.

He bought a hot dog and soda and sat down on a park bench near a tulip bed. The homeless man in the baggy tweed coat stumbled toward him along the sidewalk, turning his head frantically from side to side. Maybe he was searching for the pigeons that usually flocked here looking for handouts; there didn't seem to be as many of the birds in the park today. Several cats were around, though, digging in the flower beds, prowling along paths, or reclining on the grass in the sunshine.

The homeless man stopped near a plump cat with tawny fur. "What!" he shouted at the cat.

The cat stared up at him with a Sphinxlike expression.

"I know," the man shouted at the cat, "I *know*!"

The cat continued to stare at him.

"What the hell, you think I don't know? You think I'm a goddamn idiot? What's the matter with you?" The man lifted his head and gazed at the sky. "You too, you son of a bitch! Get off my case!" He wandered over to Don's bench and sat down next to him. "What's up with you?" he asked calmly.

"Not a whole lot," Don replied.

The older man peered at him. "Oh yeah—you're the fella what lost his job."

Don shifted his weight on the bench, surprised that the old guy remembered. "That's right, and guess what—looks like I'm getting a divorce, too. My wife walked out on me last night, or maybe it was the other way around, not that it matters. Anyway, she's back in our house at the moment, so I guess that means that technically I walked out on her." If he wasn't careful, he thought, if he didn't get himself back on a firm footing with a new position soon, he might end up like this old geezer, wandering around homeless and ranting at the world. It was almost as if Household had sent the old guy his way as a warning.

The old man said, "You wouldn't happen to have another dollar, now would you?"

"As a matter of fact, I would." Don finished his hot dog, then reached into his jacket pocket for his billfold. "Smallest I have is a five—take it."

"You sure?"

"Sure," Don replied, feeling that he was temporarily buying off fate.

"Thanks." The man pocketed the money. "And I won't spend it on booze." He sighed. "Miss my old home."

"Live around here?" Don asked.

"Not that far from here. Shared the place with a coupla folks, and a nice little place it was, too, before they let someone else in and everything changed."

Don glanced at him. "So you moved out?"

"You could put it that way, or you could say I just wasn't welcome there no more."

"Couldn't you get along with the new tenant?"

The old man wrinkled his nose. "No, I couldn't get along with that friggin' bastard."

"Maybe you should have had a lease, or some kind of written agreement."

"Wouldn't have done me no good."

It would have been better than being homeless, Don thought. The plump tawny-furred cat wandered over to the bench and sat down in front of him. More cats lay on the grass a few feet away—a calico, an orange cat, and two cats with thick dark brown fur.

"Where you stayin'?" the homeless man asked. "Now that you're not in your house, I mean."

"At a friend's place, at least until he kicks me out. I suppose you could say that makes me homeless, too."

The man cackled, showing his few stained teeth. "Not if you got a pal to put you up." He gazed intently at the cat. "You got something to say to me? Huh? How's about it, kitty, you got something to say? If you don't, get lost."

"Lots of stray cats around," Don said.

"You can say that again, Buster. I was over to the street near the animal shelter, and you should have heard all the noise, like a million cats was going at it. Sounded like they wanted to bust out. Wouldn't blame them if they did. That city shelter is a shithole."

Don looked more closely at the tawny cat. "This one doesn't have a collar—no ID at all."

"Hope the shelter don't pick him up, then," the old man said. "Probably wouldn't be no room for him even if they did." He rubbed at his face. "You work for that insurance company, don't you." He waved his hand in the direction of Don's office building.

"I do until tomorrow night."

"There's this alley behind that building I sacked out in last night," the homeless man said, "and you wouldn't believe all the kitty cats this morning. All over the place. Must have been empty tuna cans in the dumpster or something. Never seen so many kitty cats." He paused. "Know what? Gonna get me one of them chili dogs." He gestured in the direction of the food vendor's cart. "Told you I wouldn't buy booze with your fiver."

"Glad to hear it."

The man shuffled away. The tawny-furred cat was still staring at Don. The animal looked well fed and well cared for, which made him wonder why it was loose and wandering around downtown, and there was definitely something weird about the way the creature was gazing at him, as if the cat was keeping him under surveillance.

The cat stretched out, rested its head on its front paws, and gazed into the distance. Don, while watching his former cat, the inconstant Vladimir, lounging about one day, had begun to wonder what cats thought about during their long stretches of lying around, and had speculated that they might be doing higher mathematics and theoretical physics. All over the world, millions of people might be living in the company of cute furry creatures that possessed the intellects of an Einstein or a Feynman without ever suspecting it. From such thoughts, it had been a short step to imagining the Catalonic Institute of Technology, familiarly known as Cattech and headed by an eminent physicist named Professor Katz, where brilliant cat physicists had already developed a Unified Field Theory and were busily devising ways to travel between the various universes, perhaps so that they could send teams here to rescue the neglected kitties of this world and convey them to the utopia of Catalonia. As he had quickly pointed out to Gena, a school such as Cattech would of course have to be located in the town of Pussadena.

Don emitted a heartfelt sigh. Maybe he should just go home this evening and see if he could work something out with Gena. Maybe they could use some counseling. But that would cost money, and better to spend his time and effort looking for a new position instead of messing around with some damned marriage counselor. Besides, if their marital difficulties were deeply rooted, as he suspected, counseling might not accomplish anything except parting them from even more of their diminishing funds.

No, the practical approach was to get everything over with as quickly and as painlessly as possible instead of dragging it out. As Jeff had told him only last night, patching things up and glossing over any truly deep problems now might only lead to getting a divorce later in life, when children might be involved and any estrangement would be a lot more expensive, complicated, vicious, and destructive.

"Hey, Don."

He looked up into Rose Cutler's blue-gray eyes. She wore a navy pants suit and clutched a half-eaten hot dog, and he remembered that she had recently moved her small office downtown.

Rose owned and ran her own business, Everything's Coming Up Roses. In spite of the name, Rose did not run a flower shop, but a gofer service—at least that was how Don had always thought of her company. Rose called herself a "lifestyle concierge," and her small band of employees did grocery shopping, took cars to garages for repairs, went shopping for clothes, purchased gifts for special occasions, handled simple but troublesome tasks not covered by public agencies for senior citizens who needed a hand, made deliveries from one office to another, picked up take-out food, found tutors for children whose parents were worried about their schoolwork, and in general ran errands for those unwilling or unable to handle those chores for themselves. Once, Don had considered Rose's business a bit silly and unnecessary, even decadent; now he found himself admiring her enterprise. It took some smarts to figure out how to take some of the more unfortunate aspects of modern life—the decline of the family, the demands on public schools, the loss of basic housekeeping and shopping skills, the failures of governmental organizations, and the neglect of the elderly—and make a buck on them.

"Mind if I have a seat?" Rose asked.

"Be my guest."

"Still separating from Gena?"

"Looks that way."

"Well," Rose said as she sat down, "if either of you needs help with any of those little errands the other one used to handle, don't forget to call me."

"I can't afford you," Don said. "I lost my job."

"Oh, my God."

"I forgot to tell you that last night. They're closing the local office, and I'm one of the folks they laid off."

Rose hastily finished her hot dog. "I think I saw something about that in the business section of the *Times-Tribune*," she said with her mouth full, "but I never have time to read the paper. You sure have had a great run of luck lately."

"I know."

"I am sorry."

Don glanced at his watch. "In about fifteen minutes, I have to go back to the office. Then I have to call Gena and make an appointment to get a few things straight between us before we call in the lawyers."

Rose narrowed her eyes slightly; she seemed to be studying him. "Listen, would you like some company for dinner later? I know lawyers who use my service that I could recommend to you."

"Nice of you to offer."

"I've got to drop off some stuff for a client at Rolling Hill Acres later this afternoon, and then we could meet at that restaurant out there, L'Auberge-whatever-it-is."

"I know the place," Don said.

"Dinner's on me. Just ask me a couple of questions about all the services Everything's Coming Up Roses provides, and I can make it a business expense."

"Great," he said, and realized that, to his surprise, he was actually looking forward to the evening. Jeff had sometimes implied, without actually being so crass as to say so out loud, that Rose, under her generally affable exterior, could be a hard and mercenary bitch. But maybe Jeff, so content to drift through life, just didn't appreciate Rose's better qualities. Gena, Don thought bitterly, could have benefitted from being a little harder and more mercenary herself and less of a clinging vine. Anyway, given his current situation, he was in no position to turn down a free meal.

A tawny-furred mass suddenly leaped onto the bench, taking up a position between them. Don met the amber eyes of the cat that had been lying near him and received a cold predatory look in return. He lifted a hand; the cat showed its teeth.

"Beat it, buddy," Don said, but the cat only stared at him.

"Nasty little cat," Rose said. "Maybe I shouldn't admit this, but I'm not a big fan of cats."

Don said, "We used to have a cat, until he decided that he preferred living with somebody else. I kind of enjoyed having the little guy around."

"Well, to each his own, but they always struck me as arrogant, like they own the world or something. Sneaky, too."

The cat looked away from Don, then hissed and lashed out at Rose's extended hand with one paw. Rose retracted her hand just in time.

"Mean little son of a bitch," Rose said. "Could be rabid for all we know."

The cat jumped off the bench, its tail twitching. Two other cats were watching them from their perch on another bench. Don didn't particularly care for the look in their eyes, as if they regarded him and Rose as prey that was unfortunately too big for them to stalk and eat. Even though he was fond of cats, these particular cats gave him the willies; he could imagine how Rose must feel.

"Six-thirty okay?" Rose asked as she stood up.

"What?"

"I'll meet you at six-thirty, if that's all right with you."

"I'll be there," Don replied.

The tawny cat snarled, then scurried away.

Eleven

The answering machine's digital voice told Gena that she had one message. The ID showed the number of Don's office phone. She pressed the Message button. She would have to change the greeting, let callers know that only one of them was at this number and where the other could be reached. That would bring on all kinds of unwelcome queries; she especially dreaded the call from Don's parents. Time to get rid of the landline and inform everybody to call them on their cell phones from now on, which would solve the problem and save money besides. How unfair of Don to insist that she wasn't practical.

"Gena, this is Don," the machine said. "I'm staying at Jeff Nardi's, at least until the weekend. We have to get together and discuss how to divide things up and all. You can call me—uh—call me—uh, you better try me on Saturday morning, because I've got stuff to take care of tonight and tomorrow. What I mean is, we have to figure out who's going to stay in the house and how to handle the bills and whatever. Anyway, call me. I just want to be civilized about this, okay? Bye."

The answering machine beeped and said, "Thursday, three-thirty p.m., end of messages."

Gena got up and wandered into the dining room. Could Don be regretting his harsh words? Was a reconciliation possible? Probably not, she thought sadly. He had sounded resigned to their separation, with his talk of dividing things up, and she wasn't at all sure that she was ready to forgive him. Maybe if she hadn't married him, she would have learned how to stand on her own two feet a long time ago.

The living room seemed darker than usual, even though the curtains on the large window were open to the outdoor light. Gena turned on the overhead light, then the table and standing lamps, but still felt uneasy, unable to shake the feeling that something unseen and malign was haunting the place. She stood in the middle of the room, not moving, afraid that if she turned around, she would see some sort of horrible, frightening apparition.

Something was behind her, waiting to pounce. She felt it now, and wanted to scream. If she could cry out loudly enough, then her own cries would awaken her, and her nightmare would be over.

"Yoo hoo!" Gena heard the back door creak open, and realized that she had forgotten to check the lock again. "Yoo hoo! Eugenia? Just thought I'd drop by."

"I'm in here, Mom," she called out. For once, she was ready to welcome an unannounced visit from her mother. She did not even feel up to chiding her for barging in instead of waiting for someone to answer the door.

Mrs. Lawlor was in her heavy-duty shopping outfit of a short gray top-coat, jeans, and Reeboks, the kind of garb she wore for serious and intensive bargain-hunting. "You ought to get over to the Doran Park Mall," she said to Gena as she shrugged out of her coat. "You've been complaining that you need a new coat, and Macy's and The Outlet are both having coat sales with huge discounts."

"Mom, I've got something to tell you." Gena sat down on the sofa and took a deep breath. "Don and I are separating."

"What?"

"Don and I are separating, okay? And he's been laid off from his job." Gena screwed up her eyes, unable to look directly at her mother and know-ing what would come next—a recitation of Don's lacks as a husband and son-in-law, a moralistic lecture on how nobody in their family had ever been divorced except for Aunt Veronica, followed by the name of an attorney who would probably be a good friend of Gena's father.

"Oh my God." Mrs. Lawlor sat down next to her and flung her arm over Gena's shoulders. "My poor baby. Are you sure?"

"Sure I'm sure. Don found out yesterday. They're closing the local of-fice."

"I didn't mean the job, dear, I meant the separation."

"Oh. Well, we had this terrible fight yesterday, and he went storming out of the house, and I went over to Tracey Birnbaum's, and then I came back here but he didn't, not that I wanted him to, because I was really upset."

"He didn't strike you, did he?"

"He just yelled and cursed at me, and I yelled and swore back at him." Gena leaned against her mother. "Anyway, he left a message. I just listened to it a few minutes ago. He's staying over at his friend Jeff Nardi's place. It's really over, Mom. He was talking about how we have to get together to figure out how to divide up all our crap." Her eyes stung. It was over, all right. If there had been any hope at all, Don would have inserted a few meows into his message.

"You poor thing," her mother said.

"We'll be rational about the whole deal," Gena said. "I mean, neither of us wants a big battle. We just want everything settled with as little trouble as possible."

"Do you mind if I make a suggestion?"

Gena sighed, wondering which attorney her mother was about to recommend. "Go ahead."

"Try to reconcile with him."

Gena drew away and sat up, surprised.

"Ask yourself this," Mrs. Lawlor went on, sounding oddly gentle as well as persistent. "Are things so bad between you that divorce is the only way out? Donald may not be the most amiable young man in the world, at least as far as I'm concerned, but he always seemed basically sane and sound and solid and quite devoted to you. Really, you could have done far worse."

"But—"

"Your father and I had our problems, but it was well worth getting past them and not allowing them to destroy our marriage. I never doubted for one moment that, if I really needed Eugene, he'd be there for me, and I hope he always felt that way about me. The world is a hard enough place without losing the people who can best help you through the bad times."

Gena gazed at her mother in wonderment. Mrs. Lawlor did not often reveal her more sentimental side; Gena could not recall hearing such mushy sentiments from her mother in years. In fact, the last time Mrs. Lawlor had overtly demonstrated any strong emotional feelings was after the death of their beloved cat Cameron, when she had wept for days; indeed, Mr. Lawlor had often claimed that his wife had shown far more affection for Cameron than for anyone else in their family.

"Mom," she murmured, touched.

"Besides, there are the economic aspects to consider." Her mother's voice had suddenly dropped an octave; now she sounded as though she was coming down with laryngitis. "Divorce isn't cheap," Mrs. Lawlor croaked. A strange look came over her face, as if she were gazing into an abyss of despair. "You'll have to sell the house. In the meantime, you'll have your usual basic expenses. Donald doesn't have a job now, and your position is not well compensated."

"That may change soon," Gena said. "Barney—my supervisor—well, he set up a meeting with me tomorrow, and he just about said that he's got some good news for me. At least he promised me it wouldn't be bad news."

"Eugenia, you're an impractical fool if you count on promises. As they say, money talks and bullshit walks. You've got to be prepared for the worst, and that means giving some hard thought to your finances." Mrs. Lawlor's eyes looked steelier than usual, and her voice carried a sudden authoritative tone of command. "Be practical. Either you resolve your differences with Donald, or else fight him in court and grab every last asset you can."

Gena tensed.

"You know what I've always said," her mother droned on in a deep, increasingly resonant voice. "More marriages break up over money than anything else."

But you've never said that, Gena thought.

Mrs. Lawlor was still barreling ahead, and now her face was twisted into a grimace, as if she herself were resisting her own words. "If you can get yourself on a firm financial footing," she went on, "work out your budgeting, set something aside for a rainy day, build yourself a nest egg, take care of your essential household business no matter how small your resources, then you're off to a good start. And if you insist on breaking up, you have to look out for your own financial interests. That's what it all comes down to, money. Give money the proper respect, and it'll always be there when you need it. I'll bet most of the divorced people in this country were just too careless with their money."

Gena was very still, afraid to move as she recalled fragments of maternal philosophy offered by her mother in the past. Marriages broke up because people were too young when they got married. People got divorced because they had their children too soon, before they were properly prepared for that responsibility. Her mother had cited cultural differences, class differences, religious differences, geographical issues, and even a lack of good manners as reasons for the dissolution of marriages. Never in her life had Gena heard her mother claim that money was at the root of most divorces.

"You thought you could beat me," Mrs. Lawlor said, her voice falling to the level of a basso profundo, "but you can't. Surrender now, admit that you've lost, or I'll move against you. You'll either give in, or I'll ruin you for trying to banish me from your life."

"I'll get you a soda, Mom," Gena whispered, then got up and fled to the kitchen to catch her breath. That had not been her mother talking; she was certain of that. Household was speaking through her mother, fighting back, a dybbuk demanding to be fed its share of proper nourishment, struggling to survive in some form no matter what happened between Gena and Don. Could Household take her over as well, somehow enter her mind and bend her to its will?

She leaned against the refrigerator, shaking, feeling that she might collapse. But Household did not have to take possession of her, and maybe she was far too antithetical to its mentality for it to be able to endure such close contact with her thoughts. Household did not need to use her when it could use others against her, force her to consider Household's needs regardless of what she did. She felt Household out there, laughing to itself inside the body of her mother, waiting.

No, she thought; Household would not get the better of her. She would not let that happen.

She spun around and strode back into the living room. "You won't do it," Gena said. "I won't let you. I know what you're doing, and I'll fight you."

"You fool," Mrs. Lawlor continued in that weird, low voice that sounded like it belonged to a large, heavily built man who might wear a top hat, carry a briefcase, twirl his mustache, and spend his days chuckling to himself as he added his mite to the world's store of misery. "You thought you could kill me off, but you didn't. Soon I'll be stronger than ever."

"You won't!" Gena screamed.

Her mother lunged at her. Gena threw up an arm, deflecting the blow, but Mrs. Lawlor struck again and hit her in the shoulder with unexpected force.

Gena fell, nearly striking her head against the coffee table, and struggled to her feet as she stared at her mother in shock. Never in her life had either of her parents lifted a hand against her.

"Mom," Gena whimpered.

Mrs. Lawlor danced toward her, raising her arm. Gena ducked just in time. "Mom!" she cried out as her mother swung at her, grazing her jaw. Gena backed off, keeping her hands up to protect her face as her mother struck at her again, terrified that she would be forced to fight back. But how could she strike at Household without harming her mother?

"Mom," she said again.

Mrs. Lawlor's lips drew back from her teeth as she sat back down on the sofa. "Keep it up," she said, "fight me. I'll make you sorry. I'll fight you until you give me everything I want from you. You think this is your place. It's mine, too, and don't you forget it."

"Stop it!" Gena shrieked, backing away and covering her face. "God-damn you, stop it!"

"Eugenia," her mother said, "don't raise your voice to me. What's the matter with you? You go running off to the kitchen, and now suddenly here you are in a state of utter hysteria. I was only trying to be constructive."

Gena lowered her hands. Her mother was herself again. Her eyes gazed at Gena with their familiar judgmental glint. Gena swallowed, trying to calm down. Mrs. Lawlor, who had always taken pride in her iron self-control even during her most menopausal moments, was incapable of lashing out as she had just done. Either Gena was completely losing her mind, or Household had tried to strike at her through her mother.

Household could fight against her through others. Her mouth went dry as she understood that threat. She had to get her mother out of the house, to deny Household a weapon.

"I'm sorry, Mom," she forced herself to say. "I've just been really stressed out. I think I need some time to think things over. Maybe it'd be better if you leave me alone for a while."

"Well, if that's the way you feel—"

"I have to sort things out for myself. Whatever happens with me and Don, well, that has to be up to us." If her mother did not leave, she might have to fight her again.

Mrs. Lawlor shook her head. "Odd," she murmured, "my arms feel like they do after my aerobics class." She stood up. "Why don't you come out to the house for dinner tonight? I'm going to heat up some leftover pot roast, and you always did love my pot roast. And Key lime pie for dessert—I was going to pick up a pie at Rosen's on my way home."

Gena shook her head. "Can't," she said, and searched for an excuse. "I promised Tracey."

"Well, I'd better go, then. Just don't do anything rash, dear, something you might regret. I meant what I said—you could have done a lot worse than Donald."

Gena herded her mother through the kitchen, waved from the doorway as Mrs. Lawlor got into her car and backed out of the driveway, then sagged against the door jamb.

Household was still lying in wait.

She closed the door and wandered back into the living room. The air was warmer now, the lights brighter, but an unseen and malignant presence remained. Household had backed off, but she would not allow it to get the upper hand again.

"I'll do what I want," Gena said, resisting tears. "You hear me? You're nothing, you don't exist, you're just something we made up. I'll fight you, I promise you that. If you ever do anything to my mother or anyone else again, you'll answer to me."

She suddenly felt ridiculous, standing there and emoting to the walls. Her stomach tightened as the room grew colder. Whatever was here was gathering its forces for another way to come after her.

There was a meow outside the front door.

Don was home!

The sense of an unseen threat melted away. She hurried to the alcove and opened the front door, expecting to see her husband, home at last and offering Catalonian meows of repentance and ready to beg her forgiveness.

"Mrrow," she heard again, and looked down to see Vladimir, the prodigal cat, sitting on his haunches as he stared up at her with his piercing green eyes.

"Vladimir," she murmured, surprised, "what are you doing here?"

"Mrree." Vladimir hoisted his small rump and strolled inside on his oversized paws, as cute as ever, with his long fluffy black and white fur and his fat black tail held high; Mr. Bowes had clearly taken good care of him.

Gena closed the door and followed him into the living room. She should have been annoyed with the cat for assuming that he could just come right back to the home he had abandoned and be welcomed, but she was relieved to see him. She had missed Vladimir more than she realized, and now she would not have to come home to an empty house haunted by the malevolent Household.

Maybe Vladimir had not deserted them in favor of their former house and landlord simply to gorge himself on delicacies. Household had scared

Vladimir off, or had surreptitiously threatened the cat. Cats were much more sensitive than people to unseen influences; if she could sense Household, Vladimir must have been even more aware of its sinister presence before he fled to Mr. Bowes.

Now he was back, just when she needed a companion and ally in her battle.

Hadn't she and Don often called Vladimir the Catalonian ambassador and their home Catalonia's embassy? Vladimir had returned to defend their endangered world.

Twelve

During dinner with Rose, Don did some serious unloading about his lost job, his failing marriage, and his vague but still thwarted youthful ambitions. He had done what he had to do instead of simply doing as he pleased. If he hadn't gone into teaching, which he had once considered, or pursued some other satisfying but less well-paid profession, it was because he had to be practical. He had led his life in a responsible manner, and all he had received in return was a kick in the ass.

"You and millions of other people," Rose murmured gently, with an expression of sympathy on her face; it was surprisingly easy to talk to her.

"Maybe I let myself get too distracted." He struggled to grasp his next thought, which was eluding him. Maybe having two of those Bombay Sapphire martinis before dinner hadn't been a good idea, even if Rose was buying. He had been about to say that perhaps he and Gena had become so involved in their escapist Catalonian musings that they had lost track of practicalities, that their envisioned feline Shangri-La might have deranged them. Cats had made them go crazy. No, that wasn't what he wanted to say. He wasn't about to start talking about Catalonia and convince Rose that he really was around the bend.

"What I wanted to say," he said, "was this. Is it really possible to imagine something that isn't real? I mean, to think up something that bears absolutely no resemblance to reality? What I mean is, like, don't there necessarily have to be elements of the real world in anything you make up? And aren't imaginary worlds contained in some sort of reality themselves, like, you know, other universes?" That wasn't what he had meant to say, either.

"Sounds like the kind of question I used to hear in college," Rose said, "usually when we were all sitting around in the dorm at three in the morning talking about stuff like the noumena and the phenomena." She finished the last of her wine. "My boyfriend back then was a philosophy major."

"If you can imagine something," Don said, "and it's logically consistent, even if it doesn't exist—" The thought was getting away from him. That bottle of wine with dinner hadn't exactly increased his eloquence, especially since he had ended up drinking most of the bottle himself. Beer had seemed an inappropriate beverage to order in a place where the waiters were all in black tie and served the restaurant's patrons with an air that made him feel as though he should have been apologizing to them for intruding with requests for service. Imaginary things might become real, fancies invented by the mind might have a way of leaking into the perceived world; that was what he was trying to say, or else maybe that somebody could, through his imagination, somehow pick up another reality. But the insight that had blazed forth in his mind with the blinding light of an epiphany now seemed muddy and confused.

"We'd better order some coffee," Rose said, "and then get out of here. I've got to get up early tomorrow."

"Coffee sounds good," he managed to say in spite of his cottony mouth.

"Maybe Gena doesn't know how good she had it," Rose went on. "It's not like there's so many great guys in the world that she can easily let one of them go. You deserve some appreciation. She might be surprised at how fast you get snapped up by someone else."

That was probably an inappropriate comment for her to make, especially since she had so recently broken up with Jeff, but Don appreciated the sentiment.

* * * *

Rose drove Don back to Jeff's apartment; he had drunk too much to drive back safely by himself. His head was clearer by the time they pulled up in front of Jeff's building, and he already regretted all of the self-pitying commentary that he had dumped on her.

"Whenever I feel down," Rose was saying, "I just tell myself that this isn't the best of all possible worlds—it's just one of lots and lots of possible worlds." That pretty much summed up Rose's philosophy of life, from what he could gather, and she had taken his clumsy attempts during the ride to explain such concepts as collapsing wave fronts and diverging continua as confirmation of her outlook, which apparently still bore the influence of her former boyfriend, the philosopher. Rose seemingly derived a good deal of comfort in believing that this world was only one of many such universes and that anything that could possibly happen here, but didn't, probably did happen somewhere else. It was as if the actual world around her wasn't quite real, since there were so many theoretical alternatives.

An intriguing thought, and one that nearly brought him to hint at the existence of the hypothetical Catalonia. After all, given that Rose's crudely expressed theory echoed the more sophisticated notions of various physicists, Catalonia might exist, in some sense.

"See you," Rose said. "Maybe we can get together again sometime."

"That'd be great. Thanks for dinner." He was about to open his door when something landed with a loud thud on the hood of the car. A cat was out there, a large white cat with bared fangs and narrowed eyes, its claws pressing against the windshield.

Rose let out a gasp. "Holy shit," she said in a loud voice. "I really don't like cats." The cat bared more teeth.

"Maybe that's not such a good thing to say right now," Don said as the cat leaped from the car.

Rose sighed with what sounded like relief. "Well, stay in touch," she said. "And if you need a few extra bucks, I could use a part-timer once in a while. But you'll find another job, and a better one, I bet. I know you'll come out on top."

He thanked her again for dinner, got out of the car, and lifted a hand in farewell as she drove away.

As he walked down the shrub-lined path that led to the apartment building's main entrance, he could not help feeling that someone was watching him, even though nobody was in sight. That cat on Rose's car had spooked him. In the quiet of the night, he was able to pick up the soft sound of a subdued growl.

He pressed the buzzer at the entrance. As he opened the door, a small calico cat scurried past him and into the hallway.

"Hey," Don said, and a sudden blurred movement at the limits of his peripheral vision made him turn around.

He saw the cats, six of them, including the large white cat, all sitting stiffly under the shrubs, all staring in his direction, with their teeth bared and their shining eyes reflecting the security light over the entrance.

Don slammed the door, then peered through the glass. The cats were still outside, watching him. Two of them suddenly bounded across the grass into the darkness; the others scurried off in different directions.

He closed the door and looked down. The calico cat that had followed him inside seemed to be waiting for him. The animal had to belong to someone who lived here, in spite of the building's ban on pets.

He pressed the button under Jeff's mailbox, then walked to Jeff's door, with the cat following him. He knocked, waited for a bit, and was about to use the duplicate key Jeff had loaned him when the door opened.

"Yo," Jeff said. The calico cat scampered between Don's feet and into the apartment. "Well, what do you know. She's back."

"Who's back?" Don asked.

Jeff gestured at the calico. "She was hanging around before, but she can't belong to anybody here."

"Maybe somebody snuck her into the building."

Jeff beckoned Don inside and closed the door. "She was just sitting there before, not meowing or anything, just giving me the stare, and I thought she might be hungry, so I let her in and gave her some tuna and water. She didn't have a collar or a name tag, so I figured maybe I'd ask the manager if I could hang on to her for a while and try to find out who she belongs to—has to be somebody in the neighborhood." Jeff frowned at the cat, who was staring calmly up at him. "Then she started poking around the sofa, and I had to do some work at the computer, and when I looked for her again, she was gone, so she must have slipped out the door to the patio when I wasn't looking."

"You left the door open?"

"Not intentionally. But maybe I opened it and didn't remember because I was in the middle of work."

"You shouldn't be so absent-minded."

"I only am about stuff that doesn't matter all that much."

Don refrained from mentioning Jeff's absence at his and Gena's wedding, but given how things were going, maybe that lapse didn't matter, either. He took off his coat and draped it over the sofa. "Did you get my message?"

"Yeah, right after I got back this afternoon. But if you're still hungry, there's some cold cuts in the refrigerator."

Don sat down. "You and Rose really are finished, right?" he asked.

"For sure." An unhappy look crossed Jeff's face as he sat down in the chair in front of his desktop computer and leaned back, folding his arms. "Why do you ask?"

"Because Rose was the one who took me to dinner—just as a friend, you understand. I ran into her downtown today, and I guess she was feeling sorry for me. Anyway, if it really bothers you—"

"It doesn't, man." Jeff brushed back a strand of dark hair. "I told you, it's over." He sounded resigned. His mouth curved into a half-smile. "You and Gena are separating, and she knows that, and she's the one who broke it off with me, so somehow I don't think she took you to dinner just to get a write-off."

"Well, I just wanted to make sure. I mean, here I am taking up space in your place, so I didn't want you to think I was coming on to your girlfriend, too."

"Ex-girlfriend." Jeff gazed down at the cat, who seemed intent on the conversation. "It isn't that I don't care about Rose. I do, but she'd keep after me about being practical and making a commitment and settling down and why wasn't I making more use of my experience and talents to nail down some real money. And she wanted the break, so what can I do? She knew what the deal was when she started with me. Now she's probably looking to plug some other dude into her commitment-to-a-practical-guy equation—maybe you."

The cat hissed. Don glanced down to see the creature staring right at him.

"I left a message with Gena," Don said. "Told her we have to get together this weekend and talk. If she goes to stay with her parents for a while, I could move back to our house."

The calico cat leaped into Jeff's lap. He scratched it behind the ears. "Don't do it," Jeff said.

"What?"

Jeff was staring at the cat; she stared back at him. "Don't let Gena move back in with her parents. They'll start messing around in your business then and give her all kinds of advice. You won't have any chance of getting back together after that."

"Think we should try to patch things up?"

"Yes," Jeff replied in a toneless voice. "It's the only way to restore what you had." The cat was purring; Don could hear it from across the room. "Was what you fought about really that important? Are you ready to throw your whole marriage away because of it?"

That didn't sound like Jeff. Don met his friend's brown eyes and saw a cold rationality looking out at him through Jeff, with a gaze as steady and unblinking as that of the cat on his lap.

"Hrrow," the cat said.

Jeff blinked, and his stare vanished. "Divorce is a real hassle, too," he continued in his more familiar laid-back tone. "If you think you've got troubles now, just wait until the lawyers and the judges and the courts finish with you. I'd say that unless your marriage totally and irretrievably sucks, you and Gena should just let it ride."

That sounded more like Jeff: no point in exerting yourself if it was simpler to leave things alone. But Jeff also had a vested interest in getting Don out of his apartment as soon as possible, and a reconciliation would accomplish that end.

"There's two parties involved here, you know," Don muttered. "Gena might not want me back." His bitterness welled up inside him once more.

"I know a divorce might be worse for you later on," Jeff said, "but it'd also be better if you didn't get divorced at all, wouldn't it?"

"Funny to hear you talking about hanging on to a relationship," Don said, suspecting an upwelling of deeply held sentimentality from his friend.

Jeff was looking down at the cat. "Just because I can't commit doesn't mean that I mind seeing other people stick it out."

The calico cat glanced from Jeff to Don. "Hrrow," the cat said, then wandered toward the glass doors that led out to the patio. "Hrree?" The cat slipped between the doors and disappeared.

Jeff said, "I could have sworn I locked those doors."

Don went to the doors and slid them shut, then made sure the inside lock had caught. "I'd better get to sleep. I've still got one day of work left, and I have to get up early enough to call a cab so I can go get my car at the restaurant—Rose had to drive me back here."

"I'll drive you to the restaurant," Jeff said.

"At six in the morning?"

"I've got to meet Cliff Beaufort early at his halfway house, go over a lot of stuff with him, and then get him to the courthouse by noon—he's holding a rally tomorrow."

"I never thought of you as political."

Jeff shrugged. "But Cliff isn't really a politician, either. Anyway, I already finished his Web site. Have to tweak it some, but the job's basically done. He isn't paying me much, but then I don't have to do that much except run his site and set up interviews and get our headquarters organized and make sure his appearances get some coverage. Cliff can ad-lib a speech better than anyone can write one for him, and he's always giving speeches at some church or for civic groups."

"He doesn't have a chance, you know."

"I know. That assclown Dorff'll get in for another four years and get his buddies even more of the city's business, as if fixing up the goddamn Blaine Building hadn't wasted enough money, but at least I'll know we tried."

Don was familiar with the Blaine Building, an old six-story Victorian structure of brick and sandstone in the center of town, only two blocks from the courthouse. His insurance company had considered moving its offices there two years earlier before deciding against it. The Blaine Building belonged to a group of investors who were supposedly very tight with Dorff; there was even a rumor that the mayor had secretly been cut in for a share. Renovation paid for by the city had transformed the Blaine Building from an empty eyesore into a stunning but still nearly empty high-tech office building that was utterly useless except possibly as a tax write-off; for all he knew, maybe that had been the main purpose of the renovation, along with throwing some business to contractors connected to the mayor. Or maybe everybody was just sitting tight until some sort of payoff materialized; some sucker might eventually buy them out.

Don recalled that Clifford Beaufort had pushed to have low-cost apartments included in the building, along with a few shops at street level, to attract more residents and shoppers to the downtown area, but Dorff and his pals had ignored those pleas, too.

Don wandered toward the bathroom, resigned to another night on Jeff's sofa.

* * * *

Gena had picked up some wine and was on her way to the pizzeria for her call-in order when she realized that she would be driving by Tracey's street. She might as well stop there first and ask her friend to dinner. She was ravenously hungry, having postponed ordering the pizza to change her clothes, dig out Vladimir's former litter box, and pick up some cat food, kitty litter, and other pet supplies at the strip mall, but she couldn't finish a large pizza with the works all alone.

She had rationalized the frightening events of the day. Her mother had been going through some weird change-of-life symptoms and Gena had misinterpreted her comments. Maybe a sudden heat flash had inspired her violent behavior, and maybe Gena, with everything that was going on in her life, had overreacted. In fact, it wouldn't surprise her if, under the circumstances, she was having a nervous breakdown. She had imagined it all, the unseen creepy presence and her mother's voice suddenly dropping into Darth Vader-like tones. Realizing that she might have only been in the grip of delusions, and that the events of the last hour or so had not happened in exactly the way that she recalled them, was surprisingly comforting.

Everything that had happened could be explained somehow. She had to hang on to the thought that she was not rationalizing, but coldly explaining everything to herself.

She turned on to Tracey's street and slowed to a crawl when she saw the cats. Three of them, hardly larger than kittens, ran across the road, and two more were sharpening their claws against a tree. She had noticed a number of cats on her own street before leaving the house; a few had even been loitering in the driveway. She had backed out slowly and carefully, fearful of hitting one, but all of the cats had nimbly scampered out of the way. Three of them had been sitting outside the front door as she drove off, almost as if they were waiting for Vladimir to let them inside.

She suddenly longed for Don. Had he been in the car with her, they might have been deep in a Catalonian discussion by now, speculating about the roles that each of those cats might play in Catalonian society. The kittens, of course, would still be in school following a rigorous curriculum, since all Catalonians were gifted and brilliant far beyond the capacities of human beings. Catalonian students mastered the languages and meows of the various breeds of cats, took courses in science and advanced mathematics, and were extremely proud of their rich literature and relatively peaceful history. Since the end of the Cataceous Age, when dinosaurs had roamed Catalonia and the cats scratching out a precarious existence among those great beasts could only dream of their future utopia, the members of Catalonia's feline culture had followed the path of non-violence except when hunting their prey. As Don had pointed out, even in such a utopia the cats had to eat, but Gena was convinced that most Catalonians lived on fish, vegetables, and an assortment of grains. They would never dream of pouncing upon the songbirds that nested in Catalonia's trees. Their stalking of birds and mice was purely recreational, she insisted, a way to get some exercise and keep their instincts honed.

So she had always assumed, anyway. Now she wondered if any cats, even Catalonians, would be so peaceful, especially if they felt themselves in danger of losing their world.

She pulled up in front of Tracey's house, her eyes stinging, and rummaged in her purse for a tissue. Thoughts of Catalonia were so intermingled with memories of her husband that she would never be able to separate them. To give up on her marriage would mean abandoning Catalonia, perhaps the only original idea her mind had ever developed.

A vision came to her then of Nicholas and Alexandra slinking away from their palace, of lights gradually flickering out all over their feline realm, of cats huddled together in the ancient catacombs under their capital city mewing mournfully as they waited for the inevitable end.

"Whoa!" Gena cried out. But would any Catalonians just passively wait for the end? Would creatures capable of building the civilization she and Don had envisioned for them do nothing to help themselves?

She was about to get out of the car when she saw how deserted Tracey's street was, abnormally so for this time of evening. Usually there was more traffic, a couple of people out walking their dogs, a few older kids wandering aimlessly around the neighborhood. She peered down the street. Under the yellowish glow of the streetlights, small groups of cats sat at curbside or reclined under trees.

A Catalonian street.

Gena slipped from the car, almost forgetting to lock the vehicle. Three cats sat under the streetlight in front of Tracey's house.

Tracey's lights were out, but her tenant seemed to be home. Gena climbed the steps to the porch, unsure whether Tracey was out, asleep, or simply working hard with the curtains drawn against distractions. One problem with having a best friend who worked at home at odd hours was never knowing what kind of schedule Tracey was following or what she might be doing from day to day.

Gena knocked on the door, waited, then knocked again. "Tracey?" she called out. "It's Gena. If you're working, just tell me to go away." Tracey was either out or asleep; she was such a sound sleeper that even a crack-of-doom kind of knock wouldn't wake her up.

She turned to leave, then saw the cats. The three felines had followed her to the door. They narrowed their eyes in unison; she wondered how long they had been watching her. It came to her that they might be spies from Catalonia, operatives from the Catalonian Intelligence Agency disguised as ordinary domestic cats, sent here to gather information about this world that might help them to preserve their own.

That was a new thought. She had never imagined a CIA for the invented realm of cats before.

She took a step toward the cats, expecting them to scurry away as normal cats might, but instead they fanned out around her. Something about their oddly precise and orderly movements unnerved her. The porch light above her suddenly came on, startling her; she backed away from the cats as the door on the other side of the two-family opened.

"Hello?" a man's voice said. A tall dark-haired man stood in the doorway, and he had to be just about the best-looking man she had ever seen in the flesh. His thick wavy hair hung almost to his shoulders, his handsome, chiseled face would have been a fine advertisement for a plastic surgeon, and he wore jeans and a sleeveless shirt that showed off sharply defined muscles. He could have posed for a Chippendales calendar or the cover of a romance novel.

"Looking for Tracey?" he asked. Gena nodded. "I heard her go out about a half-hour ago."

"Oh." Gena grinned uneasily. "Guess I'd better come back some other time."

"She might be back any minute. I'd invite you in, if you wanted to wait, except for my place is kind of a mess right now. I just got back this morning." He stepped outside his door and thrust out a hand. "I'm Roland Tewksbury."

"Roland Tewksbury?" she said, flustered.

"Tracey's tenant. I rent this place."

"Uh, I'm Gena Lawlor." She took his hand and shook a firm and solid grip. So this was Roland Tewksbury; the man didn't look anything like what she had expected. "I can't stay anyway," she murmured. "I was just on my way to pick up a pizza." She searched for something else to say. "I was going to ask Tracey if she wanted to share it with me."

"The thing is, I wouldn't mind sharing it with you myself, but I've still got groceries and all to pick up—I'm out of everything." Roland Tewksbury smiled, showing perfect white teeth. "Are you an artist like Tracey?"

Gena smiled back, still feeling uneasy. Could he be coming on to her? She had been married too long to pick up signals or recall how to behave.

"Well, no, actually I'm not," she replied. "I work for St. Luke's Hospital, in Billing and Accounts Receivable," she added, flushed with embarrassment at having such an ordinary position. "How about you?"

"I'm a performer with Strut My Stuff."

She dimly recalled hearing about them; they were yet another company of male strippers. "Really?" she asked.

"Yeah. I'm with the road company, but sometimes they call me in to do a gig at the Strut My Stuff club in Manhattan. That's one reason I live here, because it isn't that far from New York. The other reason is because this town isn't one of the stops on our tour."

"Oh. I guess that makes sense."

He chuckled. "The thing is, I don't exactly want to live some place where people might see the show. I mean, it could be, like, kind of embarrassing."

"That's assuming people would recognize you with your clothes on," Gena said, amazed at having that witticism rise so readily to her lips just when she needed it.

Roland Tewksbury laughed again. "Actually, it's kind of a wholesome show for the most part. We show a lot of cheek, but we don't flash or any-thing—got a thong covering the goods at a minimum. But the ladies in the audience sure go wild. Had one shove a fifty-dollar bill in my jock a couple of nights ago."

"Well," Gena said, blocking any thought of stuffing money into his jock.

"Hope you don't mind my asking, but are you doing anything tomor-row?"

She tensed. "What?"

"Doing anything tomorrow?" Roland Tewksbury said again. "Could we catch a movie or something?"

She was about to decline his movie or something, then realized that, as someone who was estranged from her husband, she could go out with whomever she liked. Besides, Don had said something in his message about being busy until Saturday, so there was no reason for her to sit around on Friday night doing nothing and feeling sorry for herself.

"And we could grab some grub first," Roland added.

A dinner invitation, she thought. Dinner and a movie seemed harmless enough, the kind of evening she might have spent with any friend even if she weren't about to get divorced.

"Sure," she said. "Why not?"

"I could pick you up after work. I'm still kind of figuring out how to get around here, being as I'm out of town so much, but I know where St. Luke's is."

"That would be great. I have to meet with my boss right after work, but I'll be in front of the main entrance around five-thirty or so."

"Great—just look for a fire engine red Ford Escort. See you then, Gena." He lifted a hand, then went back inside.

A date, Gena told herself. A wild elation filled her; a man other than Don had asked her out for the first time in ages. Maybe it was just as well to be getting a divorce now, before she was past her prime.

She danced down the steps. A small form darted toward her feet with a snarl. A cat grabbed at her jeans-covered left leg and she felt its teeth biting into her.

"Get away!" she cried, shaking the cat off herself.

"Mrrow," the cat replied before running off into the darkness.

She reached down to check her leg. The cat's teeth had punctured the denim fabric just above her ankle, but hadn't broken the skin. She would not have to worry about rabies, she supposed, but that didn't seem much of a comfort.

She hurried toward her car. A big orange cat lay on the hood, its paws against the windshield. As she went around to open her door, the cat launched itself at her. She threw up her arms and dodged to one side, then fell against the car. She had a brief glimpse of the cat flying past her before it landed in the street and bounded away.

Her hands shook as she opened the door, slid in behind the wheel, and rested her hands against it.

Two cats had attacked her. She should report the attacks to animal control, but her instincts warned her against that, and not just because any cats the city might pick up faced a better than even chance of being euthanized at the city's shelter. Catalonian operatives would have ways of striking back at anyone who betrayed them. She did not want to think about exactly how.

Stop imagining things, she told herself as she started the car and flooded the engine. She waited, quelling her fears, and it started on her next try.

* * * *

Maybe she had been too precipitous, Gena thought as she pulled into her driveway. Accepting a date with somebody she had known for about three minutes might be reckless. She would search for Roland Tewksbury's phone number and if she couldn't find one for him, Tracey would surely know what it was. She could call him up and give him some sort of excuse for not going out with him.

She juggled her pizza and bottle of wine as she opened the back door. Vladimir was in the kitchen, lapping at the water in his porcelain bowl. She tensed at the sight of the cat, then relaxed. This was her beloved Vladimir. He might readily disembowel helpless mice and happily chomp on the bones of any baby birds unlucky enough to fall out of the nest in his vicinity, but he would never harm his people.

She set her provisions down on the counter and went to hang up her coat. The house seemed homier and more welcoming with Vladimir around; she no longer felt some unseen and malign presence lurking in her home's darker corners, the wounded entity of Household waiting to ambush her.

Could it be that Vladimir had come home to protect her from Household? Maybe Household had resented Vladimir enough to frighten the cat away from this house, but now Vladimir was back, prepared to be her ally against their common enemy.

Stop it, Gena told herself. There was no Household.

She returned to the kitchen, uncorked the wine, and carried the bottle and the pizza into the dining room, telling herself that she wasn't taking such a big chance by going out with Roland Tewksbury. They would be in public places, and he would not want to get on the bad side of his landlady's best friend.

She sat down to open the pizza box when the doorbell rang. Don, she thought, not knowing whether to be overjoyed or apprehensive as it dawned on her that, with Vladimir back home, she and Don might wind up in a vicious battle over custody of their cat.

She went to the front door and opened it to see Tracey with a bottle in her right hand and balancing a large pizza box in her left. "Had to pick up some art supplies," Tracey said, "so I thought I'd drop by with some supper from Giuseppe's and cheer you up."

"You sure picked the right time," Gena said as she led her friend inside. "I've got a sixteen-incher from Franco's in the dining room."

"So we can gorge and I'll take my leftovers home for tomorrow." Tracey threw her coat over one chair. "See you got some wine, too."

Gena fetched plates, glasses, and napkins from the kitchen, then sat down at the table with Tracey. As she was about to tell her that she had stopped by and met Roland Tewksbury, she noticed that the row of Russian cats on the sideboard seemed angry and accusatory. She was now a traitor to Catalonia, they were saying. She was silent, guilty as charged.

Vladimir wandered into the room and stared up at Gena, then settled himself under the table. Tracey leaned over and squinted at him. "That cat looks just like Vladimir," she said.

"That cat is Vladimir." Gena poured the bottle of wine. "He came back home today. Heard something outside the front door, and when I went to check it out, there he was. Came right in and made himself at home just as if he'd never been away."

Tracey tucked a strand of long brown hair behind her right ear, then reached for a slice of Gena's pizza. "What a day. Spent most of it online at home and then in the library reading up on cats and their behavior. Figured that might help my illustrations, getting more insight into what's on their minds. Cats always seem to have their own private agenda."

Gena glanced down at Vladimir. He watched her intently, following the conversation. "Speaking of cats, have you noticed any strange ones in your neighborhood?"

"There seem to be more of them around. At least that's what I assumed, but maybe I'm just noticing cats more, given the illustrations I'm working on now."

"I meant any strange ones that—well, that seem more aggressive than usual."

"Can't say I have. They all look and act just adorable as hell, if you're into cats, and Olive Preston down the street would have told me about anything weird." Olive Preston was a nosy old woman who constantly left messages in Tracey's voice mail about activities and doings in their neighborhood that were really none of her business. "Why do you ask?"

"Nothing," Gena said. "Um, I met your tenant before, on my way to Franco's. Stopped by to see if you wanted to have dinner with me, and he introduced himself."

"Roland?" Tracey said with her mouth full. "That's interesting. He always struck me as kind of shy."

"Why didn't you tell me about him?"

"What's there to tell? He isn't around most of the time—he's been on the road for the last two months, and when he's home, he's very quiet. He goes out to a gym a few times a week and that's about it."

"You weren't ever interested?"

"I'm just as happy to be celibate for a while, now that the fucking bastard, may his name be forever cursed, is out of my life."

Gena dropped her bombshell. "Well, guess what. He asked me out. We're going to dinner and a movie tomorrow."

Tracey gaped at her. "Are you out of your mind?"

"What's wrong with that?"

"You're married."

"Separated."

"Not yet, at least not legally. You're pissed off. Being highly pissed off at your spouse for a couple of days doesn't qualify as a separation. Don't you think you could at least wait until it's official?"

"Oh, come on." Gena finished her slice of pizza and helped herself to a piece of Tracey's pie. "It's just dinner and a movie. I'm not rushing to get involved or sleep with him or anything."

"But still—"

Gena heard a snarl. She looked down at Vladimir and saw his ears go back. He showed his teeth and snarled at her again as his eyes narrowed.

"Did you even tell Roland you were married?" Tracey asked. Gena shook her head. "How's he going to feel when he finds out? He might have second thoughts about going out with a married woman."

"Separated."

"Whatever. Look, I know how I felt after the fucking bastard, may disaster swallow him, called it quits. I didn't even want to be around guys going through serious marital issues, let alone go out with them. It's too many damned complications. Roland might feel the same way. He might think you misled him."

"He's a dancer with Strut My Stuff. He's probably more sophisticated than that."

Tracey shook her head. "Maybe not. You don't know anything about him. He's my tenant, and I don't know much about him except that he's polite and quiet and pays his rent on time."

"Hrree!" Vladimir said. He scrunched down, as if getting ready to pounce. Maybe another mouse had gotten inside the house. Vladimir had caught a mouse in the basement not long after they had moved to this house, bringing the carcass upstairs and depositing it on her pillow while she and Don were sleeping. The cat had been bewildered by her screams when she had awakened to the sight of a bloody dead mouse right in front of her face, given that he had paid her the honor of presenting his prey to her. Or maybe Vladimir was stalking an insect. She hoped that it wasn't a cockroach. That was all she needed; if the house was becoming infested, she might have to call in an exterminator. Don had always attended to such matters, diagnosing the situation and then calling up and working out the arrangements with exterminators, electricians, or plumbers. She remembered then that the kitchen faucet was starting to drip just a little and that Don had promised to take a look at it a few days before their last battle. She might end up having to fork over major bucks to a plumber to take care of a problem Don could have handled with a wrench and some plumbing doohickey or other.

"Well, what did you expect?" a voice very unlike Tracey's said. "You're going to have plenty of other problems to worry about."

"What?" Gena asked.

"I said," Tracey replied in her usual voice, "that you have enough on your mind without Roland."

Vladimir got up, rubbed against Tracey's ankles, then leaped into her lap.

"Down, Vladimir," Tracey said absently. Vladimir's head was just above the tabletop; his green eyes stared at Gena with a gaze so hypnotic that she could not turn away.

"You miss Don," Tracey went on. "I can tell." She was sitting perfectly still now, her hands resting on the table on either side of Vladimir's head, palms down but with her fingers curled, as if her hands were paws. "You've been with him for a number of years, after all. You made a realm for yourselves, a place of kindness and warmth, a retreat from all the evils that bedevil this unhappy world. You actually succeeded in bridging the gap that separates this continuum from another, and now you may lose that precious refuge. Even worse, you may bring about a schism that will forever divide its inhabitants, that is already bringing discord to their paradise."

Gena shivered. That did not sound at all like Tracey, who had become a fatalist about divorce, considering it nearly as inevitable as death and taxes. Her friend's voice was high-pitched and alien, almost—she had to search for the word for a moment—feline.

"Don't let it happen," Tracey said, "I beg you," and Vladimir keened a mournful meow.

"Stop it." Tears slid from Gena's eyes; she was powerless to stop them. "I can't bear it."

"You can't bear it." That deep rolling voice was also coming from Tracey. Vladimir howled as he jumped from her lap and fled from the room. "You haven't seen the half of it," the deep voice continued. "Thought you'd get rid of me—you have no idea how much trouble's heading your way."

"Household," Gena whispered.

"I know your weak spots, yours and your mate's. That's how I survive, feeding on your fears and phobias and obsessions. All of you have them, you know. With some, it's impatience or envy or suspicion of anyone different from themselves. With your mate, it's fear of…"

Vladimir flew through the air. He landed on top of the table, barely missing the edge of Tracey's pizza box, then threw himself at her. Tracey shrieked and knocked him aside.

"Vladimir!" Gena cried. The cat launched himself at the table again, skidded across its surface on his paws, then crouched down. Gena jumped up, threw herself across the table, and grabbed him. He twisted in her hands, howling.

"That cat can't stop me," Tracey said as she rose to her feet. "Nothing can stop me."

Gena felt claws digging into her arm. She let go of Vladimir. He jumped from the table, scurried across the floor, and retreated to one corner, his tail twitching.

"Oh, my God," Tracey said in her usual voice.

"Are you all right?" Gena asked.

"I'm fine," Tracey said as she sat down. "It's just that…I don't know what happened, feel like I'm just waking up. That wine must be getting to me. I thought Vladimir was trying to attack me."

Gena forced herself to stay calm. "That's all you remember?"

"Vladimir was on my lap, and then all of a sudden he was going for my face, and now you're suddenly sprawling across the table." She glanced toward the corner, where the agitated cat was staring past them, his ears and tail twitching. "It was happening from a distance, like a dream." Tracey shook her head.

"Maybe he's just not used to the house yet," Gena said. She slipped off the top of the table and retreated to her chair. Her knees shook as she sat down. "He's never done anything like that before, at least not without being provoked." First her mother, and then Tracey; Household was trying to use them against her. She wasn't safe in her own house; if anything, she was in even more danger here. Household was warning her; the next attack on her might be lethal. If Household took over someone with more physical strength—

No, she thought. She was tired and overwrought, misunderstanding and misinterpreting Tracey's efforts to be helpful. She gazed at the substantial remains of their two pizzas, having lost her appetite.

"Oh, God," Gena moaned, thinking of Don with both longing and apprehension. "What am I going to do?"

"Jeez," Tracey said, "you're worse off than I thought." She leaned across the table and patted Gena's hand. "Look, life goes on, you know? It's rough for you now, but when it's over, believe me, you'll feel as though you can get through anything. You'll be stronger."

"You know what bothers me most? How I could have been so wrong and made such a huge mistake. We loved each other, we really did."

"I know. You two were the last ones I thought would ever break up, but it happens."

"I never thought it could happen to us."

"That's what everybody thinks in the beginning."

"This was different, Tracey. We were as close as two people could be. We had—" Gena paused, knowing that she could not speak the name of Catalonia.

Something brushed against her leg. She looked down to see Vladimir gazing up at her, green eyes searching her face, looking for all the world like a Catalonian psychoanalyst whose practice was to encourage cats to log a lot of couch time in his office, since lying around was one of their favorite activities anyway.

"Mrrow," Vladimir said as Gena sighed and covered her eyes.

* * * *

Tracey stayed with Gena until midnight, consoling her, mentioning the names of lawyers and psychologists, and providing yet more gory details about how she had managed to extort a halfway reasonable settlement from her estranged husband, the dastardly fucking bastard Johnny, might he never find peace. Gena knew that her friend was only trying to comfort her, but almost everything Tracey was saying seemed beside the point, profoundly depressing, or mostly about her.

After Tracey left, Gena put her leftover pizza in the refrigerator, checked the locks on the front and back doors, turned off the downstairs lights, then climbed the stairs to the bedroom. Vladimir scurried up the stairs after her, slipping past her to leap onto the bed as she entered the room. Having the cat with her made her feel that she had a protector. She needed a protector. Something was still in the house, waiting for another time to strike.

"Stop it," she said, "you're imagining things." Now I'm talking to myself, she thought. She forced herself to go about her usual routines of undressing, removing her makeup, and washing her face; she would shower in the morning.

How could she and Don have come to this? she asked herself as she got into bed. The more she tried to analyze the situation, the more confusing and mysterious it became; the longer she dwelled on the matter, the more unsure she was of why they were breaking up at all. The whole damned business had started with an argument about Household. Surely they could put such pettiness aside and reconcile.

Vladimir made a sound between a meow and a whimper. A revelation came to Gena as she hung between wakefulness and unconsciousness. Household had somehow come alive in this house, manifesting itself first through Don and then through others, seeking revenge for her action against it. Perhaps Household's intention was to drive her and Don apart, or maybe only to punish her before restoring her husband to her, but none of that mattered. No true reconciliation was possible unless Household was utterly vanquished, banished from their lives entirely, its hold broken. Without a total victory over Household, she and Don would be enslaved for the rest of their lives, even if they did get back together.

"Mrrow," Vladimir said softly.

Household also knew its true enemy, Gena realized. Household had seen the strategic threat that Catalonia posed to Household's existence. Household would not rest until that entire whimsical realm of kitties was banished and forgotten, because Catalonia was a refuge, however temporary, from their deepest fears, fears that Household drew on to dominate them.

That was how the entity they had somehow provoked must live, she realized, gaining strength by draining everything from the lives of its victims and getting rid of anything that threatened its existence. Household was a kind of vampire, perhaps one that could survive only by forcing its victims to surrender their entire purpose in life to him. She wondered if the occasional tales she had read of impoverished misers found dead with thousands of dollars stuffed in their mattresses, of quiet modest men revealed as serial killers, and of people suddenly assaulting or murdering family members had been stories about other victims of entities like Household.

"Mrree," Vladimir said.

"That's how I survive, feeding on your individual fears and phobias and obsessions." Household had made Tracey say those words, too. There was something else she had to remember, a recent incident that might somehow be connected to the thing haunting her house, but she could not recall what it was.

Gena floated, not quite awake and not really asleep. Vladimir was trying to tell her that Catalonians would not stand by as their world was endangered. The cats she and Don had imagined were waking from their dream, bursting out of what they had once believed were the bounds of their reality, preparing to confront their creators. They would struggle to stay alive. Like Household, they would also fight against any threat to their existence.

"I understand," Gena murmured, and the sound of her own voice brought her sharply awake. In the dim illumination provided by her night light, she saw Vladimir sitting near the edge of the bed facing the doorway, a feline sentry on guard.

* * * *

The light woke Don. He turned over on the sofa, then opened his eyes. Jeff had left his desktop computer on; the screen displayed an iconless landscape of hills under a bright blue sky.

The visual had to be some sort of screen saver. Don sat up, wondering why Jeff had left the machine on, then why the computer wasn't in stand-by mode, since Jeff had retreated to his bedroom at least an hour ago. He stretched, then stood up and flexed his arms, trying to work out the kinks. If he had to spend any more nights on the sofa, there would be orthopedic hell to pay; his neck and upper back were already aching.

Then a tiny image scurried across the screen—an animated figure of a cat.

Don tiptoed across the room and sat down in front of the computer. The scene on the monitor deepened, becoming three-dimensional; beyond the hills, he glimpsed the towers of a distant city. He put his hand on the mouse and suddenly felt himself carried aloft.

The sky opened up above him as the hills swept past him. He was flying toward the city. He had somehow logged on to a computer game, to a game so lifelike that he could feel the wind whipping past him even though he was still sitting in the chair.

I'm dreaming, he thought. He had dreamed of flying before. He had to be dreaming.

The city was still far away. He dropped toward a valley, soared over a meadow, and landed near a grassy expanse dotted with yellow and violet flowers. A pathway lined by small stones wound through the meadow, and a cat with orange-gold fur sat in the middle of the path. Don focused on the cat, sure that he had seen this cat before, and took a step toward the creature. Odd, he thought to himself, that he now felt as though he was inside another body, one that compelled him to move on all fours.

I'm dreaming, Don told himself again.

"I have a warning for you," the cat said as those words appeared on the screen inside a pale balloon. An instant message, Don thought, and yet he had heard the words as well, uttered in a soft feline tone. This had to be a dream.

"We are aware of the threats to our existence," the cat continued in its subdued voice as more words appeared, "and we will defend ourselves. You may remain our protector, our connection to your continuum, or you may choose to surrender to our enemy. That choice is yours, but consider the possible consequences of any action you take. We will not stand by passively as our world dies."

The screen went black. He was back inside himself

Don jumped up, nearly knocking over the chair. He struggled to steady himself.

No matter how real it had seemed, either he was dreaming, trapped in one of those dreams he occasionally had in which he was convinced that he was actually awake, or he was going nuts.

He stumbled back to the sofa, telling himself that he was still asleep.

Thirteen

When Gena came out of the bathroom, Vladimir was sitting in front of the door to Don's home office. This was not his usual behavior, which was to awaken early, run downstairs, and emit sharp insistent meows until somebody came down to the kitchen to serve him fresh food and water.

"What is it?" Gena asked.

"Mrree?" Vladimir poked at the closed door with one paw, then hissed.

Gena crossed the hallway and opened the door. "See," she said, "nothing's the matter," and then saw that something was the matter.

The computer was on, its monitor showing her an image of green hills and blue sky. Vladimir bounded past her and leaped into the chair in front of the computer. A small figure strolled amid the hills; the face of a man suddenly filled the screen. Vladimir let out a yowl and jumped to the floor.

The man's moustache twitched. With his dark hair and beady dark eyes, he looked disconcertingly like a stereotypical villain. "You won't make it," the man said. "You don't have it in you."

She approached the computer and said, "You must be Household."

"How perceptive of you."

She felt hypnotized. I'm dreaming this, she thought. In a moment, she would wake up in her bed and know—

"You've always been afraid," the man continued, "afraid of leaving home, of being on your own, of having to look out for yourself, of being in strange and alien territory, of taking any chances in the wider world. You always needed somebody to prop you up, you always needed your protective cocoon. I can let you stay here in your safe little home, or I can make your life a lot more uncertain and unstable. Which is it going to be?"

He was right, she realized. Her mouth was dry; she forced herself to swallow, recalling how often she had grown homesick at college, welcoming the summers and the breaks between semesters when she could return to her parents' house. Her job had been the result of a couple of phone calls from her parents to a pal at St. Luke's, and she had clung to that tedious position even when other opportunities might have been pursued. Better to hang on to what she had; better not to disturb the tranquil little life she had made for herself, however tiresome it might sometimes be. All she had to do now was give in to Household, and—

"Mrrow!" Vladimir protested from the floor.

"Feline parasite," the man said. "We would all be on a firmer footing without you and your kind."

"That's enough!" Gena shouted.

The familiar desktop of Don's computer appeared, with its icons of programs and folders. She sank into the chair, reached for the mouse, and shut down the machine.

Her dreams of the preceding night were coming back to her now, bits and snatches of reveries about cats creeping through tunnels and gathering in groups and preparing for a battle yet to be fought. She recalled that a storm had raged around her as cats ran past her in their desperate quest for shelter. She had dreamed of standing in a long hallway with a row of closed doors on her right and a railing on her left as several large and vicious-looking cats slinked toward her, leaving her no way to escape their deadly claws except to plunge over the railing into the darkness below.

She forced her mind back to reality. The man…the thing…leering at her from the monitor had emphasized the underlying peril of her situation. Life was going to be a much harder struggle from now on. Even Vladimir would be a drain on her resources, beginning with the bill Caterina Lucci would soon be sending for his recent visit to the vet in the company of the estimable Mr. Bowes.

Vladimir rubbed against her leg. She leaned down to pet her companion in adversity. She would not count the cost of supporting him now that he was home again and with her during her time of need.

Don was at Jeff Nardi's. All she had to do was call Jeff and ask him to intercede for her, tell him that she was ready to make amends with her husband, that all she wanted was for Don to come home, and Don would then know that he could come back without any loss of pride. If that meant having to endure the tyranny of Household, then she was prepared to make that sacrifice.

It's too late for that. She had not heard that particular voice before, a high-pitched sound not unlike that of a violin being played. *Too late, too late. Your only hope now is to stand your ground.*

Vladimir pawed her leg. Yes, she told herself, it was definitely too late for retreat. She had struck the first blow in this battle and had to follow through. Fear was the weapon Household wielded against them, her fear of the unfamiliar and Don's fear that he would end up dooming himself to his father's economically insecure life. Fear was a powerful weapon; it could paralyze them, make them powerless even to defend themselves. She could not give in to fear.

She stood up, clinging to her newfound determination. She was ready to forgive Don—in her heart, she had already—but they would have to resume their life together with a new understanding. They would have to become more like the Catalonians they imagined, who were fearless and brave and willing to risk everything to preserve what they valued.

The air in the room felt colder. Vladimir arched his back and hissed. Gena knelt next to him. "What is it?" she asked. Vladimir lifted his head to be petted, then scrunched down on the floor, paws out in front of him. Irrationally, she wondered if it was safe to leave Vladimir alone here with whatever might remain of Household. Perhaps she should call Caterina Lucci and ask if she could park Vladimir at the vet's animal infirmary for the day, but Vladimir would hate being penned up in such a place, and she could hardly reveal to Caterina her true reason for bringing him there.

I'm going nuts, she thought, thinking of Household as an actual being haunting her house, having dreams about cats preparing for some sort of indeterminate struggle that involved her. She had to put such ideas out of her mind.

The phone next to the computer rang. She waited for the ringing to stop, then picked it up. The answering machine down in the kitchen should have kicked in by now.

"Hello?" Gena said as she held the phone to her ear.

"I warned you," a deep voice said, "but you think you can ignore me. You'll learn better."

She slammed down the phone, then took several deep breaths as she struggled to calm herself. Just a crank call, she told herself.

"Mrrow," Vladimir said, and then she heard, very briefly, the sound of distant meows from outside the house. Drawn by the sound, she stood up and went to the window that overlooked the back yard.

At least ten cats were there, sitting in a row and gazing up at her.

Maybe she was crazy, but the sight of those cats was strangely reassuring. Vladimir would be safe, at least for now; Household would not dare to move against him.

* * * *

Larry Philmus was the first to tell Don about the pity party he and the others had planned for that evening: drinks at Thirsty Tom's and then dinner at Vitello's, where Larry and those who were still employed would pick up the tab for their laid-off colleagues. Larry and two of the actuaries had also volunteered to be designated drivers in case Don and any of his laid-off colleagues ended up getting completely faced while drowning their sorrows. Larry left Don's cubicle before Don could tell him that he suddenly didn't want any party, that all he really wanted to do that evening was go back to his house and see if he could mend his fences with Gena.

The force of that desire surprised him. He had dragged himself off Jeff's sofa that morning determined to make it through his last day at the office with some dignity, and also looking forward to that evening's get-together, which would mark the beginning of his new life. It wasn't as though he didn't have any social prospects; Rose Cutler had just about admitted that she was amenable to going out sometime, and there was nothing to stop him from approaching Stella Przhewalski now that they were both unemployed. He didn't have to sit around feeling sorry for himself while he looked for a new job.

But he was sorry about the life he had lost with Gena. A sudden desire for her rose inside him; he hadn't felt such passion for his wife in months. What he really wanted to do was go home and spend the whole weekend in bed having sex in just about every position their bodies would allow, as they had when they were first living together.

It was almost lunchtime. He could leave now, go back to Jeff's place and call from there to tell Larry that he was taking the rest of the day off and didn't feel well enough to go out that night. Larry would understand, and he wasn't going to get much done here, anyway. The personal items he had in his cubicle amounted to an old desk clock, a couple of coffee mugs, a couple of citations, a bronzed softball he had won for being on the winning team of a local softball league two summers ago, a Philadelphia Phillies baseball cap, a leather pen and pencil holder, a pair of Nikes he had almost never worn, and a photo of Gena with Vladimir, all of which he could pack up in about five minutes.

His gaze fell on the photo of Gena. He had shot it himself, and for once Gena had smiled instead of covering her face or blinking at the flash. Vladimir, sitting on her lap in Sphinx mode, had managed to look simultaneously mysterious and adorable. Don sighed. All he had to do was head over to the house that evening and tell Gena that he did not want a divorce. She probably wanted one even less than he did, given her past dependence on him and her general incompetence at leading her own life.

He frowned. That was what had started this whole deal to begin with, her incompetence and her extreme dependence on him and her profound lack of any practical sensibility. They would be right back where they had started, with nothing resolved.

It was eleven-forty-five, close enough to lunchtime. He would pack up his stuff, leave it in his car, and decide what to do after lunch.

* * * *

The park in front of the county courthouse was slightly more crowded than usual. A few people sat on benches, but others had gathered near the courthouse's front stairway. A couple of men were putting up a banner between two of the courthouse's marble columns that read: BEAUFORT FOR MAYOR. A third man fiddled with a speaker.

Don stopped to watch them, recalling that Jeff had mentioned this rally. If it had been a rally for Mayor Dorff, that wily incumbent would have assured himself of a good turn-out by offering free food, coffee, and soft drinks. Clifford Beaufort's campaign wouldn't have the resources for such a repast, which was probably why there was already a line at the hot dog vendor's stand.

The crowd seemed about evenly divided between black people and white folks, with a sprinkling of people who looked Asian or Latino. Beaufort presumably had most of the black vote locked up, which didn't do him a whole lot of good in a city where less than fifteen percent of the population shared his African-American heritage. He was likely to pick up more votes among civic-minded do-gooders, but not enough to put him over the top, and he had made some powerful enemies. There had been his controversial and vociferous term on the school board, after his appointment to finish the term of the token black member who had suddenly died; Beaufort had managed to get much-needed funds for repairs to school buildings and for hiring more teachers only at the cost of alienating many of Stan Dorff's cronies. Then there had been the battle against a zoning commissioner and a contractor, both of them buddies of Dorff's, that had ended in their being indicted for bribery. There had also been Beaufort's campaign for a civilian police review board, a battle he had only narrowly lost. He had agitated for an addition to the city's inadequate animal shelter, only to see funds that might have been used for such a project diverted to the white elephant Blaine Building. Come to think of it, Don mused, the higher-ups at his insurance company didn't owe Beaufort any favors, either, after the shitstorm he had raised about the difficulties many in his neighborhood had in getting needed coverage.

Two cars from a couple of the local TV stations were parked near the hot dog stand, meaning that the rally would get some coverage, if only a sound bite or two. A somewhat battered looking beige panel truck pulled up to the west of the courtyard and stopped; Jeff climbed out from the passenger's side. A broad-shouldered brown-skinned man with a shock of wiry white hair got out on the driver's side; Don recognized Clifford Beaufort. Stan Dorff would have come tooling along in either his Lincoln or his Jeep Grand Cherokee with one of his aides at the wheel.

Beaufort didn't have a chance, but Don found himself admiring Jeff for going to work for the underdog. Jeff could have e-mailed his impressive résumé to the mayor's staff, put on one of the expensively tailored suits he used to wear while working for the insurance company, polished his spiel for his interview, and nailed a better paid if less influential position with the Dorff campaign. Yet here he was, fighting the good fight for a guy who probably had too much integrity and concern for people ever to get elected to anything.

Don wandered toward the hot dog stand. The homeless man in the tweed coat was loitering near the end of the line. "Got a couple of bucks?" the man asked him.

"Guess you already spent what I gave you the other day," Don replied.

"And maybe unlike me you got enough on the ball to live for a day or two on just a five-spot? Maybe you could offer a goddamn money-management clinic on how to do that." The man looked skyward. "Gimme a break!" he shouted. The people near them were already edging away. The tweed-coated man turned to Don once more, staring past him and at the ground. "And just what the hell are you, anyway, the Pied Piper?" he asked.

Don took a step toward him. "What?"

"Well, where'd they come from?" the man said.

Don turned around slowly and saw the cats. They stood in a row behind him, short-haired and long-haired, large and small. There had to be at least thirty of them, and they were all giving him the same cold, disdainful, and vaguely hostile stare.

"Not my cats," Don said.

"Didn't say they was. All I see is you walkin' over here with a herd of kitty cats following you like a goddamn Pied Piper or something."

"It was rats that followed the Pied Piper," Don said.

The old man peered at him.

Don added, "The Pied Piper had rats following him, not cats, and I don't know why they're following me."

"Same difference."

The cats scattered; a few bounded over the grass and others scurried toward the flower beds. They seemed awfully organized for such individualistic creatures, taking up positions from where they could observe everything that was going on.

"Don't know where they're coming from," the homeless man continued. "Tried to get in a nap before all this started, and I can't even lie down on a goddamn bench without some kitty cat climbing up on top of me and tryin' to put the whammy on me."

"The whammy?"

"Starin' at me with the goddamn evil eye."

Don shoved a five-dollar bill at the man. "Buy yourself a hot dog." He moved toward the sidewalk, deciding to treat himself to a pastrami on rye at a nearby deli when a balding guy in a brown corduroy jacket approached him. Don had seen the man before, but couldn't remember where.

"Hey," the balding man said.

"Hey," Don replied.

"What's with the cats, anyway? And I don't mean just the ones here, I mean the ones at your home."

Don frowned, confused.

The man continued, "I'm one of your neighbors. I've seen you around, just never got around to introducing myself. Phil Donovan—number 12, the white Colonial with the side porch."

Don dimly recalled seeing someone who looked like this man in number 12's driveway. "Don Martinson," Don said. "What cats?"

"At your home," Phil Donovan replied. "At least twenty of them sitting around in front of your house this morning, and now there's more cats hanging around here. Are you some kind of cat magnet?"

Don shrugged, trying not to look as uneasy as he felt. "I didn't notice any cats at my house," he replied, not wanting to admit that he had not been at his home last night because he and his wife were on the verge of a divorce.

"Then you must have gotten up at the crack of dawn and left for work before they got there, because the little buggers were all sitting out there by the time I left for the office. Look, it's not that I don't like cats. Never had a cat myself, but I don't have any particular animosity towards them or anything, but strays can mean trouble. They start scratching little kids and rooting around in garbage pails and going into heat and picking up fleas and getting into fights with each other, and pretty soon they're a real problem. And they don't exactly help property values any."

"I see your point," Don said, "but I don't know what you expect me to do about it."

"They're on your property. I mean, I haven't seen them hanging around on anybody else's—not more than one or two of them, anyway. There must be something around your home that's attracting them."

"I'll see what I can do," Don said, trying to sound conciliatory. "I could call up animal control or a local animal group and see what they suggest, and let you know what I find out."

Phil Donovan gave him a weak smile. "You do that." He pulled a wallet from his back pocket and handed Don a card. "My phone number's on that."

"I'll be in touch."

"Staying for the rally?"

"I don't know."

"Beaufort doesn't have a chance, you know." Phil Donovan drifted away.

Don moved toward the courthouse steps, deciding he wasn't that hungry. The crowd had remained sparse, no more than fifty people, but Clifford Beaufort was moving among them, shaking hands and clutching arms as if delighted that even that many had shown up. Several cats were on the steps, draping themselves gracefully against the marble. Wherever these cats had come from, they didn't look like feral cats; they were too well-groomed for that. Feral cats would be a lot more shy of people. These cats were staking a claim to the courthouse.

"Hey, Don."

He turned to see Jeff coming toward him. "Thanks for showing up." Jeff glanced at the small crowd. "Hoped we'd get a bigger turn-out than this."

"It'll look like a bigger crowd on TV." A man and a woman with camcorders were trailing Beaufort, who bounded up the steps, then turned to face the crowd, arms spread wide. A few people cheered. The cats lifted their heads expectantly.

* * * *

"If people voted for the best speaker," Don said, "you'd win in a landslide."

Jeff had just introduced him to Clifford Beaufort. The pair with the camcorders had left before the end of the speech, and already most of the crowd was gone. Only the cats had stayed behind, still perched on the courthouse steps. None of them had uttered a single meow during Beaufort's oratory, but Don had noticed the cats looking away from Beaufort to stare in his direction, to the point where it was soon creeping him out. They were still staring at him. He was suddenly relieved not to be in the courthouse park alone with only the cats for company.

"Thanks, son," Clifford Beaufort replied, recapturing Don's attention.

"But in all honesty, Reverend Beaufort, I don't think you have much of a chance."

"Call me Cliff, and I know that. Jeff here told me after we got our first informal poll results. But I don't have any truck with using polls to guide my actions. Gotta try. Slim is better than no chance at all."

"You're right about that." Don had to admire the big man's composure. He also had to admire his delivery; the candidate had given his speech without notes or a microphone. True, the crowd had been small, but Beaufort possessed a deep and resonant voice that carried to the far ends of the park. Clean government, better and more efficient social services, a more diverse and responsive police force with civilian oversight, better public transportation instead of more parking lots marring what had once been a graceful old city, a mayor who would think about the working people of this town and how to open up more opportunities for them instead of catering only to the business types who thought everything should be run for their own convenience and profit—no wonder the guy was going to lose. Still, it made Don feel better to know that somebody like Clifford Beaufort was trying.

"But it might have helped," Beaufort said, "if we'd had more people and not so many cats in the crowd." He glanced in the cats' direction, then turned back to Jeff and Don. "My dear wife Lorette, may she rest in peace, always had a cat or two sharing our quarters, and she found homes for lots of others. 'You look after the stray people,' she'd tell me, 'and I'll look after the stray cats.' I used to tell her that the city oughta have put her in charge of animal control, and she'd say that then the shelter would get awful crowded, because she wouldn't have been able to put any of those kitty cats to sleep." Beaufort paused. "Those cats there don't look much like strays, though. Don't act much like normal cats, neither."

"Maybe we should contact animal control," Jeff said.

Beaufort shook his head. "Wouldn't be room in the animal shelter for them even if Steve Kolbida and his staff got off their rumps long enough to come and round 'em up."

Jeff nodded. "You're probably right about that."

"I better get back to my people shelter," Beaufort said.

"Go ahead," Jeff said. "I'll take the bus over later to pick up my car." Don looked around, trying to spot the homeless man in the tweed coat, but didn't see him. Maybe Beaufort could have found a bed for him at the shelter.

"Good to meet you, Don." Beaufort shook Don's hand again, then headed for his panel truck.

"I'm going over to campaign headquarters," Jeff said. "Want to come along?"

"I didn't know you had a campaign headquarters."

"We do now. It's that empty storefront next to the Blaine Building. A shithole, but it's all we can afford. Have to be there when the phone company comes, and we could use some help cleaning the place up."

"Have to get back to work."

"It's your last day. Who's going to care?"

Except for Larry, probably nobody would care, but old office habits died hard. "There's a party tonight," Don said, "for everybody who got laid off. I might as well hang around until we go out later."

"I understand."

"Tell you what," Don said. "I'll come over and help out this weekend. I'll have plenty of free time."

"Cool." Jeff grinned. "See you later back at my place."

Don nodded as his friend left. He had spoken impulsively, but felt a little better for volunteering, not that working for Beaufort would do him much good. It certainly wouldn't make him a more attractive employment prospect to many members of the local business community.

He heard a growling, threatening sound, and looked down to see two cats at his right staring up at him. Something snarled behind him. He turned to see more cats behind him, standing in a row, all watching him.

He backed away from them. A couple of them crept toward him, narrowing their eyes and showing their fangs, then crouched down as if they were large cats getting ready to spring. The park suddenly seemed awfully empty; he had a sudden urge to call out for help. His throat tightened. He was inside one of those nightmares in which he was trying to shout for help and run but couldn't make his legs and voice work.

The cats were trying to say something to him. A ridiculous idea, but even as it came to him, a few of the cats bared their teeth and hissed. He had the feeling that if he turned to run, all of them would bring him down.

The cats stared at him, then fanned out through the park, some scurrying and others padding along at a more leisurely pace until they disappeared from view, lost amid the shrubs that dotted the park. Don hurried away, glancing uneasily around himself, still feeling stalked.

Fourteen

Most of Gena's coworkers in Billing and Accounts Receivable had fled the office wing of St. Luke's just after five o'clock, but Jeannie Biggs was still at her desk, finishing up some paperwork, while Yolanda Gutierrez, wearing her headset, sat at her computer making calls. Gena walked down the aisle between the work stations to Barney Litzer's office and tapped on his half-open door.

"Come in," Barney called out.

She entered the small office and stood in front of the desk as Barney shuffled papers and affixed paper clips to them. She continued to stare at the bald spot on his head until he looked up.

"Oh, do sit down," he said. Barney had his weird half-smile on his face, indicating that he was about to tell her what he considered to be good news. "Well, Gena, I think you're going to be very pleased with what I have to tell you," he continued, confirming her supposition.

"Um," Gena said as she sat down.

"You've been doing a nice job as one of our administrative support associates," Barney went on. "A very nice job. Pleasant, punctual, reliable, a good, steady worker, and you've been with us for some time now, haven't you."

"Uh huh," Gena replied. Too damned long, she said to herself.

"So I've decided that the time has come to move you up a level, put you into collections and making calls. That'll mean a bit more pay for you down the road, even if it does mean giving up a Saturday now and then, but you'll get overtime for that, and a few evenings when we need you to make calls then, but getting some more shuteye on those particular mornings ought to make up for that, eh?" He squinted and blinked in a way that made her wonder if he had dislocated a contact lens. "And you'll also continue to do much of what you're doing now, so…" He beamed at her, as if expecting her to leap up and dance for joy.

Gena cleared her throat. "But—" she began.

"But what?"

"Um." She had to choose her words carefully. "But I'm perfectly happy with what I'm doing now. I really don't mind staying at level five."

"Well, we don't need you at level five, we need you at level four. We need you making calls, and right now I'm unable to hire a new person for that, so I'm moving you to collections to pick up some of the slack and I'll have Jeannie train you in on the phone next week. I'm sure it won't take you long to pick up the necessary skills—after all, you've probably overheard a fair number of calls after all this time."

"Um," Gena murmured, and then, "What you mean is that I'll have to do what I'm doing now, plus start making calls, so that means even more work for me, but that's okay, because I move up one level and eventually get paid more." She knew what the pay rate was at level four. It wasn't that much more than she was getting now, but with a divorce pending and an uncertain future ahead, she wasn't in any position to be choosy. "I'd rather just stay where I am."

"Well, you can't, because we're eliminating that particular position, because right now we can't afford to hire a new person to fill it."

She looked away for a moment. "Um, I really don't want to make calls."

"But why?"

She turned back to him. Barney's forehead wrinkled; he looked more puzzled than annoyed. She said, "Because I can't."

"You can't? Why not?"

"Because it's soul-destroying." She should not have said that; those words had come from her unbidden. "Because if I had to call up and pester people whose only crime was having bad luck and no medical insurance, or having crappy insurance that won't pay their bills, I don't think I could live with myself." She could not hold her words back.

Barney's eyes widened. Now he looked completely bewildered. "Are you sure you're feeling all right?" he asked.

"I'm feeling fine." She stood up. "I don't have a choice, do I. Either I take on making those phone calls or I leave." She reached for the strap around her neck from which her ID badge dangled and slipped it over her head. "Here." She handed the badge to him. "I quit."

He stared at the badge, then lifted his head, his eyes wide with shock. "You quit?" he croaked.

"Yes."

"Without any notice?"

"Yes, and I remind you that I've got a week of vacation time banked, so I'll be expecting a check for that, too." Her memory had somehow retained that bit of information even as she was growing more aware of her utter recklessness.

She spun around and hurried from the office before whatever perverse impulses now controlling her impelled her to say even more. Principles had a price, and practicality would be unprincipled.

Jeannie was gone. She went to the coat rack and grabbed her coat. As she passed Yolanda's work station, the other woman called out, "Have a good weekend."

Gena halted. She would miss her fellow workers. "You, too," she said, then took a breath. "I just quit."

Yolanda's mouth dropped open; then she grinned and said, "Good for you."

"I'm probably going to be really sorry tomorrow."

Yolanda shook her head. "No, you won't, not if you have any sense. If it weren't for my kids, I'd be walking right out the door with you. Good luck, Gena. I'll miss you. Come by and see us sometime."

"I will—I promise."

"And let us know when you find something else." Yolanda adjusted the earpieces of her headset and turned back to her monitor.

Gena strode into the next room, threading her way through the maze of work stations and partitions toward the exit. Usually a few of the accountants were working late, but this entire wing was apparently deserted. She turned toward the corridor of executive offices and saw only closed doors on either side of the lighted hall.

Her heart pounded; she felt feverish. She could go back and catch Barney on his way out. If she was contrite enough, he would overlook her outburst, if only because it would save him the trouble of hiring and training a new person. She continued toward the exit, hands in her pockets and head down, terrified of what she had just done, sick with fear and ready to surrender to her cowardice. Barney usually came this way; all she had to do was wait for him and then apologize and beg for her job back.

"You sure do look like you got a mad on, lady."

She stopped and looked up. An old man in a baggy tweed coat stood just inside the door. She wondered why she hadn't seen him before.

"Who buzzed you in?" she asked.

"Nobody."

He looked familiar, but she could not recall where she might have seen him. "Somebody must have let you in," she said. "You can't get in here unless you're buzzed in or you have an ID badge."

"Well, here I am, and I wasn't buzzed in, and I got no badge to swipe open the damn door." He smiled and she found herself smiling back. She was alone in an empty wing with a stranger who had managed to slip past security, and yet he seemed harmless, even kind of congenial. "Guess I got my ways of gettin' into places. Anyway, you don't have to worry about me, I ain't here to bitch and moan about no emergency room bill."

She took a step back, wondering why she wasn't more afraid of him. Maybe it was because she had already been so impulsive and reckless, pretty much destroying in only a few moments what little stability remained in her life. Why should she fear anything now? She was already dangling from the precipice.

"That is why you guys got all this security, isn't it?" the old man continued. "To keep out folks with complaints who might be kinda angry and threatening."

"No, it isn't," Gena replied. "That's what I thought when I first started working here, but it was actually to keep union organizers out of the building some years back."

"I ain't no union organizer, neither."

"Too bad," she said. "If you were, I'd be more than happy to help you distribute pamphlets in praise of unionization to every work station in this wing."

"Guess you don't like your job much."

"I quit my job. In any sane world, that job wouldn't exist." She stepped past him and opened the door.

He followed her outside. "You quit your job?"

"That's what I said."

He laughed, showing yellow teeth. "Maybe there's some hope for you after all." He shuffled away before she could ask him what he meant. She gazed after him as he crossed the half-empty parking lot, then hurried in the other direction, toward the main entrance, where she had promised to meet Roland Tewksbury.

* * * *

Gena glanced at her watch. It was past five thirty, but the traffic on Western Avenue, the street that ran past St. Luke's, was moving at a crawl; Roland was probably stuck somewhere. She could still put in a call to Barney. He would be gone from the office by now, but she could leave a message in his voice mail, and if she sounded sorry enough—

I can't do it, Gena thought. She reached into her purse, pulled out her cell phone, and hit Caterina Lucci's number. Caterina had most likely gone home by now, even though she did sometimes stay late if a cat or two needed emergency care or somebody was late picking an animal up. She most likely had filled the job that she had so casually offered to Gena by now, or decided that she could limp by a while longer with her part-timers.

"Dr. Lucci's office," a bored-sounding female voice said.

"Is Dr. Lucci in?"

"Just a minute, okay?"

Gena waited on hold as music from "Cats" played in her ear. Whoever was answering Caterina's phone had not even bothered to ask who she was or what she was calling about. A singer launched into a heartfelt rendition of "Memory." She was about to hang up when she finally heard the veterinarian's voice.

"Caterina Lucci here."

"Caterina? It's Gena Lawlor. Is that offer of a job managing your office still open?"

"Sure is. Not that I haven't had applicants, I just couldn't tell if they were really cat people. Does that sound like discrimination?"

Gena drew in her breath. "I'll take it."

"Don't you want to discuss any specifics?"

"Oh, Caterina, I know you'll be fair. What I'm getting at St. Luke's and two weeks vacation—that's what you mentioned before."

"I guess I can afford what St. Luke's pays at your level. You'd have to stay on Wednesdays until nine and come in on Saturday from ten until two, but Thursdays are all yours."

"Fine with me."

"Can't pay for medical, but you have Don's plan."

"Maybe. There might be some changes there." She did not feel like going into the sorry tale of Don's job loss and their impending divorce right now.

"Or maybe I can get you a lower rate on my plan later on if you can pay for the insurance yourself, or at least for part of it. I'll have to crunch some numbers and talk to my rep to see what I can do."

"I'll try to stay healthy and see how it goes first."

"Thanks, Gena. This'll really help me out. How much time do you need to give notice to your boss?"

"I already quit. Today."

Caterina was silent for a while. "Well. I've got kind of a full slate on Monday, so just be here at eight-thirty on Tuesday, and I'll show you the ropes then. Bye."

Gena slipped the phone back into her purse, feeling a mixture of elation and terror. She had just thrown away an opportunity to have a relatively secure, even though soul-destroying, job at St. Luke's for a position that depended entirely on how well Caterina did in her practice, which the vet had admitted was having its problems. Yet there was something wonderful about Caterina's job offer nonetheless. Somebody was offering her work based purely on an assessment of her as a person, rather than insisting on lengthy interviews, background checks, and all the usual hassles. That had to count as a small miracle. She would also be in daily contact with cats, feeling that she was contributing to their welfare and thus to the general happiness of the world in her own small way.

That thought reminded her of all the cats she had seen on the front stoop and in the driveway as she was leaving the house that morning. Seeing a few cats in the back yard from upstairs had been one thing, but it was unnerving to see so many more cats watching her as she went to her car, hanging around as if her house belonged to them. She wondered again if Vladimir had anything to do with their appearance, if the cats somehow knew that he was inside and that he might need protection from a malign entity.

No. She had to stop obsessing about Catalonia and Household and all the rest of it. Catalonia and Household were no more than imaginary auto-suggestive constructs that had lately gotten completely out of hand because she was so stressed out.

A car horn beeped. She blinked and then spotted Roland in the nearest row of traffic, behind the wheel of a red Ford Escort. He pulled up to the curb, leaned over, and opened the door on the passenger's side. "Gena?"

"Hi, Roland." She got into the car and pulled out the seat belt.

"Hi, yourself. Thought we could tie on a feed bag at Vitello's. And they're showing that new Disney picture over at the Cineplex—I'm a sucker for animated stuff. Sound good to you?"

"Sure."

Roland pulled away from the curb, and she noticed that he was wearing a navy blue sports jacket, a light blue shirt, a tie, and an extremely potent and musky men's cologne. Gena wished that she had worn something dressier to work than a pair of slacks and a sweater, and then suddenly wished that she had not accepted this date at all. Separated or not, she felt treacherous and disloyal to Don, as though she had leaped into her new social life much too hastily. She wanted her husband at her side, not this stranger, however handsome.

She said, "There's something about me you should know."

"Go ahead."

"I, uh—well, you see, I'm separated from my husband. I should have told you before that I'm still technically married. Like, I feel as though I misled you."

"But if you're separated," Roland said, "that means you're getting a divorce, doesn't it?"

"Well, that's just it. The truth of the matter is that I keep hoping we can get back together. I mean, we only broke up this week. We haven't even gone to any lawyers yet. I'm sure if I told you that yesterday, you wouldn't have asked me out."

"Probably not."

She forced herself to look at him. He had stopped at a red light and glanced at her, still with a kindly smile on his face. "So what I'm saying," she went on, "is that if you just want to drive me home, that's fine. You certainly don't have to buy me dinner and take me out to a movie now that you know the truth."

Roland was silent. The light changed and he drove another block before getting stuck behind a city bus. "Hey, that's okay," he said at last. "At least you're being honest. He isn't, like, abusive or anything, is he?"

"No," she said sadly, "Don wouldn't hurt a fly. He would never lift a hand to me. He's a kind and gentle and good person, and responsible, and intelligent, too. I was attracted to him right from the start."

"Then why'd you break up? I mean if you don't mind my asking."

"Because we had one of those stupid fights where you get angry and say a lot of things you shouldn't and then can't take them back."

"I guess I know what that's like."

"So if you just want to drive me home, that's fine with me."

"Well, the thing is," Roland said, "I was kind of looking forward to chowing down at Vitello's, and I hate to eat alone in restaurants. So I could still take you to dinner—just as a friend, I mean."

Gena managed to smile. "That's very nice of you."

"And we can pass on the movie if you want. I mean, I can take you home first and then go see it by myself."

"That'll be fine with me."

"The thing is," he continued, "the main reason I asked you out is that I get kind of lonely when I'm home. I'm not around here long enough to really get settled in and make friends before I have to go out on the road again." He cleared his throat. "Not that I wasn't, like, attracted to you or anything."

"I understand." Now all she had to do was figure out what to tell Don tomorrow when they got together to settle matters. She would apologize, without preliminaries, and throw in a few meows as a convincer. Maybe Don would apologize first, in which case she would forgive him immediately. They would never allow Household to come between them again.

Thinking of Household made her uncertain once more. What would Don say when he found out about her new job with Caterina? He would tell her that St. Luke's would have given her more benefits and considerably more secure employment. He would say that he was right, that she had no practical sense, that as soon as he was out of the picture, she had gone running off to do something as unfeasible as going to work for Caterina. She would again hear Household's hard words from his mouth.

* * * *

Gena dined on scallops and pasta in a cream sauce topped with grated Romano while Roland told her more about himself. He had joined the Strut My Stuff company after his junior year in college, when he had decided that he didn't want a degree in physical education after all. His idea had been to travel and see more of the world, but much of what he had seen had been a series of hotel and motel rooms. He had been with Strut My Stuff for eight years, staying with the troupe largely out of inertia, knowing that a college dropout wasn't likely to get a better-paying job with as much time off in any other profession, especially with a work history as a male stripper.

"It isn't, like, that I get nothing out of it," Roland said as he cut himself another bite of hazelnut chicken. "I stay in shape, got some money saved, and I sort of enjoy being on the stage. The thing is, I've always been shy, but when I'm on the stage, it's like I'm somebody else. I can really go to town and enjoy my dancing. But it's getting to the point where it's time to move on, put down some roots or whatever. The thing is, I'm not getting any younger. Thought I'd only be in Strut My Stuff for a couple of years at the most."

"So what are you thinking of doing?" Gena asked, relieved that Roland was carrying the conversation without any awkward moments of silence.

"Well, that's just it. I don't really know, haven't had much chance to figure that out. But since I got some money saved, I'm thinking of just hanging around for a while and putting down some roots and trying on some other jobs for size, I mean if I can find anything. The pay wouldn't matter so much, just the experience."

Gena sipped at her wine while Roland downed more spring water; being on the road and having to stay in shape had kept him on the wagon. "The truth is," Roland continued, "that…"

"That what?" Gena prompted after a few seconds.

"Well, the fact of the matter is that settling down is kind of a major priority for me. I mean, what I really want is a home and somebody to care about and maybe some kids, one or two kids anyway. That'd be the main thing, whatever my job was. And if my wife wanted to spend her time climbing the corporate ladder or anything, that'd be fine with me. I'd be glad to take on more of the duties at home."

Amazing, Gena thought, wondering why some enterprising woman hadn't grabbed this prize catch a long time ago, even if his being on the road so much might have put a crimp in the development of any long-term relationship. Then again, she didn't really know the guy. Maybe Roland had run into the same problem that women who were drop-dead gorgeous encountered, namely not being taken that seriously as anything but adornments.

"You'll find somebody," Gena murmured, "But I don't know if you'll find too many women in this town who want to climb corporate ladders. It's not that exciting a place."

"That's what I like about it," Roland said. "Oh, I don't mind, like, spending a couple of days in New York afterwards when we've got a gig at the club, but I'm always glad to come back to some peace and quiet, like, you know, a slower pace of life."

Gena thought of all the times she had complained to Don about living here, of how unenterprising and unadventurous she felt because she still resided in the same area where she had grown up. Now she would consider herself fortunate to have things as they once were, to be reconciled with Don and to have her old life back, to have Household doing its job as an occasional annoyance rather than an unseen threat, and to have Catalonia restored to its peaceful state.

That thought gave her a turn. Even here, in this dimly lit restaurant with its warm red walls and the soothing sounds of murmuring diners accompanied by the orchestrated scores of Italian operas, the thought of Household and Catalonia roused her apprehension. She thought of the cats who had come after her at Tracey's house, and the ominous feelings she had while alone in her own house. She wondered which would be worse, becoming convinced that she was going crazy or actually believing that the imaginary constructs of Catalonia and Household had gained a foothold in her reality and would now stop at nothing to preserve themselves. Even Vladimir might not always be her ally; he might decide instead that joining with other cats to confront Household was more to his benefit. Cats, she reminded herself, weren't actually all that domesticated. It had occurred to her not long ago that if she were only a small creature, and Vladimir the size of a lion, he would have had no compunction about swatting her around with his paws for a while, just for fun, then tearing her little limbs apart and gnawing on her liver.

"Gena."

She started.

"You okay?" Roland went on. "You looked kind of funny."

"I'm fine."

"Want some coffee?" he said as he finished his last bite of chicken.

"No, thanks. And no dessert, either—I'm full."

"So am I. Gotta save some room for popcorn at the movie." Roland glanced at his watch. "I'll take you home and then head over for the next showing." He looked away for a moment. "I did have fun," he said. "What I mean is, this evening kind of helped me get my stuff together. Anyway, I hope things work out for you."

"They will," she said, wanting to believe that.

"And stay in touch, you know? I mean as a friend."

"Sure. I'm over at Tracey's a lot, so we're bound to run into each other."

Roland settled the bill with the waitress while Gena held on to her new feeling of determination. She would meet with Don tomorrow to mend the breach, vanquish Household, preserve Catalonia, and no longer be troubled by delusions.

Roland led her away from the table. He had parked behind Vitello's; they went out the back door of the restaurant into the small parking lot. Three people loitered near one car as a beige Toyota pulled in next to them. The door on the driver's side was opening when Gena heard someone in the group call out, "Hey, Don."

Gena froze, realizing now that the car was Don's Toyota. She shrank next to Roland, hoping that his height and the poorly lighted parking lot would save her from detection. Don emerged from his car, looking in her direction.

Roland continued obliviously toward his Ford Escort while Gena struggled to control her terror. Don could not have seen her. If he had, he would already be running over here, demanding to know what she was doing going out with some other man so soon after they had separated. She kept near Roland's side, not wanting to attract any attention to herself. He couldn't have seen her, she thought as they came to Roland's car. But somehow, unreasoningly, she knew that he had, because justice demanded it.

* * * *

"Sure are a lot of cats here," Roland said as he pulled up in front of her house.

There were even more cats in the vicinity than Gena had seen that morning. Twelve cats sat under the corner streetlight. More cats, at least forty of them, roamed the sidewalk in front of her house, padding back and forth over the pavement as though they were sentries on guard.

"Oh, my God," she said under her breath.

"Sure is one heck of a lot of cats." Roland got out of the car and came around to her side to open the door. "Better be careful not to step on any of them. They're all over the place."

Gena unfastened her seat belt and was suddenly afraid to get out of the car. Roland reached for her arm and helped her out. Cats sat on the steps that led to her front door, and all of them were watching her. She looked down. A few cats were at Roland's feet, arching their backs and looking distinctly hostile. She lifted her head and glanced toward the light illuminating Mrs. Seligman's house, but saw no cats there or anywhere else along the street.

A cat hissed; another snarled. Of course these cats would not be anywhere else except near her house. Here was where they would have to make their stand if they were to defeat Household and preserve Catalonia. Here was where they would strike at anything that might threaten their world.

Gena knew then that she could not let Roland get closer to the house.

"They don't look too friendly," Roland said. "That's the thing with cats, they can be, like, cute, or they can be kind of creepy. Saw this old movie on TV once, where this guy keeps shrinking, and he has this cat, and then when he gets really small, his own cat starts chasing him like he's a mouse or something and he has to run and hide in the basement or become eats."

"I'll say good night to you out here," she said. "You don't have to come to the door."

"I'll just wait until you're safe inside." Roland peered down at the cats. "Jeez, maybe I should call animal control when I get home."

"Oh, don't bother," Gena said quickly. "It's my problem. Don't you worry about it." She hoped that she didn't sound hysterical. "Thanks for the dinner."

"Thanks for the company."

She inched her way toward the door. Miraculously, the cats opened the way for her, moving back along the pavement and steps until she had a clear path. She reached into her purse for her key, unlocked the door, then looked back at Roland.

He stood by his car, a cluster of cats at his feet. He could not have taken one step in her direction without stepping on a cat.

They began to poke at his legs with their paws, as if trying to push him away. At last he went around to the driver's side and opened the door. Gena slipped inside the house and closed the door behind her.

She could not have imagined those cats; Roland had seen them, too. She turned on a light, then spied Vladimir in the alcove.

He crouched on the floor two feet away from her, his fur up, his green eyes wild. His long thick fur looked disheveled, almost as if he had been in a fight. Lifting his head, he emitted a soft meow completely unlike his usual arrogant and demanding cry.

An answering chorus of meows sounded from the other side of the door. Vladimir's eyes narrowed as he slowly sat up.

"Vladimir," she said as she knelt next to him. He allowed her to pet him, snuggling near her for a few moments as if in need of such comfort, then stretched himself and padded toward the back of the house, tail held high.

She turned off the hall light and flicked the switch next to it; the living room's ceiling light came on. Something was wrong; she could feel it. As she followed Vladimir toward the kitchen, a shadowy shape fluttered across the walls after her.

"You can't handle this house alone," a voice said. The deep voice seemed to be coming both from inside her head and from a place outside her. "You'll never make it. You'll just keep sinking, never able to—"

"Shut up," Gena muttered, "just shut the hell up."

"—get it all together," the voice continued. "There's one way out for you. Turn this place over to your husband and throw yourself on the mercy of your parents."

"I won't listen to you," Gena said.

"Or you might be better off staying with your husband," the voice whispered, "assuming he'd even take you back, as long as you both stop lulling yourselves with thoughts of all those useless, wasteful Catalonian creatures, refusing to face up to the hard facts of the world. All that foolishness just feeds your impracticality. Purge Catalonia from your thoughts and imaginings, and there might be some hope for you."

"Stop it," Gena said.

"You've already damaged your little fantasy world. Now its inhabitants fear what may happen to them and are turning against you. They no longer trust you."

She heard a sharp screech. Vladimir flew across the room, legs extended. He landed on the floor and tumbled across the rug, screeching and yowling, clawing at an invisible foe, then leaped into the air and did a back flip.

"Vladimir!" she cried.

The cat hissed, leaped onto the sofa and then into the air again, twisting his body as he landed on the floor. "Mrree!" he shrieked, his ears flat against his head.

The house was silent. Vladimir was still except for his tail, which continued to twitch from side to side. The feeling of an invisible threat was gone; they were safe for now.

There was no Household, Gena told herself, clinging to her sanity. There was no invisible entity trying to bend her to its will. Household did not exist.

Fifteen

on sat in his car outside Jeff's building, reluctant to go inside. The whole farewell party had totally bombed as far as he was concerned. At the bar, he had limited himself to one bourbon on the rocks, determined to keep from sliding into a mire of self-pity fueled by alcohol. He would enjoy the evening, have a good dinner, keep himself sober and steady for his meeting with Gena tomorrow. Better, he thought, not to dwell on that too much, not to worry about what to say. He would know what to do when he saw her.

So he had thought, before catching that glimpse of her with that tall dude in the parking lot at Vitello's. Maybe that didn't mean anything. Maybe the guy was just a friend from work, and his dinner date with Gena as innocuous as his own get-together with Rose the other night, but somehow he didn't think so. Maybe the guy had started homing in on Gena the way Rose had begun to show more of an interest in him after finding out that he might soon be available. If the whole situation was perfectly innocent, Gena would have at least glanced in his direction, maybe even greeted him and introduced him to the man. Instead, she had looked guilty and as though she was trying to hide behind the guy, and before he could even decide whether or not to confront her, she and her boyfriend had disappeared.

It was pure luck that none of his coworkers had noticed her, that none of them knew Gena well enough to have recognized her in the dim lighting. A scene in the parking lot wouldn't have accomplished anything, either. Maybe it was just as well that he had avoided an encounter with her date, who was at least a couple of inches over six feet in height and had looked as though he had a forty-pound advantage on him.

Somehow he had gotten through dinner, though he hadn't had much to say and Larry had given him a couple of funny looks. He had kept his intake of booze down, too, limiting himself to a bottle of beer. No sense in lowering his inhibitions to the point where the whole sorry story of his separation from Gena and his wife's betrayal would come pouring out of him, or where he'd start putting the moves on Stella Przhewalski in order to get even.

If the man were just a friend, Gena surely would have mentioned the guy to him at some point, but he could not recall her telling him about any man at work except for her supervisor, Barney, who was almost fifty and going bald, and a coworker named Gary who was shorter than any of the women in the office. Her dinner date was definitely not going bald, and only an Amazonian woman would have topped him in height. She had not even waited until they were officially separated to start seeing somebody else.

Worse than that, Gena might have had something going on with the guy even before their big fight. Maybe she had only been waiting for an excuse to dump Don and hook up with somebody else. Maybe her decision to close out Household was actually a crafty, underhanded maneuver to provoke a confrontation and break up their marriage. Maybe she and the guy were already back at his house.

"Holy shit," he said, grinding his teeth. But a devious plot was not in Gena's nature; she was neither cold-blooded enough nor Machiavellian enough. This guy had to be a short-term thing. Maybe he'd had his eye on her for a while and had finally seen a chance to make his move. But if the bastard was willing to horn in that quickly, he wondered how Gena, who had never had anything even remotely resembling a decisive and forceful personality, would resist him.

For a moment, he was tempted to drive right over to the house, throw the guy out on his ass, and take Gena with the fiery uncontrollable ardor of a warrior reclaiming his mate; but after a few more deep breaths, he reached inside his coat pocket for his cell phone.

He hit his number, heard the phone ring three times, then listened as his digitalized voice recited the phone number at the other end. She probably wasn't home yet; maybe her date had taken her to a movie after dinner, or to a club. Maybe they were at his place. Somehow he could not believe that she would be insensitive enough to mess around with the dude inside their house, amid all the reminders of lost Catalonia.

"Gena, this is Don." His voice caught on the words. "Uh, just wanted to check back with you and set up a time to get together tomorrow, so—"

"Don," her voice sang into his ear.

"Gena?"

"I was just heading upstairs when I heard your voice."

"Oh." Surely she wouldn't have answered the phone if she and her date were getting down to serious business. "Anyone else there?"

"No. Why?"

"I thought Tracey might have come over. I mean—"

"Actually, there is someone else here." Don dropped the phone. "You won't believe it. Vladimir came back," the phone murmured.

"Vladimir?" he said, bewildered, snatching the phone up.

"I opened the front door last night and there he was. I guess he finally decided to abandon his life of gluttony with Mr. Bowes."

"Well, what do you know." He did not know what else to say as he gripped the phone. There was a chance Gena might think that he hadn't seen her at Vitello's, given how dark it was, and maybe seeing him there had made her feel guilty enough to ditch her date early. If so, it would be better for him not to mention anything about this evening, at least not until he might need it for ammunition.

"Don," Gena said, her voice wavering, "I have to tell you—"

He waited for a confession.

"Well, there are all these cats around our…around the house, don't ask me why. I saw them this morning and there were even more of them there when I came home. There must be at least fifty of them."

Don almost dropped the phone again. "Strays, probably," he said, but he was thinking of the cats he had seen at the Beaufort rally.

"They don't look like strays."

"Maybe they'll be gone by morning. Maybe they're friends of Vladimir's." He chuckled, but his laugh sounded hollow, even to him.

"Some really weird stuff has been happening around here. It's almost like—" Her voice trailed off. "Well, at least Vladimir's home now. That helps."

"Listen, we should decide what time to get together tomorrow. Is three o'clock all right with you?"

"Fine."

"Then I'll come over to the house. Unless you'd rather meet some place else."

She was silent for so long that he thought their connection had been lost. "Gena?"

"I guess over here's all right," she said at last. "It's just that—"

"That what?" he asked after another long pause.

"It's nothing," she said, in a tone that told him it was something.

"Tomorrow at three, then. Give old Vladimir a scratch behind the ears for me."

"I will." Her voice quavered.

He hung up quickly, before sentimentality got the better of him. Vladimir, he thought, had picked one hell of a time to return. Now they would have to decide which of them got the cat on top of everything else.

There was a thump on the hood of his car. Don peered through the windshield and saw a cat staring in at him with an accusatory gleam in its eyes, as if ready to smash its way through the windshield to get to him. The cat leaped from the hood and vanished.

He opened the door, got out, and locked the car. In the distance, he heard the sound of meowing, but there wasn't a cat in sight.

Sixteen

Gena moved through a vast hallway bright with light, then found herself standing in an atrium. The marble floor was cold against her bare feet. Someone was speaking; she concentrated, trying to separate the indistinct murmurs into words.

We have to save ourselves.

But only by ridding ourselves of the one trying to control our people.

Maybe that won't be enough.

Gena struggled to wake herself. The hallway faded as she forced herself to open her eyes.

Cats sat on her bedspread, on her belly and her chest. They covered the bed, sitting, reclining, staring at her. She could not see Vladimir, and tried to call out to him, but was unable to make her voice work.

Perhaps the only way we can save ourselves now is to strike directly at the two of them, so that they will never threaten our existence again.

She tried to cry out. Two of the cats nearest her suddenly slashed at her eyes; their claws raked her face. Needles stabbed at her arms and legs; there was the sharp pain of claws tearing at her as more cats swarmed over her.

She screamed and swam up from the room full of cats. She continued to scream as they fell away from her, then found herself staring into the darkness of her bedroom. She sat up and turned on the light next to the bed.

Vladimir sat at the foot of the bed; his eyes were slits. He was alone.

She lay there, taking deep breaths. She felt her face and arms but found no injuries. She drew in more air, calming herself.

Vladimir crept to her side, settled down next to her, and began to purr. His purring, instead of soothing her, seemed ominous. He might have sounded equally content if he had just killed a bird and was dreaming of other prey.

She had been dreaming. There couldn't have been any cats in the bedroom; Vladimir would not be lying there so peacefully now if other cats had invaded the house. At last she closed her eyes, lulled by the rhythmic sound of Vladimir's purrs as she drifted into sleep.

* * * *

The phone was ringing again. Gena had turned off the ringers on the phones in the bedroom and home office, but could not escape the insistent chirp of the one downstairs in the kitchen. She rolled over, peered at the clock radio on the night table, and saw that it was almost nine-thirty. She had slept much later than usual, and wondered why Vladimir hadn't awakened her as he usually did with his resonant morning meows.

She raised herself on her elbows. Vladimir sat at the foot of the bed, his back to her, flicking his tail from side to side. She thought of her dream, of the cats she had seen on her bed, of how real they had seemed. Even now, she was having trouble thinking of the incident, still vivid in her mind, as a dream rather than an actual event.

Vladimir leaped from the bed and ran from the room. Gena forced herself to get up. By the time she was out of the bathroom and in a bathrobe, Vladimir was meowing at full throttle from the kitchen. She hurried downstairs, set out his food and water, then went to the phone and saw that there were two messages.

She hit the message button. "Gena and Don, this is Rita Seligman," a raspy voice said. "Your neighbor," Mrs. Seligman added redundantly. "I don't know what's going on over there, but it looks like there are even more cats on your property than there were yesterday. Now, I don't know what you intend to do about it, but something has to be done. I've a good mind to call the city's animal control department before they start showing up in my yard or on somebody else's lawn but I thought I had better call you first." Mrs. Seligman was silent for a moment, suddenly out of steam. "Good-bye."

"Eight-fifteen a.m.," the phone machine said. "Message two."

"Elden Bowes calling," a man's voice murmured. "Sorry to disturb you, but it appears that Vladimir has vacated my premises for parts unknown, and even though a cat is a free being, I am most concerned for his welfare. At first I was reluctant to bother you about this matter, but as time went on it occurred to me that you would be as concerned as I am about his safety and might be able to aid me in locating the little fellow. Please get back to me when you can."

"Nine-twenty-five a.m.," the machine said. "End of messages."

Gena began to make coffee, then wandered toward the window facing the back yard. Cats of various sizes and furry hues reclined on the grass and under the shrubs, at least sixty of them, probably more. She glanced at Vladimir, who had stopped eating his food and was staring at the door.

"Hrrow," he said as he hunkered down on the floor, clearly sensing the intrusion of other cats on his turf.

She hurried to the front of the house and looked through the living room window, afraid of what she might see. There were cats on the sidewalk and sitting along the curb. A passing car slowed down in front of the house, as if the driver might be trying to get a good look at the strange sight, and then picked up speed as it rounded the corner.

She went back to the kitchen and had just poured her first cup of coffee when the phone rang again. She sidled toward it, listening to Don's recorded voice reciting their number.

"This is Rita Seligman again," her neighbor announced. "I swear, there are even more cats around your house now than there were an hour ago." Gena, about to pick up the phone, thought better of it. "Something has to be done. I don't want to meddle in affairs that are none of my business, but having so many stray cats in the neighborhood is everybody's business." Mrs. Seligman let out a breath. "Well, I've said my piece. Good-bye."

Gena stood by the phone and drank coffee. Caterina was probably at her office by now; maybe she would have some suggestions.

She dialed the vet's number.

"Caterina Lucci, doctor to cats and friend of all kitties," the vet answered.

"Caterina? This is Gena."

"Don't tell me you want to come to work today. If you do, I can certainly use you."

"I wish I could. Actually, I called about a problem—kind of a cat control problem."

"A cat control problem?"

"A whole bunch of cats have invaded my property, at least fifty or so in the back yard alone, and they're in front of the house, too. I haven't fed any of them and don't know where they came from, and now one of my neighbors is starting to complain."

"I've never heard of that many feral cats in one neighborhood," Caterina said, "but maybe—"

"I don't know if they are anywhere else in the neighborhood," Gena interrupted. "They seem to be attracted to this house in particular. Oh, I forgot to tell you. Vladimir came home the other day. All these cats started showing up right after that. Do you think he could have anything to do with it?" She had to ask that question, even though she was already certain that Vladimir was blameless.

"You mean like horses forming a herd around a dominant stallion? That would be most uncatlike behavior. It's probably just a coincidence." Caterina was silent for a moment. "I suggest that you just keep an eye on them. If you go outside, be very careful and wear protective clothing and don't get too close to them in case any of them are disease carriers. If they're still there in the afternoon, call me and maybe I can get over there."

Gena thought of her meeting with Don. "I have something else I have to do this afternoon," she said.

"Call me whenever you can, then. Got to finish my accounts and order some more supplies, so I'll probably be here until late afternoon. If those cats are still hanging around your house, I can come over then."

"You think they might leave?" Gena asked.

"Well, one can always hope. Maybe they'll find something more enticing at a neighbor's place, and then at least you'll be off the hook. Looks like another patient's here. Later."

"Thanks," Gena said as Caterina hung up. She should probably get back to Mrs. Seligman now, but didn't feel up to that, and decided to call Mr. Bowes.

His phone rang twice before he picked it up. "Elden Bowes speaking."

"Mr. Bowes, this is Gena Lawlor. Just wanted to let you know that Vladimir's over here at my house and he's all right. He came back a couple of days ago. I should have called you then."

"I'm relieved to hear it. I've been quite concerned about Vladimir, especially since he got into a battle not long ago with a big gray cat and some of that assailant's feline accomplices. It was necessary to take him to his veterinarian for a look-see."

"So I heard," Gena said.

"In any case, I considered it the better part of valor to restrict Vladimir to the indoors after that fracas, in the interests of his personal safety, but somehow he managed to escape. I know he didn't get through an open door, since I am always most careful about that."

"Maybe your tenants let him out."

"They assured me that they didn't. I suspect that he managed to crawl under a loose unlatched window in my basement and got outside that way, but I'm still mystified as to how he was able to push the window open."

"Vladimir is a very intelligent cat," Gena said.

"I am well aware of that, but pushing that window open would have required strength as well as intelligence. I don't know how he could have done it alone." Mr. Bowes paused. "But then Vladimir was acting quite unlike himself after his fight, pacing the house, peering out of the window and meowing piteously whenever another cat showed up on my property, and I must say that for a day or so before he made his getaway, a number of cats were trespassing on my property." He sighed. "Apparently the little fellow was determined to make his way back to you."

"A cat is a free being," she said, trying hard to avoid her former landlord's intonations.

"Anyway, I'll be sure to notify you should Vladimir have second thoughts and decide to return here."

"That's very kind of you."

Mr. Bowes muttered a halting farewell; Gena hung up the phone. The old man's talk of trespassing cats and a mysteriously engineered escape pricked at her.

She finished her coffee. Don would be coming over later to discuss their separation. If they could not come to an agreement about custody of their cat, they might have to give him back to Mr. Bowes.

She felt fur against her legs and looked down to see Vladimir rubbing against her. He looked up with a wide-eyed stare that seemed both unhappy and accusatory. "I know," she said, wishing again that she could take back everything that had happened between her and Don over the past days.

* * * *

Gena went out the back door, slipping around the side of her house and down the driveway belonging to the Archibalds, her neighbors on that side, instead of along her own driveway, where Mrs. Seligman might spot her. She would scope out the cats in front of the house first.

She pulled the door shut, but didn't hear the lock catch. She pushed it open and closed it again; it took her three more turns at closing the door before the lock caught. A new lock was probably needed, and Don had said something recently about having a locksmith put in a deadbolt, yet another domestic detail that had been part of Don's domain.

Normally she would have spent at least part of the day at the Operation Whiskers shelter, but had called to say that she was unable to come in. Jennifer Baxter had expressed her regrets, then gone on to mention a rumor that several cats had somehow escaped from the city's animal shelter. "Wish they could make their way to us," Jennifer continued. "At least we wouldn't euthanize them. Unfortunately we probably wouldn't have any room for them." Gena had decided not to mention the cats outside her house.

Following Caterina's advice, she had put on a pair of jeans made of heavy denim, thick socks, a long leather jacket, and leather gloves, even though the spring weather was mild enough for her to do without such garb. The cats sitting or reclining in the back yard watched her in silence as she crept past them and pushed her way through the shrubbery that separated her property from her neighbors' driveway. From earliest childhood, she had loved cats, growing up as she had with her family's beloved Cameron, but the way these cats were looking at her made her wary of turning her back to them. There was something profoundly unsettling about seeing so many cats in one place, all of them so silent and watchful.

"Hey, Gena."

Brad Archibald, wearing the uncoordinated athletic attire of a Tampa Bay Buccaneers jacket and a New York Yankees baseball cap, lurked in the driveway. Although only twelve years old, he was nearly as tall as she was and probably outweighed her by at least thirty pounds.

"Hey, yourself," she said to the boy, whom she rarely saw outdoors; she had grown accustomed to the distant sounds of blasts and explosions that emanated from the TV and the computer in Brad's bedroom whenever his window was open.

"What's with all the cats?" Brad asked.

"I really don't know."

Brad screwed up his eyes. "My dad said if they don't beat it, somebody's gonna drive by and take potshots at them."

"I certainly hope not," she said uneasily. She didn't really know the Archibalds, since she rarely saw Brad's parents outside the house either, except when they were leaving for work or returning home in the evening.

"You never know." Brad shrugged.

"Anybody trying to harm those cats would get into a lot of trouble," she said in as stern a tone as she could muster.

Brad shrugged again. "I guess."

She continued down the driveway. Brad trailed after her. That was another possibility she hadn't considered, that somebody might harm the trespassing cats.

Ackley Avenue was, as usual on a Saturday morning, devoid of traffic, with a few cars parked next to the sidewalk. She crossed the street and looked back. Most of the cats in front of her house were sitting on the sidewalk or lounging about near the stoop, but a few padded back and forth along the curb. None of them was clawing at trees or shrubs, or digging around in the flower beds. She watched them for a while, estimating that there were at least thirty of them there, and probably more.

What did they eat? Would they leave to find shelter somewhere else if the weather turned bad? They couldn't keep the house staked out forever.

"Why're they hanging at your house and nobody else's?" Brad asked.

"I have no idea."

"What you gonna do?"

"I don't know."

"What does Don think?"

"He hasn't told me."

Brad, looking bored, shuffled back across the street and went inside the Archibald house. Gena walked along the sidewalk, not stopping until she was almost two blocks away from her house, then turned around. A Persian, a tortoiseshell, and three tabbies came to a halt behind her and sat back on their haunches.

"What is it?" she said to the cats. "What the hell do you want?" They looked up at her, all with the same unsettling direct stare. A car passed, and she felt foolish, standing there in the expectation that the cats might actually answer.

She continued down the street until she came to the gas station at the end of the block, then turned back. Occasionally she looked around to see the five cats still trailing her. She reached the corner across the street from her house to see that the feline multitude was still there.

Her mother's blue Volvo was parked just behind Gena's car in the driveway.

Anger and resentment rose inside her. As usual, her mother was there without any advance warning, and on top of all of her usual implied criticisms of her daughter, there would now be the issue of all the cats around her house.

She took a deep breath. Her mother had to be at the back door, since she wasn't on the front stoop, and if she waited long enough, maybe Mrs. Lawlor would give up after a few knocks and "yoo hoos" and be on her way.

She loitered on the corner, then realized after a few more moments that Mrs. Lawlor must have taken advantage of the back door's problematic lock to let herself in.

She hurried across the street, telling herself that she would finally have it out with her mother about these unannounced visits. The cats retreated as she approached and regrouped behind her. A few of them paced in front of the back door, mewing softly, as if in distress. She stomped up the steps and pushed at the door with one hand while fumbling for the keys in her pocket with the other.

The door swung open. Mrs. Lawlor lunged at her, closing her hands around Gena's neck.

Gena let out a strangled cry. The door slammed shut as she fell against it. Vladimir was on the counter top near the sink, howling. She struggled with her mother, trying to free herself.

"You won't get rid of me so easily," Mrs. Lawlor said in a deep voice, "not you, and not those cats, either."

Gena grabbed her mother's wrists. The small but strong hands gripping her throat were making it almost impossible for her to breathe. She fought for air, then managed to break her mother's grip.

Mrs. Lawlor crashed to the floor, then bounced to her feet again, as agile as an actor in a kung fu movie. A hand chopped at Gena; the high kick of a foot caught her in the chest. Mrs. Lawlor snarled, her upper lip curling back from her teeth.

"Mom," Gena gasped, but it was not her mother; something had taken her place. She dodged another blow, sick with the realization that she was fighting Household. Something hard struck her jaw. She staggered back, then swung her right arm in a roundhouse curve.

Her feebly clutched fist connected with the side of her mother's head. Mrs. Lawlor toppled forward and fell to the floor.

"Mom," Gena whispered. Her mother wasn't moving. "Mom!" Tears stung her eyes. "Do whatever you want to me!" she shrieked, terrified. "But if anything happens to her, you'll pay for it! I don't care how long it takes, I'll finish you off for good!" She fell to her knees at her mother's side. "Goddamn it, you won't get me!"

If her mother was seriously hurt, Gena would never forgive herself. If Mrs. Lawlor was unharmed, she would never allow herself to get mad about any of her mother's visits again; she would not care if her mother dropped by at three in the morning with a laundry list of suggestions for self-improvement.

"Mom," she murmured, "please."

Mrs. Lawlor rolled over, then slowly sat up. Gena searched her face for signs of the madwoman who had attacked her, but found only a dazed look of confusion.

"Eugenia," Mrs. Lawlor said in her normal voice, "what the hell is going on?"

Gena stood up and helped her mother to her feet. "I don't know, Mom," she replied.

"I came into town to shop and meet a couple of friends for lunch and thought I'd stop by to see you first. Then suddenly I'm lying on the floor." She rubbed at her face. "And my head is pounding."

"You don't remember anything else?" Gena asked.

"What else is there to remember? I stopped by, knocked on the door, and when I saw that it wasn't locked I let myself in. And then all of a sudden—" A look of bewilderment passed over Mrs. Lawlor's face. "I think I'd better sit down."

Gena seated her mother at the kitchen table. Vladimir crouched on the counter top, glaring at Mrs. Lawlor through slitted eyes.

"Are you all right?" Gena asked.

"Of course I'm all right."

"Are you sure?"

"I'm already feeling better."

"Maybe you'd better rest for a while." But her mother couldn't stay here, not with Household ready to seize her again.

"I seem to be missing something here," her mother continued. "I knocked on the door, and let myself in, and then suddenly there I am on the floor. I should probably call my doctor, not that there's any chance of reaching him today." She frowned. "What is going on, Eugenia? What are all those cats doing around your house?"

"I don't know, Mom."

"And what's that one doing inside?" Her mother peered at Vladimir. "That cat looks just like the one you used to have."

"He is the one I used to have. It's Vladimir—he came home."

"You shouldn't let him up on the counter." Mrs. Lawlor was sounding more like herself. "And what are you going to do about all those cats outside?"

"I don't know. I talked to our vet, and she told me to call her back later if they were still out there. I'll ask Don what to do when he comes over."

Her mother arched her brows. "Is a reconciliation in the works?"

"I don't know." Gena leaned against the counter, still wary of getting too close to her mother and knowing that she had to get her out of the house. "Mom, I have a lot to take care of today, so if you don't mind, I'd really appreciate it if you—"

"Of course," Mrs. Lawlor said, sounding miffed. "I only wanted to help."

"Mom, listen to me. I've said this before, but it's really important now. Please don't drop by without calling up first and giving me some warning."

"Really, Eugenia. It's not as if—"

"Mom, I mean it. And promise me you'll stop at that urgent care center before you meet your friends."

"Very well." Mrs. Lawlor stood up. "And you'd better do something about all those cats outside before your neighbors start to complain. You're probably violating some sort of ordinance just by having them there."

"I didn't invite them. They just showed up."

"Well, I suggest that you call the city animal control department." Mrs. Lawlor went to the back door. "Do let me know about you and Donald. You know that your father and I will do everything we can if you need us." She pulled the door open. "Good-bye, dear."

"And remember, don't come over here without calling first. It could be really—" She paused. How could she possibly tell her mother that coming over on the spur of the moment might be dangerous, that an unseen entity she thought of as Household might again try to take control of Mrs. Lawlor against her will? Her mother would think she had gone completely around the bend. "Bye."

She closed the door, thinking of how tight her mother's hands had been around her throat. Vladimir's ears were back, his tail twitching. She thought of how close she and her mother might have come to serious injury, even death. Those stories of people going berserk, throttling or shooting family members for no reason—maybe that was how it happened.

Then she finally grasped the memory that had been eluding her. She remembered Peter Harman, the man who had strangled his wife, who had insisted that something else had committed the act, who had hung himself in the county jail.

She was suddenly afraid to have Don inside the house, alone with her and Vladimir and Household and the horde of cats outside.

Seventeen

Don parked next to the Blaine Building. A couple of cars and Jeff's Honda sat near the storefront that was Clifford Beaufort's campaign headquarters. There were no other vehicles on this street, which was typical for a Saturday morning, when the downtown area, except for shoppers at the Dunhill and Stein department store, was deserted. An empty parking lot separated two boarded-up brownstones across the street, where he spotted one lone pedestrian, a burly man in a leather jacket, shuffling toward the corner of Main and Berland.

Don had slept late that morning; Jeff was gone when he woke up. He got out of the car and rubbed his aching neck, hoping that he would be able to sleep in his own house that night.

That of course would depend on what he could work out with Gena. He had been depressed as hell earlier, brooding about his marriage, his lost job, the state of his finances, the entire course of his life.

He wanted his wife back. Nothing else mattered. He could live with the rest if he patched things up with her.

"Hey."

Don looked around. The now familiar craggy face of the white-haired homeless man poked out from behind an open door of the Blaine Building.

Don walked toward him. "What are you doing in there?" he asked.

"Catchin' some shut-eye. What time is it anyway?"

Don glanced at his watch. "Almost ten-thirty."

"Guess I slept late, then."

"How'd you get in there, anyway?"

The old man offered him a crafty smile. "Got ways. The security here sucks, and there's nobody workin' here on Saturday anyway. Hardly nobody workin' here the rest of the time, neither."

"I know," Don said, looking up past the doors at the arched windows and sandstone edifice of the six-story building.

"Tell you somethin' else you don't know." The old man beckoned to him with one finger. "Some kitty cats broke out of the city shelter last night."

Don started, thinking of all the cats he had sighted lately. There had been another cat on his car this morning when he had left Jeff's building, lying on the hood and giving him the iciest of stares.

"Don't know how they did it," the homeless man continued, "but they busted out, a whole bunch of them. Busted right on out of the big house." He snickered. "Maybe they had some help."

"How do you know—"

The man suddenly waved a hand at him. "Go on now. Cops gonna drive by any minute." The door closed. Don peered through it and caught a glimpse of the old man shuffling across the skylit lobby before he disappeared into the shadows.

* * * *

Paint was peeling from the walls inside the Beaufort campaign head-quarters. The tiled floor looked to Don as though it hadn't been cleaned in years. Two phones and a fax machine had been installed, but sat on the floor, since no desks had yet arrived.

"We have to get some computers in here," Jeff was saying to another worker, a thin young guy in a sweatshirt and cargo pants who was thumbing a BlackBerry. "I've got a laptop I can contribute to the cause."

"I can bring one in, too," the guy in the sweatshirt said.

Jeff glanced at Don. "This is Tom Alcott," he said. "He's our treasurer."

"I'm Don Martinson," Don said, thinking again that this campaign didn't have a chance.

Two older women in jeans and sweaters, a slender black woman and a small gray-haired white woman, were mopping the floor near the back of the room. Jeff led Don toward them. "You can either mop," he said, "or scrape paint off the walls."

"I'll scrape paint." Don climbed up a ladder leaning against the wall and got to work on the part near the ceiling.

By a quarter to one, he had finished scraping one wall clean and was ready to brush on primer. He felt better after the physical labor. He had learned that Tom Alcott was an Army vet who had crashed at Clifford Beaufort's halfway house a couple of years ago before getting back on his feet and landing a job as a computer technician. Lashana Wills, one of the older women, was a cousin of Beaufort's; Helena Rothenberg, the other woman, had introduced herself as "a do-gooder from Rolling Hill Acres." Jeff had gone out to get them all lunch and returned with sandwiches and beverages. The women were perched on two folding chairs next to the front window while the men sat on the now shiny floor.

"Good of you to come and help out," Lashana said to Don as they ate.

"Glad I could help," Don replied, surprised to find that he meant it.

"Think you could help us move some furniture in next week?" Tom asked.

"Probably," Don said.

"If we don't get more volunteers," Jeff said, "we'll have more desks than people."

"I'll see who I can round up at school," Helena said, "but you know how it is. Everybody's busy, and Cliff's going to lose anyway, and in the meantime the kids have to be prepped for those damned competency tests and then for their final exams."

Don turned toward her. "You're a teacher?"

"I was," Helena said, "over at Danvers Middle School until I retired—sixth and seventh grade math and science. But they've been calling me in to substitute, so I'm over there most of the time anyway, and now they're trying to get me back full-time."

The cell phone in Don's pocket suddenly bleated the first four notes of Beethoven's Fifth. He pulled it out and held it to his ear. "Hello?"

"Don," Gena said, "I have to talk to you. Something really strange is going on here."

"Just a minute." He got to his feet. "It's my wife." Jeff raised his brows, but said nothing. Don retreated to the back of the room. "What's up?" he said in a low voice.

"Well, this is really weird. There are all these cats hanging around our house, I mean a ton of cats, more than were here yesterday. They've taken over the back yard and they're out in front of the house, too. This morning, I had two calls from Mrs. Seligman complaining about them, and then I called Caterina Lucci, and she told me to be careful not to get too close to any of them. So I went outside a while ago to scope things out, and ran into Brad Archibald, and he started talking about how somebody might take a potshot at them, and then a few of the cats followed me across the street while the others stayed near the house, and then—"

"Gena," Don said, "get to the point."

"The point is we've got at least a couple of hundred cats on our property, and I might be underestimating. Could be even more, because I stopped counting after a while. I don't know what's making them come here, and that isn't the only weird thing. I—"

He waited. "Well?" he said at last.

"It's about the house. I don't know how to put it without sounding like I'm crazy."

"Stick with the cats, then," he said, thinking of the ones he had seen at the Beaufort rally, the neighbor who had claimed to have spotted a large number near his house, and the old homeless guy's tale of cats escaping from the city shelter. "Did you notice anything unusual about them? I mean, besides the fact that there's so many of them."

"They don't look or act like strays, and they almost seem to be—organized, if that makes any sense. They look like they've been taken care of, and even the long-haired ones are well-groomed. They don't meow a lot, or chase birds, or mess up the flower beds. They're just sitting there staring at—oh, my God."

"What is it?"

"A van from WKTG just pulled up across the street." Gena was silent for a bit. "Now a guy with a camcorder's getting out of the car."

"Do you want me to come over now?"

"Where are you?"

"Downtown with Jeff."

"I don't know. I don't know what to do." He heard her let out her breath.

"I'll be there in half an hour," he said.

Eighteen

Before he got to the corner of Ackley Avenue and Bancroft Street, Don saw that he would be unable to park anywhere near his house. A crowd had gathered on Bancroft, blocking access to his driveway and making it impossible for anyone to drive along that road, and a smaller crowd stood on the other side of Ackley aiming digital cameras and cellphones at the front of his home. There were cats by his front door and on the steps leading up to it, and more cats on the sidewalk. Even more cats lay on top of Gena's car and on the blacktop around it, while still others had taken up sentry-like positions at the edge of the driveway. His neighbor Phil Donovan was in front of the WKTG van talking to a man holding a microphone and another man wielding a camcorder.

Don cruised down Ackley Avenue, finally found a space three blocks away, parked in front of a split-level with a "For Sale" sign on its patch of lawn, then walked back to his house. Maybe if he crept up a driveway, he could cut across a few back yards and make it to his back door without being seen.

He stayed on the sidewalk. As he neared his house, he pulled up his collar and kept his head down, then saw that he had to leave the sidewalk and walk into the street to avoid the cats. He couldn't help noticing that they were all giving him the same kind of stare he had seen in the felines around the courthouse. He felt their eyes following him as he walked past them. The people across the street didn't pay much attention to him, but as he rounded the corner, Phil Donovan waved his arms.

"That's the guy," Phil shouted. "Don something—he's the guy who lives there." The man pointing the microphone at Phil glanced at Don, then came toward him. Don recognized the man now; he was a reporter on WKTG's "News at Eleven" program.

Don froze, not knowing what to do. "What's this all about?" he asked the WKTG reporter.

"What's it all about?" the newsman replied. "The cats, buddy, the cats. Where'd all these cats around your house come from?"

Don tried to grin. "You came over here just because of a bunch of cats?"

"Slow news day," the reporter said, "and you have to admit it's a lot of cats. I never saw so many in one place outside of a cat show. Your name?" Don did not reply. "Is this your house?"

The cameraman bore down on Don, his lens pointed. Don thrust up his arm, warding off the cameraman, then spun around and ran toward his house. Amazingly, the cats scurried away, giving him a clear path. He looked back. The cameraman and the reporter were still standing next to the curb, their way blocked by several cats that were rubbing against their legs and pawing at their trousers. More cats retreated from Don, allowing him to pass and then regrouping behind him. He hurried around the side of the house and up to the back door.

The door opened before he could take out his key. He slipped inside as Gena slammed the door behind him.

"Jesus Christ," he said, "what the hell is going on?" He suddenly felt a strange solidarity with his wife.

"I don't know." Gena was pale, her dark hair pulled back from her face. "And every time I look outside, I see even more cats. What are we going to do if the police show up?" Her "we" sounded good to him.

Vladimir wandered into the kitchen and gave Don the once-over with his green eyes. Don gazed at the cat. "So you finally decided to come home," he said. Vladimir narrowed his eyes slightly. "I don't suppose you had anything to do with all of this."

"I don't see how," Gena said. "It has to be a coincidence. Anyway, Caterina says it isn't likely."

"Having all those cats hanging around our house isn't likely, either," Don said.

"What are we going to do?" Gena whispered, sounding conspiratorial.

"Damned if I know." Don left the kitchen and went through the dining room into the living room. Gena had closed the front window's curtains, but he could still hear the muffled sounds of voices outside, and was struck with a vision of turning up on "News at Eleven," fleeing from the cameraman as though he had just been indicted. Such footage would make a great impression on anybody in the area who might be interviewing him for a job in the near future.

He took off his coat, threw it over a chair, and sat down on the sofa. A feeling of dread rose inside him. He was without a job, had some serious unresolved marital issues, and now had to deal with a mysterious cat infestation, so feeling the way he did was certainly appropriate. But this was the most powerful feeling of doom and impending disaster he had ever endured.

Vladimir had followed him. The cat jumped up next to him but kept his distance, eyeing Don with what looked like extreme suspicion.

"Can I get you anything?" Gena asked from the entrance to the dining room. "Do you want some lunch?"

"I had lunch already."

"A soda?"

"I'm fine. Look, now that I'm here, we might as well have our discussion. We can worry about the cat situation afterwards."

"Okay." She came into the room and sat down on the chair where he had thrown his coat. She looked small and frail and childlike in her baggy sweater and loose jeans. "Are you sure you don't mind talking here?"

"Have you got a better idea?"

"It's just that—well, some very strange things have been happening here lately. I don't mean just with the cats." Her eyes darted nervously from side to side.

"Gena—"

Vladimir leaped from the sofa and trotted over to her, settling down near her chair. "You start," she said.

"This coming week," Don said, "I've got to make phone calls and set up some interviews and get my résumé out. Hope I find something sooner or later, but it may take a while, and in the meantime—" He paused. "I'm sorry."

"I'm sorry, too."

She sounded truly contrite; maybe there was some hope for them after all. All the way over here, he had been thinking of how to bridge the divide. Financial issues had been largely responsible for the breach, so maybe the simplest solution was to let Gena do whatever she wanted with whatever she earned. Anything was better than getting into pitched battles over what was or wasn't a household item.

Who are you kidding? his inner voice asked, underlining the feelings of doom and dread that had settled over him almost as soon as he was inside the house.

"Anyway," Don continued, "it'd be a lot harder for me to conduct a job search from Jeff's place. He doesn't have much room, and we'd just be in each other's way, so what I'm thinking is that I should come back here and get myself organized for the job hunt. That's the only practical thing to do."

"Then you want the house," she said.

"What I'm saying is that I need to stay here while I'm looking for a job." What he should have said was that he wanted to come home and put the past week behind them forever.

A little late for that, his inner voice murmured.

"I see," Gena said.

"But I wouldn't mind if you—"

"Maybe that's best. I haven't exactly been feeling all that secure here for the past couple of days."

He looked up. Gena's head was bowed, her eyes hidden. His doubts nibbled at him again as he thought of her date last night at Vitello's. She meant that he could have the house because she was moving in with the other guy; that had to be why she was sounding so passive about the whole business. She already had an option other than moving back in with her parents.

Vladimir moved closer to Gena and stretched out next to her feet, staring across the room at Don as if he were an intruder.

"I'll have to look for a place," she said.

"It'll cost you." He could feel his buried rage beginning to rise.

"Look, if you're going to be living here, then obviously I have to move somewhere else."

A plaintive and almost inaudible voice in the back of his mind was telling him to bag this whole line of discussion, but his rage at Gena's fiscal irresponsibility was starting to smolder. "Use your sense," he said. "You don't have to spend money on rent. Your parents have plenty of room—you could move back in with them."

"I can't," she said. "They'd be trying to run my life."

"You'd save money."

"You sound just like Household," Gena said in a whisper.

"Mrrow," Vladimir interjected, glaring at Don.

"I can't move back in with my parents," Gena continued, "because if I do, it'll be too easy to retreat and never stand on my own two feet again."

"I'm just trying to be practical," Don said. "They'd help you out, and you'll have your car to get to St. Luke's. You won't—"

"I don't work at St. Luke's any more."

He started. "You got fired, too?"

"I quit."

"You quit?"

"I quit and now I'm working for Caterina Lucci. She offered me a job as her office manager, so I took it. I start there this week."

"Caterina Lucci?" Don wondered if he had heard her correctly. "Caterina Lucci?" he repeated. "What did she offer?"

Gena frowned. "I don't know if that's any of your business at this point."

Don bristled. "It will be when my lawyer meets with your lawyer. And just what kinds of benefits is Caterina offering?"

"She said that I could have two weeks of vacation time my first year."

"Oh, that's just what you need, two weeks of vacation." He could feel himself getting worked up now. "Any 401K plan? Any retirement plan? I'll bet she isn't offering any health insurance, either." She was not denying his contentions. "That's brilliant. You give up a relatively decent and secure job to go to work for Caterina, where's there's no room for advancement. You chuck a position with some potential for a promotion and more benefits so you can go to work for a cat doctor."

"Hrraow," Vladimir said, then got up and padded across the carpet.

"What's so wrong with working for a cat doctor?" Gena's voice had taken on more resonance. Don kept his eyes on her as she slowly got to her feet. "It beats working in Billing and Accounts Receivable. It beats having to call up people and listen to their hard luck stories and having to keep to one of those damned scripts with all its euphemisms for telling them they're deadbeats and they'd better pay up right now if they know what's good for them, which is what I'd have to do if I stayed there. Barney said so yesterday. That's why I quit."

"It occurs to me," Don said, trying to keep his anger under control, "that you might have to call some of Caterina's clients from time to time to remind them of their outstanding bills."

"That isn't the same." Gena took a step toward him. "Caterina cuts people some slack if they need it. Look how long she waited for us to pay her."

"In other words, she's just as impractical as you are." He couldn't hold in his rage any more. She's going to ruin you, a voice was murmuring inside him. Time to show her who's boss. Time to let her know that she's not going to drag you down with her.

He abruptly found himself standing over her, his hands tightened into fists.

"Mrrow!" Vladimir howled from the floor. Don stepped back, appalled at himself, at the violent urges seething inside him.

"Oh, my God." Don stumbled back to his chair and covered his face with his hands.

And then a strange sound came from outside the house, a crescendo of cries, an eerie and alien shriek that rose to a high and piercing pitch. He suddenly knew the sound for what it was, the sound of a chorus of meows, of a multitude of cats crying out in protest.

Catalonia, he thought. He could avoid that thought no longer. The feline virtual world he had seen in Jeff's computer, the cats at the Beaufort rally, the horde of cats around his house—he knew what they had to be. They were here because of him and Gena and their impending separation. Catalonians were here to defend and preserve their threatened realm. He wondered how far they were willing to go in their own defense.

"Gena," he said. He was afraid to look at her, afraid to think of how close he had come to hitting her, maybe worse. His hands fell from his face. He had expected to see fear on her face, or possibly anger, but her gaze was steady and her face hard as she watched him.

"I'm getting my coat," she said, rising to her feet, "and then I'm going out the back door, and I would really appreciate it if you'd come with me." Before he could say anything, she had gone to the front closet. She returned with her jacket over one arm. "If we move fast and head toward the Archibalds', we might be okay."

"I don't know what got into me. What's going on?"

She left the room without answering. He got up, grabbed his coat, and hurried after her. She opened the back door and slipped out ahead of him, glanced quickly to her right, then ran down the steps toward the Archibalds' driveway. He followed as the cats in the yard gazed after him. Apparently nobody was staking out their back door yet, perhaps because of the obstacle that the cats posed.

He kept near her as they hurried across the Archibalds' back yard and the yard next to it, then crept down another driveway toward the street. He took her arm when they came to the sidewalk and she moved closer to him.

"All right," he said. "Maybe now we can try to figure out what's going on."

"I've got some ideas about that," she said. "I'll tell you if you promise not to tell me I'm crazy."

"I promise," he said, even though he wasn't being so rational himself. Never before had he come so close to hitting Gena, no matter how angry he had been.

"I had to get you out of there first. Too many weird things have been happening inside our house." She paused. "Yesterday morning, when I got up, Vladimir was sitting in front of your home office door, so I went in to check things, and your computer was still on."

"It couldn't have been," he said. "I turned it off days ago."

"Maybe you were so distracted by breaking up with me that you forgot to check."

"I didn't forget." They walked down the street. Don looked back, relieved to see no one was following them. "The computer couldn't have been on," he continued, "because I remember turning it off right after checking some scores at ESPN."

"Well, the computer was on, and then a man's face appeared on the screen. He looked just the way I've sometimes imagined Household might look, if that makes any sense. I swear it's true, I saw a man and I heard the same scary voice I've heard—" She halted for a moment, then resumed walking. "It was Household, fighting back, and that isn't the only way it's fighting back. Mom came over twice, after our big fight and just this morning. Both times she attacked me, and she was speaking in this weird low voice before she did. The first time, it wasn't too bad, but it was worse this morning. She had her hands around my neck to strangle me. She's never done anything like that in her life, never lost control like that. Now I'm afraid to have her anywhere near the house."

"I believe you," he said, prepared to accept almost any improbability now, even if only to let it collapse on its own.

"And then, just before, in the living room, you started talking in that same weird low voice about how I was dragging us into ruin and you were going to get back at me for what I did and then you came at me looking like you wanted to kill me."

"I don't remember saying anything like that," he protested.

"That's because it wasn't really you. It was Household, or whatever you want to call the thing that's doing this. First it was Mom, and then it tried with Tracey but couldn't really get inside her for some reason, and then it was Mom again and then you. I think it's getting better at it, too, stronger every time it tries. And all those cats outside—they're Catalonians, they have to be. All those times we made up those stories—Catalonia seemed so real, I could see it in my mind, I could have drawn a map of the place. Now I know why. We made it real. I've been seeing cats for days now, here and there, just a few at a time, whenever I think about Catalonia. That's where all those cats around our house probably come from. A few cats didn't make enough of an impression, so now they're out in full force."

"That's crazy," he said, wondering how long it would take for a wagon from the nuthouse to arrive.

"You promised me you wouldn't say that."

"I didn't say you were crazy. I mean that this whole situation is crazy. But here's the problem. What do we do about it?"

They walked on in silence until they reached his car. He unlocked the door on the passenger's side and opened it for her. Even though they were over three blocks away from their house, there was probably less chance of anyone in the crowd spotting them from a distance if they were inside the car.

Gena got into the car. He went around and got in next to her. "What are we going to do?" he asked again.

"I don't know. Either we can assume we've both gone completely insane, or we have to act as though Catalonia's real, and that Household's as real as all those cats outside our house."

"Assuming we're nuts," he said, "doesn't give us any constructive way to deal with all of this, does it."

"No. Not unless we just run away from it."

"That would be kind of impractical, abandoning everything." He paused. "Pardon me for sounding like Household."

"And maybe it wouldn't work anyway. Maybe—" She folded her arms across her chest. "Every once in a while, even before our big fight, I'd get the feeling that something was haunting our house, something cold and heartless and scary, something like how I imagined Household might be. I think Household might be what made Vladimir run away, I think that's why he left us for Mr. Bowes. And then he came back because—"

"This really is crazy," Don said. "We're both out of our minds."

"The cats around the house are real enough, aren't they? The people who came to take a look at them are seeing the same thing we are. They can't all be crazy."

"So what do we do?" But he was afraid that he already knew the answer to that question. He and Gena had imagined Catalonia together, somehow brought their imagined world into existence, and now their creatures had found a way to enter this world.

"They're here to get us back together," Gena said, completing his thoughts. "And to get rid of Household for good."

He thought of the cold stare he had noticed in the eyes of all the strange cats he had sighted, of how the cats surrounding the house had looked at him. Maybe they had something else in mind besides a reconciliation and getting rid of Household. Maybe, if they got desperate enough, they would try to accomplish whatever they meant to do without overly concerning themselves with his and Gena's welfare.

"We'd better get back to the house," he said. "I'll leave the car here. Between the cats and the crowd, I wouldn't be able to get it into the driveway anyway."

"Don—" She rested a hand on his arm for a moment. "We have to be careful of Household. It'll try to hurt us again."

He said, "I know."

* * * *

They managed to sneak across the Archibalds' back yard and up to their back door without being seen. Nearly every inch of their back yard was now occupied by cats, including several Persians and Himalayans he had not noticed earlier.

Vladimir was in the kitchen when they entered the house, huddled under the table, his ears back. Don closed the door as Gena squatted next to their cat.

"Are you all right?" she asked Vladimir. "Even Vladimir's worried," she said to Don as she stood up again.

"Of course he's worried." He took Gena's jacket from her and went to the front closet to hang up their coats. He could hear the low murmur of the crowd outside. He wouldn't have thought so many people would be interested in hanging around to stare at cats.

He returned to the living room. Gena came in with Vladimir cradled in her arms. Vladimir had never been amenable to being carried around like a baby, but he was not protesting that indignity now. His ears were still back, and Don knew that the cat was sensing the vague feeling of menace that clung to the house.

He had read enough stories and seen enough movies and TV shows about homes afflicted by spirits, poltergeists, and other mysterious beings.

Then he thought of that story about the man in their former neighborhood who had killed his wife, who had claimed that something else had made him do it before killing himself in jail.

Whatever was lurking in this house might have been here all along, just waiting for new residents to torment. Maybe the being had taken on the manner of their imagined entity Household because that was the only way it had of communicating with them, or maybe it had somehow picked up on Don's obsessions and was using them as a way to control him. None of these speculations offered a clue about how to restore his life to something resembling normality.

As Gena sat down with Vladimir, the phone rang.

"I'll get it." Don hurried to the kitchen and picked up the phone. The phone number on the handset's tiny screen was unfamiliar. "Hello?"

"Am I speaking to a Donald Martinson of 22 Ackley Avenue?" a man's voice asked.

"Speaking. Who is this?"

"Stephen Kolbida. I'm head of the city's animal control department, and I've had five calls at my home today from people telling me there's hundreds of stray cats at your house and they weren't about to wait till Monday to call and complain. One call, I'd think the caller was a wacko, and two, I'd think some kids were jerking me around, but five, I begin to wonder. Are there anywhere near that many stray cats around your house?"

"There are a lot of cats here," Don admitted.

"Hundreds?"

Don went to the window behind the sink and looked outside, hoping unreasonably that the cats might have somehow disappeared, but the feline multitude was still occupying his back yard.

"There's a least a hundred or so in my yard," Don said into the handset, "and more in my driveway."

"That number sounds like every stray in the city is camped out there."

"They're a mighty strange bunch of strays, then, because I spotted a few Persians among them—Himalayans and Burmese and Siamese, too. Some of them look like awfully valuable animals for strays."

"They could have been kidnapped and then got loose. So maybe we can find their owners. Maybe we can put out an APB or put up posters or get some notices out in the newspaper, but in the meantime we have to find some place to put them. Can't leave them in your yard being a public nuisance. So I'm going to have to see what I can do about rounding them up."

"I don't think you'll be able to round them up very easily," Don said, "even if you do have more room at the city shelter now."

"What do you mean, more room at the shelter?"

"I heard that some of your cats escaped."

There was a long silence at the other end of the line. "Where'd you hear that?" Stephen Kolbida asked.

"Around."

"Exactly where around?" Stephen Kolbida did not sound happy.

"Just around."

"Then maybe you can understand why I'm worrying about the calls I'm getting."

"These cats don't look like they came from any shelter," Don said.

"Maybe I should be the judge of that. I'm supervisor of animal control, and that means being in charge of controlling animals. We can't have cats wandering around loose and taking over everybody's lawns and private property."

If the cats were rounded up and taken to the shelter, most of them would be quickly euthanized, given that Kolbida wouldn't be able to find enough homes for all of them. That, of course, was assuming that Kolbida even managed to round them up. The cats did not look like the sort of creatures who would surrender peacefully. And if they were Catalonians, if his insane suppositions about them were true, they might have ways to fight against those who threatened them. They might even blame Gena and him for loosing the animal control department on them.

"It's the weekend," Don said, feeling desperate, "and it's not an emergency. These cats aren't ripping things up or peeing all over the place or actually bothering anybody, they're just out there sitting around. And it's my property they're on—they aren't annoying anybody else as far as I can tell." He decided not to mention the newspeople or the sightseers outside his house. "You could at least wait until Monday and see how it goes. Maybe they'll be gone by then."

"Kinda hard to think about how hundreds of cats could just disappear."

"Kinda hard to think about how some cats could break out of the city shelter."

Kolbida was silent for a moment. "Okay, look," he said. "I can wait a little while, but if I get any complaints of damage or they start wandering into your neighbors' yards, or some higher up gets after me, I won't have any choice. I'll have to bring them in or else figure out some other way of dealing with them. And the police may get after you in the meantime."

"I guess that's fair enough," Don said.

"I'll call you back if I get any more complaints."

"You do that. So long."

Don hung up the phone, then peered through the window over the sink again. A few cats stretched, then settled down again. Other cats seemed to be sleeping, but most of them were watching the house.

He returned to the living room. "That was the animal control supervisor," he said to Gena.

"I guessed that when I heard what you were saying." Gena sighed. "What are we going to do?"

Don sat down on the sofa across from her. "I don't know."

"I could call Caterina. She said she'd come over if I needed her. But—" She gave him a nervous look. "I worry about having anybody come inside the house now."

He did not ask her to explain what she meant. She was thinking of Household, or whatever it was that was haunting their house.

"Would she still be in her office?" he asked.

"She said she'd be there most of the day." Gena got up, went to the window, and drew back the curtains slightly. "Even more cats are on the sidewalk," she said softly, "and more people are coming around the corner. Now a van from one of the other stations just pulled up."

"Jesus Christ." Don covered his eyes with his hands. "Call Caterina and ask her if she has any advice."

Nineteen

ena hung up the phone. "Caterina isn't answering," she said to Don as she returned to the living room. "I left a voice mail."

"Maybe she went home."

"She told me she'd be in her office until late afternoon." She wandered toward the window, but did not pull back the curtain, knowing what she would see.

"Maybe she wouldn't be able to help us anyway," Don said.

"Cats are her business. She might know—"

"Just what we need," he said. His voice was deeper, threatening to turn into Household's. "All this bullshit isn't going to make it any easier for me to find a job." His voice sounded as though he was standing right behind her; she tensed. "Won't help us sell this house, either—all those cats'll just make people think there's something wrong with the place. I'm going to end up the way my dad did, always having to hang on by my fingernails, and it's your fault. It would have helped if you—"

"I think we should go over to Caterina's."

He grimaced, as though struggling with himself. "Something else is going on here," he said, "and we're just pasting our Catalonia over it. That's got to be it."

"No, no," she said. "What about Household…"

"I've still got to see that," Don said. "All I've seen so far is cats."

"Believe," a deep voice said within him, making her shiver.

"What is it?" she shouted.

"I heard…Household," he said in a whisper. His lips twisted in an uneasy smile. "Maybe I shouldn't be surprised. Financial devices can get out of hand."

A bad joke, she thought, and almost expected a maniacal laugh, but the threatening silence worked as well. She took his hand and squeezed it. "We're going over to Caterina's."

The angry expression on his face softened. "I don't know if Caterina can—"

"Do you have a better idea?"

"No." He sounded more like himself. "But there's no point in both of us going. We'll be lucky if even one of us can get out the door. Besides—"

"You've got to get out of this house," she said, afraid that the Don she knew would disappear and be taken over entirely by Household.

He gazed at her blankly. "I'll go," he said at last, "and you can keep trying her office. If you get her on the phone, tell her I'm on my way there."

"All right."

Don offered her what looked like a forced smile. "Besides, somebody should stay here to look out for Vladimir." He glanced at the sleeping cat, who was curled up in one corner of the sofa.

Gena thought of Vladimir's antics of the night before and could not bring herself to smile. "You're right," she said. "With everything that's been going on, I'd be afraid to leave him alone for too long."

Don went to the front closet and returned with his coat. He rummaged in his pockets, pulled out his cell phone, then thrust it into a side pocket.

"Be careful, Don."

He disappeared into the kitchen. She heard the door close behind him, and waited a few moments in case it suddenly opened again, but apparently Don had made a successful escape.

Vladimir opened his eyes, looked up at her, and yawned. His eyes narrowed and his ears went back. "Hrurr," he said, then settled back, flicking his ears forward and resting his head on his front paws.

The cat looked calmer, and Gena, looking around the warm light of the living room, felt a little better herself. It was as if the cold unseen presence she thought of as Household had left the house with Don.

That thought brought her up short. Gena shivered, while Vladimir emitted a soft snarl. She was probably safe inside the house at least for the time being; the real threat was outside. She wondered which she should fear more, the crowds that seemed docile enough now but might not remain that way, or the strange cats with their cold and observant eyes.

* * * *

Don was halfway across the yard adjoining the Archibalds' lawn when he heard a voice call out, "There he is!"

Don halted and looked back. Brad Archibald was out on the deck overlooking his parents' back yard. "Hey!" the boy shouted, pointing at him. "He's over there!"

Don ran, thrashed his way through a hedge, and barely missed a collision with a trellis. He fled down the next driveway toward the street, then slowed as he reached the sidewalk. His chest heaved as he panted for breath; he was getting out of shape.

A glance in the direction of his house revealed that nobody was after him.

He pulled up his collar and strode toward his car, forcing himself not to run, telling himself that anyone who might have heeded Brad's call would now be looking for him in back yards and wasn't likely to come after a guy who looked like he was only out for a stroll. He caught his breath, still feeling that a consultation with Caterina Lucci was wasted effort, whatever Gena thought. He did not feel particularly angry with her for sending him on this wild goose chase, even though he had felt his rage building up to a dangerous level back at the house. In fact, outside of a few scratches on his hands from that damned hedge and being a bit short of breath, he felt considerably easier in his mind than he had only a few minutes ago.

He was out of Household's range, if he assumed that Household was an actual entity. But the whole idea of Household and Catalonia inhabiting any space outside his imagination went against all his assumptions about reality. Whether such entities had always existed in some sense, or Gena and he had somehow willed them into existence and enabled them to become part of this reality, was a minor problem in comparison to the problem of having to question much of what he had been taught and had come to believe about the universe.

Still, Don told himself, the alternative would be to assume that he was going out of his mind. Accepting their existence as a fact at least held out the hope of a solution to the problems Household and Catalonia posed, while assuming that he was completely nuts would only leave him helpless to act, aside from voluntarily committing himself.

He came to his car and got in, leaned forward, and started the car.

* * * *

Caterina's office was in a small glassy building next to a rambling Victorian structure that housed the west side branch of the city's library. A black silhouette of a cat and gold letters that spelled out "Caterina Lucci D.V.M." above the silhouette and "THE CAT DOCTOR" below it adorned the door, while the front picture window was festooned with stick-ons of cats and kittens sleeping, stretching, consuming bowls of food, leaping into the air, and chasing balls of yarn.

The door was locked. Don jabbed the doorbell several times, then turned back to his car just as a mud-spattered white minivan barreled into the nearly empty parking lot and screeched to a halt.

"Hiya, Don." Caterina Lucci emerged from the van and hurried toward him, swinging her arms and stomping feet shod in a pair of Doc Martens; although a small woman, she possessed the forceful and aggressive gait of a stevedore. "Gena called me this morning. She said you have a ton of cats hanging around your house. Told me Vladimir came back, too."

"That's what I'm here about," Don said as Caterina unlocked the door. "The cats around our house, not Vladimir. We tried to call you a little while ago."

"This seems to be my day for consultations about weird behavior by cats." Caterina pushed the door open; Don followed her inside. "I was just over at Operation Whiskers. They wanted me to come over because the cats in their shelter were yowling and trying to bust out." China cat figurines of varying sizes sat on the desk in the reception area, while the walls were decorated with reproductions of Leonardo da Vinci's drawings of cats. Caterina pulled off her trench coat, threw it over a chair, and plopped down in another chair. "Actually, that isn't the whole story. Apparently there were some other cats outside the shelter, and the ones inside started howling, and then the cats outside tried to climb up the walls. Jennifer Baxter—she's the person who called me—went to the door, and you won't believe this, but a couple of the cats outside the door tripped her, and while she was down a couple more started leading cats outside before she could stop them, and she said it looked just like a planned prison break. The only reason more cats didn't escape was that most of them were in their cages, but even there, the locks on a few of the cages were unlocked somehow, and Jennifer doesn't know how that could have happened."

Don was silent, hoping for the vet's expertise.

"I know that sounds pretty unbelievable," Caterina said.

"Not any more unbelievable than what's going on around our house," Don said, shaking his head. "Did you hear anything about cats escaping from the city shelter?"

"Jennifer told me she heard something about that."

"Just a rumor," he quickly added, not wanting to tell her that his source was an old homeless guy. "But I had a call from the animal control supervisor today, and he basically confirmed the story. At least he didn't deny it."

"Steve Kolbida?" Caterina shook her head again. "If you ask me, any self-respecting cat would be better off roaming the streets and hanging out with a pack of feral cats instead of being stuck in that feline concentration camp. If I were a cat and he corralled me, I'd rather cash in than hang around that dump." She paused. "So what's the deal?"

"What?"

"About the cats around your house. How many of them are there, anyway?"

"We haven't counted them," Don said, "but there seem to be more now than there were this morning. They don't look like strays—in fact, some of them look like purebreds and show cats. They've taken over the back yard, most of the driveway, and the sidewalks around the place. Gena and I were able to sneak out our back door earlier, and the way they were all staring at us gave me the creeps."

"You snuck out the back door?"

"We had to, because now we've got all these sightseers hanging around. There's even a couple of cameramen and reporters from the local TV stations.

I had to park my car three blocks away from the house." He took a breath. "I mean, things are getting completely out of hand. Gena thought you might have some advice, but I don't see what you can do."

"Reporters?" Caterina said.

Don nodded. "One came after me with his camera after a neighbor pointed me out. That's apart from all the people shooting pictures with cameras and cell phones."

"I'll come over and see what's what." Caterina stood up. "After all, cats are my calling."

"Park way down the street and sneak across some yards and just hope nobody sees us."

"Don't you worry about that," Caterina said as she pulled on her coat. "I'll get to your house one way or another. Lead the way."

* * * *

Gena put down fresh water for Vladimir in the kitchen, then went back to the living room. She had enough food for dinner, enough cat food for Vladimir, and probably enough supplies to last the weekend; with the multitude of cats, the knots of people, and representatives of the news media loitering outside, she wouldn't be able to take more than a few steps from her door. Outside the house, she could hear the muffled sounds of people calling out to one another:

"Yo!"

"Check out all those cats, man."

"Here, kitty, kitty."

"Ever seen so many cats? Animal control's gonna have a field day."

"What if they all start fucking?"

"Look, up in that tree—there's a whole bunch of them lying on the branches!"

"Such a cute widdle kiddy cat."

"Man, the way they stare at you weirds me out."

"You're from WOOW, aren't you? I watch your news all the time!"

"Hey, over here—it's a gal from the *Times-Tribune*."

Gena heard a thud against the back door, and then the familiar squeak of one of the hinges as it opened. "Don?" she called out.

"It's me, it's me," he shouted back.

"Did you see Caterina?"

"I ran into her in her parking lot. She was just coming back from Operation Whiskers—says they had some cats escape from their shelter." He stomped into the living room and proceeded to the front closet. "Said she'd come over," he called out from the alcove. "She was following me, but I think she lost me at a red light."

"She knows the way."

"She'll have to park somewhere else. My car's about six blocks away from our house now." Don came back into the living room and sat down on the sofa. "How she's going to get from her van to the back door, I don't know."

"We'll wait for her." Gena sat down across the room from him. "You'll stay for dinner?"

"Might as well."

"There's plenty to eat. I have most of a big pizza with the works from Franco's in the fridge."

"Great," he said with a distinct lack of enthusiasm. "I'll call Jeff later so he doesn't wonder what happened to me."

Gena watched as Vladimir emerged from the kitchen and hopped onto the sofa, settling in next to Don to be petted.

Maybe the crisis was past, with no more delusions about an invisible presence in the house. The cats outside would disappear and everything would be as it was.

"Where were you?" she asked. "I mean when I called you before." Perhaps as an estranged wife, she no longer had the right to ask him such questions.

"Downtown, at the Beaufort for mayor campaign headquarters," he replied.

Gena gazed at him in surprise, having never known Don to be especially interested in politics. "That's interesting," she said, not knowing what else to say.

"Jeff signed on as his campaign manager. Reverend Beaufort seems like a good man. Of course he doesn't have a chance." Don paused. "Gena, I have to ask you this. Who was that guy I saw you with last night at Vitello's?"

So he had recognized her in the parking lot after all.

"Um, he's Tracey's tenant," Gena said. "Rents the other side of her two-family. I went over there on Thursday to see Tracey, but she wasn't home, and then Roland—that's the guy—came out and introduced himself, and we talked for a bit, and then he asked me out."

"So you only actually met him a couple of days ago."

"Well, yes."

"In other words," Don said, "you went on a date with somebody you'd known for about five minutes. You sure didn't waste any time."

"Look, I didn't know—" Her voice was rising. "Look, he seemed like a nice guy and Tracey would have warned me if he was seriously weird and as far as I knew you and I were separated so I couldn't see what was wrong with dinner, but then I started worrying that it was, like, too soon to start seeing anybody and maybe I was misleading him or whatever about my marital status, so when he came to pick me up I told him that I was still married and not legally separated yet and that maybe we shouldn't go out because of that but he said we might as well have dinner together anyway because he didn't like to eat at restaurants all alone, and then he took me home and he didn't come inside the house or make any advances either so that was the end of it, that's all that happened."

"And you probably complained to him about what a nasty husband you have," Don said when she ran out of breath.

"No, I didn't. All I said about you was how sorry I was about being separated from you. Most of the time Roland was talking about what he wants to do after he quits the job he has now."

"What does he do, anyway?"

She sighed. "He's a performer in Strut My Stuff."

Don groaned. "Oh, Jesus. You went out with a male stripper?"

"It's not what it sounds like," she insisted. "They don't take everything off."

"And I suppose you'd think it was just fine and dandy if I was going out with some babe who was the centerfold in *Playboy*."

"That isn't the same," she said.

"No, it couldn't be," Don muttered.

"Besides, it won't be any of my business who you go out with if we're separated. Anyway, I'm not going out with Roland—I told you. That's the only date we'll ever have, if you can even call it a date."

The voices outside had risen in volume. She went to the window and peered through the slight opening between the curtains. Caterina stood in the center of the street, surrounded by people, while a man and a woman with microphones and a third woman with a pad and pen pushed their way toward her. One of the cameramen had climbed onto the roof of the WOOW van, while the other roamed at the edges of the crowd.

"Caterina's out in front of the house," she said, seeing the vet gesture with her arms as the microphones pointed in her direction. "She looks like she's giving an interview," she continued, "or a speech." Caterina turned, shook back her long black hair, and waved a hand in Gena's direction, then began to make her way toward the house. "I'd better be ready to let her in."

She hurried to the front door. "Look at them," she heard Caterina say in a loud voice. "Just look at how well-groomed and obviously healthy they are. They can't possibly be wild feral cats, and at the moment they're not causing any trouble outside of attracting crowds, so I suggest that you all just go home and leave them undisturbed."

"Can't just leave them there," a man's voice said. "Aren't they what you'd consider to be a whaddiyacallit—a public nuisance?"

"I suppose so," Caterina replied, "but somebody could say the same thing about all of you, couldn't they? Couldn't we all be doing something a bit more constructive? You, there—you could run photos of these cats in your newspaper with a phone number so their owners can contact you.

And you should tape some footage for an announcement on your next news broadcast. The rest of you could post some photos on Facebook or videos on YouTube or whatever. And if that doesn't smoke out some of the people who belong to these cats, you might at least get some volunteers offering to adopt them. And I'd be more than happy to offer my services as their vet."

Gena heard footsteps outside the front door. She looked through the peephole, then quickly pulled the door open. Caterina's back was to her, and several people, including the reporters, stood on the pathway leading up to the front steps. On either side of the pathway sat rows of cats, their eyes focused on Caterina.

Gena tapped the veterinarian on the shoulder. Caterina jumped, then turned to hurry inside. Gena slammed the door just as the reporters were coming toward the steps.

"I don't believe it," Caterina gasped. Gena ignored the pounding on the door as she took Caterina's coat, hung it in the closet, and then led her into the living room. "I really thought you were exaggerating when you told me how many cats you had hanging around here."

"You should have come to the back door," Don said. Vladimir sat up on the sofa and squinted at Caterina. "I warned you that you might have to sneak through our neighbors' yards."

"Well, hello." Caterina crept over to Vladimir and chucked him under the chin. The cat purred so loudly that Gena could hear him from the other side of the room. "Hello to you, Vladimir, you naughty little boy. I'm glad to see that you finally came to your senses and returned to your people, you bad, bad boy." Vladimir's purrs were rapidly approaching the decibel level of a good-sized motorboat engine. "I don't suppose you have anything to do with all those cats outside, now do you?"

"I don't think so," Don said.

"I don't, either." Caterina sat down next to Vladimir and scratched him behind the ears. "Well, I have to admit one thing. Weird as all of this is, it might be a public relations coup for me. I made sure that those reporters got my name right, I even spelled it for them just to make sure. WKTG has higher ratings than WOOW, but between the two of them they get the lion's share of the local news viewers, so it doesn't matter all that much that WSIG isn't out there. Anybody who hasn't heard of Caterina Lucci the cat doctor before will be well aware of me after watching the evening news, and what's even better is that all of these cats turned up at the home of my newly hired office manager."

Don sighed. "I suppose you told them that, too."

"That I just hired Gena? Of course. I didn't miss a trick." Caterina offered the brightest of smiles. "I couldn't have paid for that kind of publicity."

"Maybe it won't be such great publicity," Don said, "especially if animal control starts getting on our case."

"Animal control." Caterina sniffed. "If you ask me, what this town needs is less animal control and more people control." She sat back as Vladimir took possession of her lap. "But I have to admit that you have a very unusual situation here. Those cats outside are definitely not feral cats. They don't seem wild at all. If anything, they're domestic almost to a fault—domestic, apparently well-trained, and organized, too, which is bizarre for such individualistic animals as cats. As soon as I came toward your front door, they moved back to allow me a path, and they were extremely orderly about it, too. I've never seen anything like it."

For a moment, Gena was tempted to tell Caterina about the world of cats she and Don had concocted together, about her suspicions that the cats surrounding their house had some connection with their invented Catalonia. But she couldn't do that, and not just because the vet would think that Gena had completely lost her marbles. She would also be betraying Don and the imaginary refuge they had created for themselves if she revealed Catalonia's existence to others. Somehow, in a way she did not completely comprehend, she was growing more convinced that she and Don were completely responsible for creating this odd and vaguely threatening situation, and wondered if anyone else could help them resolve it.

Caterina gently picked up Vladimir from her lap and moved him to her right. "Do you mind if I take a look out back?" she asked.

"Not at all," Don said. "You won't even have to go outside. You can see plenty of cats from the back door and from the window over the sink."

He got up and led Caterina toward the kitchen. Gena followed, with Vladimir padding along beside her. Don drew back the window curtain and stood next to Caterina as she looked outside.

"Wow," Caterina said. "They've taken over the whole yard."

"And most of the driveway," Don said.

"A couple of Persians, three Himalayans, and there's a Siamese and a Manx. Some of those cats could be best of show in a competition. Amazing that anybody owning them wouldn't have taken more precautions to keep them from escaping."

"There's a few more tabbies out there now," Don said, "and I—" He looked back at Gena. She saw apprehension in his widened eyes before he looked away.

Gena went to the window; Don moved aside. Two cats sat in the midst of the feline crowd, encircled by the others yet separated from them by a small grassy space. One was a long-haired cat with pale golden fur; the other was a small and sleek black cat with large hazel eyes.

Nicholas and Alexandra, Gena thought wildly.

She glanced at Don, who was looking at her, and she knew that he was thinking the same thing.

"Did you see them before?" Gena said very softly. "The two cats in the middle, I mean."

"I know which ones you mean," Don replied, "and no, I didn't see them there before. And I think I would have noticed them even if I was in kind of a rush."

"Well, they would have to come and go," Caterina said, "if only to eat and take a dump. They haven't been digging up your yard to bury turds, and I have no idea what they're using for food, so they must be dealing with all of their bodily functions and physical demands elsewhere. But where would they go? I don't suppose they could be starting to move into your neighbors' yards, could they?"

"I don't know," Don said. "I sure as hell hope not."

"Curioser and curioser," Caterina murmured. "Cats breaking out of shelters, a mob of cats that are obviously not of the stray or feral variety showing up here—" She shook her head. "I'd better go and find out if these cats are beginning to invade any adjoining territories. You two should probably stay inside if you don't want to deal with those reporters."

Gena was as worried about her neighbors as the reporters, but didn't feel up to dealing with either. "Go ahead," she said as the vet retreated from the door. Caterina was probably looking forward to getting more face time on the newscasts and more free advertising for her practice.

"I'll let myself out." Caterina was already heading toward the front of the house, Vladimir at her heels.

"Don't let Vladimir out, too," Don called after her.

"I won't," she called back. Gena heard the front door slam shut. She stood with Don for a long time in silence as they continued to stare at the cats in the back yard.

"It's Nicholas and Alexandra," he whispered at last.

"I know."

The two cats sat in the grass, still as statues, surrounded by those who had to be their loyal subjects.

"And somehow I don't find their presence reassuring," she added.

She thought of the dream that had come to her last night, of the cats she had seen on top of her bed. She struggled to recall the earlier part of that dream, but remembered only that she had sensed a threat, that there seemed to be some disagreement among the cats in her dream. Something involving a mysterious antagonist of the cats had been part of her reverie, but she couldn't quite get a handle on that detail. Some of the cats had wanted to preserve their world by appealing to their creators, and others had been asking if disposing of their creators might accomplish the same end.

She tensed with fear.

"They don't want us to separate," Don said, "because that would destroy Catalonia. There is a kind of logic to that."

"That's what we have to do, then, reconcile." She backed away from the window and sat down at the kitchen table as Vladimir wandered back into the kitchen. "I'm willing to apologize and forget everything that happened. We'll put it all behind us." Saying such apologetic words wasn't quite as difficult as she had expected, and she was willing to sacrifice every last scrap of her pride for a reconciliation; it was becoming increasingly harder to recall all of the details of their fight anyway. "We'll make a fresh start."

"Maybe you're right," Don said, but he was not sounding all that contrite. He crossed the room and seated himself across from her. "It won't happen again, I'll make sure it doesn't happen again. I won't be so careless this time." The pitch of his voice was dropping. "Everything will be under control, under my control. I'm not about to let a bunch of cats control me, or anything else control me. And you'll do as I say as long as you live here, and if you're not willing to do that, you had better leave now, or I won't answer for anything I might do."

The room felt colder now.

"Stop it," she said. "That isn't you talking, it's Household."

"Mroow!" Vladimir howled, his ears back.

"And that goes double for you, buddy," Don replied. "You'll be lucky if I don't scare you away from this house again."

"Stop it!" Gena shouted, rising to her feet. "Don't let it—"

"Gena." His voice was weak; his face contorted. His eyes were now looking at her with his more familiar kindly but bewildered gaze. "I'm all right. Can't remember, but it must have—" He covered his forehead with one hand.

The doorbell was ringing. She hurried from the kitchen to the front door.

Caterina was back. Gena let her in. "The cats haven't invaded your neighbors' yards," Caterina said, "and the crowd's thinning out, so maybe you'll finally get a little peace and quiet. I don't know if there's much I can do here."

"Thanks for coming over anyway," Gena said.

"The only advice I can give you is to stay inside and watch for any changes in the behavior of those cats. If you notice anything out of the ordinary—"

"Isn't this already out of the ordinary?"

"I meant anything that's even more out of the ordinary." The vet rummaged in her purse, pulled out a business card and a pen, and scribbled something on the back of the card before handing it to Gena. "Here's my cell phone number. If you need to get hold of me later, just call and I'll get back to you as soon as I can."

"Thanks."

Caterina let herself out and closed the door.

It did seem to be quieter outside. Gena returned to the living room and peeked through the crack between the window curtains to see a police car at the corner. The WKTG van had already left, and it looked as though the WOOW team was packing up their equipment. Some people still loitered in the street, but most of the others had drifted away. She tensed, worried that the police might pay her and Don a visit, and then the police car made a U-turn and disappeared down Ackley Avenue.

Her hand dropped from the curtains. As she moved toward the kitchen, the house seemed to grow colder and darker.

Household was fighting back. Maybe it wouldn't stop at trying to take possession of Don. Maybe it was preparing to attack her in some other way. She entered the kitchen almost expecting a mustachioed geezer wearing a top hat and clutching moneybags to take physical form in front of her, ready to strike. A briefcase and a bag full of coins would make good weapons.

"But this isn't about money," she heard herself say aloud, "not really." Her voice was coming from somewhere outside herself. "That's just what it's using to make itself known, all your worries and fears about scrimping and saving and barely getting by and living the way your parents did. That's what it's using against you. And we're not the only ones it's fighting. The cats—"

"What are you talking about?" Don stared at her in puzzlement.

"Don't you feel it?" But the kitchen was warm again, the cold presence of Household gone, at least for now.

"What's going on outside?" he asked.

"Most of the crowd's gone. There was a police car outside but it left. The TV crews are leaving, too."

"This is going to cost us," he murmured, "I just know it. Those cats are going to take over the neighborhood, and we'll end up with people suing us for damages or getting after us for harboring a public nuisance because the cats showed up on our property first." He spoke in a more muted manner now, nothing like Household's voice.

"Caterina didn't see them around anyone else's house. The crowd's leaving now, and the TV crews, and maybe the cats will leave, too. Maybe they'll all head back to Catalonia." She tried to smile.

"If people are leaving," he said, "I might as well go get my car."

She could not sense any strange unseen presence inside the house now; even Vladimir was chomping away at his food, seemingly oblivious to anything else. But this had to be a temporary armistice of some kind, with Household only waiting for a better chance to attack.

Twenty

After Don left, Gena put on her jacket, slipped her keys into a pocket, and went out the back door to observe the cats at closer range. The ones on the steps drew back to allow her passage, then regrouped behind her. There did not seem to be quite as many in the back yard, but the ones that remained milled around restlessly. She did not see the small black cat and her golden-furred companion; Nicholas and Alexandra, or their counterparts, had vanished.

She walked down the driveway to the sidewalk. Cats paced back and forth as if on guard. The street was empty, although she was certain that some of her neighbors were still watching from inside their houses.

The sky was getting darker; a streetlight winked on. A rumble in her stomach reminded her that it was getting close to dinnertime. She wondered how the local news broadcasts would deal with the cats and the crowds, whether the story would be just a snippet or a major human interest piece, and decided not to watch the news that evening. Maybe she and Don would luck out, and the story wouldn't air at all.

"Gena!" Rita Seligman suddenly appeared from behind the hedge on the other side of the driveway. "I phoned you twice, but you never got back to me."

"Sorry," Gena mumbled.

"Exactly what do you and Don intend to do about these cats?"

Three gray-furred cats and one long-haired cat with white fur took up positions between Gena and the older woman, as though creating a barrier.

"Well," Gena began, "Don talked to the city animal control guy this afternoon, and he told Don he'd look into it. And my vet was here this afternoon, and she says they aren't really doing any harm and don't seem to be bothering anybody else in the neighborhood."

"Your vet?" Mrs. Seligman raised her eyebrows.

"Caterina Lucci—she's Vladimir's vet. You know, Vladimir, our cat—or maybe you don't remember him. He ran away not long after we moved in and went to live at our old landlord's place. He finally came back home a couple of days ago."

"About when all these cats showed up."

Gena nodded.

"Do you think your cat could have anything to do with this?"

"Oh, I don't see how he could."

Mrs. Seligman looked down at the four cats that sat between her and Gena. "You never know with cats. They're such strange creatures."

Don's Toyota rolled down the street toward them. "There's Don," Gena said, anxious to escape from her neighbor. "He had to park his car a few blocks away while that crowd was still here. I'd better go—it's almost time to make supper."

"About time for the news, too," Mrs. Seligman murmured. "That's all we need, being on the news and then having even more sightseers showing up to take a gander at all your cats."

Gena stepped aside as Don pulled into the driveway. "See you," she said to the other woman, then hurried toward Don. The cats had not only vacated most of the driveway, but had also made space enough on one side so that Don could get out of his car without any obstruction.

She walked toward him. The cats were gathering again, pushing nearer to them, giving them both the stare. "They seem jumpier," Don said to her in a whisper.

"I know." She looped her arm through his as they approached the back door, then pulled out her keys. "Maybe that means they're getting ready to move on. Maybe everything we're imagining about them is completely wrong, and there's a perfectly reasonable explanation for all this."

Inside, the kitchen light was still on, and Vladimir was still munching on his food. "I need a drink," Don said.

"There's some beer left," Gena replied as she closed the door, "or wine if you prefer, and we still have some Scotch."

"Guess I'll have a beer." He sat down at the table. "All those cats aren't even our worst problem at the moment," he said wearily. "If I still had my job, maybe they'd just be a minor annoyance."

Gena brought him a bottle of beer and sat down across from him. "You know you never liked that job. How many times have you told me that you hated it?"

"It was a lot easier to hate it when I still had it."

"Look, I'll be getting a fresh start with my job for Caterina, so you can get a fresh start, too."

Don swallowed some beer, looking even more depressed. "Yeah—a job with no benefits and no room for advancement."

"It's a big improvement over the job I had before. At least I can get up in the morning and look forward to going to the office. At least I can live with myself." And maybe with you, she did not say.

"You can live with yourself as long as Caterina does well in her practice, and if I don't find something soon, neither one of us'll have any benefits."

This whole conversation was threatening to degenerate into a discussion of one of Household's favorite topics. "Look," she started to say as the phone rang. She glanced at it but stayed in her chair.

"You'd better take that," Don said. "It might be important."

Gena got up and picked up the receiver, sighing as she recognized the number. "Hello?"

"Eugenia," her mother's voice said, "the urgent care people told me I'm fine, but now I'm really worried about you. What on earth is going on over there? We turn on the news to see Donald hiding his face and running away from a news crew and even more cats around your house than I saw there this morning. What are you going to do about it?"

Gena sighed. "I don't know, Mom."

"WKTG must have given that story a whole two minutes at least. That's more than they gave the president's press conference. I'm surprised you weren't recording the news."

"We don't have to, Mom. We're right in the middle of it."

"What are you going to do?"

"I wish I knew."

"I mean, surely they can't stay there. Surely animal control—"

"We already heard from animal control," Gena said, "but right now, the cats aren't really causing that much trouble. The crowds are gone, and Caterina Lucci, you know, our vet, was over here to check things out, and she—"

"Oh, yes," her mother interrupted. "I saw her on the news. You would have thought she was the star of the show."

"Anyway, please don't worry about us." Gena wandered toward the back door and peered outside. In the shadows of evening, she could see only about forty cats. Perhaps they would leave. Perhaps she would wake up tomorrow with only relatively normal problems to face. "Maybe the cats will all just go away."

"But they'll have to go somewhere. I should think—"

"Mom, we'll be all right, really. I have to get dinner ready now."

"Oh. Of course." Mrs. Lawlor's voice dropped to a lower and more conspiratorial pitch. "Have you and Donald patched things up, dear?"

"I don't know." Gena wandered out of the kitchen and into the dining room. She whispered, "Maybe things'll work out."

"Well, I'll keep my fingers crossed. That veterinarian was talking about finding homes for all those cats. I couldn't bear the thought of having another cat after Cameron's passing, but time does heal such wounds, and it would be nice to have a cat or two around the house again."

"I'll let you know what's going on, Mom." Gena went back to the kitchen. "Bye."

* * * *

Gena made a salad to go with the microwaved leftover pizza. By the time she had the food on the dining room table, two more phone calls had come in, one from Don's former supervisor Larry and the other from a neighbor named Phil. She let Don take the calls, which seemed to be mostly questions about the local news stories and the cats.

He was silent as they ate. She tried to concentrate on her food, afraid that saying anything would only provoke another discussion that might give Household an opening. Maybe Don was thinking about how to handle Household and also assure the cats surrounding the house that Catalonia was in no danger. The entire situation was insane. How did you get rid of a malevolent spirit that could take over and control other people, however briefly and intermittently? How did you communicate with cats that presumably had arrived here from some fabulous elsewhere?

Toward the end of the meal, Vladimir padded out from the kitchen and sat down near the table, obviously looking for a handout. "No pizza for you," Don said to the cat. "It's not good for you, anyway."

"Mrrow," Vladimir replied.

"I have to say something," Gena said. "To you," she added, in case Don thought she might be preparing to address Vladimir. "I told you I was sorry, and what I'm sorriest about is the cruel things I said to you." She took a deep breath and plunged in, hoping that he would not interrupt her. "I think we can work things out, I damn well hope we can work things out, but one thing I won't do is spend the rest of my life arguing with you over Household or finances or who's in charge of what or any of that stuff again. I'll do the best I can, and try to be more practical, but I'm not going to have nitpicky concerns about all that crap ruin my life. And maybe working for Caterina isn't very lucrative, but at least I'll be able to look forward to my job and feel as though I'm helping people, or helping their cats anyway, and that's worth more to me than money."

She waited, not knowing what to expect. Some sort of apotheosis, at the very least, some sign that Household was at last vanquished and that the cats outside would now go back to their homeland, although the details of exactly how the cats would go about embarking on such a return voyage eluded her.

"Are you saying all of that because you really want to patch things up," Don said, "or just because all this weird shit is coming down and you're afraid to face it alone?"

Both hypothetical motives had something to do with it, but she couldn't very well admit to that. Before she could say anything at all, the telephone rang. She decided to let the machine take it, then heard Tracey Birnbaum's voice on the speaker.

"Gena, are you there? This is Tracey."

Gena sighed and hurried into the kitchen. "I saw the news," Tracey went on, "I couldn't believe it. All those cats! At first I didn't know what to think and then—"

Gena picked up the phone. "I'm here, Tracey."

"Good, because I've got some news for you, but first things first. I saw Don on the news, too—are you guys back together?"

"I don't know," Gena said in a whisper.

"Well, I hope you resolve your issues. Anyway, after I watched the news, I called Shauna Leopold. We'd been planning to touch base soon anyway, get together to bat around some ideas."

"Shauna Leopold?" Gena said.

"You know, the children's book author, the one who wants me to illustrate her books and do the paintings for her calendars. The one who writes about this imaginary world made up of cats. So I called her, and it turns out that she was about to call me. Apparently CNN picked up the story about you and all the cats that are so mysteriously camped out around your house."

Gena felt stunned and disoriented. "CNN?" she asked.

"It was only a snippet, maybe ten or twenty seconds, but it was enough to light a fire under Shauna when she remembered that I live here. She's just dying to check things out, so she asked me to make a reservation at a local hotel for her. We're coming over to your place tomorrow."

"Tomorrow?"

"She's driving up from Manhattan tonight, so she can get a good night's sleep and be at her best. She's already got her publicist lining up a couple of local interviews, and I'm pretty sure I can get a photographer at the *Times-Tribune* to shoot her with all the cats."

"With the cats? You mean the cats around my house?"

"Hello! Of course the cats around your house. You have to admit that it would make a great jacket photo."

"Tracey," Gena said, "I don't know if that's such a good idea. There's something really weird about those cats."

"Well, I know that. I could see that on the news."

Gena searched for words, trying to think of how to keep her friend from coming over. "I don't even know if the cats will still be hanging around here tomorrow. Already I don't see quite as many of them outside as there were before, and if they're still here in the morning, animal control's probably going to come after them."

"Well, Shauna's driving up, and at the very least it gives us a chance to schmooze in person, which can't hurt. And Caterina Lucci said something on the news about hiring you."

"I'm going to be her office manager," Gena said.

"I have to admit, connections with some cat people won't hurt me with Shauna. I'll try to call tomorrow before I bring her over, and we won't show up at the crack of dawn. Don't worry about entertaining her or anything, she'll be there mainly to check out the cats and maybe do a photo shoot, so you don't have to go to any trouble."

"I still think—"

"I hope things work out with Don."

"I hope so, too."

"See you." Tracey hung up.

Gena went back into the living room. Don looked up at her. "I'd better call Jeff," he said. "He was expecting me back at his place tonight."

Gena's heart fluttered. Was Don actually ready to reconcile?

"I mean," Don went on, "that I might as well stay here until we figure out what we're going to do."

"About all the cats?" She tried not to sound too anxious.

"About all those cats and about ourselves." He looked down. "We've got to think this through. First is that all those cats being out there is just some kind of weird natural phenomenon with a rational explanation, and we're spooking ourselves for no reason."

"But what about Nicholas and Alexandra?" she objected. "You saw them, too."

"What I saw was two cats that match the way we imagine Nicholas and Alexandra look. Anyway, consider the possibility that those cats have nothing to do with Catalonia. That's what any sane person would think."

"And what about Household?" she whispered.

"Even Household could probably be explained. The human mind can invent all kinds of weird stuff under stress."

She nodded.

"Or we're both completely nuts, which would account for Household, but not for the cats. I mean, everybody else in town can see the cats, unless we're hallucinating all of that, too, and that isn't likely. And maybe those cats really are from Catalonia, or from some place so much like what we dreamed up together that it's a distinction without a difference."

"And if they're here to save Catalonia," Gena said, "then they ought to leave if we get back together, because they'll know—"

"Know what? That we got back together because we're afraid of what they might do? How could they even be sure we'd stay together? Maybe it's gone too far for that, maybe they don't know if they can ever trust us again. Anyway, what kind of basis is that for a relationship, being forced back together by a horde of cats that might decide to show up again out of nowhere if we ever have another major disagreement? We'd be letting those cats run our lives, never to be masters of our own fate again."

"Does it matter?" Gena asked, knowing that it did.

"It does to me. And it probably wouldn't solve the problem of Household anyway. Remember, nobody besides us has seen or encountered what we think of as Household." He stared at his empty plate. "I'll get out the cot and sleep in the office tonight," he said, "just so you don't think—"

"You won't be very comfortable."

"It beats the hell out of sleeping on Jeff's sofa, which reminds me—I'd better call him." He stood up. "Thanks for fixing dinner."

She had an impulse to burst into tears, tell him that she didn't care whether or not a multitude of cats was responsible for any reconciliation, as long as they were back together. Instead, she began to clear the table, methodically, as she had seen Don do it.

Twenty-One

"I saw the news," Jeff said over the phone, "so I figured you might be staying over there tonight."

"Gena shouldn't have to deal with this alone," Don said. "Besides, we still haven't decided who stays in the house if we do break up. And everything that's happening is just going to make it even more impossible to sell later on."

"I wouldn't worry about it. A month from now, nobody'll even remember your cat infestation."

"Unless this is a sign of something else," Don said. "Maybe it's the first sign of an environmental catastrophe."

"I doubt it. This doesn't seem connected to anything else. I did an online search and the story about cats at your house was the only story like that I found."

"Anyway, I'm stuck here until we resolve this cat issue one way or another."

"Well, good luck," Jeff said, "and maybe you and Gena'll patch things up. By the way, thanks for coming downtown and helping out. If you feel up to it tomorrow, we'll be down at headquarters again in the afternoon. You could come over here first, or we could stop by my place afterwards if you want to pick up your stuff."

"I'll think about it," Don said, "and let you know tomorrow. I can probably come over." He could at least escape his problems for a while.

Jeff hung up. He went back into the kitchen and hung up the phone. Gena had already loaded the dishwasher and was leaning against the sink facing the window, her back to him.

She turned around. "Tracey told me that this writer she's going to be working with wants to drive up from New York to see our cats."

"Our cats." Don shook his head. "So now we're getting sightseers from out of town. I wish I could figure out how to make some money off this. Maybe we should charge admission. Maybe that would satisfy the spirit of Household enough for it to leave us alone." A chill passed over him.

"Tracey said they'd probably come over tomorrow, but not to put ourselves out for them." She sighed. "I'm going upstairs and read until I can fall asleep."

"The cot's still in the basement, isn't it?" he said, and saw a pained look cross her face.

This is ridiculous, he thought. Gena showed every sign of being in the mood tonight. There was no real reason for him not to put the past week behind them and make a fresh start, especially with the strange situation they were facing, yet something still held him back.

"You'll just be postponing the inevitable," something said inside him, "if you give in now without settling some things first. How long do you think it will take before she lapses into her careless and impractical ways? Do you really think you can trust her not to make the same mistakes again?"

Don shuddered, afraid that Household, or whatever the unseen presence might be, was trying to seize control of him again. He knew now that he could not risk going upstairs with Gena. What if it took possession of him while he was in the middle of having sex, when all his inhibitions would be breaking down? He couldn't risk it.

Gena narrowed her eyes. For a moment, she looked afraid of him, and then he realized that she understood the risks to them both. "Maybe I should head over to Jeff's," he whispered.

She shook her head. "We can't keep running away from—" She paused. "The cot's still in the basement," she continued, "with the air mattress, and there are plenty of sheets and a couple of blankets and pillows in the linen closet. Good night." She left the kitchen quickly. Her footsteps sounded clumsy as she went up the stairs.

Vladimir came into the kitchen, ears back. "Hrurr," he said then crept under the kitchen table and glared up with angry green eyes.

"Guess I'd better see what's on TV tonight," Don said to the cat. Better to act normal, he thought. Would that keep Household at bay? "I'll pick something without too many loud sound effects."

Vladimir stretched, then went to the back door and began scratching at it. "Murree?"

"Can't let you out, little buddy," Don replied. "Those cats outside could make mincemeat out of you."

"Murree?" Vladimir sounded more tentative. His usual technique was to increase the volume of his meows and to paw at the door ever more frantically until someone either let him out or distracted him with a bribe of food. Instead, he paced in front of the door, pausing every so often to look up at Don. He could almost believe that the cat was attempting to give him a warning.

"What is it?" Don asked.

"Mrrow."

Don turned the knob and opened the door just a crack, prepared to slam it shut if Vladimir tried to escape. Instead, the cat backed up and then sat down.

"Hrurr," Vladimir said, still staring at the door.

There had been enough times, when he and Gena were still renting from Mr. Bowes, that Vladimir had padded to the door even before the landlord knocked, was first to know when the mail had been delivered, or had sensed that Laurie Lawlor was outside and ready to pay one of her guerrilla ambush visits.

Vladimir was trying to tell him something.

Don closed the door, went to the front of the house, got his coat, made sure his keys were still in the inside front pocket, then returned to the kitchen, where Vladimir was still watching the door. He opened the door again, keeping an eye on Vladimir, but the cat remained where he was.

"Mrrow," Vladimir said, almost as if he were encouraging Don to proceed.

Don slipped outside, then turned to lock the door. The cats on the back steps seemed restless; several of them pressed against his legs as he descended. In the darkness, he glimpsed the glow of several pairs of eyes. There seemed to be fewer cats in the back yard, but they were as restless as the others, masses of moving fur, and he thought he heard a few soft meows.

Someone was shadowing him. He could not escape that feeling, even though a quick glance revealed that no one was behind him.

As he came to the sidewalk, the cats there retreated from him, scurrying away to take up positions at curbside.

Then he noticed two cats across the street, cloaked in shadow. They had appeared there suddenly, or so it seemed, but cats often performed such tricks, appearing out of nowhere when you least expected to see them. Vladimir had pulled such stunts often enough. The two cats padded toward the curb, where the light from one of the streetlights caught them. They were the same pair he and Gena had seen before, in the yard, the golden-furred cat and the black one.

Nicholas and Alexandra.

I'm going crazy, he thought. He crossed the street, then glanced back. The cats were regrouping by the back door and the front stoop, as if to protect the house from intruders, or perhaps to prevent anyone else from going outside.

Why had that thought come to him? He suddenly feared for Gena.

The night was quiet. Apparently most of his neighbors had decided to go to bed early, given that no lights in the nearby houses were on. He turned toward the two strange cats he thought of as Nicholas and Alexandra. They watched him without moving. Something rustled at the edges of his mind. Unreasonably, insanely, he was sure that the two cats were trying to communicate with him.

He heard the screeching of tires before he saw the vehicle. A panel truck came down Bancroft Street and braked to a stop at the side of his house, near the driveway. He watched as two men got out on either side of the vehicle, each of them holding what looked like a cat carrier.

The two strangers crept toward the cats. One of the men was tall and lanky, while the other was built like a beer barrel. Maybe they had come there to pick up a couple of pets for themselves, or maybe they were part of a rumored local gang of dog fight aficionados who allegedly stole small animals to use in training their canine fighters.

"Here, kitty, kitty," one of the men said. They approached his back yard and stopped under the maple tree that stood between Don's property and Mrs. Seligman's. "Here, kitty, kitty."

Don crossed the street. "Guys," he said, "you better stay away from those cats."

"And what's it to you?" the taller man said.

"This happens to be my house, and you're on my property."

"Then maybe we're doing you a favor, taking a coupla these cats off your hands." The man stepped toward him, swinging his carrier.

"That depends on what you plan to do with them." Don stood his ground and ignored the fact that he lacked even the most basic of self-defense skills.

"What we do with them is our business. There's plenty more where they come from."

"Get off my lawn." Don pitched his voice low to sound threatening.

"When we're good and ready," the tall lanky man said, sounding a bit more tentative.

Several of the cats near them went into a crouch. Don heard a rustling sound from the tree limbs overhead. "And maybe I don't feel like leaving without a cat," the shorter man said, in a voice much deeper than that of his companion.

"You're trespassing."

"So we're trespassing." The stocky man's lip curled.

Don took a step toward the back door. "I'll call the police."

"Call the police." The shorter man's voice had dropped even lower. "Won't do you any good," he continued in a deep bass voice. "Go on, throw a punch, and get sued for assault and battery. You can't afford to have anything else go wrong."

Household, Don thought, as the man swung his carrier at Don's head. He threw up an arm, knocking the carrier out of his assailant's hand. The man rushed at him. Don toppled over backwards and quickly rolled to his knees. The man's hands were around his neck; his breath smelled of whiskey.

"You'll never be free of me," said a deep resonant voice. Don struggled to break his grip. "Thought you'd be rid of me, but you've only made me stronger."

He could not breathe. The man's fingers suddenly fell from his neck. He gasped for air as the stocky man danced in front of him. Two cats were on the man's shoulders, clawing at his face.

Don got to his feet. The taller man staggered past him; two cats rode his back while two more clawed at the bottoms of his jeans. "Get the fuck offa me!" the stranger yelled, shaking one of the cats from his leg. "Get 'em offa me!"

His stocky accomplice, now free of his feline assailants, retrieved his carrier and retreated to their vehicle. "Come on!" he shouted back in a tenor voice. "Let's get outa here!" The lanky man stared at Don wildly as the two cats leaped from his shoulders; there were deep scratches on his face. Cats circled him, snarling, ready to attack again. He spun around, grabbed his carrier, and ran toward the truck.

His friend was in the driver's seat, gunning the motor. The lanky man pulled the door open and shoved his friend over, then slammed the door shut. The truck rounded the corner and disappeared down Ackley Avenue before Don could get a good look at its license plate number.

His neck felt bruised. He managed a couple of deep breaths. Household, or whatever the malignancy haunting his house was, could attack him outside his house. It had increased its strength and its range. He wondered how far away he would have to get from the house to be safe. Perhaps there was no refuge for him, if the entity was somehow part of him and might turn his own mind against him without warning. He could not live in constant fear that he might involuntarily do Gena harm, go suddenly berserk like Peter Harman and others who had suddenly killed their wives, or mothers who had murdered their own children. How many Households were able to torment and take possession of those whose fears they could exploit and who were susceptible to their commands?

The street was now very quiet. Either his neighbors hadn't heard a thing or anyone who had was afraid to intervene. He looked across the street, but the two cats he thought of as Nicholas and Alexandra were no longer there.

The cats in the yard were still pacing restlessly. "Thanks, guys," he said, but the animals did not seem to care. Several of them were even eyeing him with narrowed eyes and baring their teeth. One of the cats meowed, and then another.

A phalanx of cats rushed at him, claws out; he felt sharp pricks along his calves as they grabbed at his pants. He stumbled toward the back door as another cat grabbed at his hand, sinking its teeth into him. He flailed around, shaking them off, and fumbled for the keys in his pocket.

Somehow he managed to get the door open. He lunged inside, hearing a high sharp shriek as he slammed the door shut. Vladimir was still in the kitchen, stretched out under the table, his ears back and his claws out.

Don gazed at Vladimir, who stared back impassively. The sense of foreboding he had felt earlier was creeping into him again, the feeling of impending doom, the fear that he would never have a normal life again.

* * * *

He found a first aid kit, a bottle of hydrogen peroxide, and a tube of antibiotic ointment in the small half-bathroom off the kitchen. The feline attackers had left puncture marks in his jeans, but his legs showed only a few faint reddish marks. He washed the minor wounds off with hydrogen peroxide anyway. There were some fingertip-sized red marks on his neck; he swabbed them down, then slapped antibiotic ointment on his injuries just to be on the safe side. Apparently he had not sustained any serious battle wounds.

He went back into the kitchen and sat down in the chair where he had left his coat. He had to control himself. He had to think things through rationally. Two guys who were presumably up to no good and probably drunk besides had come by to steal a couple of cats, but he had managed to scare them off. The cats occupying his yard, which had to be suffering from lack of food or water by now, since there were no provisions, had come after him out of desperation or fear. That was the way a sane person might regard what had just happened. And even if he assumed that Household had been his first assailant, taking over one of the catnappers and using that man as its weapon, why would the cats, which had up to now been a fairly benign if somewhat problematic presence, attack him?

The cats had concluded that getting rid of him was the only way to save themselves and remove the threat that Household posed to them.

"Mrree," Vladimir said from under the table.

He got up and crossed the kitchen to the open doorway that led to the basement. As he looked down the darkened stairwell, he shivered, suddenly afraid to go down there.

He flicked on the light and crept down the stairs, passing Vladimir's litter box and then the washer and dryer. The cot was propped up against a wall next to their small shelf of canned goods. He reached for the cot and heard scraping at the basement window just above him.

Don looked up and met two pairs of glowing eyes. In the light shining through the window from the basement's overhead fluorescent bulbs, he recognized Nicholas and Alexandra. The cats scratched again. Don backed away, grabbed the cot with both hands, and fled through the basement and up the stairs, banging the cot's edges against the walls.

* * * *

He sat in the living room in front of the TV, drinking his fourth beer of the evening. While making up the bed in his office, he had stopped himself from crossing the hall to the bedroom to wake Gena. She would be safer behind the closed door.

Household was after them; he could feel it. Gena thought that Household might be trying to control others, but apparently it hadn't been able to take her over, at least not yet. Maybe her basic outlook on everything was so antithetical to Household's that it had failed to dominate her. Others would have to be its weapons, Don among them.

Steady, he told himself. In an effort to distract himself, he had just finished watching a DVD of "Back to School" with Rodney Dangerfield, a movie usually just about guaranteed to crack him up, without emitting a single chuckle. Vladimir, curled up at the other end of the sofa, stared at the screen as if the whole idea of Rodney Dangerfield, or movies in general, deeply offended him. Usually he slept through whatever Don happened to be watching, or retreated upstairs if the sound was too loud, but the cat had stayed wide awake this time.

Don switched channels with his remote and found himself watching WKTG's "News at Eleven." There he was running into his house looking guilty as hell; there was Caterina mouthing off and promoting herself and her practice; then came a pan of all the cats along the sidewalk and the ones occupying their yard, followed by the face of the reporter while he yakked at his unseen audience and then another long shot of the cats.

He finished his beer, wondering if he should have another or call it a day. Maybe the cats, by some miracle, would be gone by tomorrow and his life could get back to normal, meaning only having to worry about finding another job and about what was going to happen to his marriage and his house.

"You have to start considering practicalities," a deep voice said from inside him. "Find a new position and start laying something aside."

Vladimir leaped from the sofa, arching his back as he landed on the floor. "Mrrow." He flattened his ears and showed his teeth. "Hrurr."

"Settle everything tomorrow." Don somehow felt that he was becoming cold and malign as the voice continued to murmur. "Get your life back on track without impracticalities slowing you down and a lot of silly delusions holding you back." It would almost be a relief to be free of Gena, and of Catalonia, for that matter. Nothing would ever be right for him again unless he closed himself off from anything that might threaten his material security and well-being. That was the secret of life, a refusal to heed anything that got in his way. He might as well give in; it was pointless to fight, especially now that he knew how vulnerable he was. He would force Gena out of this place, scare her away if necessary. He would hang on to this house and wall himself off from anyone who might threaten his hard-won security.

Vladimir leaped into his lap and pawed at his chest. Then Don heard a high-pitched scream from upstairs.

He jumped to his feet as Vladimir leaped to the floor.

"Gena!" he shouted. He raced for the stairs, bounded up them two at a time, and pushed the bedroom door open.

The night light was on. Gena was sitting up in bed, still screaming. Don slapped on the overhead light and hurried to her side. "Gena!" She stared at him with a wild look in her eyes. "Gena!" He grabbed her by the arms. "What is it?"

"The cats!" she cried.

"What cats?"

She squinted at him, then shook her head. He sat down on the bed facing her and took hold of her hands.

"They were on the bed and all over the room, hundreds of them." She freed herself from him and stretched out again. "And I heard them, what they were thinking. They were after me, to kill me, to get rid of us both because it was the only way they could save themselves."

He shuddered, thinking of the cats that had come after him, of how merciless the look in their eyes had been. He had no doubt that a good-sized group of even the smaller cats could bring him down as easily as a pride of lions going after a gazelle, and just a few of the little guys could probably inflict some serious damage. He decided not to tell her about what had happened to him outside.

"It was so real," Gena continued. "I can't remember it all, but they were saying something about taking their fate into their own hands."

Don tried to smile. "You mean into their own paws." She gave him a blank stare. "That makes a kind of sense, I suppose. They can't count on us to preserve Catalonia any more, if you want to put it that way."

Her fingers dug into his arm. "I'm really scared now."

He sat with her for a long time in silence, then said, "Okay now?"

"I think so."

"Want me to go downstairs and make you a cup of tea? That might help you get back to sleep."

She released his arm. "I'm afraid to go back to sleep. But I could use some tea."

"I'll go get it."

"Don't turn out the light."

"I won't."

He plumped up the pillows under her head, then left the room. Vladimir was sitting just outside the door; he followed Don down the stairs and to the kitchen. The cats of Catalonia could no longer trust in the bond between him and Gena to preserve their existence; that was the message of her dream, if in fact it was a message. He filled their small kettle with water and put it on the stove, wondering if making up with Gena and abandoning any divorce plans would be enough to ward off attacks from Catalonia.

He did not want to be without her. He suddenly despised the pettiness and superficiality displayed by their recent arguments.

"I'm a sap," he said to Vladimir, who sat calmly by his bowls. Somehow, admitting to his sappiness aloud made him feel a little more optimistic. "What it all comes down to is that I still love Gena."

"Mrrow," Vladimir replied.

"Whatever faults she has, she's the only person I could ever be myself with, who I didn't have to put up a front with."

Vladimir seemed to agree.

"You're mistaken," a voice rumbled as the overhead light dimmed.

"No," Don said. His rational mind insisted that only a madman's logic would tell him that the cats outside were after him because he had brought the malevolent presence he thought of as Household into existence, that only a complete renunciation of that entity could save him and Gena. Very well; he would accept the insane logic.

"You can't live without me," Don whispered, and laughed. Vladimir hunkered down, flicking his tail from side to side. "The more I gave in to you, the stronger you got. Maybe you were always here, waiting for some way you could control me, and the more you played on my fears, the more I was willing to let you dominate me. That's over—I'm telling you that right now. This is it."

The light above him brightened; the kitchen felt warm and cozy again. He suddenly felt foolish, standing there and talking to himself. The kettle suddenly whistled at him. He took it off the stove and began to make Gena her tea.

But he had the feeling that this wasn't the end of his battle. Always at the bottom of his concern over financial security had been a fear that he could not allow himself to be dependent on anyone, that he had to be ready to face the world alone, that he was safe only behind a barrier between him and everyone else. He was caught in a situation that he would have to handle by himself, with no help from anyone else.

He stared at the tea as it steeped, feeling defeated again, then removed the teabag, stirred in a spoonful of sugar, picked up the cup, and left the kitchen.

Twenty-Two

Gena awoke to the aroma of coffee. She lay unmoving, surprised that she had slept.

Don had sat with her after bringing her tea. Vladimir had followed him upstairs, hopped onto the bed, and started purring, as if to reassure them that no malign spirit was haunting them, at least for now. Don had been ready to go across the hall to his office to sleep, but she insisted that she did not want to be alone and that she probably wouldn't be able to sleep anyway. So he stayed with her, lying down on the other side of the bed on top of the coverlet, saying little as she talked of how sorry she was for what had happened. Whatever was ahead, she would face it with him.

"Let's face it," she had told him, "I'm kind of a fraud." Don had objected. "No, it's true. I've been playacting at being an equal partner when the whole time I was basically counting on you or my parents or someone else to be there if I messed up."

"Maybe I was playacting, too," he said. "We should decide things together, but what I really wanted was to make all the decisions and have you agree with them."

"Is that really what you want?"

"No, not any more."

"Well, it isn't the way I want things, either."

She could not recall falling asleep, and didn't even know if Don had remained at her side throughout the night or had finally retreated to the cot across the hall.

Something was after them both; that had been part of her nightmare. But she could no longer remember much except that the dream had frightened her badly. Cats had invaded a house that had resembled her own, but with rooms that opened up at odd angles and long dark passageways. She had been running to hide from the cats, getting lost in long twisting underground tunnels that suddenly released her into green hills or darkened forests that seemed both familiar and yet alien.

She felt a sudden movement against her feet and sat up. Vladimir was pawing at the coverlet near her ankles.

"Gena," Don's voice called out. Footsteps sounded on the stairs. "Are you awake?"

"I'm awake."

"Good, because it's almost nine-thirty, and I made breakfast." He poked his head inside the door. "Actually, I went shopping for it and then came home to heat it up, but it's ready. Spinach and mushroom quiche, bacon, and blueberry muffins—how does that sound?"

"Very unhealthy and extremely delicious."

"Come on down, then." He disappeared, and her heart leaped. Surely he wouldn't have brought home such a bountiful breakfast if he still wanted a separation. Or maybe he was trying to soften the blow.

Gena put on her robe, quickly ran her fingers through her hair, and got out of bed. Her two china cats, the miniature Alexandra and her mate Nicholas, were still in the top dresser drawer. She opened the drawer and dug around in the layers of nightclothing until her hand closed around the china cats. She gazed at them, then put them on top of the dresser next to each other, feeling that she was making a symbolic gesture of sorts to appease the spirits.

Vladimir leaped from the bed and followed her out of the room and down the stairs. Don had laid out the breakfast on the dining room table. He came out from the kitchen with two mugs of coffee as she sat down.

She sipped coffee, then peered at her husband.

"What's up?" she asked at last.

"Well, first of all, there was a special on the bacon and the muffins. Not that I wouldn't have bought them anyway." He helped himself to a piece of bacon. "And luckily I was able to get in and out of the supermarket without anybody saying they saw me on the news. And, finally, I made a decision last night."

Gena put her fork down and stared at her quiche.

"I don't want to argue about household expenses any more," Don continued, "never again, I swear to God. You handle your money, I'll handle mine, and we'll work out whatever expenses need to be taken care of as we go along on a whoever-can-better-afford-it basis." He heaved a sigh. "I don't want to lose you, even if that means ending up in the poorhouse."

"You're saying that now," she said, "but you might change your mind later."

"I mean it. You know, I never could stand control freaks, and maybe that was because I'm one myself. I didn't keep that stuff in its place, I let it take over. I let things get out of hand. Besides, the way things are going, I'll have plenty of other stuff to worry about."

"What's going on outside?" she asked.

"Still awash in cats, if that's what you mean." He rubbed at his neck, where she noticed a couple of small marks that resembled bruises. "Even more of them were hanging around when I got back from the supermarket. I don't want to worry you or anything, but I'm getting a lot more nervous about those cats. They let me get to my car, but I didn't like the way they were watching me, and last night—"

The doorbell rang.

"Should I get that," Don said, "or just ignore it?"

"I'm not dressed." She covered her eyes for a moment. "Damn it, I bet it's Tracey. She said she was coming over today."

Don stood up. "I'll tell her we're indisposed." He went to the front door as she picked at her quiche. The doorbell sounded again. "Hi, Tracey," Don said from the front of the house, and then, "What the hell?"

"Just wanted to say a quick hello," Tracey's voice boomed out. "I told Gena not to go to any trouble, but I just knew she'd want to meet—" The door slammed. Gena clutched at her robe as Tracey, clothed in a long trench coat, charged into the dining room, followed by a small red-haired woman in a black leather coat and high-heeled boots, a lanky blonde in slacks and a parka, and a young dark-haired man in a plaid lumberjack shirt who held a camera.

"This is Gena Lawlor," Tracey said, throwing her arms wide and almost hitting the blond woman in the chest, "my best friend, the one who's going to work for Caterina Lucci, the veterinarian I mentioned before. And that's her husband, Don Martinson. Now, don't you get up, Gena, I told you not to go to any trouble." Tracey helped herself to a muffin. "I just wanted you to meet Shauna Leopold." She beamed at the small red-haired woman. "And this is Torie Shea and her colleague Lance Oldman from the *Times-Tribune*." She waved a hand at the blonde and the man with the camera.

Gena tried to forget how she looked without makeup in her old terry-cloth robe. Tracey flung her arms open again, then pointed at the floor. "And that lovely charming little kitty cat there is Vladimir."

The cat offered Tracey his iciest stare.

"What an adorable cat," Shauna Leopold purred as she fluttered around Vladimir, who seemed profoundly unimpressed. "Haven't I seen you somewhere before?"

"I used Vladimir as my model for Beelzebub in the *Manfred and Beelzebub* illos you saw," Tracey said.

"Of course!" Shauna Leopold shrieked. "What an adorable kitty he is!" She batted her heavily-lashed eyes at Gena. "Tracey told me that he was quite an exceptional cat, and I can well believe it."

"Did he have anything to do with all those cats outside this house?" Torie Shea asked.

"Absolutely not," Don replied. "To be honest, Vladimir doesn't much care for the company of other cats."

"You're sure?" Torie Shea said. Lance Oldman aimed his camera in Gena's direction. Gena threw up her hands. "Don't bother with shooting indoors," the reporter continued. "We're here to shoot Shauna with all those cats outside."

"I'd be careful around those cats if I were you," Don said. "They haven't caused much trouble yet, apart from attracting crowds, but I don't know how much longer they'll keep behaving themselves."

"They do behave themselves, don't they? Why, they even moved aside so that we could get to your door." Torie Shea smiled at him, then at Gena. "Maybe we could use a shot of your cat," she added, gazing down at Vladimir.

"Go ahead," Don said as Vladimir lifted his head, striking a pose. "Vladimir already knows he's the center of the universe. He'd be disappointed and insulted if you didn't shoot him."

Gena shrank back in her chair, trying to be as invisible as possible as Lance Oldman took a few shots of Vladimir. "Shauna Leopold is my daughter's favorite writer," Torie Shea announced to nobody in particular. "Nailing this interview is going to impress the hell out of her, and Shauna said she'd come over and autograph some of our books before she leaves."

"Better get our shooting done outside," Lance said to Torie. "Kinda looked like it was starting to cloud up."

"So nice to meet you," Shauna chirped, addressing her remarks mostly to Vladimir.

"Just watch it with those cats," Don said.

"We'll have to come back for a longer visit sometime," Tracey said, her mouth full of muffin, as she herded Shauna toward the living room. "Thanks for everything, guys." The reporter and the photographer hurried after them and Don followed them all to the front door.

The door slammed shut. "Looks like another crowd's gathering outside," Don said as he returned to the table.

Gena sighed. "What are we going to do?"

Don sat down. "Right now, I think we'd better fortify ourselves with some breakfast."

* * * *

Shauna Leopold was still outside with Tracey after Gena got dressed, posing for Lance and talking to Torie while the reporter took notes. By then, the crowd had grown, and vans from all three of the local TV stations had shown up, along with a satellite truck from the Fox station upstate. Gena could see it all from the living room window, where she had opened the curtains halfway.

Vladimir, perched on top of the small table near the window, seemed equally fascinated by the assemblage of people, cats, and communications technology. Normally he wasn't allowed on the table, but Gena hadn't bothered to dismiss him from his post. The cat was still, his only movement an occasional twitch of his ears.

The house was quiet, the living room devoid of any threatening shadows. Yet she was beginning to feel that the unseen entity, although dormant, was still nearby, waiting.

"I didn't get a chance to tell you before," Don said from behind her. "I was outside last night just in time to catch a couple of bozos trying to kidnap some cats. They came after me, and then the cats went after them. Fortunately, that was enough to scare them off. But then a few of the cats went after me and chased me back inside."

"Oh, my God."

"I'm fine—a couple of scratches, that's all. But I saw Nicholas and Alexandra again, those same two cats we saw before, and they didn't look all that friendly."

She turned back to the window, thinking of the cats in her nightmare. The dream danced at the edges of her consciousness, evading recall. "Might as well admit it," she said. "We made Catalonia up, and then all those cats started to appear. Maybe we'll have to go through the rest of our lives with mobs of cats following us everywhere."

"I don't think so," Don said. "For one thing, animal control is going to get after them pretty soon."

"We can't let them go to a shelter," Gena said. "If we do, those cats'll find some way to get back at us. I know it sounds crazy, but they will, they'll blame us for whatever happens to them and they'll have their revenge somehow."

"It doesn't sound crazy," Don said. "You may be right."

Shauna Leopold moved through the crowd, offering the TV crews some face time. Some people in the crowd were drifting away, but others had gathered on the corner and along the sidewalk across the street, a few of them holding cell phones to their ears. A group of teenagers horsed around, waving their arms at the WSIG cameraman, who stood on the roof of his van recording the scene. Tracey, swept along in the wake of Shauna's procession, waved to a broad-shouldered man at the edge of the crowd. Gena tensed as she recognized Roland Tewksbury. He waved back at Tracey while making his way toward her.

"That's the guy, isn't it," Don said suddenly.

"What guy?" Gena said, knowing exactly who he meant.

"That tall guy there, the one you went out to dinner with. The guy from Strut My Stuff."

She let out her breath. "Yes, that's the guy. His name is Roland Tewksbury, and he probably just wants to ogle the cats along with everyone else. I'm sure he's not here on my account."

"Don't get so defensive. Besides, it looks like we've got even more trouble."

A blue Jeep Grand Cherokee had just pulled up, and the driver was parking it in the middle of the intersection at the corner. People retreated from the vehicle; a few waved. The thick wavy white hair of the man seated next to the driver was instantly recognizable.

"Oh, my God," Gena said softly, "it's Mayor Dorff."

Don said, "And I'll bet that's the animal control guy with him."

* * * *

Stan Dorff finally approached the house. Gena continued to watch him from the window. The mayor had spent the past few minutes walking up and down the sidewalk, greeting his constituents and pressing the flesh. He was a tall barrel-chested man who towered over most of the people around him. Every time Mayor Dorff looked down at the cats, his eyes narrowed and he pursed his lips.

A thin balding man trailed after Dorff, shaking his head at the cats that sat on the sidewalk and lay alongside the curb. The mayor nodded at Tracey and Shauna and stopped to offer a few words to Torie while Lance shot a few more photos.

Gena started as the phone rang. "I'll get it," Don said as he headed toward the kitchen. Probably a call from her in-laws, Gena thought. Don's parents usually called him on Sundays, and maybe some news footage featuring their cat infestation had even managed to reach the Pacific Northwest by now.

"Yeah," Don was saying as he wandered back into the living room with the phone, "but it doesn't matter. I could come downtown first and stop at your place for my stuff on the way home." He paused. "No, that's okay." He fell silent again. "Yeah, I know." He glanced at Gena. "I'm talking to Jeff. He says he's glad we're back together so I won't be cluttering up his place any more."

Gena smiled, hoping that their newfound resolve to keep their marriage together would last. Their bond had to last, she told herself.

"But we still have all those cats around our house," Don continued, "so I don't know when I'll be able to get downtown. Tracey was over here with a writer from New York and a couple of people from the *Times-Tribune*, and now there's a crowd outside and some TV crews. This is really going to do me a hell of a lot of good when I'm looking for work. You won't believe this, but even the mayor's over here checking out the cats." There was another pause. "Mayor Dorff. Yeah. As a matter of fact, he's just outside our house right now."

Gena peered through the window. She could no longer see either the mayor or his companion.

The doorbell rang. She glanced at her husband, then crept into the front hallway and peered through the peephole.

Mayor Dorff and the thin balding man stood waiting.

She backed away and motioned to Don.

"Just a minute, Jeff. What is it?"

"We've got company," she said. "The mayor's outside, ringing our doorbell."

"What?" Don said into the phone. "Gena was talking to me," he went on. "Mayor Dorff just rang our doorbell. As if we didn't have enough trouble. Yeah, I…Jeff? Jeff?" Don let out his breath. "He just hung up." He set the phone down on the table next to Vladimir.

"What are we going to do?" Gena asked.

Don shrugged. "Answer the door."

* * * *

"Glad to meet you," the mayor said as he stepped through the doorway into the alcove, "and in spite of the unusual circumstances, it's always good to meet a constituent." He grinned, revealing large and gorgeous white choppers that could only have been the result of either splendid health or extensive and expensive dentistry, then extended his hand. "Donald Martin?"

"Martinson," the thin balding man with Dorff muttered. "Donald Martinson."

"A pleasure to meet you, Mr. Martinson."

"You, too, Mayor Dorff." Don shook Dorff's hand. The mayor turned toward Gena and held out his hand to her. "And you must be his charming better half."

"How do you do." Gena took Dorff's meaty hand and shook it, grateful that the mayor did not possess a bone-crunching grip. "I'm Gena Lawlor, Don's wife."

"She kept her own name," Don said.

"Glad to meet you, Mrs. Lawlor—Ms. Lawlor." Dorff beamed down at her. "Now I just want to reassure you and your husband that we're here on your behalf, to do whatever we can to help you solve your little problem." He gestured at his companion. "This is Steve Kolbida, our animal control supervisor. Now Steve tells me that he gave you a call yesterday, after getting some complaints."

"I spoke to him," Don said.

"And Steve says you told him that the cats weren't causing any real trouble for your neighbors, but it seems they've become quite an attraction, as we saw for ourselves today, so—" Dorff lifted his thick eyebrows.

"Uh, please come in," Gena said. "We can sit down in the living room."

Steve Kolbida shrugged out of his windbreaker. Dorff took off his trench coat, revealing a well-tailored dark blue suit, and handed the coat to Don, who hung it up in the front closet with the windbreaker.

Gena led the men into the living room and watched with dismay as the mayor sat down in Vladimir's favorite chair, which was sprinkled with cat hairs. "Can I get you anything?" she asked. "Some coffee?"

"No, thanks," Dorff replied. "I don't want to take up too much of your time." Gena seated herself in a facing chair as Don and Steve Kolbida sat down on the sofa. "Now, about all those cats around your home. Steve says that they haven't been causing any particular problems for your neighbors, and the people I spoke to outside have confirmed that, but we can't just leave them there, sitting around and attracting sightseers and all manner of disruptive public attention. Your neighbors may not have any complaints about the cats right now, at least none that they've voiced to me, but some of them are getting just a tad concerned about the crowds, not to mention all the media attention." The mayor showed his teeth. "Even the pleasures of television coverage can wear a bit thin after a while. So many cats—wish they could vote!"

"And the fact is those cats aren't acting normal," Steve Kolbida said. "I called up this guy I've consulted before, a biologist in the state environmental conservation department, and he's already wondering if these cats might have some kind of disease, something new that hasn't been seen before, something that could make cats act funny."

"They don't look sick," Don said. "If anything, they seem the picture of good health. Our vet, Caterina Lucci, was over here yesterday, and she said that they looked healthy enough to her."

"But they're not acting normal," Kolbida insisted, "and your vet didn't do any tests on them, did she? Maybe they're sick and just not showing any overt symptoms yet. Or maybe there's something else that's attracting them to your house."

Vladimir was still sitting on the table near the window. The animal control supervisor and the mayor were both eyeing the cat now. Vladimir stared back at them with cold green eyes.

"It can't be because of Vladimir," Gena said quickly. "Our cat, I mean. I'm sure they're not here because of him. Besides, we've been keeping him indoors."

"Oh, I'm sure it's not because of your cat." Dorff leaned toward Don. "Mr. Martinson—may I call you Don?"

Don nodded.

"Don—and Gena." Dorff flashed his broad smile. "Now we'd like to do our best to resolve this situation with as little trouble as possible, and Steve's come up with a plan. A plan, I might add, that shouldn't unduly disrupt your lives or those of your neighbors. Obviously we can't just leave all those cats out there."

"I suppose not," Don said.

"And of course we want to remove them as quickly and humanely as possible," Dorff continued.

"Of course," Don said.

"But there may not be room enough for all of them at our shelter," Kolbida said.

"Not even after losing those cats that escaped from the city shelter?" Don asked. "Or were you able to round them all up again?"

Kolbida and the mayor exchanged glances. Dorff scowled at Kolbida, and Gena had the feeling that the mayor had not known about any fugitive cats until now. "We're looking for them," Kolbida replied. "We'll find them."

"There's the local humane society," Don said, "and Operation Whiskers. They could help out with these cats."

"Even if they were willing to pitch in, we'd still need more space." Kolbida kept his eyes on Don. "Anyway, there's more to consider here than just getting those cats into a shelter. After I talked to that biologist, I called a couple of guys I know in his department, and they told me they wouldn't mind getting their hands on those cats. In fact, they think they can cut through enough red tape to get a truck and crew down here by sometime tomorrow or the day after at the latest. They can cage them and load them into the truck and cart them upstate and take them to a lab and find out just why they're acting the way they are."

"That's the beauty of Steve's plan," Dorff added, although he was still regarding Kolbida with a wary look in his eyes. "The state can handle most of it. It won't be the city's problem."

"I really pushed them to get after this," Kolbida said, "and find out just what's going on with all those cats. It could be darned important."

"Mr. Kolbida," Gena began.

"Steve."

She swallowed. "What's going to happen to them in the lab?"

"Well, they'll have to do some blood tests and such, and keep them quarantined in case it's anything contagious. They'll probably have to put some of them to sleep and see if the autopsies show anything out of the ordinary."

"No," Gena said, unable to stop herself from speaking. "They can't. We won't let them."

The mayor said, "I don't see how you can stop them."

"We'll find a way. There has to be another way to find out if there's something wrong with them. You don't have to kill them." Maybe this was what her dream had been trying to tell her, not that the cats were a danger to her, but that others posed a deadly threat to the cats. "We'll tell the people from that lab that they can't come on our property."

Kolbida heaved a sigh. "This is the state, lady. You're talking about state government workers coming down here on an emergency basis to take care of a public nuisance that for all you know might be a health hazard, too. There's no way you can stop them."

"I'll claim they're all my cats. They can't take away animals that belong to me."

"Be reasonable," Dorff murmured. "If you owned that many cats, the city health department and the humane society would both be after you, not to mention the law. You can't feed them, and—"

"We'll find other homes for them, then. I don't care how long it takes, just as long as they don't end up dissected in some lab." She was being irrational. Gena knew that even as she spoke, yet could not help feeling that she had to protect the cats.

"Gena's right," Don said. "There's no reason to take them to a lab, especially if you can house them in your shelter and have them tested there. Besides, I don't think these cats are likely to let themselves be carted off without putting up a fight."

"Are you saying they're potentially aggressive and violent?" Dorff asked. "That's even more reason to get rid of them."

"I didn't say that," Don said, looking a bit flustered. "I only meant that they might try to defend themselves."

"Mrrow," Vladimir added from his perch on the table.

The mayor shot the cat a poisonous glance, then stood up. "You two are being unreasonable," he said in a low but commanding voice. "The state lab boys are coming for those cats, and there's nothing you can do to stop them." His voice had dropped another half-octave. "Be practical. It'll go a lot better for you if you cooperate in having this public nuisance removed. Just hope that the lab boys don't start worrying about what your cat there might have been exposed to, or maybe they'll decide they'd better take it away, too."

"How dare you," Gena said. "How dare you threaten Vladimir."

"I'm just telling you what could happen," Dorff continued in Household's voice; she shrank back in her chair. "I have your best interests at heart." He moved toward the front door; Kolbida got up and followed him. Don strode after them, pulled the closet door open, and handed them their coats.

"Good-bye," Don said as Dorff opened the front door. "Somehow I don't think I'm going to be voting for you this November." The mayor stepped outside, Kolbida at his heels.

Don closed the door. "Threatening Vladimir," he muttered as he wandered back into the living room. "That was the last straw."

"I don't know if that was the mayor speaking then," Gena said. "It might have been…" Her voice trailed off. "You know what I mean."

He started, then sighed. "It doesn't matter. He's right—there's not a hell of a lot we can do. And I probably just killed my chances of getting a job with any of Dorff's business cronies." He turned toward the window. "Holy shit."

"What is it?"

"Take a look."

She got up and looked through the window. Jeff Nardi was in front of the crowd, and she recognized the big man standing next to him.

"Clifford Beaufort," Don said before Gena could speak. "That must be why Jeff hung up so fast. He wanted to get Beaufort over here to take advantage of the TV coverage."

"Mayor Dorff isn't going to like that," she said, which was probably an extreme understatement.

Twenty-Three

As Don reached the end of the Archibalds' driveway, he saw that Mayor Dorff and Steve Kolbida were still trapped outside his front door. Several cats sat on the steps below them, while more people had massed in front of the house.

Don had slipped through the back door ahead of Gena, down the driveway, and out to the sidewalk, hoping to make his way to Jeff's side unobtrusively. But now the TV cameramen were aiming their camcorders in his direction and his neighbor Phil Donovan was busily pointing him out to everybody.

"That's him!" Donovan hollered above the murmuring sounds of the crowd, "Don Martinson, the guy who owns the house." Great, Don thought. He would be instantly recognizable to any personnel department interviewer who watched the local news as that guy with all the cats around his house, a detail that would certainly enhance his résumé.

Rose Cutler stood in the distance, talking to Mrs. Seligman. Larry Philmus was next to the Fox station's truck, while the tall thin form of Elden Bowes could be seen across the street. A white-haired man in a baggy tweed coat who looked almost exactly like the homeless old geezer he had talked to yesterday was at the edge of the crowd. Maybe everybody he knew was going to show up for this jamboree.

"Let me assure you," Dorff called out to the crowd, "that we're doing everything we can to get all these cats away from here and to a safe place so that your lives can get back to normal."

Don looked around for Gena, who had been right behind him, then saw her elbowing her way toward him.

"Where they gonna go, Mayor?" a man shouted from the sidewalk. "What's gonna happen to them?"

"I'm pleased to announce that we've made arrangements with the state environmental conservation department to handle the problem at one of their facilities near the capital."

A few of the cats near the front steps began to dig at the ground with their front paws.

"They're going to take them to a lab," Gena cried out. "They're going to take all these cats away and put them in cages, and run tests on them and dissect them. That's what they're going to do."

Don turned toward his wife, feeling a powerful mixture of love, pride in her unexpected boldness in challenging Dorff, and terror at what her public defiance was likely to cost them. More of the cats were milling around now, pawing at the ground and flicking their tails; Don thought that he heard a few ominous-sounding snarls.

"Is that true?" a middle-aged woman to his right asked. "Are you going to have all these nice kitties put to sleep?"

"I didn't say that," the mayor replied. Don heard a few angry murmurs behind him.

"They'll gas 'em to death," a tenor voice said from the center of the crowd. "It'll be a kitty holocaust!" A hushed and shocked silence brought up the muted snarling and hissing of cats. Some of the cats definitely lacked the demeanor of nice kitties; a few of them even had a murderous look in their eyes.

"Are you going to put them where they'll be tortured?" the woman near Don persisted. "Or just cart them away and gas them?"

"A cat is a free being!" Don knew that voice, but hadn't realized that his former landlord was capable of such vast vocal projection. "A cat is a free being," Mr. Bowes repeated, "not to be imprisoned and manhandled."

"You might not feel that way, mister," Kolbida replied, "if they were all camped out around your house. Listen, those animals could be a serious health hazard. You don't even know what's wrong with them."

"They look healthy enough to me," Mr. Bowes said, "but even if they are not, surely you could insist that the laboratory house them in reasonably pleasant surroundings and treat them humanely while they're being examined."

"And what did those cats ever do to you?" the woman next to Don said. "Why can't you just keep them in the city shelter until you find homes for them?"

"Because there isn't enough room at the shelter," Mayor Dorff replied. "And not enough homes."

"Be reasonable, lady," Kolbida added. "The city shelter can't handle all these cats."

"You could handle more of them than you're admitting," Don shouted, unable to restrain himself any longer. "I know that some of the cats in your shelter escaped the other day, so you should have more space there than you did."

"Cats escaped from the shelter?" someone in back of Don called out. "Is that where all those cats come from?"

"Of course not," Kolbida replied.

"How do you know?" someone else asked. "How do we know?"

"You could work something out," Don said to Dorff and Kolbida. "You have more room in the shelter than you did, and we could find places for the others. You could run tests on a few cats at a time while we try to find homes for the ones that get a clean bill of health." Even as he spoke, he knew the futility of such a plan. These cats—he now accepted that they had to be Catalonians—would never allow themselves to be taken away peacefully, to the shelter or anywhere else, to wait passively for people to adopt them. They would put up a fight, as they had the night before. He wondered how many injuries they could inflict on their would-be captors before they were finally subdued.

"You're speaking of a course of action that would be quite costly," Mayor Dorff said, "the burden of which would be borne by the city's taxpayers. And since we've already had some cats apparently escaping from the city's shelter, there's no point in housing these cats there until we make sure that can't happen again."

Don could think of no answer to that.

"My friends," Dorff went on, "let me assure you—"

"Mayor Dorff," a deep voice called out. The mayor's face reddened and he scowled, his lips drawn back from his teeth, before he regained his composure.

Clifford Beaufort moved through the crowd, trailed by TV reporters and cameramen, along with Torie Shea and Lance Oldman; the two newspaperpeople had apparently abandoned Shauna Leopold for fresher game. A few people cheered.

Somebody clapped Don on the shoulder. He turned to see Jeff Nardi.

"Here's where it should start getting good," Jeff said in an undertone. "Dorff kept saying he wouldn't go mano-a-mano and debate Cliff, but he can't avoid it now. Thanks for telling me he was over here."

Gena reached Don's side. "Hi, Jeff."

"Yo, Gena."

"Hi, Gena," a voice murmured at Don's left.

Gena looked down for a moment. "Uh, hi, Roland."

Don turned his head, annoyed, but the tall and handsome Roland looked down at him with an open and friendly gaze so devoid of deviousness or hostility that Don could feel his resentment of the man fading away. Gena had said that there was nothing between them, and he could take her word for that. He had to, if their marriage was ever to get completely back on track, and right now, he needed all the friends he could get.

"I'm Roland Tewksbury," the newcomer said.

"Don Martinson."

"Gena told me some good things about you when we were at dinner the other night. Glad to see you're back together. The thing is, I wouldn't have asked her out in the first place if I'd known what the deal was with you guys." Roland glanced at Gena. "Not that I wouldn't have been interested."

"I understand."

"Mayor Dorff," Beaufort proclaimed from the front steps, "I have a question." He stood next to the mayor now, and even Dorff seemed a bit smaller in the imposing presence of his opponent. "May I ask exactly why we can't house these animals in our shelter?"

"I already told everybody why," Dorff answered; petulance had crept into his tone. "Because we don't have enough space for them at the shelter, and also because some cats managed to escape from the place recently. We have to investigate that and find out exactly how it happened before we bring in more strays."

"I remind you that I was pushing a couple of years back to have a much-needed wing added to the shelter," Beaufort continued, "and some renovation of the building done, before you encouraged the city council to direct the money that might have been allocated for that work elsewhere." He drew himself up. "Specifically, into the renovation of the Blaine Building."

"We needed more downtown development," Dorff said.

"I agree," Beaufort said. "We still do. We also need low cost housing for people of modest means, for young couples just starting out or senior citizens who might like to live in the center of town in easy to care for apartments, people who would patronize more of our troubled downtown businesses and help to revitalize our city. What we didn't need was another empty office building, however attractive, refurbished at taxpayer expense."

"Which is probably just a goddamn tax shelter scam anyway," a young man wearing a Boston Red Sox baseball cap shouted. Beaufort shot him a reproachful glance. "Excuse me, Reverend."

Dorff said, "The Blaine Building is an important part of our ongoing effort to attract high-tech businesses to our community."

"As if this place is ever going to turn into Silicon Valley," someone else replied.

"But you can't measure the opportunity to breathe new life into our downtown streets only in dollars," Beaufort continued. "I say that if you create a place where people want to live, businesses will follow. As it is, given the congregation of homeless cats that have gathered here with apparently no place to go, improving the animal shelter would have been a far better investment than renovating the Blaine Building." He took a step towards Kolbida. "Mr. Kolbida, why haven't you spoken out and pressed for more improvements? Apparently some cats have managed to get out of your shelter, which indicates a failure of—"

"Yeah!" a man called out. "Who let out the cats?"

"We don't know how they got out," Kolbida replied. "They were all locked up, I tell you. I would have been wondering if somebody let them out myself, except that there wasn't anybody on duty at the time."

"You don't have a staff member there at all times?" Beaufort shook his head. "Doesn't that constitute neglect of the animals in your care?"

"Look, we can't afford—"

"You can't afford anything," a small woman with long blonde hair called out, "but we can provide a better shelter and more care for the animals with volunteers and donated funds than you can with a line in the city budget."

"Give me a break," Kolbida replied. "I've got a heck of a lot more animals to handle than you folks do."

"Well," the woman said, "I'm surprised you actually recognize me." She pushed her way through the crowd until she had reached the front steps, then lifted a hand. "I'm Jennifer Baxter of Operation Whiskers, and I'm amazed Mr. Kolbida even knows who I am, given how little time he spends at the city's shelter. He's almost never in his office whenever I show up to plead for a little more time to find homes for the animals there."

"Lady—" Kolbida began.

"Steve Kolbida is a hard-working public servant," Dorff interrupted.

"Steve Kolbida isn't any kinder to dogs," a short boyish-looking man called out from across the street, "than he is to cats. I worked in the city shelter, and he never hung on to a dog for more than three days if he could help it. Some of us used to adopt dogs or cats temporarily just so we could have more time to find homes for them on our own."

"I remember you." Kolbida waved his arms. "I *fired* you."

"You did me a big favor, Kolbida. If you hadn't given me the axe, I wouldn't be managing the Doggone Kennel and Obedience School now and spending my days with happy dogs and making more in a couple of weeks than the city paid me in a month."

"My friends," Dorff said in a loud voice, "I assure you—"

"If you try to move any of these cats to some lab," Jennifer Baxter shouted, "you'll do it over my dead body."

The crowd muttered angrily. "Save the cats," someone called out. Don looked around nervously, wondering if people were going to get worked up enough to start some real trouble.

Beaufort thrust out his arms, as if to bless the multitude. The angry mutters faded and died.

"Fellow citizens," Beaufort said in his deep and commanding voice, "I have a question to pose to you. Does anyone here have a specific complaint against these cats?"

"They're here," Mrs. Seligman responded.

Beaufort regarded her with a look of compassion. "Ma'am," he said, "that hardly counts as a complaint, given that they aren't occupying your property."

"They're attracting too much attention," Mrs. Seligman said. "This used to be a nice quiet neighborhood. Now look at this crowd."

Beaufort lowered his arms. "That's hardly the fault of the cats, is it? How can they be blamed for what people do in response to their presence?" Don saw that a few people were scratching themselves. Fleas, he thought; that was all they needed now.

"Doesn't matter whether they deserve the blame or they don't." Christopher Archibald, Don's next door neighbor, was speaking. "I mean, there they are, and you can't blame people for coming by to check them out, and sooner or later they're going to have to feed themselves, aren't they? They'll start roaming around looking for handouts and messing around in our garbage cans. And maybe they'll attract even more stray cats to this neighborhood."

"You have a point," Beaufort said. "All I'm asking is that these cats be dealt with in as kindly and humane a fashion as possible. Aren't these cats God's creatures? Doesn't the good Lord watch over them the same way he watches over all of us and over every lily in the field and every blade of grass and every bird that soars to the sky?"

The crowd was silent, as if expecting the Lord to comment, or worse. Even the cats seemed to be entirely focused on Beaufort. The cats nearest to him settled down on their haunches, their heads raised. Those along the sidewalk and lying on the hoods of a couple of parked cars were staring at him with wide attentive eyes.

Dorff managed a forced smile. "I'm not interested in harming any of these cats," he said. "I just want to remove them."

"You want to euthanize them," Jennifer Baxter shouted.

"I have to make certain that they pose no risk to public health," Dorff shouted back. "That's part of my responsibility as mayor. It's our good fortune that the state's willing to expedite the matter."

"You want to kill them," Jennifer Baxter repeated. "Can't you at least give us a chance to try something else?"

"A cat is a free being," Elden Bowes called out.

"Save the cats!" a man at the edge of the crowd hollered. Others took up the cry.

"Save the cats! Save the cats! Save the cats!" Some tough-looking shaven-headed young men in leather jackets were chanting more enthusiastically than anyone.

Don grabbed Gena's hand and held onto it.

"Save the cats!" Shauna Leopold moved her arms as if conducting an orchestra. "Save the cats!"

"Save the kitties!" someone added.

"Save the cats!"

"Save the kitties!"

People at one end of the crowd were performing a wave, bobbing up and down in turn. "Save the kitties!"

Terrific, Don thought as he watched the crowd, which seemed on the verge of becoming a crazed, out-of-control mob. Maybe some of them did care about saving the cats, but others looked as if they were ready to riot over anything just to make the day a little more lively.

"Brothers and sisters!" Beaufort raised his arms. "Calm yourselves! There's no reason—"

"Save the cats!"

"Up the kitties!" a desperate male voice cried out in an agonized shriek, silencing the crowd for a moment with his heartfelt entreaty, pained and woebegone beyond all tolerance.

"What was *that*?" somebody asked.

Don leaned toward Gena. "Listen," he said in an undertone, "this could get ugly. You'd be safer inside. Think you can make it to the back door?"

She looked about to argue with him. "I might need you there," he went on.

Her eyes widened slightly. "I'll get inside," she whispered back.

"Be careful."

Gena began to work her way through the crowd along the sidewalk toward the corner, to sneak down the Archibalds' driveway to the back door.

Elbowing, Don pushed his way toward the front stoop. "Inciting to riot," Dorff muttered to Beaufort as Don approached. "I could have you charged for that."

"He's only trying to calm things down," Don said. He climbed up the steps toward the two men. "Back off and tell these people that you'll consider—"

"Save the kitties!" people shouted.

Dorff shot Don a venomous look, turned away, pulled a cell phone out of his pocket, murmured a few words into it, nodded, and slipped the phone under his coat. "I've just put in a call to the chief of police," he said to Don in an almost inaudible tone. "Two squad cars will arrive at this corner, and there'll be another at the end of Ackley Avenue for backup, and if that isn't enough to break up this crowd—"

Don said, "Are you trying to make things even worse? Can't you just ask everybody to leave?"

"I agree with this young man," Beaufort said. "We should give all these people the opportunity to disperse peacefully. Using force to deal with them may also endanger the cats."

Dorff sneered. "Screw the cats."

"Brothers and sisters," Beaufort announced, "leave peacefully."

But the crowd, Don saw, was already beyond appeal. A few of the cat partisans were engaging in angry verbal exchanges with Phil Donovan, Christopher Archibald, Rita Seligman, and other residents of the neighborhood.

Dorff wheeled on Don. "You started this," he said. "You're the one who's responsible for all these cats being here." It was not the mayor's voice. "You wouldn't listen, you got careless, you and that wife of yours tried to destroy me. You thought you'd be free of me at last. Well, you won't get away with it."

Dorff's hands were suddenly around Don's neck. "Hold on, man!" Beaufort shouted. The minister's fingers gripped the mayor's shoulders. Don struggled to breathe and break Dorff's grip.

He fell against the door. It flew open. Don tumbled into the alcove, with Dorff on top of him. He glimpsed Gena, her hand to her mouth, stifling a scream.

"Hold on!" Beaufort called out again, and then cats streamed through the open door, screeching and meowing.

Don struggled against Dorff as the bigger man pinned him to the floor. "You won't get the better of me," the mayor growled in a weird deep voice. "I'll destroy you once and for all." A cat leaped onto Dorff's head. Dorff rolled to one side and slapped the cat away.

Don freed himself and got to his feet. Cats swarmed through the door and over Dorff, then ran toward the living room. Cats clung to the mayor's arms and legs as he struggled to stand up.

"Get 'em off me!" Dorff yelled. He dropped to one knee, then got up again. Beaufort reached for Dorff's hand as Gena stumbled toward Don. Cats clung to Dorff, clawed at his pants and hung from the edge of his trench coat.

"Shoo!" Kolbida danced just outside the open door. Cats ran past his legs. "Scat!"

Holding Gena's hand, Don turned and staggered toward the living room as more cats surged past them. Somebody outside screamed, but other people cheered the cats on. "Go get 'em!" somebody shouted. Cats leaped onto the sofa and tore at the upholstery with their claws; a standing lamp crashed to the floor. Cats hung from curtains, showing sharp teeth as they yowled.

"Household," Don muttered to Gena.

"What?"

"The mayor—that was Household." He jumped as the table near the window fell over. Vladimir had been sitting on it earlier before Don had gone outside. He looked around the living room, fearing almost as much for Vladimir as for himself and Gena, sure that the cats tearing up the room could sense his fear.

"I shouldn't have opened the door," Gena said. "I was only trying to let you inside."

The cats began to howl.

"Brothers and sisters!" Beaufort shouted from the doorway, his back to Don. "This is no time to fight among yourselves!" Don looked toward him; Beaufort was supporting the mayor with one arm. "Cease and desist!" The sound of a siren pierced the air as more cats rushed through the open doorway, then abruptly skidded to a halt.

The cats howled like hundreds of crying babies. Don saw the golden-furred cat then, along with his small black-furred mate. The two padded toward him and paused at the entrance to the living room. The horde in the entryway and the living room suddenly fell silent.

"This is crazy," Don said uselessly. He stared at the two cats who so closely resembled the feline sovereigns he and Gena had imagined. "I really have lost it, I really am out of my mind." Go ahead, he wanted to say to the cats, you've won, trash the house, do whatever the hell you want, I have no control over you now, never did. You can survive without us.

The cats stared back at him. "Over here," Beaufort shouted from the doorway.

Entranced, Don knew what he had to do.

He made his way past cats that sat on the dining room table and cats nestled among the carved Russian cats on the sideboard and entered the kitchen. Cats gazed at him from the counter tops as he went to the back door. "Go," he said as he opened the door. "Get out of here, go home, go back to Catalonia or wherever the hell you came from."

The cats in the back yard were already vacating the premises, scurrying toward the sidewalk and bounding down the driveway. "There they go!" a man called out above the sirens.

Don went outside. Cats followed him from the house and fanned out around him. Packs of cats were scrambling in all directions, some down Bancroft Street, others toward the nearest yards, still others around the corner. Children screamed with what might have been either delight or terror. People ran after the cats, trying to evade the two police cars that now sat in the middle of the street. The lights on the hoods of the two vehicles flashed as the sirens continued to wail.

"Attention," an amplified voice called out, "this is the police, attention," but nobody in the rapidly dispersing crowd seemed to be heeding that summons.

He turned toward his house. The cats he thought of as Nicholas and Alexandra padded down the steps, followed by more cats, then fled in the direction of the Archibalds' house.

Don stumbled up the steps and into the kitchen. Gena stood in the middle of the room, her face pale. He slammed the door, hurried toward her, and pulled her close.

"Are you okay?" he asked.

"I'm fine."

"What about Vladimir?"

"He ran down to the basement when I came inside before, so I closed the door behind him."

"Good thinking."

"It just seemed like the thing to do."

They linked arms and went into the dining room. There were scratches on the tabletop and the sideboard, and two of the carved wooden cats had been knocked over; Don righted them as he passed. The living room sofa bloomed white upholstery where the fabric had been torn open; the bottoms of the curtains were shredded. Shards of glass glittered on the floor, but the overturned lamps seemed largely undamaged except for their broken bulbs.

Don could no longer hear the sound of sirens. In the alcove, Beaufort and Dorff stood with a policeman; one uniformed man was just outside the door with Kolbida. Beyond them, Don spotted Torie Shea, a knot of people, and a man with a camcorder.

"We could have had a worse riot out there," the policeman was saying to the mayor and the minister. "Good thing we got here when we did."

Don led Gena toward them. "Mayor Dorff," Torie Shea called out, "can you tell me why you suddenly attacked that man?" She pointed her chin in Don's direction.

"I don't know what you're talking about," Dorff said.

"I got it all," the man holding the camcorder said. "You were standing there in front of the door, and suddenly—"

"Don't be too hard on the mayor," Beaufort interrupted. "Pressure can get to anyone, especially in such an unprecedented situation." His arm was still slung over Dorff's shoulders. "But the crisis is past."

The mayor shrugged Beaufort's arm off himself. Beaufort, Don thought to himself, was no fool. Not only had he been quick to take advantage of a chance to get some free coverage, he had also been able to take command of the situation with a show of mercy and good fellowship.

All of this would affect Dorff's campaign, especially with an attack on Don captured on video and witnessed by most of his neighbors. He could sue the mayor, or insist that the policeman standing outside haul Dorff in on an assault charge, but there seemed little point in doing so. Contesting such a case would be another drain on his shrinking resources, and the mayor and his cronies could make his life miserable in the meantime.

He also knew, deep down, that during those few brief moments of possession by Household, Stan Dorff had not been responsible for his actions.

He shuddered, wondering how much more damage his unseen antagonist could cause.

The cameraman aimed his camcorder at Don and Gena as they came to the door. Don threw up a hand. "I've got nothing to say," he said before anybody could question him.

"I don't, either," Gena added. Don peered past the people on the stoop to the street, now almost empty except for scattered bottles, cans, cigarette butts, and food wrappers. Shauna Leopold stood on the sidewalk, waving her arms while hogging the attention of the reporter and cameraman from WSIG, while Tracey hovered at her side. Elden Bowes stood in the middle of the street with Rita Seligman, probably reiterating to her that cats were free beings. Jeff was standing by a police car with Larry Philmus, a cop, and the cameraman from the Fox station.

"We'll track those cats down," Kolbida was saying.

"They ran in a million different directions," the policeman near him said. "Be kinda hard to find them all."

"We'll round up whatever cats we can," Kolbida replied, "and tell the state lab we won't need their truck down here after all. Not unless those cats all start showing up somewhere else."

"You don't suppose they'll come back to this house," Torie Shea said.

"I hope not," Don said wearily, with no idea of what would happen next.

"Save the kitties!" cried a distant voice.

Twenty-Four

Don sat brooding on the front steps. Avoiding the reporters had been surprisingly easy, as they had seemed much more inclined to question Dorff and Beaufort than Don or Gena, who were of lesser interest without their mob of feline trespassers, while the two mayoral candidates had been only too happy to offer comments. The mayor, Don concluded, would gain a few points for having called the cops, who had been able to disperse the rest of the crowd peacefully, and that might make up for his public attempt to wring Don's neck. But Beaufort would also gain by having logged some camera time to display his eloquence and self-possession.

Tracey and Shauna had finally left. Jeff and Beaufort had headed off to campaign headquarters to confer with other campaign workers on how to use any good video of their candidate. Rose Cutler, who had been quick to strike up a conversation with Roland Tewksbury, had slipped him one of her cards before her departure. Elden Bowes was inside with Gena, having a cup of tea and visiting with Vladimir. Don supposed that he should go inside, too, just to say a few words to his former landlord, before going downtown to Beaufort's headquarters to help with more of the clean-up and repairs, as he had earlier promised Jeff he would do. At least there he could be doing something constructive instead of moping around.

A police car turned the corner at his left and stopped in front of the house. Don sighed. Maybe somebody had come up with some sort of charge against him, or else Dorff had discovered a way to have Don arraigned for assault and battery.

The cop on the passenger side got out of the car, looking around as he came up the pathway. "Haven't seen any of those cats around since they beat it, have you?" the officer asked him.

Don shook his head. "But I haven't checked out the back yard since then."

"I looked back there when we drove by. Not a cat in sight." The policeman scratched his head. "Myself and Joe, we've been driving around all these streets, looking for cats and asking people if they've seen any, and it's like they all just disappeared. That just doesn't seem right, that so many cats could just, like, vanish without a trace. You'd think we would have found at least a few of them, here and there, I mean."

"They weren't exactly your usual cats," Don said.

"You can say that again. Anyway, I don't know how much luck animal control's gonna have finding them. Mind if I ask you something?"

"Go ahead."

"You notice anything unusual about them while they were all sitting around your home? I mean apart from, like, that you had so many of them hanging around, I mean."

"There were a lot of unusual things about them. I never saw any of them eating any food, for one thing, or taking a piss, or chasing birds." Don waved an arm at the patch of grass and shrubbery to his left. "Look at that part of my lawn. There were cats all over it, and now there isn't a sign they were ever there. The thing is—" He hesitated for a moment, not sure of how much more he should say. "I don't know how to put this. Sometimes I'd look out and see certain cats, ones that stood out from the others because they were an unusual breed or had some unusual trait, and then, just a few seconds later, they'd be gone and some other cats I hadn't noticed before would be there in their places. And there were all sorts." He frowned. "But cats can do things like that sometimes, appear and disappear. They're predators who stalk their game, so they know where your blind spot is, that's how they do it. You don't see them because they're standing in your blind spot, and then suddenly there they are."

"That still doesn't explain how all those cats could just disappear."

"Cats are pretty good at hiding, too."

"If any more strange-acting stray cats turn up around here, could you let us know? The city, I mean. It could be animal control or public works or whatever, it doesn't necessarily have to be the police department."

"I'll let you know," Don said. But somehow he doubted that any more of the strange cats would show up around his house.

"Thanks."

The policeman walked back to his car. The partners drove away.

At least one of his problems was solved, Don thought. He could go about his business without crowds of sightseers and cats camping out around his house. But his old worries were gnawing at him again, his fear that he had thrown away any chance of getting his professional life back on track and his worry that what little money he had would trickle away with nothing coming in to replace it. Once unemployment and his settlement ran out, Gena's new job with Caterina wouldn't keep them afloat for very long. They might even lose the house if he found himself among the long-term unemployed. Would Household pursue him even after any foreclosure, or settle for tormenting anybody who moved in? Household's deep and forceful voice was laughing in the dark corners of his mind, mocking him.

At last he got up and went inside, picking up the low murmurs of Gena and Mr. Bowes in the back of the house. "That may be," Mr. Bowes was saying, "but after I brought the little fellow to Dr. Lucci's office, he took it upon himself to return here, so I don't see why I should pay the cost of his visit now."

"How about half the cost?" Gena said. "I mean, you did have Vladimir's companionship all that time."

"Oh, very well," Mr. Bowes replied.

"Thanks," Gena said. "I mean, I want to be fair, but I have to be practical."

As Don entered the kitchen, the telephone rang. Gena, sitting at the table with Mr. Bowes and two cups of tea, reached for the phone.

"Hello?" Gena said. "Oh, hi, Hal." Don sighed; he had been hoping that his parents wouldn't call today. "Yes, he's right here," she continued. "We have company at the moment, so I can't stay on, but please give my best to Verna." She handed the phone to Don with the air of someone reprieved.

He took the handset from her, nodded at Mr. Bowes, then wandered back into the dining room. "Hi, Dad," he said.

"Don," his father said, "just thought I'd touch base. Your ma and I saw this weird story on the news yesterday, about all these cats hanging around some guy's house in your neck of the woods. Hundreds of the little bastards, it looked like."

"And camping out there and not leaving," Don's mother added from the extension.

"Hi, Mom."

"Hi, Donnie."

"What the hell's going on back there?" his father asked.

"What did you see on the news?" Don asked.

"Just a shot of a red brick house," his father replied, "with all these damn cats sitting around on the lawn and the front steps and the sidewalks. The reporter said nobody was feeding them and the cats weren't doing a whole lot, just hanging around and such, but there sure was a bunch of them. It looked like that old movie with all the birds hanging around and going after people and taking over, except it was cats. You know anything about it?"

"Yeah, I do," Don said as he sat down at the dining room table. At least his parents had been spared the sight of him on camera.

"What the hell's going on there?"

"Well, as it happens, all those cats showed up in my neighborhood. As a matter of fact, it's my house where all the cats were hanging out. That's my house you saw on the news."

A long silence ensued. "Your house?" his mother finally said.

"Yup."

"What the hell's going on?" his father asked.

"It's hard to explain," Don said, "but I think the problem's resolved it-self. All the cats ran off today. There's no telling where they went, but at least they're not here any more." He did not feel like going into more detail.

"They just ran off?" his father said. "Well, I guess they would of had to sooner or later, especially if they started getting hungry. Did they mess up your property any?"

Don lowered his gaze to two long scratches on the tabletop. "Not much. Main problem was that they were attracting crowds and media coverage."

"Well," his father said, "at least we finally saw where you live, even if it was just on the TV."

Don felt a stab of guilt. "We should have you here for a visit soon," he said, "maybe next Christmas, or just after New Year's." He recalled that Gena had said something about her parents planning to head for Florida at about that time. "I've been kind of stressed out by a lot of stuff lately, but by then everything should be a little calmer." He could only hope it would be calmer, and was suddenly relieved that he had not informed his parents about his lost job or the near-breakup with Gena. He would get past all of this somehow, even though he didn't have a clue as to how. "And what's up with you?"

"Oh, the usual," his father said. "Had more guys at the firehouse for the pancake breakfast this morning than we had in some time. The bowling team's doing pretty well. We might even win the league championship this year." He paused.

Don's mother said in a gentle voice, "Why don't you tell him, dear? About Devvie."

"Actually, there is some more news," his father continued. "Got a post-card from your brother a couple of days ago."

"Really?" Don said, surprised.

"Devlan addressed it to me instead of your mom for a change. Didn't say much, just he's happy and he misses us. Gave me his new e-mail address and phone number and said he's doing okay in Key West. Woulda called him right then, but maybe he should get some warning first so's he'll feel like picking up the phone, so I'll e-mail him when my goddamn computer's back from the shop tomorrow." His father was having trouble concealing his emotions; his voice had dropped so low that Don could barely hear him. "At least he's writing to me, so I guess he's not mad at me any more for what I said about his lifestyle and such after he finally came out."

"That's great, Dad." Don felt that another weight had been lifted from his shoulders.

"How's everything else?" his mother asked. "Are you getting along with Gena's parents?"

"I guess so."

"That's good. I'll admit it—I worry that living that close to your in-laws isn't a good idea."

"Depends," Don said.

"Even if they are perfectly nice people."

"It depends."

"I miss you, Donnie," his mother said, "but that's the way with kids. You have to let them go. That's what the people were always saying on my stories." By "stories," she meant her favorite old soap operas, from which she had apparently gleaned this grain of wisdom. "Hang on and you cause trouble. Let them know you love them, but let them live their own lives. That's what I kept saying to Hal about your brother, and it's time I said it to you."

"We'll get you both here for a visit," Don said impulsively, "maybe head to New York City for a day or two to take in a show and see some of the sights." He had no idea whether he would even be able to afford such a junket by then, and almost expected to sense the deep disapproval of Household. Instead, he felt uplifted, another burden removed. At this rate, he would soon be inviting his parents and his brother here for Christmas and asking if Gena's parents might put them all up at their house. Either he was wiser, or just worn down.

"That'd be nice," his mother said. "That'd be wonderful."

"I'd better go," Don said. "I'll call you next week."

"Good-bye, Don," his father said.

"Bye."

He disconnected, got up, and returned to the kitchen. "I don't know why he hasn't come upstairs," Gena was saying to Mr. Bowes. She looked up at Don as he put the phone back in its cradle. "Vladimir's still in the basement," she said. "I opened the door as soon as we came in here, and put down his food, and he still hasn't come up." She glanced apologetically at Mr. Bowes. "You'd think he would show a little more gratitude for all the treats you gave him."

A wisp of a smile passed over the older man's face. "Gratitude," he said, "is something I have never expected from any cat."

"You've got that right," Don said. "I'll find him." He went to the doorway that led to the cellar, flicked on the light switch, and hurried down the steps. "Vladimir," he called out, since the cat would never respond to a summons of "here, kitty, kitty" or any other call he considered beneath his dignity. "Come on out." He peered behind the hot water heater and furnace, then behind the washer and dryer, where Vladimir had concealed himself in the past. "Vladimir."

He held his breath, listening for any sound that might betray Vladimir's presence, then felt a cold draft and noticed that one of the basement windows was open. As he went toward the window, he heard a crunching sound under his feet.

There was broken glass on the floor. A pane had been knocked out of the window, he realized, and had shattered on the floor.

He stared at the window. It had to have been broken from outside, but he doubted that anyone would have tried to break in while all those cats were in his yard; in any case, the window was far too small for anyone other than a small child to squeeze through. Or anything larger than a cat.

He searched, already certain that he would not find Vladimir.

* * * *

"He's gone," Don said as he closed the basement door. "I looked everywhere, and he's definitely not downstairs."

"But how could he get out?" Gena asked.

"One of the windows was broken, don't ask me how. He must have gotten out through that window."

Gena's eyes widened. "Oh, no."

"Look, he'll probably come back. He escaped enough times after we first moved here."

"He might have returned to my house," Mr. Bowes said proudly. "I'll search for him there. Since I walked over here, it would be no trouble at all for me to look for him on my way home."

"I'll come with you," Gena said.

Don shook his head. "You'd better stay here, just in case he shows up. I'll walk around the neighborhood and see if I can spot him anywhere."

"I hope he's all right," Gena said.

"Look, don't worry too much," Don said, seeing the distress in her eyes. "You know how independent he is. Start worrying is if he isn't back tomorrow or the day after." But he was worrying about Vladimir himself, more than he cared to admit, thinking of the broken basement window and the cats that had so mysteriously vanished.

* * * *

Don covered three blocks in his search before admitting to himself that his efforts were useless. A truly thorough search would require trespassing; knocking on a few doors and asking about a small long-haired black and white cat with green eyes and oversized paws had yielded only irritating results. The first two people he had asked had shaken their heads regretfully. The third had burst out, "Aren't you the guy who had all those cats around your house?" and had started pestering him for more details of his confrontation with Mayor Dorff before Don beat a hasty retreat. The next two people had looked distinctly unhappy at being asked about cats at all, or at having anyone knock at their door.

He walked home, hoping against hope that he might find Vladimir there, sitting outside the door and meowing for admittance, but the front stoop was empty. He went around to the back door and let himself in; Vladimir's bowl of food looked untouched.

"Gena?" he called out.

"Did you find him?" she said as she came into the kitchen.

"No." He sat down at the kitchen table.

"Mr. Bowes called a couple of minutes ago. He hasn't seen him, either." She seated herself across from him. "We could run off some flyers with a photo, offer a reward."

"If he isn't back by tomorrow, we'll do that." That would be yet another drain on his finances, offering a reward large enough to interest people. He wondered how much reimbursement he would get from his insurance policy for repairs to the broken basement window and damage to their furniture. Given that his insurer was also his erstwhile employer, probably as little as the company could get away with paying out.

"You know what I was thinking about while you were gone?" Gena asked. "About what the real estate agent told us when she showed us this house, about the atmosphere and how the people who lived here before us felt almost as though someone was watching over them, almost as if they had a guardian of some sort, and how they really hated having to move away."

He nodded. "I remember." He had felt something like that himself at the time, about this house somehow being the right place for them. "I know what you mean. I used to feel that way, too."

"We lost that feeling somehow. We let other things in."

"It won't happen again," Don said. "I won't let it." He thought of Household. "Nothing else is ever going to get in here and drive us apart."

"I think that's why Vladimir cleared out before, because we let other things in, and now he's left us again. A bad sign."

"He'll come back." Don wanted to believe that. "You know Vladimir. He'll probably show up at the most inconvenient time possible and make us feel like idiots for worrying about him." He took her hand. "Listen, I promised Jeff I'd help out down at Cliff Beaufort's campaign headquarters. Maybe you should come with me."

"Go if you want. Vladimir may not know his way around this neighborhood any more. One of us should be here in case he shows up. I could start calling people, asking them to let us know if they see him, and he might still turn up at Mr. Bowes's house."

"Okay." Don stood up. "If the little guy puts in an appearance, call me on my cell. I shouldn't be gone too long."

"Not that I would mind going with you." Gena thrust out her chin. "Right now I'd do just about anything to keep that bastard Dorff from being reelected."

Twenty-Five

"Thank you all for your help," Clifford Beaufort said to the campaign volunteers. More people had dropped by during the afternoon to help out, and now telephones and laptops rested on desks, the walls were painted, and the cleaned and polished floor tiles were several shades lighter and a lot shinier. "As you know, we've got an uphill battle ahead of us, but I appreciate your support."

"Maybe it's not quite as steep a hill as it was," Helena Rothenberg said. She, along with the other volunteers, had heard Jeff's detailed report about Beaufort's encounter with Stan Dorff, the mayor's attempt to throttle Don on the doorstep of his own home, and the subsequent exodus of cats from the neighborhood. "I think you might have more support after today." She glanced in Don's direction.

Beaufort smiled wryly. "The mayor's still out front. He's also got plenty of time for folks to forget what happened today." He shook his head. "Got to see some folks at the shelter, and then I'm heading home to watch myself on the news."

"That news story ought to make some impression," Tom Alcott said from the back of the room.

"Oh, it'll make an impression, but what kind of impression, and a lot of that's going to depend on how it's edited." Beaufort lifted a hand, then left to a chorus of good-byes.

Don, sitting on one of the desks, was feeling the onset of his usual late Sunday afternoon depression. This particular affliction had plagued him as far back as he could remember. As a child, he had dreaded the approach of Monday morning, when he gave up his weekend of homemade experiments and reading library books about science and mathematics to return to his overcrowded school. Most of his classmates were either apathetic or disruptive, while his teachers, with few exceptions, thought of education as the imposition of rigid order, conformity, and strict discipline. As an adult, Sunday evenings had meant preparing for another tedious and mind-numbing day at the office. Right now, it meant feeling completely bummed because he would have to spend tomorrow checking out job prospects with the two strikes of his recent notoriety and Stan Dorff's enmity against him. He realized then that about the only time he hadn't been depressed on Sundays was when he had been in college and looking forward to his math and science courses, at least until his senior year, when practicality and fear of poverty had convinced him to load up his schedule with all the business courses that he would need— and had largely neglected.

Most of the volunteers were leaving. "I'll lock up," Jeff was saying to Helena Rothenberg. "I have to get home and record all the newscasts, in case there's some footage of Cliff we can use in the campaign."

"I'd better get my show on the road, then," Helena said. "I wouldn't want to miss the news, either." She smiled at Don as he nodded a farewell and wandered toward the door. "And I've got a long day of substitute teaching tomorrow."

"Any prospects for the math teacher job?" Tom Alcott asked as he pulled on his Army camouflage jacket.

Helena shook her head. "I'm afraid not. At first we tried to find somebody with at least a little teaching experience as well as the required courses, but whenever we did, we'd always lose them to a suburban school. Then we tried for people with just a degree in the subject matter, but they're pretty hard to find in this part of the state. Now we're just hoping we can grab somebody with a halfway suitable undergraduate degree, and we may come up empty on that, so I may have to consider getting back in full-time harness for the next school year, which means my husband isn't going to be happy. He was hoping we could start spending our winters in Florida."

"But if you're retired—" Tom started to say.

"I know." Helena sighed. "But I can't just leave the students to the teacher they're likely to get if I don't come back. If you don't get them in middle school, chances are you've lost them for good. Not that I have anything against Coach Roosa, but he's just not that well equipped to teach math and science and he doesn't really want the job. He's just in line to get stuck with it if we can't find a new teacher."

"Don majored in math," Jeff muttered just as Don was about to step outside. Don stopped and turned toward the others.

Helena lifted her brows. "Really?"

"Got a bachelor's degree in math from the University of Rochester," Jeff said.

"You majored in math?" Helena was gazing at Don with an expression of having just come upon a great and rare treasure. "At the University of Rochester? Is that true?"

"Yes, it is," Don admitted. "They gave me a scholarship, that's why I came east, otherwise I never could have afforded it. I was supposed to be a business major, but I ended up with a minor in business instead. I could have just about had a minor in physics, too, but I didn't have enough room in my senior year to take more courses in that."

"You were a math major and almost minored in physics?" Helena still had that glazed but ecstatic look in her eyes.

Don nodded. "But business was more practical. At least that's what I thought before I lost my job." He did not feel like explaining that he had made an early vow to achieve the financial stability in his early years that had come to his father only later in life, and that his dad had taken great pride in seeing him nail down a well-paid white-collar position. What a mistaken quest that had been, given how things had turned out.

"You don't have a job now?" Helena looked ready to throw her arms around him. "Have you ever considered teaching?"

Don felt a sudden rush of emotion. "I thought about it more seriously after graduation, but figured I had to be practical and look for something that paid better instead of taking out another loan to go to grad school. Then I thought—"

"You could consider it now," Helena said eagerly.

"I don't have certification."

"Screw the certification. If you look like a good prospect, we could get you into an education course or two at the local state college this summer and get a waiver until you complete the requirements. We might even be able to help you cover some of the tuition for your other ed courses later on, but we couldn't promise that, at least not right away."

"You almost sound as if I already have the job," Don said.

"If you can get through the interview and make a good impression, and your transcript looks good, and you don't have any felony convictions or child abuse scandals in your past, it's as close to a sure thing as you can have these days. We're desperate."

"But how can you be so sure that I—"

"I do have the inside track here." Helena clapped a hand on his shoulder. "Don't look too blissed out, Don. You wouldn't get much to start, and our student body has some hardassed and hostile kids. Their parents are either apathetic or else only too ready to give you a hard time, and you'll also have all the fun of preparing the kids for those damned proficiency tests. And you'll be plenty worn out at the end of the day and wondering if you ever got through to anybody."

"I know." Helena's school sounded somewhat like his own former school. He also knew how much, or how little, he was likely to make; the scale of salaries for teachers in the city's public schools had been published in the *Times-Tribune* not long ago, just after a recent round of negotiations with the teachers' union had yielded a minimum of concessions from the city council. With what Gena would earn from Caterina, they would be barely squeaking by for some time to come, and there was a chance newly hired teachers might be laid off in a year or two if the economy did not improve. Household's dire words of warning waited for him.

It didn't matter, he told himself. Whatever the hassles and conflicts with students and administrators, however frustrated he might be, and whatever financial hits he had to take, at least he wouldn't have to come home depressed about the unconstructive nature of his work and forced to rationalize its uselessness to society by telling himself that he was being practical.

"Besides," Helena said, "I think I can pull enough strings to get you in."

Don was profoundly moved. "That's awfully kind of you, especially since you barely know me."

"Don't feel too impressed. We haven't exactly been flooded with suitable applicants, so there really isn't that much competition."

"I might be kind of notorious at the moment, too," Don said. "Your administrators might not want to hire somebody the mayor tried to strangle."

"There's always the chance we'll have a new mayor by next year." Helena smiled. "Well, how about it? Do you want to try?"

Don smiled back. "Yeah."

* * * *

Jeff locked the door of the storefront, then turned toward Don. "Sure you don't want to come over and grab your stuff now?"

"Tomorrow," Don replied. "There isn't that much there I need right now. Besides, I want to pick up some food at that new Chinese place around the corner." He and Gena could drink up the bottle of champagne in the refrigerator and celebrate their reconciliation and his new job prospect. With any luck, Vladimir might show up by evening, and then they could toast his safe return, too. They could forget their other worries for a while.

"Just give me a call, then," Jeff said.

"By the way, thanks."

"For what?"

"For mentioning my degree to Helena Rothenberg. For being a pal."

Jeff shrugged. "Just telling her the truth, bro." He grinned, then hurried across the street to his car.

Don walked down the street. He had parked his car almost a block away from the Blaine Building, since Beaufort's new volunteers had taken all the spaces near his headquarters, but the street was empty now. The long purple shadows of late afternoon that cloaked the asphalt made the abandoned street seem even more desolate.

"Hey, you," a voice called out from the shadows. Don turned to see the old homeless man, still in his baggy and torn tweed coat, standing in an open doorway of the Blaine Building. "Yeah, you, the guy what lost his job."

"I might have just found me a better job," Don said.

"Good for you. Can't say I ever cared for a nine to five myself, but good for you. Course your wife'll come after you for a good chunk of change once you're dragging your asses through the divorce court."

"We decided not to get divorced," Don said.

"Good for you," the old man said. "If you ask me, there's too many folks runnin' around gettin' divorced these days."

"What are you doing in there?" Don asked.

"Told you before. Got my ways."

Don took a step toward him. "Listen, you shouldn't be hanging around here. The police could pick you up for loitering and breaking and entering." He thought for a moment. "I could drive you over to that place of Clifford Beaufort's. He might have a bed for you."

"No thanks. Not that I got anything against the reverend, you understand. I just don't care to be around a lot of bums and drunks and crazy people." The old man cupped a hand around his mouth, looking conspiratorial. "Besides, I got somebody here you might want to see." The old man rummaged in his pockets, waved his arms, then patted his pockets again.

A cat suddenly poked his head out of one pocket; Vladimir's green eyes gazed out at Don from his familiar furry face. The old man plucked Vladimir from his pocket by the scruff of the neck and then cradled the cat in his arms. The whole business had all the appearance of a magic trick; even more miraculously, Vladimir was not trying to escape from his captor and seemed perfectly content to allow the old guy to hold him.

"Vladimir," Don called out. "That's his name," he added.

"Figured that much, 'cause it ain't my name."

"He's my cat."

"Figured that, too." The old man ducked behind the door and was gone.

Don strode toward the entrance and tried the door; it was open. He stood there for a moment, considering what to do, then reached into his coat pocket for his cell phone. He hit his home phone number.

"Hello?" Gena's voice said.

Don said, "I just found Vladimir."

"You did? Is he all right?"

"He's fine."

"That's wonderful! But where?"

"Downtown, in front of the Blaine Building, believe it or not, so you can stop calling around to ask if anybody's seen him. Listen, don't get weirded out or anything, but this old man got hold of him somehow."

"You mean somebody kidnapped him?"

"I don't think so."

"Well, how else could he get there?"

"I don't know. This old man's got him, but I'm pretty sure he didn't kidnap him or anything. He seems like a harmless old guy, and Vladimir looks perfectly fine, he's not even putting up a fuss—seems to like the guy."

"That doesn't sound like Vladimir."

"They're inside the Blaine Building now, because this old man figured out how to break into the place, so I'm going in to get Vladimir. With any luck, we'll be home in less than an hour."

"Shouldn't you call the police?"

That was the logical thing to do, but something was warning him against such a move. "I've got my cell," he said. "I can call the police if I have to later, but right now I just want to try to get Vladimir back without a lot of complications. I kind of know this old guy anyway, I talked to him outside the courthouse a couple of times. I even gave him a few bucks for food."

"Maybe he thinks he can get more money from you by holding Vladimir hostage."

"Look, he's a harmless old man. If I call the police, they'll just throw him in the can. I'd rather see if I can get him to someplace where he can get some help first."

"Are you sure you know what you're doing?"

"I'm sure," Don said.

"Just be careful."

"I will."

"Bye. Be careful."

He disconnected and slipped the phone back into his pocket, then pushed the door open.

The lobby was a narrow atrium, illuminated by a skylight overhead and by a soft light glowing from the sixth floor. Wrought iron staircases angled up to each floor, where the hallways were bordered by iron railings. The old man was already inside one of the elevators, one hand gripping the elaborate ironwork of the cage as the lift rose toward the second floor.

"Hey!" Don shouted as he ran toward the elevator bank. "Give me back my cat!" The elevator continued upward. Don opened the door to another elevator and pulled it shut behind him, then looked up. The moving elevator had passed the second floor and was moving toward the third. He pressed the button for the third floor; the elevator let out a squeak as it began to rise.

He watched the other elevator as it passed the third floor, then the fourth; apparently the old man was heading all the way to the sixth floor. Perhaps he should call the police, but there was a chance the old guy might harm Vladimir if he felt threatened. He didn't seem like the kind of person who would deliberately hurt an animal, and Vladimir's conduct indicated that he wasn't afraid of the man; Don had always suspected that cats had the ability to sense when someone intended to harm them. Still, it wouldn't hurt to be careful, especially since Stan Dorff would welcome a chance to throw a breaking and entering charge at Don if he were found inside the Blaine Building.

Don's elevator slowed to a stop. He hit the button for the sixth floor, wondering exactly how he was going to reclaim Vladimir and get the old man to a shelter. Maybe he would just have to grab the cat and leave the guy to his own ways.

The elevator climbed and creaked to a stop on the sixth floor.

The old guy was waiting for him, standing by an opaque glass door on which a sign read "Arethea Technologies" in gold letters, even though that company had moved out of the building months ago. Vladimir, amazingly, was draped over the man's shoulder in a striking resemblance to a small fur boa. The cat squinted at Don, purring.

"Look," Don said, "I just want my cat back."

"I ain't stoppin' him," the old man replied, "but looks like the little critter's kinda happy where he is. Besides, he's got company."

"What do you mean?"

The old man waved at him with one hand. "Turn around and take a look."

Don moved away from the elevator and went to the railing. Through the grillework of the railing on the other side of the building, he saw hundreds of cats, sitting in rows and staring at him across the open space of the atrium.

"Holy shit," he said.

The old man came to his side, with Vladimir still clinging to his shoulder. "Sure is somethin' to see, so many of them all together. And there's even more of 'em down there."

Don looked down to where the man was pointing. More cats were on the fifth floor level, and he saw then that the two cats he thought of as Nicholas and Alexandra were with them. The others had left a space around the feline couple. All were in a crouching position, as if prepared to bring down prey.

"What are they doing here?" Don asked.

"Don't ask me, son. Ask them. But I think I got kind of an idea."

"Why?" Don was not sure he really wanted to know or that the old guy could tell him.

"Well, it's kind of like this. Once those kitty cats were goin' about their business, keepin' to their own territory and not bothering anybody, and then all their peacefulness and quiet got kind of fucked up. One day, they were lyin' around sleepin' and thinkin' and enjoyin' their chow and rompin' around with their kittens and doin' whatever other stuff cats do, and then all hell broke loose. I'm talking power failures that'd take whole cities full of kitties offline for days. I'm talking tornadoes wreaking devastation. I'm talking earthquakes way over eight point five on the goddamn Richter scale and tidal waves and volcanoes and all kinds of disasters. Can't let that kind of thing go on if there's somethin' you can do about it, and looks to me like those cats decided to do somethin' about it."

"That still doesn't tell me why they're here," Don said.

"It does if you think about it. Somebody was lookin' out for them, from a distance, not meddling or anything but kind of keepin' their welfare in mind, and then that somebody wasn't lookin' out for them so much no more. Even worse, that somebody was kinda putting their whole way of life in jeopardy, if you know what I'm sayin', gettin' ready to tear everything apart. I mean, there is such a thing as self-defense."

Don said, "I don't know what you're talking about." But he did know what the old man was talking about; he and Gena had arrived at the truth some time before, even if they had been reluctant to confront it directly. "But there's no reason for them to be here now," Don continued. Somehow he had to convey his thoughts to the old man. "Because Gena and I aren't going to break up. They don't have to worry about that now, they can trust us, we made up our minds about that. They can leave and go back to Catalonia or wherever they came from, and nobody'll disturb them again."

"You sound awfully sincere, son."

"I am sincere."

"Maybe you mean what you say," the man said, "but how the hell can they be sure of that now? They could go back to where they come from and end up with even more quakes and twisters and volcanoes blowing their tops. All they have to go on now is your say-so that they don't have to worry. So I'd guess they're thinkin' that maybe it's time to cut out the goddamn middleman, so to speak, and take control of their own shit."

"They can't," Don said, unable to look away from the hundreds of glittering cats' eyes gazing through the iron grillework across the way. "We imagined them. They wouldn't even exist except for us, we dreamed them up, they were our invention."

"That's one way of looking at it," the old man said, "but inventions can sometimes get away from the folks who made them, and turn into something else. Or to put it another way, they can maybe kinda start pickin' up some of their own steam and end up with what you'd call free will. Or maybe you didn't have that much to do with making them what they are. Maybe what you started making up about them and imagining about them started getting in the way of what they actually were or wanted to be. Maybe that's why they're kind of pissed off at you now."

Don said, "But I didn't do anything to them."

"Maybe they don't know that. And if you want to know the truth, I'm kinda pissed off at you myself. Maybe I'm not as angry as they are, but that's only because I didn't lose as much. They had to mess with all manner of natural disasters and threats to their world and such. I only lost a place to live. I only lost my house."

Don searched his mind for a way to make sense of what the old man was telling him. Maybe the guy had filed a claim with Don's former employer for some badly needed funds; maybe the insurance company, aided by some of Don's own calculations, had denied his claim and thus doomed the old man to a life of penury and homelessness. That was possible; he had trained himself after a while not to think too much about the people who lay behind the claims that reached his office.

But that wouldn't explain the presence of the cats, or what the old man had said about their reasons for being here.

"Whatever I did," Don said, "I'm sorry, I really am." He gazed at Vladimir, who seemed completely uninterested in any appeal Don might make. "If there's anything I can do—"

"Oh, there's something you can do. I just ain't exactly sure what it is, or if you can do it even if I could figure it out."

Vladimir suddenly leaped down from the old man's shoulder. Don moved toward the cat to grab him. The old guy held up a hand; Vladimir hissed.

"Nope," the old man continued, "looks like there ain't a hell of a lot you can do. Not unless you're ready to fight."

Don said, "I don't want to fight."

The old man shook his head. "I don't want to fight neither, especially with you, but maybe you and me don't got that much to say about whether we fight or not."

Rage welled up inside Don, threatening to choke him. He looked down at Vladimir and was suddenly seized with the urge to wring his furry little neck.

"Hrrow," Vladimir said.

"It's my place," Don growled, "not yours." That deep, heavy voice was not his own. "If all you can do is just sit around and let everything go and not even try to exert your power, you deserve everything that's happened to you. If you're so weak that you can't even use what power you have to control those around you, then you deserve to lose everything."

Something was using his voice, and he could not stop himself. "Get out of me," he went on, still in that same deep voice. "Get out of me!" But the thing was embedded inside him now, squeezing what little was left of his own will into a tiny point. He wanted to lash out, rid himself of the old man and Vladimir and all of those evil-eyed cats for good.

The old man said, "You see, son, you did it, you were responsible for a lot of the trouble. You opened the door and issued a goddamn invite. You let that thing into your home, and it forced me out on the street." He gazed past Don. "And then you messed around with the world of those cats, you and your wife, whether you knew what you was doing or not, and just because of what was going wrong with you two, they had to suffer. Can't expect something not to fight back, can you?"

The thing inside Don shrieked.

The old man said, "This time, I win," and lunged at him.

Twenty–Six

The downtown streets were deserted, as they always were on Sundays; even Dunhill and Stein had recently posted a notice saying that the department store would now be closing at three on Sunday. Gena drove to the intersection near the courthouse and turned left, passing a glassy rectangle that housed a bank and then a storefront with a poster of the Stars and Stripes and a handpainted sign saying "Beaufort for Mayor" before stopping at the Blaine Building. She had her cell phone with her to summon help, and Vladimir's carrier was in the back seat.

She parked in front of the building. What should she do now? Don's car was parked down the street, so he had to be inside.

He had sounded so strange on the phone, full of a bravado that had not entirely masked the hesitancy and anxiety in his voice. It had taken her only moments after hanging up to decide to go after him.

Again, she wondered, as she had throughout the drive, how Vladimir could possibly have made his way downtown by himself. That old man Don had mentioned must have stolen the cat somehow.

The old man could be dangerous, whatever Don thought. That he had somehow got hold of Vladimir and managed to hide out in the Blaine Building, however odd, wasn't nearly as strange as everything else that had been going on around them.

At last she got out of the car and approached the building's entrance. She pulled at a door, expecting to find it locked, but the door swung open.

She slipped inside, peering fearfully around the lobby. The muffled sound of voices reached her; she looked up.

Two men on the uppermost level were struggling on a landing near a staircase, arms locked around each other.

She nearly cried out, then clapped a hand over her mouth, afraid of startling Don and his white-haired assailant; both were close to the edge of the landing. She ran toward the nearest elevator and stepped aboard, closing the door and hitting the button for the sixth floor. Then she heard another sound, a strange combination of a high-pitched whimper and a howl. The cry echoed through the empty building, rising to the pitch of a high wind.

The elevator rose. She slapped at the side of the cage, willing it to rise faster. The eerie wail became a shriek as Gena saw masses of cats, hundreds of them, crouched outside the rows of office doors on the fifth and sixth floors. The jaws of the cats were open, their sharp teeth visible as they continued to howl.

Don was still wrestling with the other man, trying to get a lock around his tweed-coated shoulders.

The howling abruptly stopped. The cats on the sixth floor fanned out, slinking along the hallway toward the two struggling men. Some of the cats on the fifth floor were moving toward the staircase, too.

Gena's throat tightened as the white-haired man knocked Don toward the staircase. Don fell, rolled down a couple of steps, then grabbed the railing and stopped himself.

"Stop!" she cried out. "Stop it!"

The white-haired stranger glanced toward her with a quizzical expression on his face. The elevator slowed and then came to rest at the sixth floor.

She knew this man from St. Luke's, just after she had quit her job. She pulled the door open and stepped out.

"Well, whaddya know," the old man said. "We got more company."

"What are you doing?" Gena shouted.

"Protectin' myself," the stranger replied. "Takin' care of business, you might say."

"That's my husband," she said, feeling her face flush. "Leave him alone."

"Your husband? You come all the way down here to look out for him? Guess he *was* tellin' me the truth when he said you wasn't gonna get divorced."

Don clung to the railing. The old man might be armed.

"Gena," Don called out.

"Mrree!" Gena turned at the sound and saw Vladimir, crouching on the floor, ears back and eyes narrowed into slits.

"What's going on?" Don asked.

Gena dug around in her pocket; her fingers closed around her cell phone. "Listen," she said to the old man, "if you raise a hand against my husband again, I'll call the police."

"No need for that," the old man replied. "Not so long as he stays himself. It's not him I'm fightin' against, anyway—it's something else, that indweller that keeps gettin' back inside him."

Don stumbled up the steps toward Gena.

"What are you doing here?" he asked.

"I had to come. I was worried about you."

She kept her eyes on the old man. At last he thrust his arms skyward.

"I don't have a gun," the old guy muttered, "if that's what you're worried about."

"I think I know what happened to me just then," Don said to the old man, sounding out of breath. "You weren't after me, you were after something else. I'm not saying I understand everything that's going on, but it won't happen again, letting that thing take me over, I won't let it happen again, this is it." He draped his arm around Gena's shoulders. "Just let us get our cat, and we're out of here. I won't call the cops. I'll even give you some money, if you need it. Just leave us alone."

"You know something?" the old man said. "I think you really mean it. Maybe you're finally on the right track, you and your wife there. But looks like you got more problems than just me." He waved a hand gracefully in their direction.

Gena turned her head. A group of cats was advancing toward them, on the prowl, eyes shining in the fading light. Don's arm dropped from her shoulders; he took her hand. They began to back away slowly from the cats. The old man pivoted, then swooped down and swept Vladimir up with one arm.

She had been here before, or in a place much like it, in her dreams, hearing cats whisper in soft feline voices, plotting their move against those who would threaten their world.

Before Gena could cry out, the cats were upon them. She screamed as claws dug into her arm, then shook more cats from her legs. They swarmed over her; she backed away and covered her face with her hands. Something struck her in the middle of her back, and then the floor dropped from under her feet.

She was falling. Her hands fell away from her face as someone caught her by the arms. Her shoulder muscles tightened in pain as her legs flailed for footing. Her fingers dug into flesh. She had a momentary glimpse of Don leaning over the railing, gripping her arms, cats hanging from his legs and his coat. He shook one leg and then the other, and then lost his balance.

The edge of the grillework caught him at the waist. Gena tried to scream, but could not. He flipped over the railing very slowly, still holding on to her arms.

They fell past one flight of stairs. She caught a glimpse of the cats crowding the fifth floor. She could not be falling; she refused to accept it. Hundreds of cats' eyes watched her coldly as she fell past them. Terror froze her, and then the building around them vanished.

She floated weightlessly, Don still hanging on to her. He slowly released one of her arms but kept hold of one hand; his eyes were wide with fear. They were surrounded by a bright and formless blue space. A wind suddenly gusted past them, and the blue space became a tunnel of curving dark blue walls.

The wind swept several cats past them. More cats filled the space around them. Some were curled up, as if on invisible cushions; others had their legs extended, as if preparing to land, while still others, their backs arched, seemed caught in mid-leap. More cats flew past, disappearing into the soft blue light below.

Two cats hovered near her and Don, a small black cat and a golden-furred cat. Gena looked into their eyes; they stared back at her, and she could not help feeling that they were trying to communicate with her, to tell her something she had to know.

She looked down. An expanse of green dotted with bright colors opened up below her, a grassy garden of shrubs and flower beds. A stream wound through the garden, and cats lay along the banks of the brook.

"Do you see it, too?" Don said, his voice barely audible above the wind. He looked past her, at the two cats floating near them, and then his face paled.

The two cats flew past them; the garden and the blue tunnel vanished.

* * * *

A hard surface was under her. She seemed to be lying on her back. Gena lay there, afraid to move, gazing up at a hexagon of dim yellowish light until she finally recognized the skylight of the Blaine Building. The levels of iron lattices and staircase railings gradually came into view and took shape in a lifting fog.

Fingers gripped her hand. She turned her head to see Don lying beside her.

"Are you all right?" he said after a long silence.

She wiggled her toes inside her shoes. "I think so." She was still fearful of moving. "How about you?"

"I'm all right. A few scratches."

Gena lifted one leg, then the other; she sat up slowly and felt her ribs with her free hand. "Guess I'm okay, too. What happened?"

"Damned if I know. I could probably come up with a rational explanation if I thought about it for a while. Right now the only thing that comes to mind is that a way opened up to someplace, we got caught inside it with those cats, and—"

"Catalonia," she whispered.

"Whatever." Don let go of her hand and sat up. "Well, what do you know." He motioned with one hand.

She looked behind herself. A number of cats sat at the other end of the lobby. A few licked their paws; others were stretched out, and still others seemed to be asleep. All of them looked considerably thinner and more disheveled than the other cats that had been inside this building.

"I had to come," she said. "The way you sounded had me really worried. I thought you might need me."

"I did." He reached for her hand and held it. "I'm sorry."

"For what?"

"For everything I did that hurt you."

"I'm sorry, too. Damn it, Don, you could have been killed."

He stood up, then helped her to her feet.

"Vladimir must still be here," she continued, "unless—"

Don gripped her hard; she felt his hand tremble slightly.

"I saw it," he said, "and you saw it, too, that garden and the cats. Maybe that's where he belongs, with those other cats in Catalonia or whatever that place is. Maybe it's better for him there, and maybe they opened that passage on purpose—or it just opened up by itself, and dropped back here for some reason. Or maybe we're both just completely nuts by now." He let go of her. "And that old guy—he has to—"

He stepped forward and lifted his head. "Hello!" he shouted up at the skylight. "Anybody here? Hey, answer me if you're still up there." His voice echoed in the atrium; there was no reply. "Hello!"

Gena heard a loud click, followed by a hum. Up on the sixth floor, one of the elevators was descending. She moved closer to Don and watched as the elevator dropped past each level before stopping at the first floor.

The door opened. The old man stumbled out, shook his head, and mumbled, "What the fuck?"

His voice sounded higher and lighter. Don ran toward him, Gena at his heels. "You're all right," Don said, then stopped and lifted his arms defensively. "Just keep to yourself."

"What you talkin' about, sonny?" The old man did not sound at all like the man she had run into at St. Luke's. He blinked his eyes and rubbed at his spiky white hair. "Where the hell am I?"

"Don't you remember?" Don asked.

The old man squinted at them, then plopped down on the floor. "The last thing I remember is sittin' in the goddamn park in front of the courthouse with a bottle of Night Train." He shook his head. "And a lot of weird-assed dreams."

"Don't you remember me?" Don said.

The old man wiped his nose. "You know, I keep thinkin' I should, but I don't."

"Got any place to go?"

"Jesus, sonny, do I look like I got any place to go?"

"Then maybe I can help you out," Don said. "I know a place that might have some room."

Gena said, "We'll have to do something about them, too." She waved an arm at the cats.

Don sighed. "Yeah."

She frowned. "Maybe Jennifer Baxter can get somebody over here from Operation Whiskers to pick them up. Then I'll call Caterina. I don't want that animal control guy getting hold of them."

Don said, "We also don't want him on our case about how we got inside this building."

The old man said, "And maybe you two could tell me if I'm batshit crazy or all that booze finally scrambled my brains."

* * * *

"Cats sure have a thing for you two," Jennifer Baxter said as the parka-clad man with her carried out the last of the cats in two carriers. "Good thing there's only twenty-three of them—any more and we wouldn't have had the room."

Jennifer had recognized several of the cats, which had escaped from the Operation Whiskers shelter only a day ago. The rest, Gena suspected, were fugitives from the city shelter.

Caterina, arms folded, stood near the old man. "Listen, lady," he was saying, "I'm tellin' you again, all I know is I was havin' me a nightcap in the park and then I was lyin' in that elevator over there." He gestured as an elevator door opened and Don emerged. Don had gone looking for Vladimir as soon as Jennifer, Caterina, and the man in the parka had showed up, but Gena knew from the look on his face that he hadn't found their cat. She had a feeling they might never see Vladimir again.

Caterina shook her head. "I still don't understand how you guys ended up in here."

"Let's just say that we were down here and noticed that one of the doors was open," Don replied. "So we came inside and found this old guy and those stray cats and figured we'd better call you."

"I'll buy that," Caterina said, "even if I don't entirely believe it."

* * * *

Gena drove home in her car. Don had called Clifford Beaufort's shelter and discovered that a bed was available. After driving the old man there, he would pick up supper on the way home. He had some good news to tell her about a possible job as a teacher in the city schools, but he had looked pensive and a bit disoriented while mentioning that possibility. She felt as if they were going through the motions of normality, only pretending that their lives would be as they once were.

Even if she and Don eventually concocted some rational explanation for everything that had happened to them, she doubted that such an explanation would ever be truly convincing. Something unknown had connected to them in some strange way. She would just have to be grateful that, whatever the reasons behind the apparitions of the cats and Household and the blue passageway, they had helped heal the breach in her marriage.

As she came down the road toward her house, she almost expected to see a throng of cats gathered near the front steps or by the driveway, but there wasn't a cat in sight. She pulled into the driveway. As she got out of the car, she saw something move out of the corner of her eye. She looked around; an indistinct human form flickered at the edges of her peripheral vision.

Gena shook her head. For a moment, she thought that she had glimpsed the old man who had been inside the Blaine Building. A small black and white cat now sat in front of the back door.

"Vladimir!" she cried, certain that he had not been there just a moment earlier. She hurried up the steps to the door. Vladimir looked up at her with an expression that might have been either impatience or exasperation.

"Hrrow!" he said, demanding to be let inside.

"Vladimir." She wanted to pick him up and cuddle him, but unlocked the door instead. He could not possibly have found his way back here so quickly by himself; it was impossible that he should be here at all. It didn't matter. She and Don had not lost him after all.

Vladimir trotted inside with his usual insouciance, flicking his tail from side to side. "Mreee," he said, giving her an I-demand-food look.

Gena got out a can of food for him and set it down with fresh water. The kitchen seemed cozier, more welcoming; the entire atmosphere of the house felt different. Perhaps that was only because she and Don were reconciled, but the vague sense that an invisible and threatening presence might be lurking inside the house was gone.

She was home. She sat at the kitchen table, watched Vladimir scarf down his food, and was content.

After a while, there was the sound of stomping feet outside the back door and then a sharp knock. She went to the door and opened it to find Don bearing a large bag of food containers in one arm and a bouquet of roses in the other.

"Don." She flushed with pleasure as she took the flowers from him. "You shouldn't have."

"I know." He came inside; she closed the door behind him. "They cost me enough. But what the hell." His eyes widened. "Vladimir!"

"He was sitting outside the door when I got home. I don't know how he could have done it, but somehow he managed to find his way here."

They stood there, grinning mindlessly and happily at each other until Vladimir rubbed up against her legs, then did a figure-eight around Don's.

"Better get these flowers in some water," Don said.

"And get this food served, too," Gena said.

* * * *

Don and Gena munched on their dim sum, shrimp in garlic sauce, and General Tso's chicken while watching a DVD of "Somewhere in Time," a movie that inevitably made both of them extremely weepy while evoking powerful romantic feelings. Don would have preferred watching more

NCAA playoffs, but such viewing didn't quite fit the spirit of the evening. At any rate, they had managed to avoid the six o'clock evening news by getting home after that broadcast was over, although he could still watch his assault at the hands of Mayor Dorff at eleven o'clock.

Vladimir basked on the floor in front of them. Life is good, Don thought; all was right with the world for the moment. The house seemed warm and comforting, even with the torn-up furniture and damaged lamps.

Vladimir got up, crept under the coffee table, then jumped up on the sofa. Don covered his container of shrimp with one hand, but for once the cat didn't seem interested in food. Vladimir curled up against his thigh and began to purr.

A sharp knock sounded at the front door. "Yoo hoo!"

Don's heart sank momentarily. The voice belonged to his mother-in-law.

"I'll get it," Gena said.

She hurried into the alcove as Don put the DVD player on pause. Laurie might be intrusive, he thought, but everybody had flaws and he knew that she had Gena's best interests at heart. Why had it had taken him so long to arrive at this obvious piece of wisdom? Being too preoccupied with his own problems, he supposed, with too many concerns that now seemed inconsequential.

Gena flung open the door. Her mother came inside, followed by her father, who looked even more immense than usual in a bulky navy blue jacket and sweat pants.

"Hello, Eugenia," Laurie Lawlor said, offering her cheek to her daughter for a kiss. "Hello, Donald."

Don got to his feet. "Hi, Laurie. Hi, Eugene."

Gena ushered her parents into the living room. "It isn't that I'm not glad to see you," she said to her mother, "but I just wish you'd call first." Her voice was uncharacteristically firm.

"Yes, dear." For once, Mrs. Lawlor didn't look as though she wanted to contest the point. "We only dropped by for a moment." Still in her coat, she sat down in a straight-backed chair, while Mr. Lawlor settled himself in the ravaged easy chair. Vladimir leaped down from the sofa, padded across the room, then suddenly leaped into Eugene Lawlor's spacious lap.

"He likes you," Don said as Vladimir kneaded a thigh with his paws, then curled up. "He isn't usually that friendly."

"Isn't this that cat you used to have?" Gena's father asked. "Vladimir? The one who ran away?"

"He came back," Laurie Lawlor said. "I forgot to tell you."

"He came back," Gena said, "just before all those cats showed up outside our house—not that he had anything to do with that."

"Didn't think he did," Mr. Lawlor said.

"Well." Mrs. Lawlor turned toward Gena. "I know I should call first. I know that I'm sometimes—well." She folded her hands. "After seeing the news tonight, we decided to drive over to make sure you were both all right."

"We're fine," Don said. "You don't have to worry about us."

"It's strange," Mrs. Lawlor murmured, "how all those cats just disappeared the way they did."

"That was on the news?" Don asked.

"Sure was," Mr. Lawlor said. "You two got a lot of play. At least your house and the cats did. Surprised you didn't take a look at it."

"We were out," Don said.

"Well, as I told you," Laurie Lawlor said, "we just wanted to stop by after dinner and make sure you were all right, so we won't take up any more of your time." She looked around at the take-out containers, half-filled plates, chopsticks, and flutes of champagne cluttering up the coffee table without, miraculously, any trace of a disapproving glance.

"Thanks, Mom," Gena said.

Eugene Lawlor gently removed Vladimir from his lap and set him on the floor before standing up.

"Don," he said gruffly, "I don't know quite how to bring this up, so I better just blurt it out. I know you're looking for a new job, so if there's anything I can do, maybe put in a good word somewhere, you let me know. I've got a few friends who won't care what opinion Stan Dorff might have of you."

"Thanks. I appreciate it."

"Come on, Laurie. Long as we're in town, I might as well buy you a drink before we head home." Mr. Lawlor took his wife's arm as she rose and propelled her toward the front door. "Let the kids finish their supper." He looked back. "We'll let ourselves out."

The door closed behind them. Despite its brevity, that had to be about the most congenial visit they'd had from Gena's parents in quite some time. His life now seemed rich in improbabilities that had become realities.

"Gena," Don said, "you know that all of this could have been something else."

"What do you mean?"

"I mean that maybe we made a lot of strange coincidences all fit together—us, our cat, Catalonia. What if we had been more attached to…bunnies, or birds, or dogs?"

"It all happened."

"And might have been…otherwise. I mean something else. Maybe it is something else completely."

"You mean a delusion?" she asked.

"Maybe the world's a delusion. We don't any of us know what reality is, really."

"No," she said. "It all happened." She paused. "Don," she continued, with a funny smile on her face, "we've got a long week ahead of us. Maybe we should go to bed early."

Vladimir jumped onto the table by the window and began to paw at the curtain. "What is it, pal?" Don asked. The cat pawed at the curtain again.

He went to the window and drew the curtain open slightly.

Two cats sat on the sidewalk across the street. Don blinked, and the cats were gone, shadows in their places. As he let the curtain fall, he almost felt as though something else was in the room with him and Gena and Vladimir, something benign, the kind of presence a credulous person might have called a guardian spirit.

Apprehension and fear, unvanquished, nibbled at his mind. He slipped his arms around Gena and held her, treasuring the moment, knowing how easily the love, contentment, and acceptance he now felt could be taken away. They would have to be careful, both of them, to cling to what they had and not allow anything to take it from them.

He had a feeling that the cats and whatever strangeness lived behind them would not be so forgiving again.

About the Author

Pamela Sargent has won the Nebula and Locus Awards, been a finalist for the Hugo Award, Theodore Sturgeon Award, and Sidewise Award, and was honored in 2012 with the Pilgrim Award, given for lifetime achievement in science fiction and fantasy scholarship, by the Science Fiction Research Association.

She is the author of the science fiction novels *Cloned Lives*, *The Sudden Star*, *Watchstar*, *The Golden Space*, *The Alien Upstairs*, *Alien Child*, *The Shore of Women*, and *Venus of Dreams*, as well as the alternative history *Climb the Wind*. *Ruler of the Sky*, her historical novel about Genghis Khan, was a bestseller in Germany and Spain. She also edited the *Women of Wonder* anthologies, the first collections of science fiction by women.

Her young adult novel *Earthseed*, selected as a Best Book for Young Adults by the American Library Association, was followed by *Farseed* and *Seed Seeker*. *Earthseed* is in development by Paramount Pictures, with Melissa Rosenberg, scriptwriter for all five "Twilight" films, set to write and produce through her Tall Girls Productions.

Her short fiction has appeared in magazines and anthologies including *The Magazine of Fantasy & Science Fiction*, *Asimov's SF Magazine*, *New Worlds*, *World Literature Today*, *Amazing Stories*, *Rod Serling's The Twilight Zone Magazine*, *Universe*, *Nature*, and *Polyphony*. Her short story "The Shrine" was produced for the syndicated TV anthology series *Tales from the Darkside*, recently re-released on DVD. Her work is available in electronic editions from Open Road Media (www.openroadmedia.com) and Gollancz's SF Gateway (www.sfgateway.com), as well as Wildside Press (www.wildsidepress.com).

Michael Moorcock has said about her writing: "If you have not read Pamela Sargent, then you should make it your business to do so at once. She is in many ways a pioneer, both as a novelist and as a short story writer… She is one of the best."

Pamela Sargent lives in Albany, New York. Her website can be found at: www.pamelasargent.com.

CPSIA information can be obtained
at www.ICGtesting.com
Printed in the USA
LVHW09s1443130818
586826LV00001B/159/P

9 781479 407002